PRAISE FOR THE CLEO COOPER MYSTERIES

Saving Cecil:

"Mims' heroine and supporting cast flesh out a rich crew of characters."—*Kirkus Reviews*

Trusting Viktor:

"A breezily entertaining whodunit."—*Publishers Weekly*

"[A] fun read."—*Mystery Scene*

Hiding Gladys:

"Readers will want to see more of this spunky geologist with a streak of independence and a passion for her profession."
—*Alfred Hitchcock Mystery Magazine*

"[A] solid debut."—*Publishers Weekly*

SAVING
CECIL

ALSO BY LEE MIMS

Hiding Gladys (2013)
Trusting Viktor (2014)

LEE MIMS

SAVING CECIL

A CLEO COOPER MYSTERY

MIDNIGHT INK
WOODBURY, MINNESOTA

FIRST EDITION
First Printing, 2015

Cover design by Ellen Lawson
Cover illustration by Ken Joudrey
Map by Bob Murray

Midnight Ink, an imprint of Llewellyn Worldwide Ltd.

Library of Congress Cataloging-in-Publication Data (pending)
978-0-7387-3427-9

Midnight Ink
Llewellyn Worldwide Ltd.
2143 Wooddale Drive
Woodbury, MN 55125-2989
www.midnightinkbooks.com

Printed in the United States of America

JUN 0 4 2015

This book is dedicated to the memory of Ron Lowery.
He was a computer tamer extraordinaire and a fine friend.
You are gone too soon.

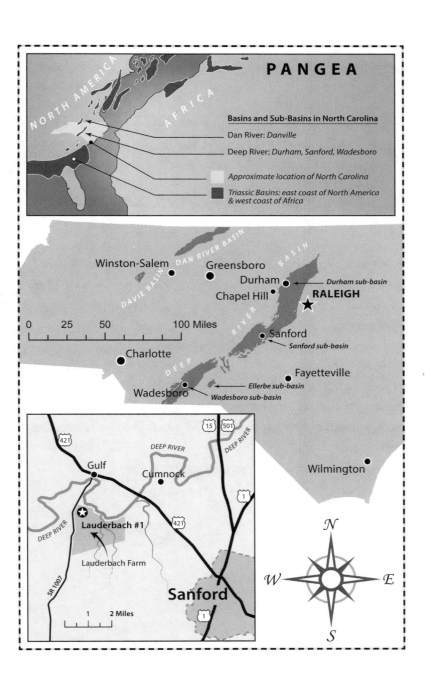

PANGEA

Basins and Sub-Basins in North Carolina

Dan River: *Danville*

Deep River: *Durham, Sanford, Wadesboro*

Approximate location of North Carolina

Triassic Basins: east coast of North America & west coast of Africa

NORTH AMERICA

AFRICA

Winston-Salem

DAN RIVER BASIN

Greensboro

Durham

DAVIE BASIN

Chapel Hill

Durham sub-basin

RALEIGH

DEEP RIVER BASIN

Sanford

Sanford sub-basin

0   25   50   100 Miles

Charlotte

Fayetteville

Ellerbe sub-basin

Wadesboro

Wadesboro sub-basin

Wilmington

421

15 501

DEEP RIVER

DEEP RIVER

Gulf

Cumnock

1

DEEP RIVER

Lauderbach #1

421

Lauderbach Farm

SR 1007

Sanford

1   2 Miles

1

N

W   E

S

"Why has not anyone seen that fossils alone gave birth to a theory about the formation of the earth, that without them, no one would have ever dreamed that there were successive epochs in the formation of the globe."

—Georges Cuvier, *Discours Aur Les Rvolutions Du Globe, Tudes Sur L'Ibis Et Mmoire Sur La Vnus Hottentote*

"Amidst the vicissitudes of the earth's surface, species cannot be immortal, but must perish, one after another, like the individuals which compose them. There is no possibility of escaping from this conclusion."

— Charles Lyell, *Principles of Geology*

"It was during my enchanted days of travel that the idea came to me, which, through the years, has come into my thoughts again and again and always happily—the idea that geology is the music of the earth."

—Hans Cloos, *Conversation with the Earth*

ONE

YOU KNOW HOW IT feels when you think someone or something is watching you? Well, I can tell you the creep factor goes *way* up when the latter is suspected. It was a Wednesday, October 2nd to be exact, and a gorgeous fall day. I was in my favorite place on the planet—that being anywhere in the woods of North Carolina. The leaves were starting to turn. The air was nippy and tinged with the faint hint of wood smoke. Normally, I'd have reveled in this pleasant assault on my senses, but instead I was distracted by another sense ... that sixth sense that alerts us to unseen dangers. Some call it ESP. I call it the jitters.

Whatever it was, the snap of a twig here, the crackle of a dry leaf there, had me on edge. Occasionally I'd stop and listen, but nothing ever revealed itself. I was trying to quell my unease, chalk it up to too much caffeine, when I detected the scent of something other than wood smoke, something deeply rooted in my memory bank.

I stopped again and sniffed the air.

The scent proved to be as frustratingly elusive as the phantom sounds. Still, I stared intently into the deep woods for a few moments. Then, deciding I needed to put a check on my imagination, I reached into the back pocket of my jeans for a freshly printed satellite photo—thank you, Google Earth—of the immense family-owned dairy farm I was currently trekking.

My hope was that the old game trail I'd stumbled upon would be a shortcut to the forty-acre pasture where I'd parked my Jeep earlier this morning. I'd already accomplished my mission of flagging a second drill site. Shouldn't be much farther now. I refolded my map, jammed it back in my pocket, and moved on.

After a while, I came to a clearing where an ancient oak spread its low-hanging branches, creating even deeper shade than already existed in the old-growth woods. Mossy undergrowth muffled my steps. My wariness momentarily waned as autumn sunlight, filtering through the dense hardwood and pine canopy above, danced in brilliant patches at my feet. Just then, another rustle, this time to my left, brought me up short again.

And the smell had returned. What was it?

As I tilted my head, trying to pick up even the slightest sound, the abrupt jangle of my iPhone—programmed with the old phone ring—sent me straight up off the ground. Fumbling it like a hot potato, I managed to answer without dropping it.

"Babe," my ex-husband, Franklin Donovan Cooper IV, chirped on the other end.

"Hi Bud," I answered, using his nickname from birth, the one that everyone who knew him used if they expected a response. "What's up?" I eyed my surroundings warily as I talked.

"I just got all warm and fuzzy thinking about last night and wondered when you're coming home. I thought I'd make you some of my famous clam chowder. We've got several bags of chopped clams in the freezer."

Now, Bud never makes me his clam chowder, being the rather arduous process it is, unless he wants something. Of course, I knew what he wanted and decided to save him the trouble. "By 'home,' I take it you're referring to my house," I said, peering around the mighty oak before I leaned against it. "Which, in turn, means you're still there and apparently planning to spend another night."

Bud sighed. "If you're trying to imitate a shrew, you're doing an admirable job. Play nice. I'm simply suggesting that we actually go over some of the wedding arrangements that are being made for you because you're too ... busy to take part ... "

"Hey!" I butted in. "I helped with the hard part, picking the actual date."

"Yes," Bud said patiently. "And we've both pencil-whipped our calendars until we could set aside a whole month for that honeymoon we never had."

I closed my eyes as Technicolor images of Bora Bora floated before them.

Bud continued, "A cozy bowl of chowder, some of your jalapeño cornbread, a little coleslaw, and we'll both feel ... fortified ... to take on the task. It won't be hard, I promise. And, if you'd take the time to meet the wedding planner I hired, I'm sure you'd like her. She's handled all types of affairs from big corporate events with a thousand people or more to small intimate weddings with only a few hundred people."

Bora Bora evaporated. My eyes blinked open. "What?" I squawked. "Bud! How many people have you invited?"

"Well, I've got a large corporate family, you know. Then there's all our friends and family, plus all the people you do business with. The kids and I have kept it down to around five hundred..."

"Are you insane?" I screeched. I could hear him sputtering something as I tapped the phone off, dropped it into my windbreaker pocket, and turned to stare square into the face of a very large wild boar.

Oink! Oink!

I froze. The blood-curdling shriek that had formed in my chest hung up at my lips and my feet were stuck to the ground. When the massive beast backed up a few steps, squinted his beady little eyes at me and clattered his tusks, my mobility instantly returned. Whipping around the massive oak, I took the only escape route available at the time, a low-hanging branch. I leaped, wrapped my arms around it, and swung up just as the boar skidded to a stop under me.

From my inverted position, I not only realized the source of the illusory musky odor, but two other things as well: an upside-down boar doesn't look any friendlier, and, this hog was *way* larger than any I'd ever seen, and I'd been to several pig pickins where wild boar was featured. Not only was this guy a plus-size shopper, he was also a fast learner. He quickly walked his front feet up the trunk and tried to hook me with his deadly tusks, barely missing my butt.

My butt—being one of my better features—is very dear to me, so, hand over hand, legs crossed at the ankles, I scooted up the limb as fast as I could. Many years spent in the field has kept me in great shape. I was quickly gaining altitude. "Ha!" I shouted triumphantly down to the vile creature.

Then the limb began to droop.

Porkulus, realizing this, abandoned his position at the trunk and returned to stand under me, drooling with anticipation. Only now, his jaw smacking was creating a frothy foam. Wonderful! Had I known when I left home that I'd be served up like an hors d'oeuvres on a toothpick to an angry member of the porcine tribe, I'd have stayed home.

Accompanied by tiny cracking noises, the branch swayed down another few inches and, great shape or not, my biceps were beginning to fatigue. I needed another plan. My cookies!

With one elbow hooked over the limb, I reached into my other back pocket and found the packet of Nekots I'd placed there before leaving my Jeep. "Hey, fatso! Want a cookie?" I tossed the pack to the ground at Porky's feet.

He never even looked down, just stomped right on my mid-morning snack. To add insult, he ground it into the dirt, pawing like an Spanish bull. Rude noises erupted from somewhere—I didn't want to think where—as he leaped and lunged at me. I hugged the limb tighter.

"Have you thought of Weight Watchers," I called down to him—humor often lessens fear—while struggling to roll up on top of the limb instead of hanging under it. Hogzilla's response: a frightened little squeal. I looked down just in time to see him hauling freight up the path, tail pointed straight in the air.

Who knew hogs were so sensitive? The small modicum of relief I felt upon witnessing his retreat gave me strength, and I managed to pull myself over the limb and straddle it. I scooted back against the trunk. When my heart rate returned to normal and I was sure Elvis had indeed left the building, I carefully stood up on the branch. Hugging its trunk cautiously, I peered to either side of it, wondering if the clever boar was just waiting down the path for me, hiding in the thick underbrush.

Why was he so big? He'd probably tip the scales at 450 pounds. Typically, wild boars average around 200 pounds. And, not discounting my fat joke, why had he run off like that? I peered through the limbs and leaves for a hunter who might have frightened him, but saw no one. Thinking more height would help, I hauled myself astride another larger branch higher above me. This, however, proved to be a waste of time and energy. The foliage was even denser up here. Then I thought I heard something.

I stopped scrambling about in the branches and listened.

Only birdsong and the whine of a far-away chain saw met my ears. I returned to the limb below and thought of my next move. Did I climb down and risk another encounter with the boar? I thought not. With balled-up fists, I gave my head little faux punches and exclaimed aloud, "Damn, damn, double damn!" Why hadn't I strapped on my Beretta this morning?

I knew better than to enter woods, no matter how small, without protection, but hell, I was practically in the suburbs. I was little more than 15 miles from downtown Sanford, the Lee County seat. To be precise, I was in a small fifty-acre patch of woods, one of many scattered about as windbreaks, separating the rolling pastures of the Lauderbach Dairy Farm.

I'm a geologist, educated at UNC in Chapel Hill, trained in the field for many years, working for several private companies in various geologic capacities. Presently, I own my own geologic consulting business. Actually I am the business, but lately I've been putting some serious thought into hiring someone to do the leg work … especially on days like today. So far, though, I haven't found the time or, honestly, the inclination to start a search.

Anyway, the Lauderbachs had contracted an energy company, Greenlite Energy out of Pennsylvania, to find gas on their farm. As is customary for operators, Greenlite hired an independent well-site geologist, me, to work with Schmid & Medlin, the contractor they hired to do the actual drilling of the well.

Lauderbach Dairy Farm comprises over 2,200 acres of gently rolling pastures and primitive woodlands situated on a sweeping outside bend of the Deep River. Two small towns, Gulf and Cumnock, are only a few miles away. Once beyond the boundaries of the farm, it was impossible to go very far in any direction before encountering an isolated house, a small farm or, for that matter, another drilling operation. I blew out a frustrated breath. That was no excuse, I should have worn a sidearm.

What an easy shot that would have been. Right between the eyes, and it would have been lights out for Porky Pig. Besides being a solid guarantee that he wouldn't charge me again, he'd have made a tasty donation to one of the many charities in the state that process game for the needy. Still, there was one bright spot. Good old fate had intervened and I hadn't brought Tulip with me.

She's a deerhound that found me in the far reaches of a pine plantation one day while I was prospecting for granite and she was looking for her owner. She'd adopted me on the spot and has been my trusty field buddy ever since. Feral hogs can make short work of hunting dogs. Thankfully, she was at the vet's, getting her annual checkup.

Just thinking of her made my heart rate slow and my frazzled nerves even out. Tense shoulder muscles relaxed. I closed my eyes, listened to the woodland sounds, and tried to convince myself of the prudence of waiting a little longer. But I didn't like being treed. It gave me too much time to pontificate on marrying Bud again, which brought back memories of how we happened to get married in the first place. Memories made me ... well, anxious. To my mind, I was more than justified in feeling this way. After all, I'd been here before, both physically and metaphorically.

Physically, I'd been in this very location. In a geological sense, that is. It was 26 years ago and I was right here in the Sanford sub-basin doing the same thing I am now, working for an exploration company engaged in drilling for natural gas. Only back then, the wells weren't production wells like they are today. Back then, we were drilling the first-ever exploration wells in the area. Without a doubt I can say that was the lowest point of my life.

Metaphorically, I was under enormous pressure to marry Bud Cooper just like I am now. Again, the lowest point of my life. The only difference: back then Bud wasn't acting like a wedding planner on steroids. I got a shudder just thinking of crowded ballrooms in a stuffy hotel, champagne flowing, drunken friends, giggling children, and the cloying smell of wilting flowers. *Okay, enough of that!* Throwing caution to the wind, I swung to the ground and resumed my hike to the drill rig. Wild boar or no wild boar, I was outta here!

Once on the ground, I quickened my pace to a brisk clip. I still needed to introduce myself to the Lauderbachs—I'd be their liaison with Schmid & Medlin. I'd already met the drill crew when I arrived this morning and they seemed like a nice bunch of guys. But then I've never met a drill crew that wasn't. They'd been here for over a month already, doing site preparation and taking care of the myriad of things that must be done before I'm needed.

Besides site prep, which included digging and lining the pits that would hold drilling mud, fracking fluid and flow-back water, they'd also dug the cellar for the well and installed the conductor pipe. One of their new generation of flex-rigs had been brought in and was now completely set up. The surface hole had been dug and the casing cemented. This was the stage where precautions were taken to prevent contamination of the ground water, generally located in the Sanford area about 200 feet down.

The drill team had drilled past the water table, inserted surface casing, pumped cement down the well until it came out the end of the casing and was forced back up between the casing and the well to the surface, thus sealing off the water table. Then the casing head, and the BOP, blowout preventer, had been installed and tested and now vertical drilling was underway.

They were cutting through surficial deposits of recent age, which wouldn't require any sampling, so I wasn't really needed on site. Once we reached the Sanford Formation, the formation overlying our target, I'd get back on site and earn my keep. I had scheduled at least three more weeks to complete this well. My plan for the rest of the day, once I spoke to the Lauderbachs, was to leave here so I could prepare to wrap up some loose ends on old projects. In particular, one in DC.

The trees began to thin out and I could almost make out the pasture I was looking for through the trees. The clanking sounds of metal on metal and occasional laughter let me know the drill crew couldn't be far away. I picked up my pace, feeling somewhat like Dorothy upon seeing the Emerald City.

The trail broadened and here and there saplings stretched their branches over it. Unfortunately, these branches also made perfect anchoring points for orb spiders to spin their webs, leaving them at just the right height to catch me in the face. I ducked under one of their sticky homes, sending its occupant scurrying for cover, and rose to my second jaw-dropping sight of the morning.

There, lying facedown on the trail in front of me, was the body of a man. A bright neon-green arrow stuck straight up from his back. I heard the startled intake of my own breath. Dropping to my knees beside him, I quickly palpated his neck for a pulse. He was still warm, but I felt no bumping of life through his jugular.

I wanted to place my ear on his back but the arrow was in the way. It had gone in a few inches to the right of his spine. Thinking maybe his pulse was just faint, I shook him gently, hoping he'd give me some sign that he was still alive.

He didn't.

Panicked, I jumped up and sprinted a few feet in the direction of the drill crew. Then sanity kicked in and I stopped, pulled out my iPhone, and called 911. I told them what I'd found and gave them directions to the drill site. Next, I hit the number for the drill foreman. I'd stored it this morning as soon as I'd met him.

"Yo!" said Jackie Floyd, a Pennsylvanian who'd been drilling holes for Schmid & Medlin since their inception in 1980. I quickly explained the situation and my location. "I know right about where you are," Jackie said. "We're on the way!"

"Be sure to leave someone at the site and someone at the edge of the woods to direct the EMTs," I said.

"10-4!"

I turned back to the camo-clad body. It looked like that of a young man but now days hairstyles aren't definitive. Moreover, his face was turned away from me. I stepped to his far side and knelt in the pine straw and leaf litter. Gingerly, I brushed aside auburn curls, revealing the face of a handsome young man. There was also an angry red wheal on the side of his neck, but that was the least of his worries. Still not convinced he was dead, I inspected him further, but the more I did, the more hopeless I felt.

Blood, which had run from his nose and mouth, was beginning to congeal and his eyes held a fixed, dull gaze. The fact that the blood was no longer oozing let me know his heart had probably stopped pumping. Still, I couldn't stop myself, I pulled his arm from against his body and placed my ear against his rib cage, hoping to hear a beating heart, however faint.

I heard something! A bumping, fluttering sound.

I reached across his back, careful not to touch the arrow, and pulled him closer, pressing my ear tighter to his side. The bumping got louder.

"Holy crap!" exclaimed one of the drill crew, sliding to a stop beside me. Disappointment flooded over me when I realized the sound I'd been hearing was only the drill crew's footfalls as they ran to my aid.

"What the hell?" said Jackie, stepping around his crewman. He looked at me, then knelt at the body and went through pretty much the same attempts to detect life as I had. Finally, he sat back on his heels. "Don't think we're gonna need medical help," he said softly.

"I'm afraid you're right," I said, looking closer at the man's face. "Looks young. Early twenties maybe, and apparently a hunter."

Jackie nodded, then stood. He studied our immediate surroundings and said, "'Cept for one thing ... where's his gun?"

"Good point," I said, joining him. "For that matter, where's his ammo pack?"

"Could've just had them in an easy-access pocket. That's what I do."

I considered checking his pockets, then said, "I would look, but I don't think we should disturb the body any further."

"I agree," he said. Jackie was in his mid-fifties and was a few inches shorter than me. He lifted his white, plastic hard hat, scrubbed his mostly bald head with a calloused paw, then replaced it with a thunk. At this gesture of finality, we all moved a discrete distance from the sad sight.

Within minutes we heard the far-away pulsing of the siren on an emergency vehicle. Like I said, the outskirts of the small town of Sanford was only a few miles away and no doubt most of its residents knew where the Lauderbach Dairy was located. It was one of the oldest businesses in the area. They were probably one of the larger employers as well.

Unfortunately, Jackie and I were correct in our diagnosis. The poor soul was as dead as the proverbial doornail. We stayed out of the way until the EMTs confirmed the death in their call to the Lee County Sheriff's Department. Then we followed their van as it pulled up a small hill that rose gently from the edge of the woods to the leveled area where our rig sat.

The van continued across the pasture to the far gate where they met cars carrying sheriff's deputies and the coroner's van. The lead deputy car and the EMTs pulled aside each other, exchanging information, I imagined. Then the caravan resumed its short journey to where one of Jackie's crew waited at the edge of the woods. He directed them to the body, then joined us at back at the rig where we all tried to get back on track.

Tried being the operative word. The crew might have been working on the casing head, but their chatter was of nothing but the body, what he might have been hunting, where his gun was, how another hunter could have made such a dumb mistake, and on and on. I hoped their distracted state didn't end in a smashed finger or worse.

Jackie and I had gone straight to the doghouse—a small travel trailer provided by the operator for the wellsite geologist.

Everything needed to conduct my job, from a table for studying maps to a small testing lab for samples, was available there. It even had a bathroom, a mini-fridge, and a cot for catnaps or for when wells came in during the dead of night as they often do. "It's stuffy in here," I said as I picked up my topographic map of the farm and a copy of the drill plan and moved to a small wooden stoop outside and into the fresh air.

Jackie followed, expressing his concerns for keeping to Schmid & Medlin's tight schedule. Just as we started going over our plans, another van and a sedan came over the crest of a far hill and through the gate.

"Good thing Mr. Lauderbach moved his cows," I said as we watched them bump down the slope toward the deputy who was motioning at the edge of the woods.

"Huh?" Jackie grunted as another deputy car pulled up to the gate.

"Yeah," I concurred. "Interesting. Detectives and a van full of crime scene techs for a hunting accident?"

Jackie squinted his eyes, tracking their progress. "Guess somebody had the same questions we did."

"Guess so," I said, directing my attention once again to the information before me in an effort to bring the day back on course. From the moment I'd seen the dead man, a sick feeling, like a deep depression, threatened to move in and take over. I shook my head, rubbed my temples, and tried to forge on.

"You feeling okay?" Jackie asked.

"Oh, yeah. I'm fine. Just a little headache is all," I said, flattening the rolled map again. "Let's make sure I flagged Lauderbach #2 where the company man wants it." I was referring to Mr. Ben Overmire, Greenlite's top executive on this job. From time to time, he'd drop by to make sure the well was being drilled according to his design.

Jackie was noting my flag on the map when the sound of another car engine robbed us of normalcy yet again. This time, it was a shiny new Ford Police Interceptor, and instead of driving to what was now becoming an ant hill of activity, it pulled up in front of us. That's when the course of the day suddenly left my control and headed off on its own with me as a passenger on a ride I didn't want to take.

A ride back in time.

TWO

THE LEE COUNTY SHERIFF unfolded himself from the Interceptor, took a few steps in our direction, then stopped. His head seemed to snap back as he lifted his shades. His jaw dropped for a second, but he was quick to regain his composure. Casually, he sauntered to the bottom of the stoop. With one hand on the railing and one booted foot resting on the bottom riser, he said, "Well, well, as I live and breathe, if it ain't Pete Margot's little girl, Cleo."

I, too, ditched my gape and now managed a polite response. "I'm surprised you remember after all these years." I wanted to say I was also surprised he was still sheriff. He had seemed old back in the dark days when I first knew him. But back then, anyone over the age of thirty seemed old.

Sheriff Clyde Stuckey and I stared at each other. I sensed he was trying to judge whether I was still holding a grudge.

I was.

"How long has it been now?" he asked.

"A little over 25 years."

"How is Pete?"

"Fine, I guess. I don't see him much." *Thanks to you.*

"Last I heard he was working in Africa or one of them dark, dangerous countries doing some kind of deep-sea work."

The fact that you keep up with him is pretty sick. "Dad's an underwater welder," I replied stiffly. "Because he's one of only a handful with his level of experience, he travels all over the world." I was ready to end this conversation or at the very least change it. I didn't have to though. The good sheriff did it for me.

"Wow. What are the odds?" he said, giving the railing a smack. "You're back working in my county and bam! Another body turns up! And you find him too. Just like last time ... "

I let a pregnant pause take full effect before asking, "Was there a point in there?"

"Not really. I'm just saying is all." Sheriff Stuckey straightened up, snapped the lapels on his sports jacket and hitched well-worn jeans up on his lanky frame. "Speaking of experience, I imagine you remember the routine, missy, but just to refresh ... I'll need to speak with you and probably these men, too, before I leave. Right now, I'm needed at the scene."

My long-dormant hatred for this man was awakening at an alarming rate. Moreover, I needed somehow to show him that he wasn't dealing with the same young girl he'd known before. I rustled up my sternest professional manner, molded my facial expression to match, and said, "It would be better for us if we could get this over right now. We've had enough interruptions for one day and Mr. Floyd and I have a tight schedule to keep."

Stuckey pulled a toothpick from his jacket pocket, placed it between his teeth and flicked it rapidly up and down. Then, with a sarcastic snort, he angled himself back into the car and headed down the hill.

Jackie blew out a long, low whistle. "He sure don't like you none and what was that about you finding a body before this one?"

"It'd be pretty fair to say Sheriff Stuckey doesn't like anyone, and about the other ... don't give it a second thought."

"No problem," Jackie said with a smart nod of his head. "And about him interrupting us again later, don't you worry none, I can keep them knuckleheads of mine on track."

I could tell Jackie and I were going to get along real good.

———

True to his word, Sheriff Stuckey did return. And true to my memory of him, his interview dragged out way longer than necessary given the fact that none of us knew much of anything. Well, I did mention the fact that I'd seen a wild boar on down the game trail a ways. I even took him to the spot, explaining I'd stopped there to answer my iPhone.

Seemed pointless to add all that extraneous information about being treed. No sense sounding all girly. I just pointed to the tracks under the tree, identifying them as belonging to a feral hog and noted that it's open season on them all year long in North Carolina. To my mind, these facts added weight to the theory that the young man was the victim of a hunting accident. I mean, how else do you end up in camos, dead on a game trail with an arrow in your back?

Sheriff Stuckey had brought a detective with him and stood by, as though supervising, while he asked us questions and took notes. The first thing that stood out about Detective Sergeant Chris

Bryant—he was a pretty boy with startlingly bright blue eyes. He looked to be in his early thirties, his dark brown hair neatly trimmed on the sides, longer on top with a charming cowlick on the right side. He, too, wore jeans and a sports jacket. He was at least four inches taller than my five-foot-nine frame and had a buffed-up physique and a friendly smile.

Every time he would try to wrap things up, Stuckey would ask some irrelevant question to engage the crew in hunting or fishing stories. It was obvious the detective wanted to tell him to take a hike but was too polite. He might not have known what was going on but I did. Stuckey was just showing me he was in control, he could take as much of my time as he wanted.

Also, I got the feeling that he was trying to get at something—I couldn't put my finger on it—that the detective was ignorant of. I wanted to ask if Stuckey knew the victim; almost seemed like he did. I refrained. Given my past with Stuckey, seemed best to stay out of things. Finally, just in case it wasn't obvious to everyone who was in charge, he turned to his detective and said, "Finish up here, Bryant, and make sure you see me in my office before you leave today."

Detective Bryant's face flushed red, but he answered with a crisp, "Yes, sir, will do."

I kinda felt sorry for the guy.

———

Just before leaving the site for the day, I informed Jackie that for the next two days, I'd be in Washington, DC, finishing a project I'd been working on for Martin Marietta Aggregates. My last task before heading to my house in Raleigh forty-five minutes away, was a quick stop by the Lauderbach home.

As I pulled up the drive the stately old white farmhouse was inviting, glowing rosy gold in the mellow light of late afternoon. I trotted up the brick steps and wondered how old they were and if they'd been mined from one of the clay pits prevalent in the area. Not finding a doorbell, I used the knocker. The door opened wide, revealing a portly lady with a round, brown face. "Yes?" she inquired.

"Hi," I said. "I'm Cleo Cooper and I was hoping to meet with the Lauderbachs. Are they home?"

"No, ma'am," she said, her manner nervous and distracted. "Not at the moment. They've, uh … they … ."

"Is there a problem?" I asked.

"Well, there was an accident here on the farm early this afternoon. A hunting accident. The police have been here and talked to them and to me. It was terribly distressing," she said, clutching her ample bosom. "Since then, they've found out it was a close friend. Why, that child has played here with their children since they was little bitty kids. He worked here in the summers in the dairy too. They've gone into town to meet with the family."

"I'm so sorry," I said sadly, explaining that I knew about the accident—without mentioning I'd found him—and why I was there.

"Well, I'm Ruby," she said, wiping her hands on her apron. "I'll tell them you came by. Would you like me to let them know when you'll be back?"

"Yes," I said. "Tell them I'll drop back by in a few days."

———

19

Later that evening in my kitchen, Tulip was finishing her dinner. Her tags made comforting little clinking sounds on her stainless steel bowl. Bud was making his own clinking noises, chopping coleslaw. He was also trying to draw me into a conversation about our upcoming nuptials. We'd planned our wedding for Saturday, November 9th. Bora Bora is spectacular that time of year. The rains haven't set in yet, it's plenty warm, and there are less tourists.

"So what did you think of the pictures of wedding cakes Henri brought over?" Bud asked as I stirred an egg into my cornbread batter. To say that Henri, my daughter, and Will, my son, ages 26 and 28 respectively, were elated about Bud and I remarrying would have been an understatement. When Bud had told the kids he wanted it to be a big, splashy affair, they'd practically floated off the ground. When he'd turned them loose with the wedding planner to do anything they wanted, they'd shot straight to the stratosphere! They were of the age when most any occasion was an excuse for a party.

I poured the batter into my mom's old cast iron frying pan and slid it into the oven. I flopped in a chair to go through the mail that was waiting for me on the kitchen table. Tulip curled at my feet and licked leftover chow from her muzzle as I shuffled through envelopes and sipped wine. Then I remembered Bud had asked me a question.

"Huh?" I said.

"The wedding cakes," he reminded me. "I asked you about the wedding cakes."

"Oh, yeah," I said. "They were really ... lovely."

"Henri's putting a lot into this," Bud said. "She's visited bakers, been to tastings, and looked through stacks of wedding magazines.

That's where she got those pictures. She tore out ones she said were 'you.' So which one are you leaning towards?"

Finding the envelope I'd been looking for, the one from the Smithsonian Institute, I slit it open, adding, "Uh, you know, the one I...uh, already said I liked." I removed the enclosed documents.

"You mean, the one with the naked cupids spiraling up the layers and the bright red heart on top?"

"Yeah, that's the one," I said, pocketing the enclosed staff pass and tossing the envelope and junk mail in the trash.

Bud smacked the bowl of coleslaw down in front of me. "Naked cupids, indeed! You haven't heard a word I've said!"

"Huh?" I startled, sloshing wine on my hand. "I have too!"

"Describe the cake. The one you say you like."

"Uh..." I looked up at him and sucked wine from my fingers—a time-tested diversionary tactic.

"Nice try. Maybe later," Bud said, refilling my wine glass before guiding me to an oversized lounge chair in the den where he gathered me onto his lap. "Tell me what's wrong and don't give me your usual 'everything's fine' crap. Clearly it isn't. Is it the wedding or your new consulting job?"

"Both, kind of...."

"Explain."

"Well, about the wedding, we've been over this and over it for a year now. I don't want this circus you and the kids are planning, and now, since you put them in charge and they're so excited, I can't stop it. They'd be crushed. I feel out of control here, Bud!" Tulip, sensing my anxiety, trotted to us and sat in front of me. I rubbed her silky ears to let her know all was fine and she left to take care of her business, exiting the house through her doggie door.

"That's the idea," Bud said. "You and I have demanding jobs and don't need to be in control. The kids are doing a fine job and they have the wedding planner, too, don't forget. Besides, they're having a grand time and I can afford it. What's the problem?"

I should explain that Bud is a very wealthy entrepreneur from a long line of wealthy entrepreneurs starting back before the Revolutionary War, growing cotton and rice in the Deep South. He's the first of his family, however, to bring them into the 21st century, diversifying the company and moving into other ventures, including everything from oil and gas investments to rocket parts.

"It ... it's just that ... "

"Look. The kids and I have tried for a long, long time to put us back together. I think they deserve this celebration of family. I know I do. It's beginning to worry me that you are so against it."

Great. Make me feel like a world-class heel. "I do feel like celebrating. Just not with two-thirds of the world's population. I wanted it to be something of a more, you know, intimate nature."

"That's what honeymoons are for. And just a heads up: Henri's convinced you haven't actually ordered a dress like you've told her you have. She's on the warpath so maybe you should do something to remedy the situation."

"Like what?"

"Simple. Choose a dress. Now, before we move on to what's bothering you about your new consulting job, have you talked to your dad yet about coming to the wedding?"

Feeling I'd lost this wedding battle, but might still have some effect on the overall war—the size and scope of things—I retreated to fight again another day. I said, "No, that's another thing. As a general rule, I can never get him on the first try, but I've called him repeatedly and he hasn't gotten back to me. I know he's getting my messages."

"You worry too much. He's probably on a job without much reception. Now tell me about the new job."

"Well, there *is* the matter of finding a body not far from our drill site today."

Bud was momentarily struck speechless. Then he found just the right words to sum up my feelings perfectly.

"I guess that was déjà vu all over again, huh?"

"Yes, and except for the fact that this was obviously a hunting accident, it gets even more 'déjà vu,' as you put it, than that." Bud waited quietly but I could feel him tense. "Guess who the Lee County sheriff is now?"

He shrugged. "I have no idea."

"The same one that arrested Dad all those years ago and threw him in jail for something he didn't do. The same one that, if it hadn't been for you, would have succeeded in having him convicted for murder one! The same one that ... "

Bud hugged me tight against his chest. "Cleo, stop. You're working yourself into a state now. The past is the past. And, yes, the old bastard is ... well, a bastard, but he's definitely not worth getting upset about, especially after all these years. Speaking of which, isn't he a little long in the tooth for the job of sheriff?"

I took a deep breath. "You're right, and to answer your question, I have no idea how old he is. He looked fairly fit. I'm trying to chalk this unfortunate event up to ... I don't know, bad karma or something because the thing is, I can't let him or the past distract me right now. I might not have money riding on this job, but it means so much to me to be a part of this new energy revolution in North Carolina. To be part of seeing that it's done right."

"As you know, Bud, the shale in the Cumnock Formation isn't like the Marcellus that lies under most of Pennsylvania. The Marcellus shale lies tens of thousands of feet below the water table. The Cumnock is just a few thousand feet below it and like one of my old professors used to say, 'You can make all the hydrologic models in the lab you want to, but groundwater has a mind of its own. It goes where it wants to go.'"

"Plus," I added, wiggling up from his lap. "Lots of people are becoming very rich. Some even millionaires. Jobs are being created and even though this economic boom only effects the energy sector of North Carolina's economy, like you always say, it spreads. I like being part of something good ... "

"That's all well and good," Bud interrupted. "Just remember, even though you aren't having to do the wedding planning, there are decisions to be made."

"Yes, yes, I'll remember." Bud rolled his eyes but I continued, "And, don't *you* forget, I'm still working on that Smithsonian project. I'm leaving bright and early tomorrow morning to drive up there and you said Tulip could hang out with you."

"I haven't forgotten," Bud said, rising to the sound of the timer to pull my cornbread from the oven. "While we eat you can tell me how you happened to find the hunting accident victim, then I'll see to it you get to bed early. I'll even tuck you in myself."

THREE

NEXT MORNING, BEFORE I could pull my Jeep out of the drive, my daughter, Henri, pulled in behind me. "Hi, Mom," she said, riding my window glass with her elbows as I powered it down. "I'm glad I caught you! Have you chosen your outfit for the wedding yet?"

Good grief. "Henri. The wedding is still weeks away, child. I have plenty of time."

"Just as I suspected," Henri snipped through pursed lips. "Stay right there."

Only because you're blocking me in. I blew out a frustrated breath and watched her trot back to her Tahoe and scramble around in the backseat. She returned with yet more magazine pictures. These had been placed neatly in a manila folder.

"Let me guess, wedding gowns?" I batted my eyelashes. "You shouldn't have gone to such trouble, precious."

"It's no trouble, Mom . . . "

"No, I mean it. You shouldn't have. You do still have a life of your own, don't you? Why aren't you with some wonderful man right now? You should be trying to find a husband and have a wedding of your own. Do you even have a date for this weekend? You and Will are entirely too twirled up about this wedding."

"It's Thursday morning, Mom," Henri replied primly. "Kind of an early start for the weekend and don't you worry about my love life, I've got that covered."

"Yeah, that was a bit over the top ... " Me worrying about Henri's love life would be akin to Madonna's mother worrying about hers.

"Well, now you're just being catty," Henri snapped. "Besides, I've got my work cut out for me, two photo shoots this week and a large wedding and all the parties leading up to it next week. Now. Back to *your* wedding, your gown, as you put it."

"Henri, I don't have time right—"

"Actually there should be no gown," she interrupted.

"Huh?"

"I don't think a gown is appropriate for a second wedding to the same man. Besides, you've fiddle-farted around for a year and now it's too late to order one. So, when you get time this evening in your hotel room, look at these couture suits. There are some elegant ones in satins and silks, and some with beautiful beadwork too. And, just so you know, I've looked into availability and any of these will have to be ordered too. They just don't take as long as a gown. Then there are the alterations ... "

Why hadn't I planned this driveway as a half circle?

"And by the way," she continued, "there are only five weeks left before the wedding, so keep that in mind when you order. Anyway, I highlighted the suits that you can see in person in several shops in the DC area." She dropped the folder in my lap. "See how lucky you are to have me to make sure you end up with something nice … and appropriate?"

"Yep. I'm lucky there," I said, pulling forward in the drive just enough to make backing around her car possible. I gave her a cheery wave from the street and headed for Washington.

———

Entering the Willard Hotel on Pennsylvania Avenue was just as impressive this time as it was when I was here several months ago. I'd been contracted by Martin Marietta to coordinate their part of a project they were participating in with the Smithsonian Museum and they'd insisted I stay here. Since they were paying the bill, I didn't quibble. Their executive in charge of the project, the man who had hired me, was a rock hound. He said I'd be impressed with the variety of marble used in the hotel.

I was. The floor, as well as the massive Doric columns in the main lobby—they had to be at least twenty feet tall—were made of beautiful golden Italian marble. Rich tones of olive and gold on the walls and in the scattered Persian carpets enhanced the natural beauty of the stone. Lacy parlor palms in sculptured pots softened the area and gave it a timeless feel.

As I waited for the desk clerk to check me in and took in the warm ambiance of the room, I couldn't help but imagine some prehistoric sea where calcium carbonate had accumulated over millions of years into a deposit hundreds of feet thick. The amount of heat and pressure required to turn it and the component of iron oxide that gave it its distinctive color into marble was mind boggling. "Welcome back to the Willard, Ms. Cooper. Is this a pleasure trip or will you be working with the Smithsonian again?"

"Working, Mr. Hansby," I said, reading his name tag. "And thank you for remembering me."

"Please let me know when you're ready, and I'll call you a cab."

"Thanks, but it's such a beautiful day, I believe I'll walk. Besides I've been cooped up in the car for hours and the exercise will do me good."

"Very good, ma'am," said Mr. Hansby, with a polite nod of his head.

———

My walk was invigorating. There's no way to go to our nation's capitol and not feel the beauty and majesty of the place. I felt honored just to be here. That I was in charge of coordinating part of a major exhibit for the world-renowned museum was pretty heady stuff. I made my way west on Pennsylvania until I hit 15th Street. I enjoyed the gardens and fountains of the Elipse as I made my way to Jefferson Street and decided, once there, to use the museum's impressive main entrance. Besides, I just love that elephant.

Hanging a quick right at the Hall of Dinosaurs, I pulled my temporary staff pass from my purse. I showed it to the guard, then hung it around my neck. The hall was closed—curtained off until the big unveiling—while the new exhibit was being constructed. It would open again in a few months with a gala event complete with movie stars as well as corporate and political bigwigs.

The exhibit, entitled *Fossils as a Natural Resource*, would focus on five natural resources: coal, diatomaceous earth, oil-impregnated sandstone, fossiliferous limestone, and phosphate. Composed primarily of fossils, they are widely used in our everyday life. A large pylon of each, twelve-feet tall by ten-feet wide by two-feet thick, would be on display, along with a wide variety of the products derived from it. For instance, items like toothpaste and Tums can't be produced without limestone. Sadly, most folks don't know that.

Each of the pylons was to appear as though taken straight from the earth so visitors could view them in their natural state. Unfortunately, when it came to fossiliferous limestone, there was a problem. It didn't exist in beds that thick in the quarries owned by the company that had donated the stone and hired me to oversee the project.

Creating a pylon that *looked* like it did called for some imaginative engineering on my part—not to mention a pavement splitter, a garden hose, and a trowel—but it had been fun.

When I didn't see the project engineer I'd met on an earlier trip, I asked a friendly young man in a Smithsonian uniform where he might be. He stopped stirring the contents of a five-gallon bucket and offered to take me to his boss.

We found him behind the twelve-foot-tall skeleton of Tyrannosaurus Rex, leaning over a set of blueprints entitled: *Smithsonian Institute after Cleo Cooper*. That might be a small thing to some people, but for me, it was a big thrill. When I leaned over his shoulder, casting a shadow on his work, he turned with a smile and told me I was just in time to see the first pieces of the pylon go up...if the cement matched.

It didn't. But, after several trial runs, adding larger and larger lumps of the original stone to the cement mix, we finally got it right. We were standing back from the pylon, watching, as the next section was hoisted into place, when someone tapped me on the shoulder. I turned to greet a familiar face. "Dr. Watson, I presume," I said, laughing at the same tired old line he'd probably heard a million times since he'd been awarded his PhD at Brigham Young back in the early 80s.

"I'd heard a rumor you'd be here for the construction of your baby. I'm glad to see it was true," said Dr. Jonathan Byron Watson. He'd been a visiting fellow in the Paleontology Department at UNC when I was there working on my master's thesis in sedimentary petrology. His office was next door to mine and we'd become friends. Now he was on staff at the Smithsonian and was one of the leading paleoentomologists in the world, specializing in insects of the Triassic Period.

After catching Dr. Watson up on the other projects I was currently engaged in, including my impending nuptials, I said, "So, tell me, Watson,"—that's what everyone called him—"what are you up to these days?"

"Ah, better to show you, my child," he said, his pale blue eyes twinkling. I joined him in the elevator, then followed his sturdy form through a labyrinth of halls until we reached his lab. He wasn't a terribly tall man—probably five-feet-ten—but despite his age, which had to be pushing hard at seventy, he was still powerfully built.

"Check out this lovely little number," he said, as he pulled open a narrow drawer in a specimen chest that reached from floor to ceiling. He couldn't have been prouder if he were introducing his own child.

"Oh, man," I said, bending over to look at the perfect impression of a mayfly in a hand-sized slab of red clay. The insect was so complete that I could make out the exact shape of its lacy wings, even to the venation. "That's a beauty. Obviously found in a red bed, but where exactly? Or, don't you want to say?"

"Oh, I don't mind saying because you'll find out soon enough," Watson said. "Of course, I'd like you to keep this to yourself, but this little fellow is going to be the subject of my latest publication. I'm basing my reputation on it being a new species within the order Ephemeroptera. Look at the size of the back wings as compared to those of the present day."

"Ah," I said. "They're larger, aren't they?"

"Yes," Watson said. "Today's mayflies have small back wings while mayflies of the Paleozoic sported back wings as large as their forewings. This guy's were somewhere in between, plus the venation was way more complex. Moreover, the only mayfly that has mouthparts similar to my specimen is an African species—which makes sense, of course, since North Carolina and Africa were connected up until the late Triassic when seafloor spreading began."

"Oh, so you found this in one of the red beds in North Carolina. Is that why you're telling me—because I'm likely to see you tromping around in the woods down there anyway?"

"Actually, I'll be in the Durham sub-basin area, to the north from where you said you were, in the Sanford sub-basin. The reason I told you is because we go way back and I knew you'd appreciate how significant this little mayfly could be to me and my career."

"Aw, thanks, Watson. I'm very happy for you."

"My dear, compared to me, you're still a teenager. You have no idea how much it means, but sadly, one day you'll find out."

"How's that?"

"One day, you'll find that advancing age makes people view you differently. They take you less seriously. It's almost like you start becoming invisible. No matter that it should be the other way around." Watson sighed. "That's just our modern culture, I guess."

"I guess," I agreed. "But like you said, this discovery will give new life to you and your career." I looked at my watch. "Let me get back to my project. Then tonight, let's go someplace nice for dinner to celebrate your new species."

Watson bent close to my shoulder. His voice took on a serious tone and he said, "Again, this is for your ears only, Cleo, but I believe this little guy may be a transitional fossil."

"Wow," I breathed. "That's some heady stuff."

"So true, my dear. Anything that helps an old educator such as myself make a controversial concept like evolution easier for the common man to understand is a God-send. It increases the hope that one day we'll all be able to relate to one another and thereby have a more peaceful world."

————

Back at the Willard late that same evening, I was all tucked in bed and ready to sleep. Unfortunately, my brain had other ideas. I was so wired from stimulating discussions on evolution and missing links that sleep was proving to be an impossible task.

Dinner at a popular upscale restaurant in town where the project engineer and his wife had connections and managed to finagle a reservation was sumptuous. They'd joined me and Watson and his wife and we'd all made a merry old time of it. Still, with a full day planned for tomorrow, including finishing the pylon, a little shopping, and the four-hour drive back home, I needed to get some rest. Then I remembered the folder of wedding suits Henri had given me. That ought to knock the excitement right out of anybody.

Thumbing through the stack of magnificent yet tasteful suits, Henri's idea of how I should look on my wedding day came through loud and clear. My eyes crossed and next thing I knew, I was answering the courtesy wake-up call I'd requested.

Friday morning flew by at the Smithsonian; however, a few problems with the pylon, calling for additional sizing of several of the top segments, prolonged my departure. It was after lunch before the last piece was cemented into place, so after saying my goodbyes I nixed my little shopping excursion and headed back to the Willard to check out. Just as I crossed Connecticut, however, a compulsion overcame me and I turned up the street, my thought being just to window shop at a few of the luxury boutiques. Then, one I recognized from Henri's folder caught my eye.

The store, specializing in couture fashion, was so enticing I was lured inside. Once there, I moved from one spectacular garment to another, farther and farther back into the store until I noticed the bridal section. Dutifully, I strolled over to look at their "appropriate" wedding suits. A beautiful sales attendant, late-fifties with her silvery blond hair swept up in an elegant French twist, approached me. "May I offer Madam assistance?" Her accent was as French as her do.

"Yes, you may," I said, shaking her proffered hand. She introduced herself as Fanny. "I'm Cleo Cooper, Fanny," I said. "And I'd like to see something in a wedding suit... perhaps ivory or maybe a light coffee color..."

"Non, non, non," said Fanny, stepping back and eyeing me critically.

"Pardon?" I said.

"This would not be for you," Fanny said, reverting to English. "You have the beautiful body, and youth is still very much on your side. You must revel in these assets on this your most wonderful day."

"Well, it is my second wedding."

"All the more reason for you to assert yourself," Fanny said, with a wise tilt of her head.

"Interesting you should say that, Fanny," I said. "Because, frankly, wearing a suit to my wedding is about as exciting as a cup of chicken soup."

Fanny smiled knowingly and said, "Tell me. If you could be a food or a drink offered to your husband on that day, what would it be?"

Without hesitation, I answered, "'96 Dom in a Waterford flute." Although Bud is generally a Bud Light kinda guy, he has his elegant moments and when he does, Dom Perignon is what he always orders.

"As I suspected," Fanny said. "Follow me."

I did. We entered a large, opulent dressing room with a raised stage flanked on three sides with mirrors. "Please make yourself comfortable," Fanny offered graciously, motioning to an ornate Baroque chair before disappearing from the room. She returned in a wink, cradling a gown with both arms.

"This, madam, is you." She held up the gown by its satin hanger, artfully flaring its skirt, allowing the hem to trail upon the lush carpet.

My astonished expression was quickly replaced with a wry smile. Fanny slipped politely from the room, but not before discreetly pointing out that undergarments with this gown were unacceptable. I stripped out of my street clothes, but kept on my thong. When she returned with a soft knock, she helped me into the gown. I stepped up on the stage and looked at myself. Turning slowly before the mirrors, I viewed the gown from all sides. A wonderful feeling of calm and confidence enveloped me and I said to Fanny, "I'll take it."

"A wise choice, madam."

Following a measuring session by a covey of tiny Asian women, I paid for my new treasure—gratefully without fainting upon seeing the price. Everything was moving along well until I realized there had been a miscommunication regarding the date of the wedding.

Fanny had thought the wedding date was to be November 9th of *next year*, not this one. This brought about a slew of international calls dominated by French swear words. When it was all over, she calmly told me the floor sample would be remade to my exact measurements in about three weeks. At that time I'd be expected for another fitting to make sure everything was perfect.

My trip back home that evening was uneventful. I spent the drive time planning out my weekend and looking forward to some quiet time with Bud. Every now and then, though, I thought of the gown and laughed and laughed.

FOUR

MONDAY WAS ANOTHER SPARKLING fall day and Tulip paced around my kitchen. She was raring to go. That mysterious internal alarm she possessed, the one that alerted her to the possibility of field work must have gone off. She fidgeted impatiently while I finished my coffee and read the obits from the online edition of the *Sanford Herald*. I noted that the funeral for Clinton Baker, the young man accidentally killed on the Lauderbach farm, had been held on Saturday. It made me sad to contemplate such a waste of a young life. I closed my laptop with a sigh and Tulip scrambled for the door.

Bud, who had just bounded down the stairs, followed me outside.

"Okay, girl, load up," I said unnecessarily to Tulip. She hopped into the cargo area of my old 1986 CJ-8 Jeep Scrambler and I pulled the fiberglass door closed and latched it.

Before I could open my door, Bud wrapped his arm around my waist, nuzzled my neck and said, "What would you do if you came home this afternoon to find a shiny new Jeep Grand Cherokee waiting for you?"

"We've been over this many times, Bud," I said, giving him a peck on the lips. "I wouldn't like it and you know why."

"Right," Bud snipped. "You don't want anything shiny and new that you can't drive through the woods and swamps for fear of scratching or denting said shiny and new finish."

"Exactly." I pushed away from him, giving him a harder-than-playful pinch on the abs before climbing behind the wheel.

"Ouch!" Bud squawked as though fatally wounded.

"What do you have planned today?" I asked sweetly.

"You're changing the subject, but I've been meaning to tell you. I probably won't be here this evening or the next. Actually, I'm going to be in and out all week with business meetings, but we'll keep in touch by phone."

"Okay then, I'll see you when I see you. And, Bud, there better not be a new Jeep in the driveway when I get home this afternoon ... or ever."

On my way to the site, I thought about our little driveway exchange and tried not to make too much of it. If our new marriage was going to be successful, it was paramount for me to keep old fears and anxieties at bay. Still, my old Jeep was very dear to me. It had safely carried me thousands of miles and gotten me out of many a sticky situation, literally. The fact that he was trying to push me around on this issue, yet again, was disappointing. The fact that he didn't understand why the Jeep was special to me was infuriating.

The issue was more than simple scratches and dents. The 1986 Jeep Scrambler had just come out when I'd met Bud. At the time I was struggling to finish my master's thesis, doing pro-bono work for a gas exploration company, and trying to manage the over-whelming family issues present in my life. Those issues were the reason I couldn't have the Scrambler in the first place. Normally, it would have been the perfect graduation gift from my parents. I know that because my dad told me so … from behind bars in the county jail while he awaited trial for murder.

Fast forward to when Bud and I separated and I'd refused to take any alimony. After all, I was the one who'd left. In desperate need of transportation and scant funds, it seemed fate had guided me to the used car lot where I found the same model Jeep Scram-bler. I bought it on the spot and from then on I thought of it as the magic Jeep. Over the years it became a symbol of my indepen-dence. That Bud couldn't understand really ticked me off.

And, it *was* a plus that I never had to worry about damaging it, squeezing down overgrown logging trails. The hefty V-8 engine had plenty of power, plus I'd added a few extras over the years, like my trusty wench mounted on the front bumper, and of course the addi-tion of a backseat and my custom hard top. No siree. No one was separating me from the magic Jeep.

———

By the time I reached the Lauderbach farm, I'd pushed the Jeep incident to the back of my mind, but I hadn't forgotten it. Tulip whined with anticipation as we approached the drilling area and parked. I grabbed my hard hat from the backseat and joined the men at the rig. Following an introduction to Jackie, Tulip went off on her merry way to check out the site and see if she could find a cow pie or two to roll in. I wasn't worried, there's always water on a drill site and I kept a towel in the car just for her.

"How'd your trip to DC go?" Jackie asked.

"Just fine. Thanks for asking. We got my pylon put together, so now all that remains is the grand opening."

"You haven't missed anything here. We're about 800 feet down in the Sanford."

"Very good," I said. "That puts us about halfway to the Cumnock. I'll start taking samples today. According to Greenlite's drill plan, we'll start making our turn at about 1,750 feet, so we have plenty of time to identify beds before we get there. Before I get started, however, I still need to run over and meet the Lauderbachs. I tried to call on them the day that kid got killed in the hunting accident but they'd gone to make a condolence call at his home. Seems he was one of their employees."

"Damn shame," Jackie said, shaking his head. "No one that young should die. Why, he'd hardly started living yet." We pontificated on the sadness of the event for a moment, then Jackie said, "You go do what you need to do. We'll be drilling on ahead."

"Good enough. I'll be back in a few."

Before leaving the site, I called Tulip to the office trailer. "You give real meaning to the term doghouse, girl," I said as I poured her some water and cracked open the windows. "I'll only be gone a few minutes, then you can go back to scouting for cow pies." Office trailers are all pretty much the same, so, feeling right at home, she hopped up on the cot, turned around a few times, and prepared to take a nap until I got back.

My second trip to the Lauderbach home was successful. Ruby, the sweet housekeeper I'd met earlier, greeted me at the door again. "Come on in," she said. "Mrs. Lauderbach is in the sunroom. I'll go ask if she can see you."

Standing in the high-ceilinged foyer, I was grateful that I hadn't been on the drill site long enough to get my boots dirty. Site preparation for a drilling operation like ours rearranges practically all the soil on three acres or more. There are mud pits to be dug and numerous areas to be leveled for pipe and casing storage as well as the rig pad itself. If it rained ... well, you get the picture.

I checked my appearance in an impressive mahogany-framed mirror, featuring intricately carved fruit and game birds, and straightened my ponytail. A glorious antique grandfather clock, it had to be seven feet tall or more, majestically ticked away the minutes until Ruby returned and guided me to the sunroom on the east side of the house.

I don't know what I'd been expecting, but Mrs. Lauderbach didn't fit any preconceived notions I might have had about what a dairy-farmer's wife ought to look like. She was tiny, frail, and appeared to be weak as a bird. I pegged her at mid-fifties, but she was so thin it was hard to say for sure. Her hair was a soft brown, naturally curly with only a few gray strands, and her eyes were a vivid green. She rose to greet me.

"Ms. Cooper," she said and gestured to a chair beside hers, which was facing floor-to-ceiling windows. The top row had been opened, allowing the cool air outside to bring the room to a comfortable temperature and occasionally billowing the gauzy cream drapes stacked in the corners.

I shook her hand, then sat in the comfy wicker chair and looked out at a lush green lawn, sloping gently to a picturesque farm pond. On the south side of the lawn were a fall vegetable garden, several rows of Muscadine grapevines, and several rows of fruit trees. On the north side, an array of outbuildings were well-maintained. Since smokehouses and chicken coops are no longer needed, I imagined these building were used for storage. Taken all together, the scene was reminiscent of a Grant Wood painting.

"I'm so sorry I missed your visit last Wednesday," Mrs. Lauderbach said. "But Clinton, the student killed in the hunting accident on our farm, was a close family friend." She paused, composing herself, then continued. "Ruby told me she explained to you our relationship with him."

"Yes, she did," I said. "It must have been devastating to your entire family. I'm so sorry for your loss."

"Thank you for your kind words, Ms. Cooper . . . "

"Please, call me Cleo."

"Thank you, my dear, and please, call me Annette. We're just one big family here at the dairy. All our employees have been with us for most of their lives. My father ran this dairy and his father ran it before him. One day, God willing, my children will run it when my husband and I no longer can. I understand you're the person we are to contact if we have any questions about the well, about how it's progressing, or if there are any problems."

"That's correct," I said. "If there is anything you want to ask me, just call this number," I handed her my business card with my cell number. "If I don't respond, it's only because I didn't hear the ring. It's often very loud on site. If that happens, just leave a voicemail or a text and I'll be right over. Of course, you can always come to the site, but I warn you, it gets pretty muddy sometimes."

"Oh, I may look a little worse for wear right now, but I can assure you, I don't mind mud or muck," she laughed, then leaned over conspiratorially and added, "We call it muck when it's mixed with cow manure . . . "

She was interrupted when Ruby stepped into the room asking, "Would Ms. Cooper like to join you for some cookies and milk?"

41

Cookies and milk? "Thanks, no, Ruby," I said. "I need to get back to the site in a few minutes."

"Ruby insists I eat a fattening snack twice a day and a big meal three times a day," Annette said. "She's trying to put the weight I lost after the accident back on these bones."

"Oh?" I said, hoping she'd explain.

"Yes. My husband and I were both injured in a car accident about nine months ago. Arthur still has a ways to go, but he's getting there. We both will with Ruby's help."

Ruby strode across the room, gave her employer a pat on the shoulder, then fussed with a wool throw that had fallen from her lap. "You gonna catch your death in this room with these windows open." She then proceeded to huff about the room pushing the top windows closed with a pole made for that purpose.

"Now Ruby, not all of them ... " Annette complained.

"Yes, not all of them," a new voice called from the doorway. A handsome man in a wheelchair pushed himself briskly into the room. "I think fresh air and sunshine are the best medicine, don't you?" he said, addressing me.

"No offense, Ruby, but I have to agree with this gentleman," I said, standing and offering my hand as I introduced myself.

"Arthur Lauderbach," he said with a firm handshake. "Call me Arthur." He instantly reminded me of the character Thurston Howell III, on the old sixties sitcom *Gilligan's Island*—my kids loved those reruns—basically an adorable older gentleman whose complete devotion to his wife was obvious. Except for being in a wheelchair, he looked fit. I did notice, however, that his legs, clad in creased jeans, appeared painfully thin. "So you're our go-to lady at the well?"

I recited my credentials and gave them a timeline of how I hoped events would unfold at the well, ending with, "… so according to indications from two previous wells dug back in the eighties, we expect to hit our target horizon, the Cumnock Formation at about 1850 feet. We'll stop vertical drilling at 500 feet above this horizon so we can make a slow, gradual turn until we are drilling horizontally in the formation itself…"

I paused because Arthur's expression became quizzical. "You can make a turn in a well?"

"Yes," I explained. "This stage of the operation will be accomplished with a steerable drilling head. Once we've reached the extent of our horizontal section, we'll remove the drill pipe and lower steel casing into the hole, pump cement into it until it comes out the shoe end of the pipe, and fills the space between the casing and the rock. When that is completed, hydraulic fracturing will proceed."

"But how do you know there is gas down there? I mean, before we spend all that money," asked Annette with a worried look on her face.

"Well, first, if Greenlite Energy didn't feel strongly about the viability of this new production field, they wouldn't pull a rig off a well-known production field like the one they were drilling in Pennsylvania to send it down here. You can rest assured they did their homework after you contacted them."

"They've studied the core samples from those first wells I mentioned and took their own samples from stream beds and road cuts on your land. Believe me, after compiling all the information available, they feel your property is a good bet. And, more importantly, there are a respectable number of wells already pumping gas into new pipelines in this area."

"God, I hope they're right," Annette said.

"Now, honey," her husband soothed, "don't get yourself worried. We're going to come out of all this just fine, you'll see."

All this? Was there something other than a car wreck involved here? "Moreover," I continued, "they like the fact that the land has been continually owned by one family, that you have enough in one contiguous tract that they can drill several wells, using the 160-acre well spacing standard. When we reach the target formation, the Cumnock, I'll take samples and subject them to lab tests. At that point, you'll know as much as anyone whether it's worth the risk."

Both Lauderbachs looked like they were standing before a roulette wheel with all their savings on the table. A timid tapping at the door caught my attention. A young girl, early twenties, in jeans and a UNC sweatshirt crossed the room and gave both Lauderbachs a peck on the cheek.

"Oh, Sara, you're home," Annette said, then introduced her daughter to me.

"Nice sweatshirt," I said, smiling. "Are you a student there?"

"Sure am," Sara beamed. "I'm a senior this year. I just dropped by to check on my folks, but I'm glad for the chance to meet you. I wanted to come out to the well and talk to you in person, look around a bit, you know, but I didn't know if that'd be okay."

"Of course it is," I said. "I'd be glad to show you around. It's your farm, after all, and you can go anywhere on it you'd like. If you're at the drill site, though, we want you to be accompanied by either me or one of Greenlite's employees so we can be sure you don't get hurt while you're there. Was there something in particular you wanted to see?"

"Well, I guess I just want to actually see the settling ponds and where the fracking fluids are stored … that kind of thing. I can't help but worry about the farm, the groundwater and all."

"I understand and appreciate your concerns completely," I said. "The farm was pristine when we arrived and it'll be pristine when we leave, I promise, but I admire you for taking responsibility and checking things out for yourself."

"So I can come by?"

"Whenever you'd like." I gave her my card. "Call my cell anytime."

———

Sheriff Stuckey's Interceptor was parked in front of the doghouse when I returned to the site. I wasn't surprised. In my mind, he'd take any opportunity to irritate and harass me. Jackie was on the stoop with him. I parked my Jeep and went to see what he wanted.

Jackie met me before I reached the steps and said, "You need me, I'll be at the rig."

"Thanks, Jackie," I said, then climbed the stairs to where Stuckey stood.

"Miz Cooper," Stuckey greeted me.

"What can I do for you?" I asked, leaning against the stoop railing. I had no intention of inviting him inside.

"Well," he drawled, "as you may remember, I'm not one for beating 'round the bush. You're my main suspect in the murder of that boy you *found* in the woods Wednesday. What do you have to say about that?"

The state should never have closed Dorothea Dix Hill Mental Hospital? His utter inappropriateness and lack of professionalism almost left me speechless. Almost. I looked him square in the eye

45

and said, "Looked to me like he was the victim of a hunting accident."

"Well, aren't you just the little detective?" Stuckey sneered. "And for your information, missy, the arrow didn't kill him and it wasn't an accident."

Now that was a surprise. "Really? How do you know that?"

"'Cause I'm the sheriff and you're just a civilian. Just soon's I saw him with an arrow in his shoulder blade yet bleeding from his mouth as well as his nose, I knew he had to have another wound. Didn't take an Einstein to roll him up and see the stab wound in his stomach. That's what caused the bleeding from the mouth."

"There you go, Sheriff," I said. "That's why you get the big bucks. Now tell me, what makes you think *I* did it?"

"Again, I'm the sheriff and you're … "

"Yeah, yeah. I get it. I'm the civilian. I'm also working here, so if you could cut to the chase."

"I look for the person with the motive and opportunity. You, and for that matter, the Lauderbachs, have the same motive, but since you found the body, that means you were right there in the area, so you go straight to the top of the list."

"I hate to encourage you, but please, enlighten me. What motive do the Lauderbachs and I both have?" I asked incredulously. "And while you're at it, you can tell me why you think I would want to kill him. I didn't even know him. Besides, I wouldn't be able to hit the broad side of a barn with an arrow, and I'm pretty sure you'd have to be very skillful to actually hit a moving target like a person."

The sheriff squinted his eyes at me and said in a knowing way, "You and the Lauderbachs both have lots of money riding on these wells and since the Baker boy threatened to stop this operation, I'd call that a very credible motive."

"You better check your facts, Stuckey," I said with a smirk. "You do check facts don't you?" Stuckey just stared at me. "Well, it doesn't appear so, because if you did, you'd know I don't have a dime riding on this or any other well in the basin. I'm just a paid employee. I was hired by Greenlite to be their wellsite geologist. And, it's none of my business, but it doesn't appear to me that the Lauderbachs are in such dire straights that they'd be willing to kill for it."

Stuckey's face fell the slightest bit so I kept up my ridicule. "And what on earth could a young college student do to stop them from drilling on their own property?"

Regaining his cocky attitude, he said, "Oh, like you didn't know Baker was a environmentalist! Everyone around here knows that. He was head of a youth movement that was planning a big protest at the Legislature to stop this damn fracking."

"Protesters are a way of life in my profession," I said calmly. "I deal with them on a regular basis and despite what you apparently think, I don't dislike them. That'd be like disliking America. Everyone here has a right to protest. Their rights, however, don't trump the law or the rights of a private citizen to do what they please with their land. As long as no rules are being broken, and the proper permits and leases have been filed, protesters are, well, just protesters. I welcome them as part of the American culture. Plus they help keep everyone on their toes so we can all be safe while we enjoy the comforts and conveniences of living in the golden age of hydrocarbons."

"Since you're so smart, "Stuckey sneered, "you want to know why he was dressed in camos?"

"Not really … "

"'Cause he was snooping on you guys, that's why. Taking pictures of some of your infractions. You saw him, found out all about him, and didn't want to take the chance he'd shut down your operation."

Infractions? Holding a tight rein on my desire to ask Stuckey where his attendants were—clearly he needed to be under close care on a psych ward—I said, "You should consider letting your detective handle this case. He has a much better grip on … reality than you. Now if you'll excuse me, I've got some work to do in the lab."

I closed the doghouse door behind me and moved to the window to make sure Stuckey left. Then I flopped on the cot beside Tulip and rubbed her bony head. "What the hell?" I breathed. "That man is certifiable." Tulip thumped her tail. "So you concur?"

She jumped to the floor and gave me one of her "inside" woofs.

I stood and patted her sides, my mood already considerably improved. "My thoughts exactly. Come on, girl, let's go collect samples and get a head start on logging. Then, because your expertise on human behavior is without parallel, I'll treat you to a burger for lunch. I know just the place."

FIVE

Now, I'm no detective. I have no special skills at rooting out evil or following clues that invariably lead me to the den of a crook or a murderer or other dastardly dude. But I am an investigator of another type. As a prospector I seek out and find valuable deposits of a geologic nature. Like a detective, I look to the past for clues to the present state of conditions deep under the ground. Then I follow up, using my lab skills to prove I'm on the right track.

So when someone like the head of the local branch of law enforcement accuses me of murder, I naturally try to put all my skills together to save myself. And if there's one thing that detectives and geologists have in common, it's that the best tool in our box is our ability to communicate. You'd be surprised what you can learn by just talking to people.

As I drove the outskirts of Sanford on my way to Chapel Hill, I stopped at a convenient mart and a bought a copy of the *Sanford Herald*. Just before reaching my destination, UNC, which was about 25 miles from the site, I spotted a Mickey D's. I hung a left off 15-501 and pulled up to the drive-through and ordered a couple of quarter-pounders with cheese, Tulip's all-time favorite. She topped off her lunch with a slurp of fresh bottled water. When she was done, I pitched the rest of the water from her bowl and headed up the street to the Mitchell Building, which houses the Department of Geological Sciences.

I wasn't sure what the current school policy was regarding dogs in the buildings. In my day, they were allowed, so I decided to chance it. Tulip followed politely at my heels. Because I keep in touch with the department, I knew that the same secretary was there from when I was a student. "Melody," I said when I saw her seated behind her desk typing away as though in a time warp. "How do you do it? You haven't changed a bit."

"Cleo!" Melody said, smiling. "What a nice surprise, and I could say the same. You look very happy too. Must be your upcoming nuptials."

"How'd you know about that?"

"Oh, now Cleo, you know how fast word travels in the geologic community. When is the big event?"

"Uh," I said, trying to remember the exact date. "Just a little over a month away now." Melody asked numerous questions about the wedding plans, none of which I could answer. I fumbled my way through them as best as I could, then steered the conversation to the reason for my trip. "Say, Melody," I said. "Do you know anything about an environmental protest group over here, particularly one planning a fracking protest at the Legislative building in Raleigh?"

"I'd imagine if there was something planned, it'd be the kids over at IE—the Institute for the Environment—doing it. Have you been over there?"

"No," I said. "But I will."

"Well, if you don't find out what you need to know over there, I happen to know where a lot of the IE students hang out."

"I don't doubt you do," I laughed.

———

It didn't take me long to find the student bulletin board on the main hall at IE. When I didn't find any notice of a scheduled protest at the Legislature, I decided to check out the Internet café, which, according to Melody, was their favored haunt.

"Perfect," I said to Tulip as I pulled to the curb a short ways down Franklin Street from the café. "They've got outdoor tables." Much to her chagrin, I clipped Tulip's leash to her collar, grabbed my copy of the *Sanford Herald*, and found an empty outdoor table. Tulip's a magnet for kids of all ages. She just smiles, wags her tail, and they can't resist.

It wasn't long before she'd lured in three dewy-faced co-eds, who, sure enough, were from IE. Their T-shirts, sporting environmental phrases, posed the perfect segue into the bug-a-boo de jour: fracking. It was like pouring gasoline on a campfire. They fumed and fussed with the usual uninformed and misinformed outrage. I waited them out, then mentioned that I had a young friend, Clinton Baker, now sadly deceased, who was also strongly against the practice. Surprisingly, they'd never heard of him.

I opened my newspaper to the obits and showed them Baker's photo. "Are you sure?" I asked. "He was majoring in environmental sciences."

"Oh, wow. He's cute!" said the tallest of the girls. "Are you sure he's dead?"

"Oh for heaven's sake, Stephanie," snapped one of her friends. "Don't be a goofball. That's his *obituary* ... hello ... under the photo!"

Stephanie looked at the photo again. "Bummer," she said.

The third co-ed spoke up. "Well, honestly, the three of us are freshmen so it could be that since he's like ... older, and a few years ahead, that we don't know him because we don't share any of the same classes."

"I know," offered the brilliant Stephanie. "Let me show this photo to Daryl and Tyler. They're seniors." She took the *Herald*, folded it to Clinton's photo, and headed to a table of guys apparently deeply engaged in iPad games. Either that or they all had to pee really bad. Stephanie shoved the paper in front of one of the squirming young men. He retracted his tongue, which had been wiggling like mine does when threading a needle, and looked at the photo. I watched as the guys passed it around the table. Negative headshakes told me I'd hit a dead end.

I thought about heading over to the records department, but decided to Google Clinton to see if I could find out what his major was. It would've been nice though if I could've talked to some students who knew him. I checked my watch. Time to get back to work. My lunch hour was long over.

———

The afternoon droned on with drilling proceeding at a normal rate. It was about five thirty and I was in the doghouse, analyzing samples and filling in my log sheet, when the phone rang. It was the company man, Ben Overmire, Greenlite's top executive on the Lauderbach job and the well designer. Fortunately he was calling from the main office in Pennsylvania and not out at the front gate. The man had a reputation of just dropping in unannounced.

I caught him up on our current down hole position. Then he surprised me, saying he'd changed his mind on the location of Lauderbach #2. He gave me the new coordinates and explained his reasoning for the move. I told him I'd take care of it and we were discussing the differences between the drill plans for the two wells when I heard a car pull up. It was Sara Lauderbach, daughter of Arthur and Annette. I excused myself and went to the door to greet her.

"Sara," I said. "Have you come for that tour I promised you?"

"If you're sure you have time and I won't get in your way," she said. "Dad would skin me if he thought I'd caused so much as a one-second delay out here. He's told me umpteen times how much money this well is costing."

What luck! When I wasn't able to find any information on Clinton at UNC, I'd considered calling Sara. After all, she and Clinton had grown up together. If I was a detective, she'd be one of the first people I'd talk to. And since I'd just been informed that very morning that I was the prime suspect in a murder, I needed to do all in my power to find out the identity of the real killer while I could.

I wouldn't put it past Stuckey, being the lunatic he was, to try to throw me in jail. I wouldn't be the first innocent person in my family he'd done that to. Never mind that it made no sense for me to kill a person I didn't even know to keep him from protesting a well that I had no financial stake in.

"You're not holding up a thing," I said. "Come on in. We'll start with the office. We call it the doghouse, which has nothing whatever to do with Miss Tulip," I said, pointing to her prone body on the cot, "and then we'll move out to the drilling pad." I showed her the lab, how I analyze samples and some of the different types of maps I use when prospecting or testing property. After fitting her with a hard hat, we moved outside where Jackie joined us. Tulip, never one to miss anything, followed along.

Jackie briefly explained to Sara how the drill works and the differences between horizontal and vertical drilling, besides the obvious. When we moved over to the pits, she asked him, "How can we be sure none of these toxic chemicals leak into the soil and spoil the groundwater?"

"If you look here," Jackie told her, directing her attention to the lining extending over the edge of the pit, "you'll see the pits are all double lined with an industrial-grade plastic lining. And remember, those chemicals comprise one half of one percent of the fracking fluid. Ninety percent is water and about 9.5 percent is sand. The chemicals are added for a variety of reasons, but primarily to increase the viscosity of the fluid, prevent bacterial growth and corrosion of the equipment, as well as minimize friction between the pipe and the fluid."

"Are the chemicals you guys put in the fluid really toxic?"

"It depends on how you use them. Many are found around your home. For instance, ethylene glycol is present in some household cleaners. Guar gum is used in ice cream to make it creamy. Isopropanol is present in most deodorants. Borate salts are found in cosmetics. And most detergents contain sodium/potassium carbonate. If you added up all of those chemicals that go down household drains and in landfills every day and compared that number to the amount used in fracking, which happens over a two-to-five-day period during the 40-year life of a well, you might be surprised."

"I see," Sara said as the sound of someone banging on a metal pipe intensified. Jackie looked in the direction of the drill crew. "Gotta go. The natives are getting restless. Always do around this time of day, when it's quitting time for most folks."

Just in case she didn't know, I said to Sara. "Once the crew and the rig are on station, work continues 24/7 until the well comes in. They work in shifts, but the pace is grueling nonetheless."

"I figured as much," she said. "One night about a month ago, it was late and Clint and I drove by the site on the way to the calf barn—we had a sick calf—and it was a regular beehive of activity."

"Speaking of Clinton," I said. "I haven't had the opportunity to personally offer you my condolences. I believe it was Ruby who said you two were childhood friends. Did you go to school together as well?"

"Thank you for that," she said. "And, yes, Clint went to UNC too. We applied together, attended orientation together and, even had some of the same classes. We're both seniors this year."

"Aw, I know you must miss him terribly," I said, sincerely. "He was like a brother, I guess."

"Oh, he was much nicer than my bratty little brothers. I've got three younger ones and one who's older than I. Sometimes I think Mom had me so I could help her take care of them!" She laughed pleasantly, then like the sun going behind a cloud, her face crumpled. She was clearly in deep emotional pain. I stood quietly beside her until she regained control and gave me a weak smile. "No," she said wistfully, "he wasn't like a brother, he was my best friend."

"I'm so sorry," I said again, guiding her back to the doghouse. I didn't know her well enough to give her a hug, but she needed one. Instead, I did the next best thing and offered her a Coke. I had so many questions for her, but I didn't want to overwhelm her or scare her away. Cracking open two canned Cokes from the mini fridge, I handed her one and said, "I never asked you what you're majoring in."

"Journalism," she said, joining Tulip on the cot and daintily sipping her soda. "I know it sounds corny, but I want to be a reporter. Only I want to be a different kind of reporter than those in the mainstream today. I want to be a reporter who tells the truth, gives the facts, and leaves out all the PC and the touchy-feely stuff."

I sat on the edge of my desk and gave her a lopsided smile. "Wow. You would be a different kind of reporter." She looked a little like I'd hurt her feelings, so I added. "It's a very laudable goal and I hope you succeed."

"Oh, I know I will. I have lots of arguments with professors and often they grade me lower because I don't take the liberal view on whatever issue I've been asked to write on, but I don't care. I just keep on. One day, they'll take me seriously. I'll teach them how important it is to only report the facts and let the public draw their own conclusions. After all, that's what the news used to be all about."

"Yes, it was. But that was way back before the earth cooled and I was just a girl..."

"...Global warming is a perfect example," she interrupted determinedly, "I wrote a paper on it last semester..."

"Sara," I interrupted, hoping to steer the conversation away from political issues and where I'd wanted it to go in the first place: to my question about Clinton Baker. I said, "Here's my suggestion. Make sure your sources are impeccable and your facts are accurate. Then stick to your guns. If you do that, you *will* be happy and, in the end, that's the top prize, being happy. Maybe for your next paper, pick a subject that's not so controversial, huh?"

"Hell—I mean, heck no! I'm writing on fracking. And it'll be just what you said, based on accurate facts, and I'll remain neutral. Only this time, those facts will be first-hand knowledge straight from the horse's mouth."

Great! "And the horse?" I asked pointing to myself.

"Yes ma'am!" She beamed. "This is gonna be so cool!"

Yeah, cool. "Say, Sara, not to change the subject, but what was Clinton's major. If you don't mind talking about him, that is."

"No, I don't mind. For a while when we first started classes in the general college, Clinton fell in with the far-left views. I was surprised because they were so different from how our families raised us. But, over time, he began to come to soften his views.

"So, he had a transition of sorts?"

"You could say that. He'd started dating a girl from NC State who was in the forestry program. She let him know in no uncertain terms that trees are a renewable resource and not "living things with feelings." They broke up later. The distance thing, you know. She was from the Pacific Northwest. Anyway, she changed his thinking. He started studying paleontology second semester sophomore year and fell in love with it. According to him, paleontology answered all the mysteries of the universe! He has—had—been into fossils ever since. It kind of served another need in him too."

"What do you mean?"

"Well, he always despised the religious sector of the far right. Bible thumpers, he called them. He couldn't in his wildest imagination see how anyone could not believe in evolution. Paleontology allowed him to fly in the face of the creationists every day. He was seriously into transition fossils, those that show a distinct link between two phases of the same creature. He'd go onto creationists' blog sites and talk about his latest examples of how evolution worked. He'd really get some heated comments flying his way, but he loved it. Fed on it, really. The nastier the better."

Sara sniffed and wiped a tear from the corner of her eye. Tulip, noticing Sara's demeanor had changed, sat up and leaned against her. She smiled and wrapped an arm around Tulip. "What a neat dog," she said. "What's her name again?"

"Tulip," I said. "And you're right. She is a neat dog." My stomach growled about that time, letting me know I needed to find some grub for both Tulip and me. I stood up and threw my soda can in the trash. Sara did likewise and headed for the door.

"So you're going to help me with my fracking paper?"

"I'm glad to help you anyway I can," I said. "Especially since I know I can count on you to only present the facts, stay neutral, and let folks draw their own conclusions."

I waved to her as she drove away, then went back to work. Before leaving today, I still had to finish analyzing my samples, clean up the office, and go over a few things with Jackie and the crew to make sure we were still on schedule.

Those things took me longer than I anticipated and it was dark as I prepared to leave the site. It was eight thirty, actually, but I didn't have anyone at home to worry about. Then, because I'm compulsively tidy, I emptied the office trash into the garbage can beside the stoop. Jackie pulled up in his pickup. He powered down his window and called, "Everything looks to be running smooth on the seven to three shift so I'll see you in the morning."

"You will," I said and waved as he pulled away.

I decided to find dinner on the way home. Hopefully it would be more nourishing than the fast-food burgers Tulip and I had woofed down at lunch. Then I remembered a small country restaurant on the outskirts of Sanford that served good down-home meals and offered takeout. I couldn't remember the name, so I couldn't call ahead, but I didn't mind waiting. One of the perks of not being married is making plans on the fly. I sure was going to miss that.

———

I pulled up to the Spring Chicken Restaurant—how could I forget that name—and went inside where I gave the waitress my order for a blue plate special to go, then sat at the counter to wait.

"Well, hello," said a cheery voice to my left. I executed a half turn on the spinning lunch-counter-style stool and looked into a familiar face. Where had I seen this pretty boy? Then I remembered, but still struggled for the name.

SIX

"DETECTIVE SERGEANT ... UH ... " I clicked my fingers like doing so would improve my memory.

"Oh, man," pretty boy laughed. "My mother told me no one could ever forget this face. She lied!"

"No. No, she didn't," I said, stalling for time and not wanting to let his mother down—bless her heart for raising such a gorgeous creature. "DetectiveseargentChrisBryant!" I said, smacking down my palm: the winner!

"Correct! For a seven-day, all-inclusive trip to Hawaii ... or a blue plate special, whichever arrives first in the next ten minutes," he said, adding, "and please, call me Chris."

"Okay, Chris," I laughed. "Since I don't expect a courier with a ticket to Hawaii to bust through that door, I guess I'll have to settle for the blue plate special. But you don't have to pay for my meal, detective. In fact, I should be buying yours, you being a prince of the court and defender of the people."

"No way. I could never eat dinner with a beautiful woman and let her pick up the tab."

"Well, thank you, anyway," I said, enjoying his compliment. "But actually I've already ordered takeout. My dog is in the car and she gets cranky if she doesn't get fed."

The waitress who'd been washing dishes a few feet from us squeezed out her greasy dishrag, walked over, and stood in front of us.

We lifted our arms off the counter so she could give it a good swipe. "You can bring your dog in, honey," she said. "It's almost closing time. Besides it's just you two in here and I know the county inspector real well...he's my husband so he won't be causing no trouble. I can feed your pooch too. No charge. I've got a big bag of dog chow in the back where I keep Buddy. He guards the place at night. You wouldn't believe the bums that try to break in here and steal my steaks. Why, I can tell you stories..."

"Gosh, Wilma, that's very kind of you to feed Miss Cooper's dog," interrupted Detective Bryant as he took my elbow and steered me toward a booth next to the wall. "That way she and I can talk without bothering you."

"Okay, Chris," Wilma said dryly. "I can take a hint." Then, to me: "Seriously, hon. Go on and git your dog. It won't be no trouble."

"Thanks," I said. "I know she's getting hungry. It has been a long day for her." I retrieved Tulip and considered my luck for the second time today. Dinner with a handsome young man—I'm getting married, not having a frontal lobotomy—who just happened to be investigating a case I was very interested in solving. Especially since I was the lead suspect.

Wilma placed a gigantic bowl of chow—Buddy-sized, I imagined—beside our booth. Tulip dug in. "I'll be back with your dinners in a few," she said and sped away on crepe-soled shoes, her ample derriere twitching back and forth furiously beneath her white waitress dress.

"So tell me," Chris said. "What's a fancy, big-city woman geologist like you doing in a small town like Sanford?"

Though I wasn't wearing reading glasses, I crossed my arms on the table, leaned over, and gave him a look like I was. "Same thing a small town detective like you is doing. Making a living. Besides, you already know from taking my statement, I'm working here."

He gave me a thousand-kilowatt smile and said, "Of course I do, I'm just messing with you. But it is nice to know—by your ringless finger and the fact you have to work for a living—that I don't have to worry about a rich husband busting my chops for spending an evening with you."

I burst out laughing. "Getting out over your skis a little, aren't you? You're having *dinner* with me, not spending an evening, and no, I don't have a rich husband." *Well, not for several weeks, anyway.* "Besides, I have a hard-and-fast rule about younger men."

"Younger? You can't be a day older than me and I'm 32. But, do tell, what's your rule?"

"Never again."

"Ah … again. Now there's a word I can work with." Wilma brought our water and utensils.

"No you can't," I said, smiling in spite of myself. This guy was obviously a player, but I had to give it to him. He seemed to be an honest player. Behind the fast-and-loose exterior, he was probably a genuinely nice guy. Of course, I'd been fooled before. Thus the reason for the newly in-place, hard-and-fast rule. Well, that and the getting married thing. I took a sip of water. "But I *am* surprised at your attempt at … flirting, charming though it was."

"Ouch."

"Seriously, is this some new method of interrogation for murder suspects?"

Chris screwed up his splendid face. "Huh?"

"I mean, as I understand it, I'm suspect number one in the murder of Clinton Baker."

"Who in the world told you a *crazy* thing like that?"

"Your sheriff," I said.

The detective leaned back against the bench and bumped the salt shaker between his index fingers. "Oh … him. Well, that makes sense."

"What makes sense?"

"The *crazy* part. Look … " Chris paused, chewed his bottom lip, then said, "I take that back. I don't have anything bad to say about our sheriff. We just have a different view on how an investigation ought to be conducted … "

Wilma laid out the specials—country-style steak, mashed potatoes, green beans, and rolls. Meanwhile, under our table, Tulip chomped and gobbled, pushing her bowl across the floor until it smacked against the wall.

Chris smiled, gave an inquisitive peak under the table, then raised his water glass. "Bon appetite," he said. We both busied ourselves with our meals for a while and I offered no further information, just waited to see what he had to add. Finally he continued, saying, "You know…it is odd. Sheriff was there when I took statements from you and your crew. He didn't have much to say then. Has he talked to you since?"

"Oh yeah. And he was very clear on why I am his number one."

"Why?"

"Motive and opportunity. He thinks I'm invested as a partner with the Lauderbachs on their well. Plus, since I found the body, in his mind, I was *obviously* there when he died."

"Huh?" Chris puzzled. "I went to the Division of Land Resources at NCDENR—North Carolina Department of Energy and Natural Resources—and looked up the permits for that well. All investors and partners have to be listed ... by law. There was no mention of you. You aren't some kind of silent partner are you?"

"No. I'm not invested with that well in any way. I'm just a hired employee and I told him so, but he doesn't seem to want to listen."

"He does have a point on the opportunity thing. Sometimes the person who finds a body is in some way connected. But since I did a thorough search on you and found no connection with the victim, I counted you out right away. I gave all this to the sheriff in a report. I can't imagine why he's wasting time looking at you."

"Again, the word crazy comes to mind. And what do you mean, you did a thorough search on me?"

"Now, now, remember. We're talking about my boss. And, yes, I Googled you. Very impressive. All those degrees and published papers. Not much there in the way of personal information, though ... "

I ignored his attempt to illicit such information because I was still processing his having Googled me. Chris continued, "You know, all this could be cleared up with an alibi. County coroner says the stabbing wound did so much damage, he probably went unconscious relatively fast even though it took a while to bleed out. Maybe up to two hours."

"Jeez," I said, shaking my head sadly.

"So if you have someone that could vouch for your where-abouts during the two hours before he died at 11:14 a.m., that'd put you in the clear with the sheriff."

"That would be difficult unless you want to help me find a very large wild boar." Chris blinked his startling blue eyes, waiting for an explanation. "Truth is, I was up a tree during those hours. The same one I took you and the sheriff to. The boar chased me up there, but I didn't want to admit it because normally I would've had my Beretta 380 and blown him into barbeque." I shrugged. "For some reason, I didn't bring it that day."

"Well, I wouldn't worry, unless you're the real murderer, of course."

"Why not?" I said, pushing my plate away.

Chris wiped his lips politely with his paper napkin and tucked it under the heavy crockery plate. "Because I'm going to find the real murderer. I'm like a Mountie. I always get my man."

"You have a record?"

"Yes. I got my illustrious start in the military, and without delving into my background I can tell you I've had many years of experience with the worst of the worst and, again, I've never missed my man ... or woman."

"Well, that's good to know. And, thank you for your service, by the way, and the meal. Now I've got to go."

"Just one more thing. When you said the sheriff said you had a motive, money invested in the well, what did that have to do with Baker?"

"Oh, yeah, good question. I asked that too. He said Baker was an active environmentalist and was planning to stop drilling by staging a rally and fracking protest in front of the Legislature building in Raleigh. Said he was the leader of a group of young environmentalists. I checked it out. Went to UNC myself and talked to people in the department and he wasn't even an IE student."

The detective raised his glossy black eyebrows.

"Institute for the Environment," I said, answering his unspoken question. "Then earlier this evening, I talked to Sara Lauderbach, his best friend—I imagine she knows him better than anyone—and she said he had no interest in environmental issues anymore. In fact, she said he'd changed his major long ago to paleo."

Chris sat up stiffly. "You've been running around asking questions about the victim? Why?"

"Because your cra … your boss said I was the prime suspect, of course. I've got to do something to protect myself."

"No you don't!" he said, raising his voice. I instantly stood and Wilma looked up from her mopping across the room. "Sorry," he corrected himself immediately and stood. "But this is my job and your poking around could jeopardize my case. But, thanks for trying to help."

"No problem," I said. "And thanks again for dinner."

After settling Tulip in the cargo area, I got behind the wheel just as Chris finished paying the tab and made it out of the restaurant. "Listen," he said, leaning into my window. "I really enjoyed dinner. Maybe we can do it again sometime."

"Well … " I figured now was as good a time as any to set him straight on my lack of availability.

But before I did, he said, "Good, glad we got that straight, Miss Cooper." He tapped the door as he strode off, calling over his shoulder. "Remember what I said. No more detective work!"

My iPhone woke me Tuesday morning before my alarm went off. "Hey, sleepy head," chirped Bud.

"Hey, yourself," I yawned, checking the clock: 6:30. "Where are you?"

"Funny you should ask," he said. "I'm in Athens."

"Yeah? What's going on in Georgia," I asked, knowing it was probably something to do with one of the family's textile mills down there.

"Athens ... as in Greece, actually."

I sat up. "What?" I sputtered. "You didn't tell me you were going to Greece. You mean Greece as in the Mediterranean Sea, azure blue skies, and all the ouzo you can drink?"

"Yep. That's the place. Sorry, babe, but some things came up over here ... an opportunity I couldn't pass up. There was no time for, well, for all the planning it would take to bring you with me. But we'll do it someday, I promise. Gotta go right now, though. It's two a.m. here and I've got an eight a.m. meeting. Opportunity calls!"

"Just as long as opportunity isn't wearing a thong bikini ... or topless," I said into a dead line. Tulip opened one eye and stared at me from her curled-up position in an overstuffed arm chair. "Don't give me that look. One thing I know about my Bud. He always prefers home cooking."

I got up, removed the protective cover from the upstairs doggy door that opened onto the master deck. She hopped through it and trotted down the stairs to the backyard, and I jumped in the shower.

———

Arriving at the wellsite, I noticed two things right off: a service truck was parked by the well that supplies water to the site and drilling had stopped. Not good. Jackie was shouting into his iPhone while some guys with jumpsuits bearing the same logo as their truck stood patiently by. Tapping off his phone, he blew out a frustrated sigh. "What's going on?" I asked.

"Well, we're down as you can see. Water well pressure is so low we can't operate the drill. I think the filter's clogged up. Happens with new wells sometimes." Drilling needs a constant supply of water to keep the synthetic mud flowing and the sample chips circulating up from the annulus to the surface where they're collected and tested by *moi*. Often water is trucked in by dozens of large water tank trucks, but sometimes we just drill a water well on site. This one had been dug before I arrived.

"That shouldn't be a big deal," I said, with a glance to the logo on the service truck, which said: Johnny's Well Drilling and Pump Service. "Why don't they just put in a new filter?"

"That's what I said," Jackie huffed. "Only problem is they don't have that particular model on the truck. Johnny ... don't know his last name ... anyway, he's the owner. He's already gone to Greensboro to get one. In order to save time, I'm going to run out to his shop, meet him, and pick it up."

"I know Johnny," I said. "His name's Johnny Lee and his place is all the way across the river in Chatham County. Might be hard for you to find, not being from around here. I don't mind going for you."

"You're probably right," he said. "I would like to ride along though. That way I can ask a few trouble-shooting questions when we get there."

"Let's go," I said.

"Okay, boys," Jackie said to his assembled crew. "Y'all have got plenty of maintenance to catch up on while we're gone."

———

"So how do you know Johnny?" Jackie asked as we zipped along the back roads of Lee County.

"I'm from these parts. I grew up not far from here. My dad was a well driller. He had a nice business. Five rigs. Anyway, Johnny and my dad were friends."

"Well, hell, if I'd known that, I'd've used your dad to drill the well."

"Thanks, but he's not in business anymore," I said. "In fact he doesn't even live here." I looked out the window as familiar places whipped past. Farmhouses here and there where I'd gone with my dad. I remembered watching, totally mesmerized, as the drill bit on his rig penetrated the mysterious depths right beneath my feet.

"Did he retire?" Jackie inquired politely.

"No … " I said, pausing. Then, for some reason talking about a matter that I usually never talk about seemed right. "Actually he had to sell his business to pay the lawyer fees incurred trying to stay off death row. He was falsely accused of the murder of one of his drillers." I paused to take in Jackie's reaction. He didn't move closer to the door or put his hand on the handle in fear of perhaps having to make a quick exit, so I continued.

"According to the prosecutor, my dad killed the man in a fit of rage because he wasn't doing his job properly. The good sheriff, Stuckey, the one you met the other day, went after my dad like a bulldog. They were bitter enemies, but, other than being rivals in high school, I never understood why. Just chalked it up to his being crazy as an outhouse rat."

"He doesn't seem to have any good feelings for you, either."

"No. I don't expect he does. If it wasn't for me ... a friend of mine, actually, he and the prosecutor would have prevailed."

"What did your friend do?"

"My friend hired a big-time New York lawyer to defend him. Problem was, my mom was so stressed by the ordeal that she had a heart attack and died. To this day, my dad blames the sheriff for her death, and he's probably right. Anyway, when she died, my dad wouldn't fight anymore. Got the big-time attorney to cut a plea deal. He served five years in the state pen and he's never gotten over the shame of it. He's a bit of a recluse now. Works out of the country, keeps to himself."

Jackie was quiet for a while, then said, "That must have been a pretty good friend you had. I mean to spring for big bucks like that."

"Yeah," I said, feeling a lump forming in my throat. "He turned out to be a pretty good friend," Then I decided I'd engaged in all the touchy-feely talk I wanted and pointed to a side road on our left. "Right up there is the old Endor Iron Furnace."

"Really? When was it built?"

"In 1862, right after the Civil War broke out. They'd take iron ore from the Buckhorn Iron Mine, about 20 miles from here on the north bank of the Cape Fear, pile it onto flat barges and tow them back up stream by steamboats. They had to navigate a whole bunch of complicated locks and canals, which are all gone now. Destroyed by the Yankees, but that's how they brought the iron to the furnace. Then they'd use coal from the Deep River coal field to fire it and make war materials."

"Was that when coal was first discovered here?"

"No, actually it was discovered in 1775, back before the Revolutionary War."

Jackie made the mistake of acting interested, especially in how the local geology tied in with the history of my home state and indeed the birth of the nation, so I pointed out several outcrops of Triassic rocks along the roadside as we crossed the railroad tracks and again when we crossed the river into Chatham County. I noted that the Deep River Basin is one of the most studied geologic terranes in the country.

"It's also a hot destination for fossil hunters," I said as we turned into the drive at Johnny's shop. "On the way back, I'll be sure to point out the Boren clay pit. In case you have time to go fossil hunting before heading back to Pennsylvania." He laughed at the absurdity of that notion.

———

Johnny Lee was working on an old rig when we drove up. We joined him and I introduced Jackie. Johnny wiped his hands on his overalls, shook hands with Jackie, and patted me on the back. "Dang, girl," Johnny said. "You're even purdier than you were last time I saw you and you were beautiful then!"

While the two of them went to inspect the part and engage in man-talk about it, I stayed beside the old rig. Just looking at it brought more memories of summer days spent with my dad. When ten minutes passed and the men hadn't come back, my impatient nature kicked in and I went to hurry things along. Stepping under the supply shed, I could tell both men were deeply engaged in a discussion about the part.

It didn't take long before I developed a few filter questions of my own. Then I spied another part. This one was sitting on the far end of a workbench. It caught my attention because I'd never seen anything like it and, being the curious soul I am, I asked Johnny what it was.

"It's a fletching jig. A right-handed Bitzenburger, actually," he said. "You probably ain't never seen one 'cause you ain't a bow hunter. You use this to make your own customized arrows if you're really into bow hunting and you don't want another hunter to be able to claim your kill."

"Oh," I said lamely. "No wonder I've never seen one on a rig!" We all laughed, then followed Johnny back to the rig he'd been working on when we arrived.

"This old double-barrel Schramm has seen better days," Johnny said, patting the hood of the rig. "But with the economy the way it is, I can't replace it. Got to keep everything patched up the best I can. Another reason I appreciate you coming by, so I could keep on working and get this old lady back on the job." We commiserated on the crappy economy and offered our own sure-fire cures, then Johnny said, "Say, Cleo, how's your dad?"

"Pretty good," I said, although in truth, I was beginning to worry about not being able to reach him for the last month. And, the few times I was able to get him on the phone before that, he'd only talk in general terms or tell me stories about some of the big game he'd seen on side trips he'd taken.

"Reason I ask is … well, you remember Buster Gilroy? Runs a machine shop over in Gulf?"

"Yes, I remember him." If Dad had a best friend, I'd guess it would have to be him.

"Well, one day, back in the spring, I thought I saw your dad and him eating together at one of the little cafés over there. I couldn't believe my eyes so I went over and spoke and sure enough, it was Pete. It sure was good to see him."

"My dad, up here?" I asked aghast. "Are you sure?"

"Yep. Sure as you're standing right here, it was him. So you didn't know he was here?"

"No. Did he say why he was here?"

"Well, that's the thing. The two of them were friendly enough. You know, asked me to sit a spell, but they seemed a little ... what's the word ... secretive to me. He did make a point of telling me he was only up for a short visit. Maybe that's why he didn't call you ... "

I was stunned into silence. Jackie came to my rescue. "I 'spect we'd better get on back. Those boys will be done with the work I gave them before long." We said our good-byes and headed for the Jeep. I got behind the wheel, but Jackie hesitated before he got in.

"Something wrong?" I asked as he finally climbed in.

"Naw. It's just my old military training kicking in, I guess."

"How so?"

"I got the feeling I was being watched. Just wanted to take a sec to check things out."

Watched? Out here? "Did you see anybody?"

"Yep."

I started the engine. "You going to tell me?"

"You know that big Ford Interceptor the sheriff drives?"

"Yeah."

"Well, I saw it pull out from behind that stand of China Berry trees at the corner of Johnny's drive. It pulled off real slow, then went on down the road. Didn't you say we're in another county here?"

"I did," I said, nodding my head.

"Curious," Jackie said.

"Yeah. Curious."

SEVEN

"I'll be in the doghouse for a while," I told Jackie as he exited my Jeep. "Then I'll either be flagging the new position for Lauderbach #2 or taking care of some things offsite."

"Okey doke," Jackie said and hurried off with the much-needed filter.

I stepped into the doghouse to grab my Beretta and field bag before heading across the farm to flag the new location for the second gas well. I'd barely gotten out the door when my iPhone clanged. I didn't recognize the number.

"Is this Ms. Cleo Cooper?"

"Yes," I said. "How can I help you?"

"Oh, I'm so glad I caught you," a slightly hysterical voice said. "This is Frank, at Giovanni's Florist. I've been trying to call Muriel..."

"Muriel?"

"Yes. Your wedding planner?"

"Oh, right, *that* Muriel," I said, shrugging my shoulders at Tulip. She cocked her head.

"I've been trying all the numbers available to me on my contract," Frank went on, "and I can't get a soul to answer. But since you're the bride... you are the bride aren't you? The Cooper/Cooper wedding? November 9th ?"

"Yes." *Safe to say there's probably only one Cooper/Cooper wedding happening in North Carolina that day.*

"Well, yippee then," gushed Frank, "you can answer my question."

"Okay. Shoot."

"Well, since peonies are your wedding flower and they aren't available locally in November—they bloom here the second week in May—and as I'm sure you're aware, they're very expensive right now, what with Thanksgiving and the holidays right around the corner. Everything positively doubles and triples in price..."

"Yeah, umm, Frank, I'm kind of busy here. If you could—"

"Get to the point," Frank laughed, finishing my sentence. "Of course, I was just wondering if you'd mind if we substituted garden roses. They look very similar and they're much cheaper and it would really save time for my staff if we could stop looking all over hell and Georgia for peonies."

"Sure!" I said. "Anything else?"

"Gosh! That was fast. Most brides would go all Bridezilla on me..."

"I think you'll find I'm not most brides, Frank," I said. "Thanks, and have a nice day."

I'd no more than hung up when the phone rang again. Henri.

"Hey, Mom"

"Hey, Henri, what's up?"

"I'm just making sure you haven't forgotten our dinner tonight."

"Of course, I haven't," I lied. Tulip gave me another head cock.

"Glad to hear it. Dad can't be here, but Will and I are still planning to meet you at the address I gave you last week. Remember? It's on your events app on your phone. I know because I put it there myself."

"Looking forward to it."

"We are too ... "

"Oh, before you go," I added, proud that I could interject something about the wedding, some decision I'd made all on my own. "Frank from the florist shop just called and asked if it was okay to substitute ... er ... garden roses, I believe he called them, for peonies ... " I heard a sudden intake of breath.

"What'd you say?" Henri gasped.

"I told him yes, of course."

"Mom! Good grief! You know better than to make decisions on something as important as this on your own. Now I've got to call him back and undo this mess. What were you thinking?"

"Umm, that it is my wedding ... "

Silence. Then, as though she were speaking to a three-year-old, Henri said, "Of course it is, Mom. I'm sorry. Don't you worry about a thing, I'll take care of this. See you tonight." Just before our lines disconnected, I'm pretty sure I heard a comment about "Fuck a bunch of garden roses!"

I hit the door with both palms and strode for my Jeep, Tulip hard on my heels. Best for me to get as far from civilization as possible until I simmered down following my conversation with Miss Henri, especially considering I was packing. With Tulip in the cargo area and the 8 x 10 copy of the aerial photo of the farm in the passenger seat, I left the site for a different pasture, this one still occupied by cows, I'd been told.

———

Winding down long dirt roads, some no wider than a cow path, I bumped along, my thoughts jumping between and the murder of Clinton Baker and why my dad hadn't called me on his recent visit home. Of course, I could simply call and ask him. Provided I could get him on the phone. But who could I call to answer the larger question of who would want to rob Clinton Baker of his life? One thing was clear. It had nothing to do with a plan to save the planet by stopping fracking in the Sanford sub-basin.

Maybe it was something of a more personal nature. An angry girlfriend or a ticked-off drug dealer, perhaps. But why was he killed in the woods, wearing camos? Someone angry enough to shoot him with an arrow and then stab him sounded like someone with a lot of pent-up hate. Or passion.

I wanted to talk to Sara again, but the words of my new friend Detective Chris Bryant about no more detective work were still fresh in my mind. Nevertheless, she'd be coming back to see me often since we were now working on a paper together. I'd chat with her then.

The dirt road I was traveling cut through the entire farm, dividing it in half. According to my GIS research, the road was here before the farm, which had been purchased piecemeal over the generations. At any rate, the part of it I was now traveling ran along the top of a long ridge. Another smaller ridge rose about ten feet above me to my left.

Needless to say, the road was subject to erosion so it was good that the state maintained it. A smooth road with few potholes and gullies was a good thing, because I was zipping along at a pretty good clip. What the heck? I wasn't bothering anyone and I hadn't seen a speed limit sign.

In fact, the drive was helping to lower my blood pressure, pushed to the boiling point by Henri's call. When I stopped to open yet another gate, I took the opportunity to check my aerial map and make sure I was in the right pasture.

As I drove through, rumbling over the cattle guard, I wondered why the gate was here in the first place. Seemed redundant. But I'm no farmer and since I'd been told all the pastures contained cows except the one where we were drilling, I dutifully closed it before resuming my joyride across the farm.

Dust clouds roiled merrily behind me and despite my attempts to put Henri from my mind I thought of the reason for her call: to remind me of tonight's dinner. I assumed the restaurant was in Raleigh. But then I'd assumed I had a say in my own wedding, too, and where did that get me? Just to err on the side of caution, in case I needed to add travel time, I pulled up the events calendar on my phone.

Or, tried to.

Bracing the wheel and holding the jiggling phone with one hand, I struggled to punch the correct app. Suddenly there was a loud bang.

The wheel jerked abruptly to the left and my phone flew off into space. Well, it just seemed like outer space, because within seconds, I was fairly certain none of the Jeep's four tires were attached to the planet and I was no longer attached to the seat. But then the laws of gravity took over again and with a crashing thud,

Tulip, the Jeep, and I hit the ground, headed down the steep ridge. I spit blood—must have bit my lip—and wrestled the wheel for control.

No dice. Looking ahead of us, I realized two things: one, control was out of the question because the wheels had fit neatly into a pair of erosion gullies, and two, if memory served me correctly, the soft, fluffy green bushes another twenty feet ahead weren't bushes. They were the tops of trees growing along Pocket Creek fifty feet below. If that was true, and I keep a very accurate internal map in my head at all times, I needed to stop. Now!

Again, it wasn't to be.

For a split second I thought the tree tops might act as a safety barrier, but the Jeep cut through them like a roadside tree shredder and we became detached from gravity again.

It's said your life passes before your eyes when you're about to die. Mine didn't. My thoughts: *Dang, this is going to hurt! And I sure hope Tulip survives.* Pitiful, I know. No grand thoughts of family or friends, just my own personal pain and a fleeting thought for my dog. Then we hit the creek.

Now Pocket Creek, a tributary of the Deep River, is not some little babbling brook. In places, it's ten to fifteen feet wide, deep and dangerous. It is especially treacherous if the water is high from runoff, which, as luck would have it, it was.

We landed nose first, tilted to the passenger side. There was a sudden stop, a crashing blow to my body, seemingly from everywhere, and the deafening sound of bending metal and splintering fiberglass. Being fall, the windows were up, thankfully. The creek was high so that was a good thing, I guess. Maybe the water cushioned the impact. I don't know.

I might have been knocked out for a few seconds. The first thing I remember was pushing away from the windshield with both hands, feeling water trickling in through its myriad of cracks. We were still wheels down, but the passenger side was definitely taking on water faster. The tilt suddenly became alarming. Then I heard Tulip barking. That was a good thing! I tried to push the buzzing fog from my head and get to her. In our current situation two things were certain: The Jeep was in the creek and the creek was coming inside. We needed to exit. Pronto!

Naturally I tried to lower the driver's side window but since the doors were buckled, that was a non-starter. I gathered my feet under me—grateful everything was still working—and prepared to kick out the weakened windshield, but I didn't have to. About that time, my optional hard top, my pride and joy, shelter for Tulip for lo these many years, detached from its clips along the roll bar. A giant gush of water flushed us from the Jeep like so much flotsam.

We drug ourselves onto the nearby bank. Tulip kept licking me as I tried to examine her. Unbelievably, she didn't have so much as a scratch that I could see, although I could tell she was tender to the touch in places. I prayed there was no internal damage. I, on the other hand, hadn't fared so well.

Both lips were swollen, the bottom having a cut inside, probably made by my teeth. Horrified they might be broken, I ran my tongue over them. No jagged edges and they felt tight so a trip to the prosthodontist wouldn't be required. There were a variety of minor cuts and bruises scattered about my body, including a goose egg forming at my hairline right above a scar I'd gotten last summer, but nothing life threatening.

My Jeep, however, was another matter altogether. It was a gonner for sure. I walked to where it had floated, then settled into shallow water not far away and surveyed the damage. The frame was definitely bent and I'd had some experience with water flowing through an engine. They tend not to work very good afterward.

Suddenly I felt shaky, so I found a piece of deadfall on the bank and flopped down on it. Tulip huddled beside me. While we watched, the Jeep rolled on its side and began to hog in, settling into the rocky bottom. It was going to be a bitch to haul out. Finally, the fog of near catastrophe cleared from my mind and a thought that had occurred to me way too many times in the past found its way front and center. What the hell happened and why does it always happen to me?

Soon, as is my way, I'd had enough of feeling sorry for myself—although I was planning on spending some quality time with a bottle of Jack when I got home. I stood stiffly, waded to the wreckage, and got on with the job of saving what I could of my possessions, starting with my Beretta. My tote, my purse, and any gear that wasn't underwater were next. I gave a cursory glance about for my phone, but suffice it to say, wherever it was, it was underwater and that meant bye-bye phone.

I spent the better part of an hour dragging salvageable equipment from the Jeep to the bank and dumping it into what was left of the hardtop. I'd managed to drag it back upstream from where it had caught on the snag. My plan was to retrieve it when I came back to get the Jeep out of the creek. How I was going to accomplish that I wasn't sure yet. I thought about going back to the site for help, but Jackie had his hands full getting the well back on track. Plus, if I pulled a crew off station, the bill from Greenlite and Schmid and Medlin would be a darn site heftier than that of a local wrecker service.

"Come on, girl," I called to Tulip and crammed my baby nine and soggy purse into my dripping tote and draped it over my shoulder. "I expect the Lauderbach house is the best place to get help."

Scrambling and clawing our way back up an embankment so steep that, at times, I didn't think I was going to make it, we finally reached the road. I was gasping for breath. The possibility that a little shock was starting to set in was enough to make me take a minute to sit down on the shoulder of the road. As soon as my lungs had filled again, I considered myself recovered. I checked my watch. Mickey had taken quite a licking over the years, but he was still ticking. It was past two.

"Funny how time flies when you're having fun, huh, girl?" I said to Tulip who had been resting beside me, but now had moved to stand behind me, a low growl bubbling deep in her chest.

"It's *not* funny?" I said, turning to see what she was upset about. The world's largest Jersey bull—and the reason for a gate as well as a cattle guard—was standing about ten feet from us. Now I happen to know a few things about bulls. This isn't the first dairy farm I've prospected so I've picked up a little cow knowledge over the years. One important fact came quickly to mind. Of all the different breeds available to cross with Holstein cows—the black and white ones—Jerseys are the most desired. They are also, with absolutely zero dissent amongst dairymen, the most dangerous, most cantankerous, most nasty-tempered bulls in the world.

No one knows why exactly, but it might have something to do with their extreme masculinity. Masculinity equals testosterone, which equals aggressiveness along with a desire to bonk every cow in sight. Anyway, those high reproductive rates are why dairymen take the risk. Their female offspring also produce award-winning milk with a low-fat content, but those silly factoids weren't important right now, considering the angry bovine now glaring at me.

In fact, he looked like he might be trying out for an award of a different sort—Bad Ass Bull of the Year. He didn't have to bellow and paw at the ground but one time for us to get his message: get outta my face!

Tulip and I fell all over each other trying to get back over the edge of the embankment. We'd tumbled and rolled about fifteen feet straight downhill, stopped only by a stand of young pines. "Shit!" I yelled. "This day just keeps getting better 'n better!" As soon as I was sure the copse of spindly little trees was going to hold us, I stood and looked back up the embankment.

All I could see was El Torro's head. He didn't have horns, but he didn't need them. He was at least 1800 pounds and every bit of it fighting-mad beef. I pulled my Beretta from my tote, then thought better of firing it over his head. Bullets that go up come down and might hit someone accidentally. I shoved it under my waistband behind my back, then remembered another fact I'd learned: Bovine are creatures of habit. He was bound to go back to his barn at feeding time. We just needed to wait him out.

After what seemed like hours, but in truth was probably only about thirty minutes, I heard the sound of a tractor approaching. It stopped right above us and I heard a deep male voice command, "Git on, Boss! Git on up now!" Tulip growled and trembled. I held her tight and waited until the voice boomed again. "You okay down there?"

"Yeah!" I called back. "But you better look out, there's a bull up there!"

"Dat's okay. I've got him under control. You can come on up."

Easy for you to say. Still, not having any better offers lately, Tulip and I struggled back to the top again and peered over the edge. Before doing so, however, I placed my Beretta back in my tote. No sense scaring someone nice enough to rescue me. A tall, heavyset black man with an electric cattle prod in one hand stood above us. El Torro stood a respectable distance away on the far side of a very large tractor, the kind big enough to have a cab. "You okay, now. Come on up," he said.

"Thanks so much," I said, allowing him to give me a hand.

"You just lucky I come along," said the man, who introduced himself as Luther Green, dairy manager and husband to Ruby Green, the Lauderbach's housekeeper. "Dis is Boss's field and dis time of the day, he's usually under his favorite tree over yonder in the corner. When I didn't see him, I come looking and that's when I seen he was up to no good. How come you out here anyway? Where's you car? Ain't you the lady that finds gas?"

"Well, something like that," I said. "I'm Cleo Cooper and I work for the people who are drilling a gas exploration well for the Lauderbachs." Then I explained how I came to be in Boss's field.

"Lawd God! And here I am going on and on. I's wondering why you was so wet. Let me get you up to the house," he said, opening the door to the cab of the bright red Massey Ferguson. I squeezed in beside Luther. Tulip balled up in my lap and Boss looked on ominously. "My Ruby can take care of them cuts and bruises and I'll come back and see to your car. I speck we gonna need a wrecker though. That's a good little ways down to the creek." Luther gave me the once over with a more critical eye now that he realized I'd been in a car accident. "You damn lucky you ain't dead!"

"I'll say."

EIGHT

HOURS AND HOURS LATER, after Ruby had patched me up, my beloved Jeep was hauled out of Pocket Creek by a wrecker and taken to a graveyard for dead cars in Sanford. I didn't call my insurance company. No point. The Jeep was totaled, it had over two hundred thousand miles on it and it was a 1986 model. In short, it wasn't worth anything to anyone but me. I'd also answered questions from a sympathetic highway patrolman who'd been nice enough to drive out to the Lauderbach farm to see me.

While I was on private property, the road itself was maintained by the state. Hence the patrolman. Following his visit, Luther had driven me to the junkyard where my Jeep had been taken.

Standing in the office of Dexter Jenkins, owner of Jenkins Junkyard, I negotiated with him for the price of the salvageable parts on the Jeep.

"All four of those tires are brand-new," I said. "They're BF Goodrich, top of the line, all-terrains."

"Well, that may be," Dexter replied, totaling the items he was willing to pay me for on a grimy plastic calculator. "But I can't give you anything for one of them 'cause it's got a hole shot through it."

"A hole?"

"Yes, ma'am," he said, tightening the rubber band on his mullet. He took a giant swig of Mello Yello. "I know a bullet hole when I see one. Must've been a stray shot from a hunter..."

"Miss Cooper!" Detective Chris Bryant interrupted from the open office doorway. "I heard about your wreck. You alright?"

"Yes," I said, a little annoyed at being interrupted mid-deal. Plus, it was late, I was continuing to stiffen up and now my head was pounding too. "How'd you hear about my wreck?"

He pulled aside the bottom of his windbreaker to reveal the detective badge clipped to his belt. "Detective... remember?"

"Whatever," I said as Luther Green stuck his head in the office too. "It's getting close to feeding time. I'm going to need to get back to the barn soon. You can borrow one of Mr. Lauderbach's farm trucks to get home tonight." Before I could respond, Chris chimed in. "No need for that. I'll see to it that Miss Cooper gets wherever she needs to go."

"Thanks," I said, grateful I wasn't going to have to create further disruption on Mr. Lauderbach's farm. "I appreciate that. But are you sure you don't mind? I live in Raleigh."

"No problem."

After I thanked Luther again for all he'd done and assured him I didn't need any more help, he left.

"What a nice fellow," I said to Chris as I waved to the departing farm manager. "And you're very kind, as well, checking to see if I'm alright and offering to take me home. I really appreciate it, but I'm glad you're here for another reason too."

"What's that?" Chris asked.

"This gentlemen says one of the tires on my Jeep was shot out. Care to join me in checking it out?"

Chris's eyes grew round. "Lead on," he said.

"I've already had it hauled down to the bottom field," Dexter said, handing us a scrap of paper. "You'll have to take that golf cart out front to get to it. Here's the row and space number."

With the sun setting behind the trees that bordered the far western edge of the immense junkyard, we zipped past row upon row of junked cars and trucks. I shivered as we navigated the neatly mowed paths between them until we reached row "F" and headed to the end, and my Jeep. Chris let out a slow, low whistle. "You must have a guardian angel," he said, looking at the mangled remains. I could hardly bring myself to look at it; I just hopped out and started checking the tires. Chris went to the opposite side and did the same. Shortly, he called out, "Here it is!"

"Let me see that," I said, squatting beside him.

"Can you tell if that's a bullet hole?" I asked, an eerie feeling forming in the pit of my stomach.

"Yep. It's a bullet hole, alright. No doubt about it," he said, standing and brushing dry grass from his jeans. "Tell me what happened."

Dutifully, I did my best to give him details.

"So you were driving along that dirt road that runs along the ridge above Pocket Creek. It's what...fifty, sixty feet down to the creek bed?"

"Something like that," I said, surprised that he knew that much about the lay of the land.

"I'm a hunter," he said, reading my mind. "Did you hear anything before you lost control?"

"Yes!" I said, suddenly remembering. "I'd forgotten, but there was a noise. It all happened so fast, but there was a loud bang, then the wheel jerked out of my hand and next thing I knew I was airborne. Actually, my immediate thought was I'd lost control because I was ... er ... "

"Texting?"

"Heavens, no," I snipped indignantly.

"Talking on the phone?"

"No."

"What then?"

"I was only *looking* at the phone! Trying to pull up ... oh, nevermind! I was on a dirt road after all ... with no traffic and ... " I started to add that I wasn't going very fast, but thought better of a lie that big.

"Okay, so you weren't holding the wheel firmly and what?"

"Well, I thought I'd hit a hole or something because there was a loud noise, then the wheel jerked violently and my phone went flying. I guess that was when my tire was shot and I ran off the shoulder of the road and headed down the ridge."

"I'll get out there tomorrow and investigate the area where it happened," Chris said, heading back to the golf cart.

I gave the magic Jeep one last look, then climbed into the cart. Chris gave me a curious look and I realized a big sigh had unconsciously escaped me. "You know, they only made 127 of those Jeeps," I explained. "I guess now there are only 126 left."

"Tough luck," he said. "But if you had to suspect someone as the shooter, who would it be?"

"Who do you think?"

He gave me another look. This one incredulous. "You really think the sheriff shot your tire?"

"Well, this morning Jackie, the site manager, and I rode over to Chatham County to pick up a part. Jackie saw him watching us from the road when we left the guy's shop."

"In Chatham County? Our sheriff?"

"Yep."

"Jesus," Chris said, stopping the golf cart beside his Crown Vic. Painfully, I unfolded myself, limped over, and climbed in with him.

———

As we exited the junkyard and headed for Raleigh, forty minutes away, he continued, "What kind of feud do you have going on with him?"

"Well, I'll tell you, but we have to use the 'way-back machine,'" I said, referring to reruns of the Rocky and Bullwinkle Show, another of my favorite cartoons as a kid. "We have to go back to 1987 ..."

"I know what the 'way-back machine' is," he laughed.

"Okay, then. Waaay back, when you were just a little bitty boy, about six years old, I was finishing my master's thesis at UNC." Another incredulous look so I clarified. "Mind you, I skipped several grades and was still ... very young."

"How young?"

"*Very* young. Do you want to hear this story or not?"

"By all means, continue."

"At that time," I said. "The first exploratory gas wells were being sunk into the Triassic Basin, right in the general area where we're drilling now, and the energy company doing the drilling was allowing me to observe and help log samples. My dad owned a well-drilling company and he'd been contracted to drill a water well out there since there was no other available source of water nearby."

"I know a little about drilling," he said as he accelerated up the ramp onto US 1. "How you have to have water to cool the bit and all that."

"Very good," I said. "There was a young man who worked for my dad on this rig. His name was Francis Gary Wayne. One morning he didn't show up for work." I had to pause. I hadn't told the story in many years, so I was a little disappointed in myself that it still took my breath to recall it. "I found his body in a hog pen not far from our rig."

"Aw, man," Chris said, with a sigh. "I'm sorry you had to experience something like that. It must have been hard on you."

"Yes, it was," I said sincerely. "We were working the back side of the landowner's property, far from any houses or stores and I'd gone into the woods to find a secluded place to tinkle. That's where I stumbled upon a hog pen. I've always been curious so I climbed the split-rail fence to see the pigs. But there weren't any, just loads of very deep, stinky mud and Wayne's body. At first I didn't even realize I was looking at a body, it was so caked in muck and mangled by the hogs."

Chris shook his head sadly.

"The owner of the pigs later testified before a judge that he hadn't seen the body because when he'd gone to move the hogs to their feeding lot he'd only opened the gate and not looked in. Fortunately there was a potential investor in the well on the site that day and he helped me put the death in perspective and understand that bad things sometimes just happen. We became close friends very quickly and, as it turned out, that was good for me because I came to draw heavily on his strength and maturity in the coming months."

"Why was that?"

"Because Sheriff Stuckey arrested my dad the very next day on the grounds that he'd killed Wayne in a fit of rage. My dad had a reputation for having a bad temper and coincidentally had chewed Wayne out the day before I found him dead."

"What did he chew him out for?" Chris asked.

"Nothing important. The kid was doing something unsafe. My dad was a real stickler when it came to job safety. Anyway, for the next few months, my family experienced more stress than most families go through in a lifetime. My dad was very courageous during the whole ordeal ... until my mom died of a sudden heart attack." I had to pause again and clear my throat. But I wanted to finish. I was actually feeling better. Who knew? Maybe there was something to the touchy-feely notion of sharing a burden by telling someone else about it.

"That's when my dad shut down completely," I continued. "And even though my friend had hired the best lawyer money could buy, Dad took a plea deal and went to jail where he could grieve in peace. He was so worried about what would happen to me, being young and suddenly alone, he made me promise to marry my friend in the bargain and, not knowing what Dad would do if I didn't, I agreed. Of course, in the end, I grew up and the marriage fell apart."

Chris was quiet for a time, then said, "I don't mean to bring up bad memories or a sore subject, but why was the sheriff so convinced that your dad was the murderer? Was there overwhelming evidence?"

"Not really," I said. "I think Dad's reputation for having a hair-trigger temper hurt him more than the wrench they had as evidence. According to the prosecution, Wayne had been bludgeoned to death with it. This was impossible to prove after what the hogs did to his body, but Stuckey said they'd found it in my dad's tool box and it had Wayne's blood on it. As icing on the prosecutor's cake, there were witnesses to his blow up with the kid the day before."

"What was your dad's defense?"

"That he was framed. I was afraid he was going to get the death penalty, although the lawyer said the chain of custody regarding the murder weapon was tainted and he could get him off. At first my dad was very positive about fighting through a long protracted murder trial, but then when mom died and he just gave up. The rest is history."

Chris turned to me in the darkened car. "You were lucky to have such a special friend," he said sincerely. "Too bad it didn't work out."

"Yep," I said. "That's what everyone said."

———

By the time we'd reached my house in Raleigh it was after eight o'clock. We pulled in the drive and I invited him in. After I fed Tulip, she hopped through her doggie door to the backyard and I went straight to the wet bar in the den to make myself a tall Black Jack.

"I'd offer you one if you didn't have to drive back to Sanford," I said, stirring ice cubes in the ice maker.

"Here, let me do that," he offered. "You go sit on that comfy-looking couch. I'll also make you an ice pack for your head. It's a little late to stop the bruising, but like my mom used to say, 'It'll heal before you get married.'"

I did as told and sat on the couch. "I hope you're right," I said. "Because I just spent a hideous amount of money for a wedding dress. I'm remarrying my first husband, my very good friend, on November 9th."

Chris might have missed a beat as he walked toward me, drink in one hand, ice bag in the other, but it wasn't noticeable. "I'm not surprised. There was no way you were unattached. I couldn't possibly get that lucky."

"Oh, not that again," I said, taking a big slug of my drink and planting the ice bag on my noggin. "I told you, I'm old enough to be your ... much older sister. Honestly, *I'm* the one who's surprised."

"How's that?"

"I'm surprised that you aren't having to beat the women away from your door with a stick."

"Who says I don't," he smiled, taking a wingback opposite me. "There are a ton of single women my age in and around Sanford. It's just that since I've been back I haven't met anyone with enough brains to carry on a conversation beyond what's new on television or at the movies or how to make the hottest new moonshine cocktail."

"Raleigh is only 40 minutes from Sanford. There are 1.3 million folks living here now. Surly among that number you can find someone who interests you."

"This is true. I just have to stop hunting and fishing long enough to look," he said.

"Ah," I laughed, "now the real reason for your longevity as a bachelor is starting to emerge ... " I paused, hearing a car door slam outside. Suddenly I realized I'd forgotten all about my dinner plans with Will and Henri. Figuring it must be them, I braced.

"Mom!" Henri exclaimed as she and Will busted into the room. "What's going on? You missed dinner—and who is this?"

"Henri!" Will snapped, taking in my sorry state. "Look at Mom! Can't you see something's happened."

"And where are your manners?" I demanded. "We'll do dinner another time. Right now I'd like you to meet my friend, Detective Chris Bryant—"

Henri, ignored my introduction and cut me off. "Not at that catering house, we won't," she snapped. "That was a tasting they were holding just for us to be sure the selections I've made are what you and Dad want and what happens? Dad leaves town and you're a no-show! Well, I can tell you, I've about had it. You have no idea how hard it is planning an event of this magnitude!"

I turned to Detective Bryant to apologize. He was staring at Henri like he'd encountered an alien being. "I'm so sorry, Chris," I said, although it was obvious I didn't have his attention. I addressed him again, more forcefully this time, "Chris." Nothing.

"Chris!" This time I snapped my fingers.

"What?" he startled, dragging his eyes from Henri.

"Tell you what," I said, standing and guiding the bedazzled detective to the front door. "I'll call you first thing when I get back on the job tomorrow and we'll make arrangements to meet at the section of road where I tried to fly the Jeep."

"Okay," he said, then pointed back toward the den. "Who was that?"

"Those two ungrateful wretches are my children. My daughter, Henri is the uber-rude one. She's 26 and my son, Will, the slightly less rude one, is 28."

"Is she ... "

"Tomorrow, Chris," I said, then thought of something. "Oh, and before you go back to where I had the wreck, you should know there is a very territorial bull in that pasture. Seriously, get the dairy manager—guy named Luther—to go with you."

Back in the den all hell broke loose.

I told both children what I thought of their transformation from normal young people into wedding vampires who sucked the life out of everyone and everything, feeding on an unnatural, unrealistic desire to create something perfect. I know, it didn't make a lot of sense, but it was the best I could do in my out-of-control state.

I mean, I'd nearly been killed in a wreck that cost me my magic Jeep, then been chased by a bull. I knew my venting was perhaps a tad over the top, but I couldn't help ending my tirade with, "And for your information, you two idiots, perfection is an illusion. You can chase it all you want, but it's unattainable."

Henri burst into tears, stormed out of the house, into her car, and left.

Will quickly made me another drink. "Tell me about your day, Mom. How did you get all bruised and banged up and where's your Jeep?"

I felt a little better after he and I had a long discussion, including a detailed account of my day, but without any mention of the sheriff and my run-in with him or the fact that a bullet had likely caused my accident. No sense worrying him. While we talked, Will made me a bowl of tomato soup and a grilled cheese sandwich. I didn't realize how hungry I was or how tired. I wanted to call Bud, tell him about my dismal day, but I was too damn done in. Tomorrow, I promised myself.

Wednesday morning dawned dull and grey, mirroring my mood and physical state. My body, as I clomped downstairs, was one stiff, sore aching muscle. And that was after a hot shower and a BC powder. Then I smelled coffee. My heart leaped. Bud was back!

When I stepped into the kitchen, I encountered Will and was instantly disappointed, which in the next instant made me feel guilty. I sighed and made myself another promise to call Bud first chance I got. Fortunately Will was busy scrambling eggs and buttering English muffins and missed my emotional struggles. "What are you still doing here?" I asked. "I thought you left last night."

Will looked up from his task and licked his fingers. "I was going to," he said. "But after I called Henri and told her what had happened to you, she insisted one of us needed to stay and check on you during the night. You did hit your head, you know. Since I was here, it made sense I stay."

"I see," I said, still ticked over last night's display.

"We're really sorry, Mom. Especially Henri. She feels just awful."

"Really?"

"Yes. It's just, well, you know how she can be sometimes. She'll call you soon. And from now on we're going to keep a tight rein on getting too caught up in this party. I mean, wedding."

Yeah and humans will soon vacation on Mars. "Fine." I snipped. "Soon as we eat, I need a ride to the iPhone store and a car rental place."

After purchasing a phone, completing the download of my contacts and other information from my computer, and renting a plain grey minivan—folks coming in for a major NC State football game on the weekend had taken the good ones—I prepared to leave the car rental parking lot.

Will slid the van door open for Tulip. She climbed in, showing a slight stiffness, too, and proceeded to check out her vast new domain.

"Drive careful, Mom," Will said with a forlorn look on his face.

"I will," I said. "And thanks for all the help, sugar."

"No problem, and don't worry. Henri'll calm down and everything will be just fine. You'll see."

———

As soon as I got back onsite, I set about trying to catch up on logging all the samples I'd missed yesterday. A knock at the door preceded Jackie's entrance with more bags of samples.

"Once we got back drilling, we made good progress," he said, dropping the samples on the table. "What's with the minivan?"

"It's a long story," I said. Jackie folded his arms over his chest and leaned back against the table as I recounted my activities after I left him yesterday. When I got to the part about my tire being shot out, his immediate reaction was to suspect the sheriff.

"Maybe you should ask Greenlite for a replacement. You know, someone to take over for you here," he said. "A gas well ain't worth getting killed over."

"I hear you," I said. "Keep in mind, we don't know for sure if it was him. But I'll take your advice and keep a sharp eye."

"Okay, then," he said dubiously. "'Course, long as you're up here around me and the boys, we've got your six."

"I appreciate it, but I don't think we need to worry," I lied. "It probably was just a stray hunter's shot. It is deer season, after all."

The rest of the day passed without incident. Chris called and left a message that the sheriff had him on another case all day, but he'd get up with me soon. I tried to reach Bud one more time before leaving for home.

I'd tried several times during the day but his phone just went to voicemail. As luck would have it, I was on the highway by the time he returned my call. When the phone vibrated in the drink holder, I resisted the urge to answer, or even pick it up. Maybe I *had* learned my lesson about messing with the phone while driving.

The very moment I pulled in the driveway, fifteen minutes later, I reached for the phone to return his call and noticed I had a message too. It was from Annette Lauderbach wanting me to stop by or call when I got a chance. I made a mental note to do so, then called Bud. Greece is seven hours ahead so it was close to midnight there. "You just getting home?" he asked across the miles and time zones that separated us.

"Yes," I said, feeling giddy at hearing his voice. What was it about that guy that turned me into a pile of mush? I didn't know. Never had. I'd loved him and hated him so intensely for so many years—the hate being for his controlling nature—that now that I was about to commit to him again, I surprised myself at the depth of my feelings for him. "What are you doing?" I asked goofily. God. I sounded like a schoolgirl.

"Laying here thinking about you," he answered, sounding just as goofy. We went on like that for a few minutes. He said his return time was still up in the air. Then he asked if there was any word regarding the boy's hunting accident and I told him what I'd learned. I considered telling him about totaling the magic Jeep, my run in with the sheriff, and the big meltdown with the kids but decided against it. There was simply no point in worrying him. When we hung up, I felt wonderful.

Love is a great healer of all types of wounds.

NINE

My plan of action Thursday morning: an early start in the dog-house, logging the samples collected during the night while I'd been sleeping and the crew had been drilling ahead. We were down hole a little over 100 feet and still in the Sanford Formation.

I'd logged sandstones and mudstones interbedded with each other seemingly forever. The grain size hadn't started to coarsen up yet and that was the indicator I was looking for. When it did, I'd know we were approaching the basal beds of conglomerates in the Sanford, including one unit containing very large pebbles, termed "millstone grit" because it was quarried back in the 1800s for that very purpose.

Around lunchtime I gobbled down the KFC snack lunch I'd bought on the way in. Tulip ate the biscuits, which, after hours in the mini-fridge, were as appetizing as cardboard. After freshening up a bit, I headed for the Lauderbachs. Besides finding out what Annette wanted, I was hoping to get some additional information on Clinton and take care of thanking Luther in a more substantial way. Once I'd accomplished those things, I'd take care of flagging the site for Lauderbach #2.

When I arrived, Annette opened the door—a pleasant surprise—and led me back to the sunroom again. Arthur put down his copy of the Herald when I entered, but pointed back to it and said, "Very informative article in there on Clinton Baker, the young man killed on our farm. Have you seen it?"

"No," I said, taking the chair he offered.

"Lots of detail about him, his hopes and dreams. Really gives some insight into what a fine fellow he was. He was interested in everything. It's just so sad," Arthur sighed deeply. "Now nothing he dreamed of will ever come to fruition."

Mentally scratching questions regarding Clinton from my to-do list, I said, "I'll have to read it later. Thank you for bringing it to my attention." Suddenly, there was a clamor outside the window. A flurry of shouting and running created by a bevy of teenage boys playing tag football lifted the somber mood in the room.

"What fun!" I laughed. "And how convenient to have those old outbuildings in just the right spots to serve as end markers. It's good they can still serve a useful purpose. Plus, it's wonderful you've preserved them."

"Thank you," Arthur said, laughing at the antics of the players. "Now days that's about all they're good for, that and homes for bats and mice, but it's important for the kids to see how things were done in the old days."

"Are all those yours?" I asked, nodding at the players.

"Gracious, no," he said, feigning astonishment. "Only three of them."

"We had one a year for a while there," Annette said wistfully.

And you're still sane. Impressive. "You have a beautiful family," I said with true admiration. Now I remembered that Sara had told me about her three younger brothers. "And you have one other son, right?"

"Yes, he's at State, majoring in Animal Science so he can take over the farm one day."

"Well," I said, moving on to the reason for my visit, "besides being here in answer to your voicemail, I wanted to drop in and thank you so much again for the help you and your employees gave me Tuesday. Without Luther and Ruby, I'm sure my day would have been much harder."

"Now, now, none of that!" Arthur said. "We're just sorry that old buzzard, Boss, got after you. And as to Annette's voicemail ... "

"Now, Arthur, I can answer for myself," Annette said. "I called just hoping you'd gotten some test results or something that would let you know that billions of barrels of gas are right below the farm, just waiting for us to tap into them."

Arthur rolled his eyes.

I laughed. "Actually gas is measured in cubic feet, billions or trillions as the case may be, and it's a little early to know anything yet."

"Oh, dear," Annette said with a nervous laugh. "I'm just a silly goose."

Arthur reached out and patted her knee, then looked at me and said, "I guess we are anxious because ... well, we've had a tough go of it since the accident ... " He paused as he collected his thoughts. "In truth, we were falling on hard times for several years before that. Just the economy, I suppose, but now, with school tuitions and the added pressure of unexpected doctor and hospital bills, we had to find some way to get financial relief. These wells are it.

We've thrown everything we have left into them in the hope of pulling ourselves back into the black."

"You see, my dear," Annette said. "We have so many people depending on us. All our employees, some of whom have worked here all their lives like Ruby and Luther and lots of others. If we go bust, we take a lot of families down with us."

"Our major problem is the equipment," Arthur explained. "In order to meet new regulations and standards required by the FDA and state and local agencies, we need to upgrade. Plus some of our barns are about to fall down. We house over 500 cows here that have to be milked and fed twice a day. Plus there are new waste treatment requirements that are very stringent. If we don't do up-keep and maintenance and modernize the equipment, they'll close us down. It's just as simple as that."

They looked so tense I wished I could offer some assurances, but there were none. Exploration is a gamble any way you look at it, even in a production field. The odds are three to one against you. Still, it was better now than it used to be.

"Big rewards require big risks," I offered. "If it makes you feel any better, you're not alone. I've been on several jobs in the Pennsylvania gas fields in the last few years. All were on large farms, hoping for the same outcome as you and for the same reason. Just keep in mind that while we wouldn't necessarily call the Triassic Basin a production field yet, several good wells have been brought in and put on line, so that kicks your odds up a little."

"And," Arthur said, reaching for his wife's hand and giving it an encouraging squeeze, "we have you. As we hear it from Greenlite, you've got a top-notch reputation for bringing in stubborn wells."

"Thanks for that, Arthur," I said. "Call me anytime you want a report on how things are going. We've got a few more days of grinding through the Sanford Formation. Then, right before we break into the Cumnock, because it's only about 580 feet thick at the most, we'll begin our turn to run horizontal. The idea being to tap into the gas-bearing shale above the last coal seam. That should take about a week, give or take a few days." I stood to leave. "Oh, one last thing. I'd like to thank Ruby again for patching me up."

"No need," Annette said. "She loves helping people and she knows you appreciated it. Anyway, she's not here. Thursday's her grocery day. Getting ready for the weekend. But if it makes you feel better, I'll tell her again for you."

"I'd appreciate that," I said. "I thanked Luther personally on Tuesday, but I feel I should stop by the barn and offer a little financial token. After all, he was in his truck, using his gas. I'd feel better if he let me repay him."

"I'm sure he'd welcome it," Arthur said. "He and Ruby have several children in college too."

Walking to the minivan, I remembered a bag of apples I'd left on the passenger side of the backseat and stepped around to get it. I took a bite of one and slid the door closed. Just then, a slight movement to my right caught my attention. Through the lacy limbs of a Hollywood cypress, I spotted another unique outbuilding, this one had not been visible from the sunroom.

The movement I'd detected was the door slowly swinging open. Just as I started to leave, thinking it was only a matter of the door being unlatched, a familiar face peered around it. You know how you can tell in an instant when someone is doing something they don't want anyone to know about?

The moment I saw Ruby step down out of an old stick-built chicken house—the kind raised several feet off the ground on stacks of rocks—I could tell she didn't want to be seen. I also knew that the chances of her noticing me from that distance and through tree limbs were slim and none, especially if I remained motionless. I watched as she warily checked her surroundings before latching the door and scurrying from sight.

That's weird. I'd thought Annette said she was grocery shopping. And why, if mice and bats infested those old buildings, would she be storing anything out there? I got back in the van, took the first left past the drive on the main farm road, and motored toward the two massive silos visible over the trees. They sat beside twin barns, both gigantic white two-story affairs with red roofs. I pulled up to the first barn and went in.

———

Apparently they were in cleaning mode. Five men of varying ages and ethnicities, all in coveralls and black rubber boots, hosed down the concrete floors and raised milking stations in the vast barn. It looked pretty modern to me, but what did I know? I asked the first person whose attention I could get where Luther Green might be. He pointed in a curving manner towards outside and shouted, "Over yonder."

Nodding thanks for the precise information, I changed my direction and headed "over yonder" to the other barn. It was a complete rerun of the goings on in the first barn. I waved down another man in coveralls and asked again for Mr. Green only to get a shrug. The guy did stop hosing long enough to holler to his co-workers but the consensus remained the same: for sure he wasn't in the barn area and beyond that no one knew where he was.

Lucky no one needs the barn manager. Deciding to come back later, I headed off to fulfill the next item on my agenda: flagging the site for Lauderbach #2. Again, I planned to kill two birds with one stone. Since my curiosity regarding the murder of Clinton Baker knew no bounds, and since, as far as I knew, I was still Sheriff Stuckey's prime suspect, I decided to reach the new wellsite by a different route than the one I used on my ill-fated attempt Tuesday.

Instead of trying to drive as close to it as possible and then hike the rest of the way, I'd go the entire distance on foot, cutting across pastures and woods. Besides, using the same shortcut I'd taken the day I found Clinton would take me back to the crime scene. Who knew, maybe I'd see something others hadn't.

———

Back at the doghouse, I pulled the relevant aerial of the farm from my file drawer. The state of North Carolina uses 160 acres as the standard drainage area for wells. Including low, wet areas and roads, the center of the drainage area for #2 was a little over three hundred acres from my present location. I made a copy of the photo, stuffed it and a bottled water in my canvas carryall, and buckled on my Beretta. Then Tulip and I left on foot.

Following the ruts across the pasture created by law enforcement and emergency vehicles, I headed for the yellow strip of crime scene tape, marking the point where the trees were sparse enough to allow their entry. Just before reaching there, the call of a Carolina wren drew my attention to the right and I noticed a game trail.

I wondered if it was the same one that passed by the crime scene and decided to follow it. At the head of the trail, I noticed something else: a marker in the form of a notch cut in a small pine. Though the cut was well healed, it was no more than a year old.

Nose down, Tulip snuffled ahead of me on the faint trail. It meandered about and though, at times, seemed to disappear altogether, I could tell it had been used lately...and by a human. An OIT—old Indian trick? No. Expert tracking technique? No. The Chiclet I'd found in the leaf litter while stooping under low-hanging limbs was a dead giveaway. The fact that it still had its candy coating meant it hadn't been rained on. Besides the gum, I had no luck with evidence upon reaching the crime scene.

Though the area was still taped off, the ground had been so disturbed I doubted if one more person poking around could do any harm. So I studied the area all I wanted, but didn't see anything beyond what I'd seen the last time I was here. My dream of finding...oh, I don't know, say a hunting knife thrown in the bushes, went unfulfilled.

Resuming my hike to #2, I passed the tree where I'd spent a few miserable hours and was reminded to be on the lookout for feral hogs. Finally I reached the far side of the woods and stepped back into the bright autumn sunshine. I looked at the base of the trees at this end of the trail. Sure enough, a scooped notch, similar to the one at the other end of the trail, had been hacked in a small oak.

It looked to be the same age as the first mark and it wasn't done by a surveyor. They use a very distinctive system of hatch marks to blaze a trial. Basically, they use one notch on each side of a tree to indicate a straight boundary line, three in a row to mark a corner, and they use a machete to make the cuts. These were made by something much smaller, like a hunting knife

Still retracing my steps of last Wednesday, I marched on until I reached my marker at the edge of a vast cornfield. The Lauderbachs grew their own feed. Corn, coastal Bermuda hay, and soybeans thrived in large, well-maintained fields. As soon as I entered this one, I was quickly swallowed up. The towering corn stalks, now dried and ready for harvest, reached over my head, giving me the childlike feeling of hiding in grass in a land of giants.

Midfield, at the site of #2, I retrieved my orange plastic marker flag, jammed it in my tote and took out my aerial. I did a quick recheck of where I'd highlighted the new #2, using the company man's coordinates.

Ahead of me, on the other side of a fifty-foot swath of open land that circled the field, was another patch of old-growth woods. Beyond those woods, another cornfield, then another pasture, midway across which was the new location for Lauderbach #2. I could have been annoyed at Overmire's changing the location after I'd already flagged his first choice, but I wasn't. Any reason to be outdoors was okay with me.

I checked my watch. It was only three o'clock. I had plenty of time so I decided to take the long way around the woods instead of cutting through them. No sense risking another encounter with some UV—unfriendly varmint.

I have a complete mental list of UVs, and at the top of it, I placed dumb hunters, vicious moonshiners, and the scourge of today's ATF, the creeps that sneak onto the property of law-abiding citizens and plant patches—marijuana. They were way worse than any of the animals that call the woods and fields of North Carolina home.

From time to time while skirting the edge of the deep, dark woods, Tulip would liven things up with a startling bay followed by an impressive scratch off. She was trotting about thirty feet ahead of me when she decided to take off on one of those jaunts. She darted into the woods, spewing leaves and dirt behind her as though she were after Bigfoot.

When I reached the spot where she'd disappeared, I saw she'd taken another faint trail. Not only that, it was marked with the same type of scooped notch I'd seen earlier. In my mind, they looked like they were made by the same person or persons. I wanted to investigate, but had work to do, so I continued on to my destination where I planted my flag... again.

On my way back to the site, I took the same route, only this time I let my curiosity get the better of me. Though it was now almost five, I still had plenty of light. Besides, I'm a scientist, if I didn't let my curiosity overrule my practicality on occasion, I wouldn't be a very good one. I pushed my way into the woods, following the trail and the sound of Tulip already off on her own fact-finding mission.

From my earlier information gathering, I remembered this section of woods to be about sixty acres. And, according to my geologic map, a significant portion of it was underlain with red beds. One of the old county maps even indicated clay digs.

Perhaps some of Arthur's relatives from generations past used the clay for brick making. I practically tingled with anticipation of actually seeing the intersection of history and geology and hurried along. I was so excited, in fact, that I pushed aside the fact that a slight musky odor occasionally wafted my way.

Tulip's nose, however, remained on duty. About fifteen minutes into our transect, she trotted back to me, the hair on her back bristling, her eyes anxious. She heeled at my right side. When I stooped to comfort her, I saw her feet and legs were coated in red clay ... the kind used for bricking. "What's the matter, girl?" I said soothingly. "Did you smell hog?" I petted her sides, stood and sniffed the air but the smell had gone. My excitement at seeing her clay boots had not.

"Let's go just a little further," I said. "Then we'll turn back, I promise." She gave me a dubious look and instead of her usual forward-scouting position, she trotted protectively by my side. I should have taken her standing hackles as a warning, but I didn't. I was only going a short ways. Looking ahead to where the path turned right, I decided that if I didn't see signs of a dig there, I'd turn back.

At the turn, the scant path merged with an old logging road and the hog odor increased exponentially. "Phew wee," I said, looking down the path. "We must be getting close to one of their wallows, and something tells me that's probably right where I want to be." Tulip whined. "Aw, come on now. I really want to see it. After all, I've got my Beretta."

I unsnapped the safety strap that keeps the gun snugly in its holster—just in case—and walked on, my hand resting on its butt. The further I went, the more pungent the odor got. But something else was mixed in with the pungent odor of hog musk and dung.

I'd smelled it before.

Now I was really intrigued. Tulip wasn't. She was growling softly as the path turned sharply left and opened into a clearing. That's when I saw that neither my nose nor my memory had failed me.

A row of a hog pens stood before me.

"What the hell," I breathed, counting the massive split-rail pens. There were five of them, attached side by side. There was also a shed—probably where the commercial hog feed, which was giving off the sweet, fermented odor I'd detected, was kept.

Upon seeing me, the hogs began to stamp and squeal. Tulip was now in fighting mode, her growl fierce, her lips curled. I tried to reassure her, but I was trembling too. "Something is out of whack here, girl," I said, stating the obvious. It was one thing to keep hog pens away from your house to avoid the smell, it was another thing entirely to have them hidden deep in the woods, a mile or more away.

The reason for the subterfuge became clear with a quick inspection from a safe distance—past experience being my teacher. The first pen held a ferocious feral boar. The next two held domestic yearlings of both sexes. Another held a large domestic sow and the last, a larger one, was packed with varying ages and sexes of a cross between the wild and domestic breeds. I suspected such interbreeding was frowned upon by the North Carolina Wildlife Commission.

Just then, I heard the sound of a truck engine. It was approaching from the far side of the clearing where the path picked up again. I ducked back in the woods so I could see if I recognized the truck. My instincts told me to get out of there, but I wanted to know who the hogs belonged to. Tulip, still trying to get me to follow, poked me with her nose. "Just a sec!" I hissed, giving her collar a warning tug. "Sit and stay!" Reluctantly, she sat and I turned back to part the branches for a better view.

The truck came into sight. It was one of the smaller variety of pickups, dark green with oversized tires and fancy rims, but it didn't appear to be new. As though the driver was looking for something, the truck rolled slowly forward across the clearing until I could see the emblem on the grill. A Toyota.

It was dirty and had scratches and dents reminiscent of my magic Jeep. One thing it had my Jeep didn't: a rear-window-mounted gun rack complete with scoped hunting rifle. Closer and closer it rolled until it was about fifty feet from me. Then it stopped. Unfortunately the tags were on the opposite end of the truck! Dammit!

A heavyset man of about fifty with mostly grey hair and a ruddy complexion got out and stood by the door without closing it. He rested his hand in the open window, an outdoorsman with the air of an executive. He was dressed for hunting with boots, flannel shirt, and heavy canvas hunting pants. "Hey?" the man called in a harsh, bullish voice. "You here?"

When he received no reply, he stepped a few feet away from the truck. Then, as if honing in by radar, he drew a bead on my location. He squinted his eyes and moved a little closer to the heavy underbrush and deep gloom concealing me.

Slowly I let go of the branches, withdrew my hands and stood stock-still, watching him. He hesitated, scanned left and right, then returned to his truck and started the engine. Figuring this might be a good time to leave, I stepped back a few feet to where I'd left Tulip. That smart hound was already at a smart trot, heading back the way we had come. I scratched off after her.

TEN

WE'D RUN A LITTLE less than a quarter of mile when I caught my boot on a greenbrier and went sprawling. The fall knocked the wind out of me. I lay still and caught my breath. After a moment when I didn't see Tulip, I pushed to my knees. There I saw another curious sight—as if I hadn't seen enough for one day.

Eye level with me on a pin oak tree was yet another trail notch. It was exactly like those I'd seen at other locations along the path. I stood and pushed the thick underbrush aside, revealing a fork in the path. I could hear Tulip's tags but I still didn't see her. I didn't want to call aloud or whistle, so I went to find her and in doing so, discovered the clay pit.

The trail followed a gentle slope to the bottom. Along the way, the soil changed from primarily sandy clay and gravel to pure red clay. It was about a hundred feet long, extending up the low rise on the other side for about thirty feet. A shallow dig, it was only about four feet deep at the most, but extended horizontally across ground for about sixty feet. I seriously wanted to explore it, but was still very nervous about being anywhere near what appeared to be a clandestine hog-breeding operation. Tulip's tags tinkled again and I saw her next to a tall clump of mare's tail weed. She was rooting under what appeared to be a large camouflage tarp.

It was about twenty feet long and covered a lower section of the old pit. Now what the heck was that doing out here? Was someone still working the clay pit? Local potters maybe. Maybe even amateur fossil hunters. Seemed logical, and I badly wanted to investigate, but I didn't feel safe.

"Tulip," I called softly. "Get over here!" I had a bad feeling about this place. Whoever the mystery hog farmer was, he surely wouldn't want me nosing around. Stubbornly, Tulip ignored me, pulling harder on whatever was under the tarp. Then with a jolt, she fell back on her haunches, rewarded with a good-sized stick. I clucked softly to her and this time she responded and trotted past me, keeping at arm's length so I wouldn't take her treasure.

On the way back, we were about halfway across the second cornfield when my iPhone rang. I had been expecting Bud to call. It was only a little before 11:00 p.m. in Greece. A rush of warmth flooded over me. He was calling to say good-night. I forgot all about hidden hog pens and camouflaged clay pits and scrambled to dig the phone from my tote before it stopped ringing.

I tapped it on quickly. "Well, hello," I said, doing my best to muster a sultry bedroom voice in the middle of a dried-out cornfield. "Are you all tucked in?"

"Uh, it's a little early for me," Chris said with obvious amusement.

"Oh, man!" I said, totally disappointed. "I'm sorry. I was expecting someone else."

"Nooo! Really?" Chris said sarcastically, then he got serious. "Hey listen. I've got some news to run by you. It's about the bullet hole in your tire."

"I'm all ears. What about it?"

"I'm not at a very good place to talk right now. Let's meet for supper at the Spring Chicken since hubby-to-be is obviously somewhere in another time zone. Ehh, you did think that's who I was, didn't you ... your hubby-to-be?"

"Of course I did!" I huffed. "I just have to finish in time to make my Krav Maga class at nine."

"Wow," he said. "Israeli street fighting. I'm impressed. Doesn't get much tougher than that."

I shrugged, though he couldn't see me. The courses were something I'd promised myself for a while. Especially in light of some of the close calls I'd had over the last few years. "You never know when they might come in handy," I said.

"This is true," he said. "You think six-thirty will leave you enough time?"

"Sure. See you there."

———

I still had time after I got back to the doghouse to pull up the online edition of the *Sanford Herald* on my laptop and find the article on Clinton Baker. Despite what the Lauderbachs and Sara had told me about him, I wanted to know more. When I finished reading the article, I did.

In fact, I felt even worse now that I'd read he was an Eagle Scout, a lettered high school athlete, a member of the debating team, an accomplished pianist and number one on the most-favored counselor list at Camp Morehead on the coast. The list of things he'd accomplished in his short life went on and on. Toward the end of the article, a mention of his passion for fossils, that he was majoring in Paleontology at UNC and even joined a local fossil-hunters group reminded me of what Sara had said about how he loved antagonizing creationists on their blog sites. Something I probably should mention to Chris when I saw him.

I checked Mickey. Time to meet Chris. Besides, staring at the article on screen and feeling sad wasn't helping me find out what happened to Clinton. Although it did fire up my determination. I turned off my laptop, locked the company logs in the floor safe, and padlocked the doghouse.

On the way to the Spring Chicken, I realized the minivan needed gas. Now seemed better than after dinner, so when I saw a small country station at the next intersection, I pulled in. Their gas was more expensive and it looked like they were having some sort of political shindig, but I like giving my business to locals.

Smoke coiled lazily from a pig cooker outside the station, perfuming the air with the delicious and unmistakable aroma of North Carolina barbeque. Under the overhang of the porch roof, the usual gaggle of old men in ladder-back chairs leaned against the outside wall of the station and smoked cigars. Inside, more folks were gathered, chattering and laughing.

I swiped my card, stuck the nozzle in the tank, and was just setting the handle to fill when Sheriff Stuckey moved into the open doorway. An obese man with a florid face and a cigar clamped between his teeth—a heart attack waiting to happen—took hold of his elbow before he could leave. Stuckey clapped him on the back as the large man pumped his hand vigorously. "You've got my vote, Clyde," he said.

"Thanks, Elton," said the sheriff, moving down the steps to shake hands with the men in the chairs.

He didn't see me and I watched as he greeted each with a comment that implied he knew them well. Then it dawned on me, this was an election year for him. That's what all the schmoozing was about. I'd almost finished filling the tank and was hoping to leave without him noticing me, but I didn't get my wish. As though sensing he might have missed a voter, he turned my way. His phony political smile vanished, replaced by a stony glare.

"Well, well," he sneered as he walked up to me. "You saved me a trip out to see you tomorrow."

"What? Aren't you going to ask for my vote too?"

"I know what you and Johnny and Buster are up to, thinking you can overturn your dad's conviction. But hear this, missy. You can't. The case against him is airtight. Besides, you won't be around much longer to do anything anyway. You'll be in jail ... "

"Whoa, whoa, whoa, Stuckey," I said, pulling the nozzle from the tank and replacing it. "You're raising the bar for lunatics worldwide. Who, pray tell, are Johnny and Buster and what have they got to do with me?"

I knew who Johnny and Buster were. What I wanted to do was goad him into admitting he'd seen me at Johnny Lee's well-drilling shop. Meanwhile, some new voters had arrived at the little gathering and gone inside the station. Heart attack man came out and called to the sheriff. "Hey, Clyde, got some new supporters here that want to meet you!"

"Be right there," Stuckey called, then turned and left, but not before squinting his eyes and shooting me with a finger gun à la Dirty Harry. He was clearly a lunatic. That he was also the sheriff was seriously scary.

I saw Stuckey's Interceptor parked on the side of the station as I pulled away. Wishing I'd seen it before making my refueling choice, I drove on, determined to get to the bottom of this latest mind-bending tidbit of information regarding my dad's long-closed case. At least I thought it was long-closed. Another call to Dad was in order soon as I got home after dinner and before my Krav Maga lessons.

———

Dinnertime at the Spring Chicken was crowded and noisy but Chris had arrived ahead of me and snagged a corner booth where it was relatively quiet. He'd also ordered me an iced tea. "Just the ticket," I said, slugging down half the tasty brew.

"You know that's not Jack Daniels, don't you?"

"Of course. If it were, I'd have sucked down the whole thing."

"Bad day at the office?"

"You could say that," I said and gave him the condensed version of my latest little altercation with Stuckey. Wilma, our waitress, arrived and we both ordered the dinner special, meatloaf, mac and cheese, and fried okra. When she left, I asked, "So how do you get along with the sheriff? Don't you think it's a little odd, his bringing up my dad's old case, right out of the blue? Then, there's his insistence that I'm the prime suspect in the murder of Clinton Baker, despite the fact that I have no motive nor any past association with him."

Chris seemed a little uncomfortable. "Well, as I said, opportunity is a consideration and you were there … "

"I *found* him. Big difference. The killer was there, too, only a few hours ahead of me if the coroner is to be believed." Wilma delivered our plates, dropping Chris's a little hard at the mention of the word "coroner."

"Yes, there is that," Chris said. "Which brings me to my reason for wanting to see you. One of them anyway. It's about the hole in your tire. I went back out to the junkyard. Dexter helped me pull the tire off the rim and we got lucky."

"How's that?"

"The bullet was caught inside."

I wrinkled my brow.

"Instead of going straight through, it hit the rim and stayed inside the tire."

"Ah," I said.

We ate in companionable silence while I considered how this might affect me. If it proved to be from Stuckey's gun, it would be so long Sheriff Stuckey. Not only would he be out of my life, but someone else, better qualified for the increasingly complicated job of sheriff in a rapidly growing county would be able to take the reins. After a while, I asked, "Can I see it?" It was Chris's turn to wrinkle his brow. "The bullet," I reminded him.

"It's locked in my desk in an evidence bag, but I can tell you it was very likely from a hunting rifle."

Is that a "no"? I considered his not offering to show it to me and wondered if he thought I was being irrational to think the sheriff could do such a thing. Then I put myself in his place, and well, it was a lot to take in. I worked on my dinner a little longer, then said, "Let me ask you something, Chris."

"Shoot."

"If you were to match the bullet with, say, one of the sheriff's hunting rifles, what would you think then?"

He drank some tea, then said, "I don't deal in hypotheticals. First I'd have to have a reason to confiscate his rifle. I can't just take it off the wall in his office and test it, you know. He'd have to be charged first. You willing to bring charges against him for attempting to kill you?"

"Maybe," I said. "Does he know you have the bullet?"

"Not yet, but I'll have to tell him sooner or later."

"Anything that says you have to make that sooner rather than later?"

"No, not really."

Well, that's something, anyway. "Good," I said sarcastically. "After all, we wouldn't want to worry him, what with his trying to get re-elected and all. And, since he's already got me in his crosshairs for the Baker murder, making him even angrier seems a little counterproductive, don't you think?" Chris fiddled with his spoon. "You have to admit, you think it's possible he's the one who shot out my tire or else you wouldn't have told me about the bullet. You'd have just chalked it up to a hunter's shot gone wild."

Wilma returned and took our plates. "Coffee?"

We both nodded in the affirmative. "I've thought of a few things I need to tell you about the Baker case," I said, changing the subject. "Remember when I told you Clinton was quite the fossil buff, even to changing his major to Paleontology?"

"Yeah."

"Well, I forgot to mention that, according to Sara, he liked to antagonize the creationists and did so on their blog sites...a lot."

Chris put down his spoon, showing renewed interest in what I had to say. "We've got his computer," he said. "I'll have the analyst check it out. What else?"

"He belonged to a local fossil hunters' group."

"What's that got to do with the price of tea in China? And, I believe I told you not to be playing detective in this case anymore."

"Jeez, I read it in the paper. Calm down, I'm just trying to help here. Plus, I've been thinking about him lately. Like, why was he wearing camo? He wasn't hunting. Was he into military gear or ... "

"Now, you calm down," Chris interrupted as Wilma set down our coffee and sped away to wipe up a spilled soda at one of the large family tables. "I told you I'd get to the bottom of this and I will, but solving cases like this—no witnesses and no real suspects—takes a seasoned detective. Not a geologist."

"Have you got some other leads, other ideas, perhaps?" He didn't answer, just watched creamer mix into his coffee in big looping swirls. I couldn't help staring at his downturned eyes. Sooty lashes so long they seemed to rest on his cheeks. Damn he was pretty—and annoying. Obviously, he wasn't planning on sharing information. Well, two could play at that game. No need to tell him about the wild hog breeding operation I'd found. Not just yet anyway.

Chris squirmed in his seat. Something, it seemed, was still bothering him.

"Problem?"

"No," he said. "But I *do* have a question for you."

"Ask away," I said over the top of my mug.

"Is your daughter married?"

Oh, good grief. "No."

"Spoken for?"

"No."

His expression turned quizzical. "You're not very encouraging."

I didn't have the heart to tell him that Henri goes through three guys like him—hot body, to-die-for face, mediocre job, scant ambition—a month. "No. Call her if you want. She's unattached. Just consider yourself warned."

"What does that mean?"

"It means she's got a lot on her plate right now. You'd be a nice ... distraction for a while but that's all there would be to it." His blank stare said I wasn't getting through. "You'll get all attached, then poof! She'll be off to the next distraction and you'll be just another piece of wreckage floating in her wake. I've witnessed this pitiful scenario *many* times."

He continued to stare, undaunted. I sighed, removed one of her business cards from my purse, gave it to him, then headed home.

By the time I got off US 1 and onto I-40, it was almost eight o'clock and I had come up with a whole new plan of attack in searching for Baker's killer. Well, it wasn't really a plan of attack, more like a fact-finding expedition, which centered around the wild hog breeding operation. The fact that he was in camo—good for spying on the operation—and found on a path that eventually, albeit circuitously, led to the pens, told me it was something to look into.

I was so deep in thought when I pulled the minivan into the drive that at first I didn't notice vehicles belonging to Bud, Henri, and Will, respectively, parked in the drive. "What the hell," I said aloud as I pulled around a catering truck and into the garage.

After lowering the door with the remote that still worked despite having been submerged in Pocket Creek, I shoved it back in my purse and opened the door to the kitchen. Delicious aromas enveloped me. "She's home!" Henri called, then disappeared through the swinging door as a chef, complete with tall white hat, starched tunic, and rotund belly, poured wine into a balloon glass for me.

"Thank you," I said, glancing around my kitchen. It looked like the set of *The Iron Chef.* Just then Bud busted through the swinging door and, before I could even sip my wine, swept me off my feet and planted a great, big sloppy one square on my lips. It felt so good, I just went with it. When we came up for air, chef and cooking crew applauded! To my great embarrassment, I giggled.

"You're just in time, Mom," Henri said, apparently having forgotten her recent claim to have had enough of Bud and me. "When Dad let me know he was flying in tonight, I started thinking. Since you both missed my last attempt at letting you sample the wedding food before the big event, I thought tonight would work perfectly. We're serving your favorite, French country cuisine. The one thing you've both actually told me you wanted." This last she muttered under her breath. "Dinner will be a little later than we expected, but as it turns out, you're both a little late, so it's all good."

"Dinner?" I said.

"You haven't eaten have you?" she asked anxiously.

"No!" I lied. "I'm famished! Let's do this thing!"

———

Late that same evening, I dropped an Alka-Seltzer in a glass of water and gulped it down as I enjoyed watching Bud shed his clothes. He tossed them onto the lounge chair in my bedroom and said with a happy grin, "I don't know who's more excited about this event, the kids or us."

Yeah, that's a tough one. "Well," I smiled, still enjoying the show. "I can only say it can't get here soon enough." Bud narrowed his eyes. "No. I mean it. I can't wait." I'd never told him about my little catfight with Henri, and didn't plan to. I was just damn glad she'd calmed down, because lately I'd taken to breaking out in a cold sweat at the thought of having to take her place in the slow torture known as wedding planning.

To be honest, no matter how much of my life had been spent as Bud's wife, I could never handle conspicuous consumption. Even after I finally clawed my way to my own financial independence, I wasn't comfortable with throwing money away on such things as five-course meals for five hundred people in a tent fit for a Bedouin sheik set up in .... I suddenly realized I didn't know where the wedding was to be held. Probably a little detail I ought to inquire into.

Had I ever known where it was to be? Probably, but since the where of it wasn't as important to me as the point of it—being with Bud for the rest of my life—I guess I'd forgotten. I didn't have long to ponder the question that night because just then Bud let me know he had other plans for me that didn't involve my memory.

ELEVEN

I'D ARRIVED AT THE site early Friday morning and was on my knees in the doghouse, spinning the dial on the floor safe. I'd left the house before Bud even woke up, wanting to get a jump-start on the day. The last tumbler fell into place and as I turned the handle I heard Tulip's toenails click on the floor behind me. She'd entered through the open office door. The weather was so gorgeous, I'd left it open. Besides, she likes to come and go as she pleases and conduct her wide patrols. Apparently a canine can never be too careful.

Still crouched, I was shuffling through the logs when she dropped an object beside me.

"Whatcha got there, girl," I said, setting the papers aside to inspect her find. At first I thought it was the stick she'd pulled from under the tarp at the clay pit yesterday. It didn't take a rocket scientist, or even a geologist, however, to see that it wasn't. It was a fossilized bone. The significance of the find wasn't lost on me either. This was huge!

The object I now held in my hand was a bone from a long-extinct vertebrate. More than that, I couldn't say. Lucky for me, however, I knew lots of paleontologists. Suddenly recalling that one of them, a close friend, might be in the area, I scooped my iPhone from my purse and pulled up the cell number for Dr. Jonathan Byron Watson.

"Cleo!" he answered brightly. "What a nice surprise."

"Not nearly the surprise you're going to get when I tell you what I'm holding in my hand," I said, barely able to contain my excitement.

"Do tell. What *are* you holding?"

"Uh, only the fossilized bone of a large vertebrate!" Stunned silence floated between us. "Watson? Are you there?"

"Yes. Yes, my dear, I'm here. But are you sure?"

"Well, I'm sure it's a fossilized bone," I said, pacing back and forth across the trailer. "And, considering the environment in these parts back during the Triassic, I'd say it's likely from one of the larger reptiles. Plus, it's remarkable in its detail. I can even make out a trace of where a tendon was attached. The rest, well, that's over my pay grade."

"I have to see it! Where did you find it? Does anyone else know?"

"I would send you a phone photo, but ... "

"No!" Watson interrupted. "It's too risky!"

"Exactly," I said. "And to answer your other question, it's hard to say but I believe the only other person who knew about it is dead now ... "

"What?"

"Long story, but for now let's go with the premise that no one else knows about this and keep it that way."

"My sentiments exactly. Until we know what we're dealing with, of course."

"When are you coming down here to your research site in the Durham sub-basin?" I asked.

"I'd come tomorrow, but if I cancel a preplanned meeting, well, it might send up a red flag. You know how it is with us old bone hunters. We're a suspicious bunch. It would be better to wait for my next scheduled trip in about a week."

"How is your Mayfly research going?"

"Terrific. Even better than I expected. But I want to be in on this find, if there is one, of course. And don't worry, you'll get all the credit."

"That's something we'll have to talk about later."

"I can't tell you how much this means to me, Cleo, to have something like this as a career topper. You know, old girl, if it does turn out that you've found a complete fossilized skeleton, it will take an entire team of paleontologists, geologists, and archeologists to bring it to light. Why, bringing such a project to fruition will take years!"

"I'm happy and honored to include you," I said as I sat at my desk, marveling at the wonderful bone before me. "Get back with me when you know your arrival time."

"Right-O!"

I'd just tapped my phone off when I heard footsteps on the stairs outside the open door.

"Hi!" chirped Sara Lauderbach. "I was hoping you'd be here. Is this a bad time?"

"No. It's not a bad time at all," I said, sliding the bone under the log sheets on my desk. "In fact, I've been thinking about you."

"Really?"

She and Clinton had been in the back of my mind ever since I'd found the clay pit. "Sure," I said. "I wanted to ask how your paper is coming along."

"That's why I'm here!" she said as if I'd be surprised. "Do you think I could bother that nice man who showed me around last time? I'd like to ask him some technical questions."

"Let me check and see what he's got going on right now. As long as we aren't having some type of problem with the well, he'd be glad to talk with you."

"That'd be super!"

"No problem. I'll step out and ask him right now."

"Want me to come with you?" she asked as I moved to the door.

"If you'd like." I looked out the open door to the drill pad. "Uh-oh," I said. "I see they're making a connection right now. Joining another three sections of pipe to the drill string. We should let them finish that first. While we wait, mind if I ask you a question about Clinton?"

"Not at all," she said, taking a seat on the cot.

"When you guys were little, did you ever play in the woods? You know, build forts, dam up creeks, go exploring, stuff like that?"

"Oh, sure."

"What about your brothers?"

"The little ones were too small back when Clint and I were kids and my older brother, well, he thought of us as a bad rash. So it was mostly just the two of us. Our favorite game was Lewis and Clark. There's not a part of this farm we don't know."

"Did you ever find any of the red clay beds, the kind used by the brick makers around here?"

"Yes," she said. "There's an old brick pit on the farm. Mom hated the day we found that! She'd get so angry at us when we'd come back to the house covered in that red sticky stuff. Even Clorox won't totally wash it out."

My pulse rate ticked up. "Can you show me?" I asked, moving to a corkboard, which covered most of the wall above my desk. I'd tacked an enlarged copy of the aerial there.

"Wow!" she said. "This is neat! I've never seen the whole farm at one time." I pointed out a few orienting markers for her like barns, roads, and creeks. "Okay then, the old brick pit would be right about ... here in this patch of woods, down in this shallow depression." She'd pointed to the very spot where Tulip had found the fossilized bone. "I'm told," she continued, "that my great grandparents used the clay to make the bricks that were used in the foundations of buildings right here on the farm. In fact ... oh, wow, you're going to love this ... "

"What?" I prompted.

"Well, there are layers of a red slate-type of rock in the clay. If you break a piece of this slate just right, sometimes you can find little impressions of leaves and bugs and stuff. I even have a few pieces in my room. I haven't thought of doing that in years ... " She grew quiet.

"Do you think Clint did? Remember that slate bed, I mean. Maybe go back and look for more fossils there?"

Sara shrugged. "Honestly, I've been so wrapped up in helping take care of my parents since the accident, I haven't had time to think of much else, but it wouldn't surprise me. He'd become so fascinated by fossils, it seems logical anyway. Why do you ask?"

"Just curious," I said, then looked back out the door. "Okay. I see the guys are finished with the connection now and I've got to get back to work. I'll take you to Jackie and you can fire away at him with your questions. He loves the opportunity to educate civilians on what a clean source of energy natural gas really is. Then, when you're ready to move on to the next stage of your paper, production and distribution, let me know."

I put the fossilized bone in the safe and locked it. Then I scurried around, logging in last night's samples and taking care of reports, phone calls to the main office, and the usual morning duties. The timing worked out perfect. Just as I finished, Sara drove her little Nissan past my office window on her way off-site. I strapped on my Beretta, tossed my camera in my field bag, and Tulip and I headed to the clay pit.

I had some documentation to do and I wanted to do it in private.

———

Instead of going straight to the clay pit, it seemed prudent to first make sure no one was at the hog pens. Besides, I still wanted to know the identity of the man in the green Toyota truck. Did he work for Arthur Lauderbach? Was he in charge of tending the hogs? He certainly didn't look the part.

It took a good half hour of fast walking to make it to the last section of woods, the one that contained the pit and the hog pens. Here I adopted a wary mode. I didn't have to caution Tulip; she was just as anxious as last time we were here.

The North Carolina Wildlife Commission considered feral hogs a serious problem that required drastic measures to correct. Hence the yearlong open hunting season. They carry diseases like hoof and mouth and pseudorabies virus. Some of these diseases can even be transferred to humans, plus they do hundreds of thousands of dollars of damage to crops every year. So why would anyone want to increase their numbers by crossbreeding?

I could only come up with one reason.

To create a larger, more impressive hog to hunt, a trophy hog, if you will. I also had a theory.

Say someone was crossing feral with domestic hogs, then taking the biggest, most fearsome boars and fattening them up, maybe even making them more aggressive with hormones and steroids, and using them as trophies in a *secret* hunting club. Since secrecy would be paramount, guns would not be allowed. Too noisy. Wouldn't that leave only bow hunters as members? Made sense to me.

Made sense, too, that an arrow could have accidentally hit young Clinton on his way to the red beds to look for fossils—wounding but not killing him. It even made some sense that the guilty bow hunter panicked—knowing his missed shot could rain down all manner of crap on everyone involved—and ran away without calling for medical help. That the bow hunter, finding Clinton wasn't dead, finished him off with a knife... now that didn't make sense. Not to me anyway. Unless Clinton recognized him...

With that happy thought in my head and holding Tulip's collar with one hand, I parted thick undergrowth to reveal the hog pens. Damn! The green truck wasn't there. I was hoping to get its tag numbers. Just then, the hogs began to oink and squeal. Crap! I'd forgotten to check wind direction, and they'd picked up my scent. Well, I never claimed to be a hunter. Time to head back the way I'd come.

When I reached the fork in the trail, I ducked under overhanging limbs and trotted down the path to the pit. The faded camouflage tarp was still where I remembered it, covering an area of the pit near the edge beside a tall stand of mare's tail weeds. My breath caught in my throat at the thought of what the next few minutes might mean to me and to Watson, but most of all, to Clinton.

Fortunately dry weather, normal for autumn in North Carolina, had been the case lately and the clay wasn't extremely sticky. I moved to each corner of the tarp to see what was securing it to the ground. Twine tied to wooden stakes held it down at three ends, but on the bottom left corner—the one Tulip had rooted under—it was broken. With trembling fingers, I lifted it …

"Well, hello there, Cecil," I said quietly.

The skull of Cecil, the cartoon dragon that had delighted me as a child in reruns of the old Bennie and Cecil Show, stared back at me. At least that was my immediate impression. A shaky breath of disbelief escaped me as I knelt for a closer look. My next thought: this find was even bigger than I'd first realized. I was staring at the *intact* skull of a rauisuchian, a meat-eating reptile from the Triassic age.

How did I, an economic geologist, have enough knowledge of large vertebrate fossils—a subject covered many years ago during my undergraduate days—to identify this one? Because a skeleton of this particular type of reptile had been big news back in 1999. A student from UNC had found it while on a paleontological field trip to a brick pit owned by the Triangle Brick Company right here in the Sanford sub-basin. The story had fascinated me then and I'd followed it ever since.

As it turned out, the lizard was one of the most significant fossil finds in the history of the state. Interestingly, by the time the team of experts who took over the recovery and restoration of the fossil had finished their work six years later, they had even learned how the giant lizard met its fate.

The skeletons of several crocodile-like creatures who attacked it lay underneath. Not only that, but the undigested contents of the rauisuchian's belly contained four other specimens. Unfortunately, most of the lizard's skull was missing, accidentally torn away by a dozer. This made Cecil, with his perfectly intact skull, truly unique.

Wanting to take in the entire creature, I untied the bottom right corner of the tarp and folded it above the skeleton. As I did, I wondered if it had been young Clinton who'd placed the tarp here. I really wanted to believe it was.

After all, he knew of the existence of the pit. He was a paleontology major. And, he was in the woods wearing camo. Then I had a thought. Since the tarp was also camo, if I could prove it came from the same place as his clothes, it would go a long ways toward proving that he was the one who'd discovered Cecil. I scanned the tarp and found stenciled on its underside: GI Joes's Army Surplus, Durham, NC. Its faded condition suggested it was at least a couple of years old.

Stepping carefully alongside the skeleton, I positioned myself between his massive legs and gazed at the miracle before me. It was as though the giant beast had just stretched out on the bank of a swamp 250 million years ago, died, and was quickly covered by a mudflow. Or, maybe the mudflow killed him. Whatever. The fact he was still here, perfectly preserved, as though waiting for someone to discover him eons later, was truly … well, I could think of no better word to describe it, miraculous.

I dug around in my tote for my measuring tape, then looked for a rock to anchor one end so I could take accurate measurements. That was when I made another find, a heart wrenching one. Under the dry leaves skirting the edge of the pit lay an Estwing rock pick.

The initials C-A-B were burned into its simulated wooden handle. Clinton A. Baker?

Exhilaration with the enormous scientific find, and sadness, fought to control my thoughts, but there was no time for that now. I pushed on, dropping a rock on one end of the tape. The reptile measured thirteen feet, six and one half inches. Since it was larger by two feet than the 1500-pounder found at the brick company, I imagined this big boy would have weighed closer to 1800 pounds, maybe a ton. I placed the pick, initials up, at varying spots on the skeleton and took a slew of photos. Before stowing it in my tote, I ran my fingers over the initials again.

I knew others might need more proof as to who actually discovered the fossil. For me, the pick was all the evidence I needed that it was Clinton. Sometimes you just have to let your heart be your guide. Vowing then and there to make saving Cecil for posterity the crowning achievement of Clinton's young life, thus insuring his place in North Carolina history as one of its greatest fossil hunters, I gave the reptile one last admiring look and covered him back up.

When I came to the corner with the broken twine, I added a note beside my measurements to bring more twine when I returned. Then, just to be on the safe side, I pulled some Carolina creeper vines from a nearby pine tree and laid them over the tarp. Us Indiana Jones types have to take every precaution.

On my way out, I was careful not to ruffle a leaf on the branches that hid the fork in the trail. Then I headed back to work. At least I was going to, but stopped after only a few feet. The proximity of the hog operation and the clay pit was really bugging me. Maybe if I went back, I might find some convincing evidence that there was a connection between the two.

You know how it is when you don't know what you're looking for, you just know you'll recognize it when you see it? Well, that's why I went back. One more sneak peek and I might just get lucky and see that truck again, get some tag numbers. Maybe see someone feeding the hogs, do some real detective work. Chris wasn't the only one with savvy in that area.

This time, before advancing on the pens, I checked the wind, noting I'd need to make a correction in my approach. The north side of the clearing would be downwind. This worked out well because, according to the aerial; it offered better cover than the south side. Then I pulled some masking tape from my tote—I kept everything in there—and taped Tulip's tags to her collar. No sense taking chances with unnecessary noise. Then, quietly, stealthily even, we made our way to the opposite side of the pens to see what we could see.

I found a good vantage point, unfortunately there was still no sign of anyone, so I sat down to wait. Tulip fidgeted behind me. "What are you doing?" I whispered and looked over my shoulder to see for myself. She was plundering around in the underbrush, but she seemed content, so I turned back to my stakeout. I was just wishing I'd brought a snack when I heard the sound of a truck engine.

The dark green Toyota truck pulled up. Just as I opened my field notebook to scribble the tag numbers, I heard Tulip thrashing about behind me again. "Quiet!" I whispered, craning my neck to see the truck, which was now blocked by a small limb. Frustrated, I rose to a find a better line of sight.

That's when I lost all sight and everything went black.

TWELVE

CAW! CAW! CAW! A couple of noisy blue jays fussed somewhere nearby. Try as I might, however, I couldn't seem to perform the simple task of opening my eyes to see them. And my head felt like it was about to explode. What was up with that? I knew I was still outside since I felt dry leaves at my fingertips. I was also leaning against something. Tulip stirred beside me.

Summoning all my strength, I lifted my arm—though it felt made of lead—and reached out. Tulip's bony head slipped lovingly under my palm. One thing, at least, was right with the world.

From close beside me came a deep, familiar voice. "Dere she is, girl! She coming around, now!" This was followed by a whimper and a tail thumping. Damn! I just *had* to get my eyes open! Then the chill of a cold, wet cloth on my forehead—apparently the stimulus my brain cells were waiting on—startled my eyelids into opening.

The smiling face of Luther Green floated before me.

"What happened?" I croaked, trying to push myself to my feet.

"Now don't go getting too rowdy, Miz Cooper," Luther said. "You must've fainted or something. I was just about to call the rescue squad. Then I thought maybe you just coming down with the flu or ... didn't eat no lunch."

"Fainted?" I struggled to replay the last things I remembered. I was watching the hog operation, hoping someone would show up .... In a flash, reality dawned and I took in my surroundings. Damn, I was sitting smack in the middle of the hog operation, leaning against the shed. Yet, strangely, Luther Green didn't seem to mind that I was here.

I glanced to the pens directly in front of me, then pushed shakily to my feet, all the while keeping Luther in my sight.

"You getting a little color, now, Miz Cooper," he said, steadying me with a firm hold on my elbow. Then he took a few steps back. "I swear if you ain't had a time of it lately. First you wreck your car, then old Boss gets you hemmed up, and now I find you down here by Mr. Lauderbach's hog pens, fainted dead away." He chuckled like he was trying out for the part of Hoke in *Driving Miss Daisy*.

"Mr. Lauderbach's?" I squeaked. "These are Mr. Lauderbach's hogs? He's crossbreeding wild and domestic hogs! Why on earth would he do that? Isn't that illegal or something?" Luther looked at me like I'd sprouted another set of ears. "And by the way, I didn't faint. I'm not a fainter!" I said, blinking, still trying to clear my head.

Unfortunately, I'd had some past experience with being chloroformed and the splitting headache I was suffering now said I'd been treated to it again. Only the last time someone tried to knock me out with that crap, I'd had the good fortune of getting the upper hand. I must be slipping.

"Crossbreeding hogs?" Luther said incredulously. "What do you mean, crossbreeding hogs? You sure you alright, Miz Cooper?

You musta hit your head when you fainted. You sure I don't need to call the rescue squad?"

"No! I'm not alright! But I don't need the rescue squad and I know the difference between wild hogs and domestic ones. It's quite startling, you know? If you don't believe me, check out this big brute over here!" I said, pointing as I wobbled to the first pen. Luther followed politely beside me.

"See!" I said without looking in the pen. Luther climbed up a few of the split rails and peered down. "What am I 'posed to be looking at?" he asked.

What? I, too, climbed up the rails and looked down into the pen. It was empty. I jumped down, moved to the next pen, and looked in. A few yearling domestic hogs returned my gaze. I trotted to the next pen. It contained the same large domestic sow I'd seen before. Then I went to the next two. They were empty. There was not a feral hog in sight.

I pulled at my bottom lip and tried to figure out what was going on. Obviously, someone was trying to hide the feral hogs and the crossbreeds. But how had they done it? I looked at the sun and tried to guess how much time had gone by since mid-morning when I'd first started my surveillance.

Luther, who had been standing patiently beside me, now moved in front of me and leaned casually against the rails. "You know what I think?" he said kindly, offering me the damp cloth. "I think you just like Dorothy in *The Wizard of Oz*. When you fainted, you must've had one of them dreams. The kind that feels so real, you can't tell it from being awake! Yep," he said, smiling at his own profundity. "I bet that's just what happened."

An overwhelming desire to get clear of the hog pens and Luther came over me. I needed time to think without someone trying to convince me I was "only dreaming." Still, I wasn't getting a vibe that Luther was a danger to me. Looking at Tulip, she wasn't getting a vibe either. At least she wasn't growling or looking anxious. No way she'd let the person who'd disabled me get close to me again, so I asked him, "Are you saying you just found me leaning against the shed?"

"Yessum."

"And these," I said, pointing to the hogs, "are Mr. Lauderbach's hogs?"

"Yessum."

"Why are they so far from the farm?" I stepped back over to the shed. Luther followed.

"Well, now … they's hogs, you know, Miz Cooper, and Miz Lauderbach, she don't like the smell none too good."

"Uh-huh. And are you the … ehh, hog manager for the Lauderbachs as well as the dairy manager?"

"Yessum."

I stooped for my tote, heaped against the shed, and slung it over my shoulder. "Maybe you're right," I said, rubbing my forehead. "Perhaps I am coming down with something."

"Sure enough, you probably is," Luther said, guiding me to his old Chevy F-150 pickup. "Let me give you a ride back to your car. You best go home and rest."

———

Despite Luther's urgings, I persuaded him that I could make the walk back to the wellsite on my own steam. I thanked him for his help—it was getting to be a regular thing—and Tulip and I set off.

While the walk helped clear my brain, I was still at a loss to know what was really going on at the Lauderbach farm. But, by the time I saw the derrick stretching to the sky and started across the last pasture, I had taken stock of what I did know regarding the hog operation.

First, it was no dream. Second, the man in the green Toyota and Luther were definitely involved. And lastly, whoever gassed me clearly didn't want to go so far as to kill me—or I'd be dead. Still, being gassed was not something I intended to take lightly. I stomped up the steps to the doghouse, knowing something else too.

The person or persons who'd gassed me had to know I wouldn't believe Luther's "you had a dream" spiel. They were working on the premise that the ordeal, as unpleasant and confusing as it was, would cause me to steer clear of their operation for the rest of my contract time on the farm. They were wrong. But before I did any more searching for answers, it was time to do something I should have done as soon as I'd wrecked my Jeep.

I'd promised Bud that in our new relationship, I wouldn't keep things to myself. That I would stop trying to do everything on my own and, most especially, that I wouldn't involve myself in anything that would normally be done by the police. Lately, I'd blatantly disregarded all those promises. Right now, while I could still explain—well, to some degree anyway—why I hadn't adhered to our new rules, I planned to rectify the situation.

I pulled my iPhone from my pocket and a bottled water from my mini fridge—I can multitask—and flopped down at my desk. "Afternoon, babe," Bud said. "How come you left so early this morning? I was hoping to have a cup of coffee and discuss what's been going on while I was gone."

"Sorry," I said. "I'd have liked that, too, but I needed to take care of some things here. I do want to talk about what's been going on while you were in Greece. Are you going to be at my house for dinner tonight?"

"Actually, I was going to take care of things at my place. I've got some paperwork to catch up. But if it's important, I'll be there. Want me to call the kids to come too? Are you unhappy about the wedding plans ... again?"

"No. No kids. And I'm not unhappy about the wedding. I need to talk to you alone."

"Ooo. Mysterious. I like that. What time?"

"Sixish," I said. Then, after checking my watch, I made my next call.

In Mozambique, six hours ahead of me, it was around nine o'clock. My dad's phone rang and rang until it went to his voicemail. I wondered if he'd seen it was me calling and decided not to answer, or if he was really busy, maybe having a little late supper. As his message played I got a catch in my throat just hearing it. Nothing to do but leave him one too. I'd already left four over as many weeks, but they'd been about my wanting him at the wedding. This one was way more important.

His message ended and I said, "Dad, it's me. I had a conversation with Sheriff Clyde Stuckey a couple days ago and he said you and Buster Gilroy and Johnny Lee are planning something to overturn your conviction ... " I paused. "Call me back ... please. Let me know what's going on." I tapped my chin with the phone and waited, hoping I'd hear right back from him. When it was plain he wasn't going to make an immediate return call, I placed my last call before getting back to the work.

Watson answered after the first ring. "Cleo! I'm afraid to ask. Did you find the skeleton? What was it? Something from the Lepidosauromorpha group? Tanystropheidae, perhaps?"

"Nope."

"One of the Archosauria group, then?"

"You're getting warm," I laughed. "It's a rauisuchian!"

"Christ! I can't believe it! We've hit the jackpot. Is … is it all there?"

"Yep! As far as I can tell, anyway. Part of it is still encased in the red rock. I've made copious photos. Trust me, it's everything we hoped for and more."

"Tell me everything!" he said breathlessly. I did, describing the rauisuchian to him in abundant detail. Just as I finished, Jackie opened the door and gave me a look like he had a question. I indicated I'd be right there just as Watson was asking another question.

"What about the landowners? Have you notified them yet?"

"Not yet. I'll do that as soon as I take care of a … small issue I've discovered near the clay pit."

"Oh my god, what?"

"I can't go into it now. Apparently I'm needed at the well, but just know I'll get to the bottom of whatever it is and speak to the Lauderbach's about Cecil before you get here."

"Who's Cecil?" he asked. I laughed and explained my nickname. Being brought up on the originals of Bennie and Cecil, not the reruns like I had, he understood right away. "Cecil it is, then! Can't wait to meet him!"

We signed off and I slapped on my hard hat. It was time for me to find Jackie and collect the day's samples like I'd planned on doing right after my short expedition this morning. Being chloroformed into unconsciousness had knocked a serious hole in my day. Just then a low rumble of thunder rolled across the sky.

I went outside and searched the site for Jackie. He was checking one of the pits for signs of leakage. He smiled at my approach. "You been busy this morning?"

"Sort of," I dodged. "Just a few things I wanted to check on about Lauderbach #2. Maps show a couple of diabase dikes in the area and I wanted to physically locate them. If they're too close, we'd have to move #2 yet again."

"Everything okay?"

"I think so. It took me a while to locate them and then make sure there weren't any others cutting across our drainage field." In truth, I'd already done this, but I certainly didn't want him to know what I'd really been doing. I changed the subject. "I see from the sample bags, you're making good progress. I'll run them and confirm where we are formation-wise. What's the depth?"

"A little over 1550 feet," he said as thunder pealed again. He studied the sky.

"If that storm is what it looks like, just a rain squall and no lightning, we won't shut down. We should be making the turn at about 1750 feet." I gave him the thumbs-up and returned to the doghouse to run the samples.

Hours later, I didn't like what they were telling me. They were saying that we were coming up on a baked zone caused by the intrusion of a diabase dike, one that didn't show up on any of our maps. Depending on the angle at which we hit it, it could damage our bit. That, I knew, wouldn't make Overmire, Greenlite's head geologist and designer of the well, happy at all. I went to report my findings to Jackie.

"I was afraid of that," Jackie said when I told him what I'd found. "Everything was going too good. Something was bound to happen."

"Well, you never know," I said optimistically. "We may hit it at more of a perpendicular angle and punch right through it, or … "

"Yeah," Jackie laughed. "It's the *or* we gotta worry about. But thanks for the heads-up. If the derrick starts shaking and bucking, at least we'll know what's up."

"You bet," I said. "I'm getting ready to send a daily report to Overmire. I'll let you know about the dike."

It was a little after six o'clock by the time I'd completed my call to Overmire. He didn't seem too worried, telling me to grind on and hope nothing happened. Suited me. We signed off and, after I passed on his suggestions to Jackie, I gathered my things to book it for home. I still had to make the dinner I'd promised Bud. "Tulip!" I called.

No Tulip.

Then I had a thought. I'd been leaving the door to the minivan open while on site. Tulip reveled in its vast carpeted interior and plush, fluffy seats. "There you are," I said, finding her stretched out on the backseat. She sat up, yawned like a Serengeti lioness, then hopped out. "I swear you're getting spoiled," I told her. "But you might as well climb back in. It's time to go home."

Rain had set in by the time I got there. I was disappointed to see Bud's Porsche was already in my drive. I'd wanted to start dinner before he arrived. Oh, well. No sense spoiling him too. I pulled into the garage and he opened the door from the kitchen and stood on the stoop with a questioning look on his face.

"I was hoping to beat you home," I said, climbing out. "I wanted to defrost some steaks."

"A minivan?" he said, ignoring my domestic prattle. "Where's your Jeep?"

"That's what I wanted to talk to you about. Well, that and a lot of things. But you have to promise here and now you won't get upset."

"Uh-oh," he groaned. "I don't like the sound of that. Come on in. I've got a nice bottle of Pinot chilling, though I'm afraid Jack Daniels might be called for."

Over steaks, salad, and a nice potato casserole—that man can really cook—I told Bud about the loss of my magic Jeep, owing my loss of control to a blown tire. He was actually very sympathetic and he seemed to take it in stride that I hadn't told him because he was in Greece and powerless to do anything but worry about me. "And what good would that have done?" I asked him.

"None, but I could have commiserated with you. The important thing is that you're unhurt. Still, I am sorry. I know how much that Jeep meant to you."

Really? "Well, I appreciate that, Bud, but there's more that I want to tell you."

"More?"

I had two major discoveries to tell him about: the fossilized reptile in the clay pit and the hog operation. I started with the rauisuchian.

"A what?" Bud asked, tilting his head. "A raunchy... "

"No. Not raunchy, rauisuchian. Raw-ih-*soo*-ke-un," I said slowly. "It's a large—very large actually—meat-eating reptile that lived back during the Triassic age." Bud made a few attempts at the pronunciation before he got it right. Then I gave him a brief geologic rundown of the Triassic Basin—much of it he'd heard from me before—and told him how I'd made the discovery. That led me to the hog operation, Luther Green, and the mysterious man in the green Toyota truck.

He, too, was amazed that anyone would go to the extremes of breeding feral hogs with domestics to get a large hunting trophy, but agreed that it was a plausible explanation. When I got to the part about going back to see if I could spot some vehicle tags...well, Bud started to get agitated.

"Stop right there!" he demanded. "I believe I've made it clear, as have a couple of police detectives you met last summer, that you are not to engage in amateur...sleuthing! Am I right?"

"Will you let me finish?" I snapped, wishing now I hadn't started. If he didn't like that I'd neglected to take the advice of a couple of cops last summer, he was really going to hate my latest disregard of a warning from the law. I got as far as the part about the chloroform, which I decided to describe—taking a cue from Luther—as fainting.

"Stop again!" Bud said, as he cleared the table and I rinsed and loaded the dishes into the dishwasher. "You fainted?"

"Kinda."

"Kinda? You pregnant or something?"

"Very funny. Are you going to let me *share* this with you or not?" I asked sarcastically. That tendon in his jaw that popped when he got annoyed was doing its thing so I hurried through the part about the missing hogs. When I finished, Bud was quiet and I knew this lack of response meant he was considering all that I'd relayed to him. It was quite a bit to take in so I gave him some time. We took our coffee into the great room and he lit the fire he'd laid in the fireplace.

Finally, between blowing and poking at his budding flame, he said "Okay, here's what I still don't understand. First you said you 'kinda' fainted, but at the same time you're incredulous that this guy, Luther, would suggest something so ludicrous. Which is it? Did you faint or not?"

"Mom!" called Henri from the kitchen.

Thank the lord for small miracles!

THIRTEEN

"COME ON IN!" I called. Time for Bud to concentrate on something else difficult, convoluted, and mysterious—like our wedding plans. Sipping my coffee, I looked up just as Henri, hand in hand with Detective Sergeant Chris Bryant, strolled into the great room. To say I was stunned would have been putting it mildly.

She was positively beaming. He, on the other hand, upon seeing me, gave me what I can only describe as a smug smile. I know I was blinking, a total giveaway to anyone who really knows me that I was confused. Trying to get my poker face in place was a waste of time.

In fact, I gave up on it altogether and gawked openly as Henri scrunched up her shoulders and opened her mouth to speak, only nothing came out. My thought: *Damn! He must be spectacular!* Bud, who'd been sitting on the couch beside me jumped up to spare us any continuation of the awkward scene. "Bud Cooper," he said, approaching Chris with an outstretched hand.

Balancing my coffee, which sloshed dangerously close to the edge of my mug, I hopped up before Chris could introduce himself. "Bud," I said. "This Chris Bryant. He's the detective who's working on the case involving the boy whose body I found."

It was the best I could do. I mean, I'd been trying to work up to telling Bud about the bullet in the tire and the detective who helped me but, honestly, there hadn't been time yet. And if I've learned anything from years of living with Bud, it's that it's best to feed him bad things in small doses.

There was another awkward pause. Chris gave me a look that said he'd follow my lead. Unfortunately, Henri, having found her voice, wasn't following anyone's signals and blurted out, "Dad, Chris is a detective on the Sanford police force. A detective *sergeant*," she beamed.

"Yes," Bud said. "I got that much … "

"And, he's the one who brought mom home after her wreck *and* found the bullet in her tire!"

Oh shit. "Bullet?" Bud said, turning abruptly to me.

"Oh," I laughed dismissively. "Didn't I mention that? We think it was probably just a stray hunter's bullet, right, Chris?"

"Uh … "

"More likely that crazy sheriff!" Bud boomed. I put my hand on his arm to calm him. "I've told Detective Bryant all about our past with Stuckey," I said. "And he's checking into it, aren't you?" Now it was time for Chris to feel a little pressure. Only he didn't.

"As I told your wife, I'd need cause to take out a warrant on our own sheriff. She'd have to jump through quite a few hoops, probably involving a judge, to get that done. I've asked her if she wants to pursue it and she hasn't gotten back to me."

The ball was back in my court. Bud looked at me, then said, "Well, maybe she's right, it could have been a stray bullet from a hunter's gun."

Henri began to babble about what a sweet guy Chris was. How he'd gone out of his way to look her up after seeing her for only a few minutes at our house the night of the accident. How he'd sensed she was stressed over trying to coordinate the wedding plans and how he'd wanted to help her and...oh brother. I didn't know whether to hate him or admire him.

Then Bud, apparently paying no more attention to *When Henri Met Chris* than I was, said, "Say, Chris, you're an officer of the court. What do you think about that hog operation Cleo found? Isn't it illegal in the state of North Carolina to interbreed wild and domestic hogs?"

Double Shit. "Bud," I said sweetly. "Could I see you in the kitchen for a sec?"

Pushing the swinging door with the palm of my hand, I resisted the urge to let it fly back in Bud's face. Instead, I held it for him, stopped it from swinging to insure our privacy, then spun around to face him. "What were you thinking?" I whispered sternly. "I haven't told him about the hogs because I need to check some things out for myself first..."

"You mean some things you're trying to keep to yourself. Some things you're supposed to let the police handle..."

"That's not fair!" I said more loudly than I'd anticipated. I lowered my voice and continued. "Telling him about the hogs would naturally lead to what I found besides them." Bud gave me a quizzical look. "Hello? Important fossil find?"

"Oh, right."

"Even if I could lie—and I believe no lying was one of your new rules—he might find the pit himself if he investigated the area. Now, you may not know this, Bud, but archeological finds like this one are very rare and highly prestigious and people have been known to actually kill to protect one!"

"Did I hear you mention killing someone to protect something?" Chris said, letting go of the swinging door and striding purposefully to where Bud and I stood by the sink.

Threatening Bud with a stern squint of my eyes, I said. "Of course not. We were just discussing ... a movie."

"No you weren't," Chris said coolly. "Maybe you'd better tell me about these hogs you found."

"I think that would be a good idea," Bud said, giving me a return squint. "After all, it is this young man's job to solve murder cases, Cleo. Not yours."

"Even if I'm the main suspect?"

"Especially if you're the main suspect," Chris added.

"Let me ask you something, Chris," Bud said. "What's your opinion of the sheriff?"

"Honestly, I've been a little surprised at his reaction to your wife. He does seem somewhat irrational in his attempt to prove she committed the murder. Generally, he's a competent officer, if not a terribly innovative or imaginative one."

"What's going on?" Henri said from the doorway. She joined us, took Chris's arm in hers, and smiled up at his handsome face. "We're going to miss my friends at Blue Oasis. The Friday night bar crawl is starting there ... "

The blue-eyed detective smiled suavely, slipped his arm around Henri's waist and gave her a light buss on the lips. Modulating his tone from interrogatory to intensely sexy, he said, "Why don't you go powder your nose, Miss Henri. I'll meet you at the car."

I braced for the "Henri blast" following this sexist request, but surprisingly she squirmed like a puppy and said, "Good idea. It won't take but a few minutes."

Clearly, I'd underestimated this fellow in so many ways.

Moreover, since I was going to have to rid the area of the hog operation before I could risk bringing in a team of paleontologists to excavate Cecil, I decided I might as well get some help. I gave him a brief sketch of what I knew of the operation, including Luther and the man in the green truck. I told him I'd stumbled upon it while flagging Lauderbach #2, but left out any mention of the clay pit.

Chris listened, arms crossed, then said, "So are you thinking these hogs were deliberately interbred, the feral and the domestic. Why?"

"To create a hunting trophy."

"A hunting trophy... huh. Interesting theory. Who would want to do this?" Chris asked.

"Luther Green and the man in the green truck, of course," I sniffed.

"Have you any proof of this?" he asked.

"No," I said. "I've been told not to interfere with police work."

"Okay," he replied, rubbing his chin contemplatively. "I'll check into what laws, if any, might have been broken. But the obvious thing, the thing that stands out, of course, is the connection to the murder. Clinton might have been killed with a knife, but he was shot with an arrow first. Arrows would be the only ammunition plausible if the hunting club was meant to be clandestine."

Then, upon hearing Henri approach, Chris directed his attention to Bud. "Nice to meet you, Mr. Cooper. Sorry it was such a short visit. Perhaps we'll see each other again soon."

"I'm sure we will," Bud said, handing him one of his business cards from his wallet. "Drop by my office any time."

Chris looked at the card. "Cooper Enterprises," he said, reading it.

"Yes," Bud said. "We're in the CP&L Building downtown."

As soon as Henri and Chris left, I decided I'd had about all I could stand of "let's share our lives" and found several creative ways to occupy Bud's mind that were far more pleasant.

———

For most workday folks, Saturdays are a day off. For those of us who toil in the energy field, however, Saturdays and Sundays are just another day. I was on my way across the farm, headed to the site by way of the series of dirt roads that connected its vast acreage when, several hills due south from me, bumping along a path at the edge of another section of woods, was the green Toyota truck.

Braking to a full stop, I watched until it rounded the edge of the trees, then followed at a safe distance. All that crap about me not doing law enforcement's job was right there, front and center in my mind. It's just that I was here and law enforcement wasn't. And hadn't Chris asked me about proof?

Seemed appropriate that a civic-minded citizen such as myself take action to help solve crimes whenever possible. Especially when the crime was murder and the prime suspect was said civic-minded citizen. Besides, I was only going to follow the truck.

This was easy to do because the soft, sandy soil and flattened weeds made the tracks obvious. Also obvious was the fact that more trucks than the one I was following had passed this way. Perhaps one, pulling a stock trailer full of hogs? Soon, the tracks turned into the woods on one of the many old, overgrown logging paths. A fleeting thought that the newly broken branches poking out into the road might scratch the van slipped through my mind, but I was so intent on not being detected, it slipped away.

Who was running the hog operation and whether it was legal in the eyes of the state of North Carolina was information I needed to know if, as I'd told Watson, we were going to be able to proceed with the excavation and preservation of Cecil. Plus, it'd be a good thing to know where the feral hogs were when I talked to the Lauderbachs. I had a feeling they had no idea any type of hogs were being raised on their land, let alone crossbred ones. I especially wanted to be enlightened about every aspect of the operation because, well, no one likes being jerked around and having their head screwed with.

After about a quarter of a mile, the road narrowed even more and concern over the van's paint job returned, so I got out and walked the trail for a short ways. Didn't look too bad, so I got back in the van and slowly eased along as broken branches and rubbery sapling limbs slapped and scraped along its sides. Tulip whined. I'd learned to take her anxiety as a warning... usually. "Pipe down," I commanded as the woods got thicker, the light dimmer, and the branches bigger. "I'm not going far."

One thing I know about logging trails: unless you luck up and happen upon a clearing, there is no where to turn around. They can snake through the woods for miles, connecting one logging deck to another. I didn't want to get trapped where I couldn't run if necessary, so after another quarter mile, I stopped and walked the path again, finding a clearing of sorts. Well, it was more of a slight depression devoid of trees. Ones too big to flatten with a vehicle, anyway.

Overhead, a canopy of limbs, all dressed out in autumn colors, intertwined tightly. I gave them a serious appraisal. No problem. I could push them aside too. Scuffing the leaf litter aside with my boot, I found the depression underlain by a very small outcrop of diabase rock. Probably what caused the stunted undergrowth. It was about three feet wide. Not optimal, but probably as good as I was going to get in terms of a place to turn around. Prudence told me to go no farther. Logic told me I didn't need to.

If the hogs had been relocated somewhere up the path, it would have to be in a large natural clearing. When I'd been knocked out, it had only been for a short while, two hours at the most. Even if they had pens already constructed, it would have taken a Herculean effort just to get the hogs loaded and moved while I was out. It wouldn't have been impossible, but highly unlikely in that short amount of time.

The more I thought about it, the more sense it made that there would be other locations on the farm where hogs could be corralled. Especially if this was, as I believed it to be, a trophy hunting scheme of some sort. Lord knows, I'd seen enough portable corral panels stacked around in various places. When a rich hunter contracted to shoot a wild boar, it was likely released from one of any number of remote locations on the farm, depending on wind conditions and what type of farm operations were being conducted nearby.

All I had to do to find these possible locations? Look on the GIS maps and aerials of the farm. Seeing the green truck and locating the trail had made finding this one on an aerial photo easy, not to mention much safer. And, I'd be adhering to Bud's rules about staying out of trouble, right?

The overnight rain had softened the ground and it squished under my boot as I climbed back into the van. I wasn't worried. With my foot on the brake, I let the van roll down into the depression, pushing aside hardwood limbs. Red, orange, and yellow leaves covered the window so thickly it blocked out the light. Tulip whined again. "Oh, don't be a wuss-dog," I said, inching back and forth in the small clearing.

Pretty soon, I'd reversed direction. I breathed a sigh of relief. It could have been a sticky situation that left me in a vulnerable spot. I thought wistfully of the magic Jeep. I'd turned it around in much smaller spots. Of course, it was much smaller and had four-wheel drive. This piece of junk didn't. The Jeep had also had a wench. Something I would add to whatever new vehicle I got. It was time to do something about getting a new vehicle. Resolving to move that task to the top of my to-do list, I headed for the site.

———

Upon arrival, I could hardly wait to check the oversized aerial above my desk. I hopped out and opened the door for Tulip. That's when I saw the damage I'd done to the van. Crap! It looked like it'd been rolled. Well, hell, I'd worry about that later.

A magnifying glass wasn't even necessary in scanning the aerial. I found what I was looking for right off. Just as I'd suspected, a large clearing, probably a loading deck for a past logging operation was still visible. I smiled smugly. Time to have a little chat with the Lauderbachs.

FOURTEEN

Before I called the Lauderbachs, I examined the last of the chip samples and pebbles brought up overnight from the depths of the ancient basin as I rehearsed in my head the way I wanted our conversation to go. Informing them about Cecil prior to bringing up the bad news about the hogs and why they had to go seemed right. I was just finishing my Schmid and Medlin work when Jackie poked his head in the door and gave me a you-got-time-for-me look. "Come on in," I said. "You've saved me a trip out to you."

"I thought I'd let you know we made it through that diabase dike with no trouble. Apparently, our mojo is still working," he said. He and I conducted a short, impromptu meeting regarding the drill plan and our next move should any problems arise. My motto: always have a plan, a backup plan and a backup to the backup. After he left, I cleaned up, then put in a call to the Lauderbach home. Sara answered and said now would be a good time to visit.

When I arrived, instead of taking me to the sunroom, Ruby guided me down a wide hallway lined with photos of generations of Lauderbachs to a room that at one time might have been a den.

Wall-mounted cases held trophies and ribbons for numerous cattle shows and county and state fairs. A wide-screen television, couch, and chairs had been relegated to the far end of the room. The rest was devoted to physical therapy equipment.

Annette Lauderbach sat in a folding chair, watching her husband as he took a few steps in an obviously homemade contraption the likes of which I'd never seen. It looked like two large horseshoes welded together at 90-degree angles with a harness in the middle. The seven-foot-tall device rested on John Deere lawn mower wheels.

Arthur, comfortably positioned in the harness, balanced himself with handles welded to either side of the horseshoe frame. Sara and Luther stood by, ready to offer assistance.

With deliberate determination, he slid one foot forward across the floor a few inches. Then, straining mightily, veins popping out on his neck, he shifted his weight until he balanced again so he could drag his back foot to the new position where he'd rebalance and start the process all over again. Once he completed a step, everyone clapped. Luther helped him into his wheelchair and pushed him to the sitting area.

My admiration for his amazing progress was heartfelt and I let him know, then asked, "Where in the world did you get this amazing piece of equipment? It looks—"

"Homemade?" Arthur laughed. "It is. Luther's quite handy when it comes to creative engineering. I wasn't making any progress going to the therapist once a week, so he came up with this and now that I can work every day, I've been doing much better."

Ruby beamed. Luther grinned proudly. I was wondering how much longer they'd hang around, and if I should come back another time, when he and Ruby excused themselves.

When I gave Arthur, Annette, and Sara the grand news about Cecil, they were at first astounded. Then they were ecstatic, especially Sara. She started to cry, she was so overcome with emotion. "I just wish Clinton was here to enjoy this."

"But that's the best part," I said. "I believe he's the one who found it. That is, if this is his." I pulled the Estwing pick from my tote.

Sara gasped. "I gave him that for Christmas a few years ago. He was so proud of it."

"It appears he's been working—maybe for years—to expose enough of the fossil to show someone who could help him with a discovery of its magnitude. Do you know if he'd been spending time with any of his paleo professors lately?" The three Lauderbachs indicated that, if anything, Clinton had become withdrawn and less social after declaring his new major.

"He didn't get all weird or anything," Sara said. "He was just very intense and focused on his studies. We still did things together, just not as often. Several times I asked him if something was up, you know, like a girlfriend occupying his time. He just said he was busy. There was one time when he was working on something important, and I pressed him on it. He only smiled and said, 'you'll see soon enough.' Now I know what he was talking about." Her chin trembled, but she sucked in a deep breath and continued, "I'll talk to his professors and see if he mentioned anything about the fossil to them—"

"No!" I cut her off abruptly. "Leave the paleo department out of this for the time being. I can't stress enough the importance of keeping this find a secret in these early days. Once we go public, there'll be a slew of professors and friends coming forth, all saying they'd worked on the fossil with Clinton. Documentation will prove whether they were."

The Lauderbachs all nodded in agreement and I continued, "Meanwhile, I've already arranged to have a crack team put together to see that the fossil is properly excavated and that Clinton gets all the credit for the find and the early work on it ... " I paused and looked at them intently so as to be sure of their feelings. " ... if that meets with your approval, of course."

"Of course," they answered in chorus.

"Good. I just want you to know that everything about Cecil is subject to your approval, Arthur. As the landowners, you and Annette also own the fossil. It will be up to you to donate it or sell it to whomever you wish."

"What about Clint's parents?" Sara said.

"Good question," I said. "But, again, for the present, let's keep the number of people with knowledge of Cecil"—I explained the nickname to them too—"to a minimum. I want to be sure we can prove Clinton discovered it first, and I've done my best to document that with photos, but no sense taking chances right now."

"Do you think someone would really try to take credit for a discovery made by a student who's now dead?" Annette asked incredulously.

"When it comes to the grant money and prestige a find like Cecil will bring, the answer is yes," I said. "But let me worry about that."

"Gosh," Annette said. "Look at the time, Arthur! Luther will be here any minute to take you to the barn for your regular visit." To me, she said, "Arthur has had to reduce his time in the barn since he came home from the hospital to Saturday mornings only."

"I understand," I said. "I've got to leave too. But before I do, one quick question, Arthur. Where on the farm do you keep your hogs?"

Arthur's brow furrowed. "Years ago, my father used to have some hog pens between the two barns in a sheltered area. Of course, we only kept a small number, just what we needed for our family use. Now days it's far cheaper to buy what you need at the store. Why do you ask?"

"Oh, no reason," I said quickly, hearing the squeaky clump of Luther's black gum boots in the hallway. "I'm just afraid of hogs and if you have any stashed in the woods somewhere, I'd like to know so I don't stumble upon them."

Arthur laughed. "Aw, you don't have to worry about us having any, but feral hogs, now, that might be something to consider. I know they're becoming a problem for farmers to the east of us."

"I'll keep my eyes open," I said, standing. "And remember, it's important not to discuss the fossil with anyone until we've crossed all our T's and dotted all our I's."

———

I decided to make this Saturday work day a short one and was straightening my office preparing to leave when my iPhone clanged. "Dad!" I exclaimed, truly stunned. "I've been trying to reach you for weeks. Where have you been? Are you alright? How's Mozambique? Are you coming to the wedding?"

"Cleo," my dad said in his matter-of-fact voice. "Settle down. I don't have much time. I'm in between dives but I'll try to answer your questions one at a time. First, tell me why you were having a conversation with that damn criminal, Stuckey."

I gave him the whole story about finding the murdered body of a friend of the family whose land I was working on and Stuckey's insane insistence that I was his prime suspect.

"Tell me he isn't pursuing you like a rabid bulldog." Dad's voice carried a hint of alarm.

"Actually, I've heard very little from him," I said. "Probably because he doesn't have a case and because he's consumed with getting reelected right now. But back to you, Dad, I know you've been up here and I want to know why you didn't come see me and what Stuckey meant about you and your friends trying to overturn your old case."

"Well, as I recall," my dad drawled, "I just dropped by to see Buster on short notice. Johnny ran into us later. It was good to see him, too, though … "

"Dad, please!"

"You weren't in town and I didn't see any need to tell you later and make you feel guilty."

Trying to recall where I was "back in the spring," as Johnny had described the time he'd seen Dad and Buster at a local café, I asked, "Where was I?"

Dad snorted a laugh. "Well, honey, you'd know that better than I would."

Frustrated, I squawked, "What about the three of you trying to overturn your old conviction? What was Stuckey talking about?"

I heard a mechanical chiming sound. "Dive manager's ready for me to go down now," Dad said, referring to his job as an underwater welder. "We'll talk about this later."

"Wait! Dad! What about the wedding? You are coming, aren't you?"

"Gotta go!"

"Dad? Hello?" I said into a dead line.

The house was quiet late that Saturday afternoon as I checked my email in my study. Reading a quick note from Watson, saying he'd be landing at Raleigh-Durham International on Friday, the 18th, around one thirty, brought both relief and a tightening in my gut. The relief came from knowing I was moving forward with my plans for saving Cecil. As for the concern, well, there were still a passel of hog hunters running loose on the Lauderbach's farm and one person was already dead. Whether Clinton's death and the hog hunters had anything in common, I didn't know, but I sure as hell didn't want to find out the hard way. I shut down the computer and moved into my bedroom.

Carefully shedding my muddy clothes—causalities of trying to squeeze a fat van along a narrow path—I tossed them down the laundry chute and pulled on clean jeans and a favorite, old sweater. I was just heading downstairs when I thought I heard a car in the drive and looked out the window. It was Chris. I hurried to the front door to meet him.

"What brings you here?" I said, gesturing for him to enter. Just then I heard a growl from Bud's Porsche and I knew he wasn't far away.

Chris turned at the sound and said, "Let's wait for your husband."

"Husband-to-be," I corrected as Bud's creamy turbo Carrera whipped into my drive and chirped to a stop beside Chris's Crown Vic.

I directed Chris into the kitchen where I offered him a beer, which he declined with a negative shake of his head.

"I'll take one," Bud said, striding into the room. I opened the refrigerator, handed him a Bud Light and was reaching for the white wine—technically it was the cocktail hour—when he dropped the bomb. "Chris thought I should be here when he informs you that Stuckey's going to arrest you for the murder of Clinton Baker in the next few days." I closed the door and made a beeline for the Jack Daniels.

FIFTEEN

BUD TOOK THE BOTTLE from my trembling fingers and poured it
into a tumbler. "Well," I said. "This blows our wedding plans all to
hell. Henri and Will are going to be so disappointed."

"What about us?" Bud said.

"You know what I mean!" I snapped back.

"Well, if it makes you feel any better," Chris said. "I've had several long talks with him, trying to dissuade him, get him to wait
until I can fully investigate but he's hell-bent." Chris rubbed his
brow in consternation. I could tell he was torn between trying to
follow orders, something he'd been doing for most of his adult life,
and using his common sense. He shifted uncomfortably. I pulled a
bar stool from under the overhang of the stove island. "Sit," I said
and he did, seemingly grateful to do so.

I needed to tread lightly here, but, well, if this thing was going
to get really insanely nasty—and I had up close and personal
knowledge of how Stuckey could take insanely nasty to unheard-
of heights—then I needed to find out now which side of the fence

Chris was going to graze on. "You sure you don't want to rethink that beer, or maybe something stronger. The clock says you're off duty. Is this an official call or just friendly support?"

Bud set a can of Bud Light in front of Chris. He popped the top. I took that to mean the latter was the case. "Remember what I told you about my past with Stuckey?" Chris nodded again. "And how if it weren't for Bud, my dad would probably be on death row?"

"Right," Chris said, taking a long pull on the beer.

"Well, it seems to me, that in light of what I told you about his actions then and how he's acting now—irrational seems the most appropriate choice of words—you could at least give me the benefit of the doubt until we find the real murderer."

"We?"

"Well, clearly you need help. I mean … "

"How do you think the DA would take my letting the prime murder suspect in a case help me clear herself in that very case? How do you think that would stand up in court? Besides, I think I can wrap up a simple case of murder without the help of you two. I've done it many times."

"But … " I sputtered.

"On the other hand," he continued. "I have to admit that Stuckey's judgment in matters concerning this case seems somewhat … "

"Biased?" offered Bud.

"Non-existent," I added.

"I was going to say, distracted … what with his election and all. Moreover, we're shorthanded. The bad economy has been bad in many ways for our department. We've had cutbacks in hiring, lay-offs, and frankly, I don't know what happens to the department's money. Anyway, it's not your problem except that instead of the six detectives we used to have, counting me, now we only have four."

"Well, there you go," Bud said. "Another reason we've got to get this case wrapped up so Cleo can stay on the job. The more wells brought in successfully in this county, the more expendable funds there are available for every sector of the economy, including government hiring."

"I see your point," Chris said. "That's why I'm going to call an audible on this thing. From now on, Ms. Cooper, any time you run across information pertinent to the case—by accident, of course, you let me know." He slugged down the rest of his beer, crushed the can and looked at Bud and me.

"That's it? That's your plan?" I asked.

"It's the best I can do," he said.

"Nothing says we can't be ready with our own plan, Cleo," Bud said.

"Yeah," I said. "What's our plan?"

"I'll have our attorney draw up papers swearing out a warrant for Stuckey's arrest for attempted murder on the grounds that you think he was responsible for shooting out your tire," Bud said. "He needs to know we are ready and willing to file them."

"Now *that's* a plan that might actually get Stuckey's attention," Chris said, rising from his bar stool. "Dueling lawsuits. Plus, he has some experience with Bud's high-powered lawyers."

"Wait," I said as he turned to leave. "I have information that I . . . accidentally came across today."

"Oh, wow," Chris said sarcastically. "Why am I not surprised?"

"Well, as I said, I only happened to see what I saw by accident, you understand."

"Of course."

"Remember that green Toyota truck I told you I first came across at the hog pens?"

"Yeah."

"Well, while I was on my way to the site this morning, I just happened to see it again."

"Just *happened* to see it? Where was it?" Chris asked.

"On one of the farm roads a few hills and down elevation from where I was driving, but, since you weren't there to investigate, I thought I'd be a good citizen and see where he went."

Chris rolled his eyes. "Okay, tell me where he went."

"Well, I followed from a safe distance until he turned down a logging road and, because I promised my fiancé"—I batted my lashes as Bud—"I wouldn't engage in activity best left to the law, I turned around and went to my office. I figured he might be going to check on some of the hogs. If so, more than likely they'd be in a clearing, which, if it was an old logging deck, I'd be able to spot on my aerial of the farm."

"Good thinking. Were you able to spot it?"

"Yep."

"You did that for me?" Bud said. "You actually turned around?"

"Certainly," I said, poker face in place. Then to Chris: "Anyway, I have a theory about multiple remote locations and why they'd be needed. Want to hear it?"

Chris glanced at his watch. "Sure," he said and sat back down as Bud dropped another cold one in front of him. "I just can't be late picking up your lovely daughter." Bud raised his eyebrows.

"It's simply a matter of wind direction and what's going on at the farm at any given time," I said. "For instance, if there's planting going on, lots of workers milling about a field near a certain patch of woods, then that patch wouldn't be a good place for a hunt. So they take the trophy hog in question, move it to a pen on the other side of the farm where nothing is going on and there's no chance of being seen. Also, if you're letting a hog loose to be hunted down, it's a good idea to do it upwind of where the hunter will be. In looking at the aerials of the farm, there are quite a few clearings where pens could be hidden."

"Wouldn't you be able to see the pens in the photos?" Bud asked.

"Not if they're placed under the overhang of the trees at the edge of the clearing. It isn't like these are large hog farms back in the woods. The one I saw had five split-rail pens. There was also a shed, but it was one of those portable kinds. Also, if there are pens scattered around the farm, they're probably made from corral panels. They're lightweight and easy to move. In fact, I've seen quite a few stacks of them at various spots on the farm. And, since they are usually painted a rusty brown color, they'd blend right in with the scenery."

"All of this is good information," Chris said distractedly as he checked his watch and rose and headed for the door.

Now or never. "There is something else," I said dismally. I hated to utter my next words, but I had to. It was time to trust the law. Or try to, anyway. Still, when it came to a fossil as important as Cecil ... well, it took everything I had to say, "I've discovered another motive for murder."

Chris stopped and turned back to us. His expression turning from impatient to deadly serious. "What?"

"A very rare, very valuable fossil."

I guess one look at my face told Chris this was not something I wanted to talk about. If he sat back down any faster, we would need to have the bar stool surgically removed. "Fossil? Valuable enough to commit murder for?" he asked quizzically.

"Yes," I explained. "I'm referring to the fossil of a long-extinct reptile. Since you have Clinton's computer, you've got access to his research files. You need to see if he has started a file regarding this species..." I stood, went to my kitchen desk, and wrote the Linnaean classification for Cecil on a piece of paper.

"What the hell is that?"

I sighed. "You might want to call Henri," I said. "This might take more than a minute and a half to explain."

Turned out it only took about twenty minutes to tell Chris the story of how I stumbled upon Cecil, how I knew Clinton was the one who had actually discovered him, how it would take a team of paleontologists to excavate it, and why I didn't feel safe doing that with a bunch of hot-headed hog hunters running around with bows and arrows.

I explained why it was so important to me, the Lauderbachs, and anyone who knew Clinton to be able to prove beyond a shadow of a doubt that he was the one to make the discovery. I gave a quick explanation of how, in the cutthroat world of academics, it would take more than an Estwing rock pick bearing his initials to prove he was the founder. I ended by saying, "There's one other thing that you could do to add strength to our proof of who actually found Cecil."

"Shoot," Chris said.

"Remember the camos Clinton was wearing?"

"Yeah."

"Well, he also hid the fossil under a twenty-foot camo tarp that was purchased from G.I. Joe's Army Surplus in Durham. If you could find that the tarp was bought from the same place—hopefully at the same time—then we'd really have something. I'd do it for you, but again, I don't have access to his computer and his credit card records."

"When do you think it was purchased?"

"Well, the tarp is very weathered, but it would be. More so than his clothes. Still I'd start looking at least three years ago."

When I finished, Chris said, "You've done some very good work here."

"Thanks," I said dryly. "Glad I could be of help. Accidentally, of course."

"If fossils are as big a deal in the world of academics as you say, this could be the break I need," Chris said. "I'll have my staff go through all his emails to see if they match up with anyone at the university ... "

"Not to mention the museum world," I said.

"Right. Suffice it to say, this opens up a whole new set of motives, don't you think?"

"Honestly, from what I've learned of that young man, I can't imagine anyone wanting to hurt him, much less kill him. Here's the thing though, secrecy, at least until we can get the legalities and the extraction team firmly established, has to be the watchword. No one can know about it. Least of all that maniac, Stuckey."

Chris held out his palm like a traffic cop. "Okay, I know how you guys feel. And I understand your desire to have the hog situation under control before you put vulnerable academic types in a situation you feel could be dangerous. Just tell me how long it's going to take you to get everything in order so that you feel comfortable going forward."

"Watson is coming in Friday, the 18th. I'll know more then ... "

Bud's text tune chimed. "Uh-oh," he said. "It's Henri. You forgot to call her." Without a word of good-bye, Chris scrambled for the door.

I smiled. "Good to see the disturbance in the force is being rectified and the balance of power in the universe is returning to normal."

"I agree. I was beginning to think Henri was losing her touch," said Bud, noticing his beer can was empty. He checked the refrigerator. "We're out of beer in here. I'll bring some more in from the garage."

"Good idea," I said. I had another refrigerator and freezer out there so I never ran low on the important things in life. I was trying to remember what I had there that I could whip up for dinner when I suddenly had a bad thought and ran to catch Bud. Too late.

He was already in the garage, standing in front of the minivan, his hands on his hips. "You've wrecked another car?"

"What do you mean? It's not wrecked," I said indignantly. "I told you, I didn't want to follow the green Toyota too far into the woods so I turned around and went back to the office where I could let my maps do the work for me."

"Where'd you turn around ... inside a cement mixer?"

"Har, har. Very funny," I said, retrieving the beer from the fridge. Then I opened the freezer, grabbed a surefire subject changer and held it up.

Bud's eyes got big and round. "Homemade chicken pot pie?"

———

Sunday was a busy day at the well. Jackie was cracking the whip on the crew as they tripped the strings of drilling pipe up out of the hole. They'd pull everything up, change the bit to a directional one, and then push it all back down again. Since we'd reached our kickoff point, the beginning of the gradual turn to the horizontal, we needed a directional bit. This process could take a few days. The good news: I didn't have to feel guilty about going home once I'd caught up with last night's samples. I needed to take care of some domestic chores.

It would take about 500 vertical feet to complete the turn and hit our target horizon at the base of the Cumnock Formation. Once we were completely horizontal, we'd continue on for a quarter of a mile, about 1300 feet, and end the drilling part of this well. Casing, cementing, and perforation would take place after that, followed by a few days of fracking. All this, assuming no unforeseen problems arose, would take another week, more or less. Then, the well would become the domain of the production and reclamation people.

I was making notes regarding a chip sample when Sara bopped into the trailer with a friend in tow. She introduced me to Mia, one of Luther and Ruby's daughters. "Nice to meet you," I said, noticing her Prada shoes and stylish Burberry sweater and muffler. "Are you in school with Sara at UNC?"

"No ma'am," said the beautiful child with the perfect manicure. "I'm at Brown."

"On scholarship," said Sara. "Mia's way smart!"

"Oh, you stop now," Mia said shyly. "It's only a partial scholarship."

We chatted a short while until my iPhone rang. I checked the screen. It was Overmire. "I have to take this," I said.

"Okay, but first may we go out to the well and see what's going on?"

"Yes, but grab two of those hard hats by the door. Jackie is entering a new phase in our drilling plan. He'll tell you all about it."

As they pulled the door closed behind them, I returned to my caller. "Mr. Overmire," I said. "What can I do for you?"

"I'm afraid we're going to have to change Lauderbach #2 yet again."

Was this guy using darts to pick wellsites? "How come?" I asked politely. "I thought your last change was well founded."

"And I think it could be a good site, it's just that this new area shows even more potential." He gave me the coordinates and I quickly located them.

Oh, no. Say it ain't so! Staring at the new wellhead site right on top of Cecil and the clay pit, I said, "Uh … let me make some on-the-ground observations and I'll get right back to you."

"I'm leaving early today, it being Sunday and all. Wife wants me to go somewhere with her. Let me know as soon as you can if you find any problems."

I tapped my phone off. Great! Now I had to either make up a reason why the clay pit was a bad place for a gas well or find a better one. First things first, however. Right now I needed to get started doing what it took to run off a bunch of hog hunters. I pulled up Arthur Lauderbach's number.

He answered right away. "Hello, Cleo," he said.

"Hi, Arthur. I wonder if you could spare a few minutes to speak with me on a matter of some importance."

"Of course. Any time in particular?"

"Now would be good."

"Oh my, I hope this isn't bad news. I'm actually headed down to the barn. Annette is taking me. Could I meet you there?"

I briefly wondered if Luther would be there. Didn't matter. He'd have to be confronted sooner or later. "Yes," I said. "That will be perfect. See you in a few."

I arrived at the barn ahead of the couple. I assumed Arthur had meant for me to meet him at the barn, which had a private office in it. Stepping inside to watch the goings on in a dairy barn on Sunday, it didn't take long to realize that as with well drilling, the day of the week makes little difference in the workload. Several teenage boys were riding herd on the gaggle of Lauderbach boys I'd seen playing tag football not so long ago. The oldest of the boys—he looked to be about sixteen—shouted orders like Coach Bobby Knight. The kids in turn complained until he'd threaten them with life and limb. Finding an empty bucket, I placed it out of the nippy breeze that whipped around the gigantic open doors and sat down to watch their antics.

One kid was making a complete mess, opening bags of feed supplements and pouring them into a mixing vat. "Hey, doofus!" shouted Coach. "Stop tearing those bags open and go get a knife from the feed room. There are several of them on the workbench." Doofus darted off to follow orders.

When he returned, I cringed to see the knife he'd been allowed to retrieve. It was an eight-inch fixed blade with a black plastic handle. I wondered if the wicked-looking curved blade, the top of which was serrated, was particularly useful around a cattle barn. Coach had said there were several of them.

"Here she is, Arthur," Annette Lauderbach said, pushing her husband's wheelchair into the barn to meet me.

"I can see that, lovey," Arthur said with forced cheer. "I'm in a wheelchair because I'm *physically*, not mentally, incapacitated."

"Oh, now, don't be such a grump, dear," Annette said patiently. "And you're only handicapped temporarily. It won't be long before—"

"Yes. Yes," Arthur sighed, reaching back to pat her hand on his chair. "I know. It won't be long."

Annette smiled at me. "He's just a little miffed because Luther called and said he couldn't be here today. He's been absent rather a lot lately. In any event, unless Sara is here, Arthur has to pick up the slack. I don't know where she is either."

"I think I might be able to shed some light on where Sara is," I offered. "She and Mia are at the well, watching the new phase of operations."

"At least they're not shopping!" Arthur laughed, some of his usual joviality returning. "Now what was it you wanted to see me about, my dear?"

"Is there a place we can talk?" Half an hour later, I'd related everything I knew about the hog operation. To say they were appalled would be putting it mildly. They flatly refused to believe Luther would be disloyal to them in any way.

"Luther's daddy and his granddaddy worked for my father and grandfather," Arthur sputtered. "It is inconceivable that he'd do anything so ... so ... "

"Cheesy," Annette said. "Ungrateful. Entirely low-life. All of those things would be appropriate descriptions of such a scheme. Even though," she patted Arthur's shoulders in an attempt to calm him, "it's probably not illegal. And, so what if he were doing something like that?"

"What?" Arthur boomed, outraged she'd even consider it a possibility.

"Calm down, dear! You're going to have a stroke. I'm not saying he is. I'm merely pointing out that if he is, it isn't illegal, he's not hurting anything, and you know as well as I do, times are tough. He's got kids in college too—"

"Actually," I interjected. "I'm still looking into whether crossbreeding feral and domestic hogs is illegal, but I'm pretty sure it is and—"

Arthur put his head in his hands, "Lovey," he mumbled. "I don't feel so well."

Alarmed, Annette felt Arthur's cheek as though feeling a child for a fever. "This conversation is over," she snapped, turning the wheelchair abruptly away from me. Then she stopped. "Cleo, I suggest you concern yourself with bringing in our very expensive well. Oh, and continue doing whatever is necessary to remove Clint's fossil ... "

"But that's just the point. I can't continue with the excavation if ... "

Completely ignoring my protestations, Annette cut me off again, saying, "As for anything else that is or isn't happening on this farm ... well, I'll keep your concerns in mind. But Luther doing anything potentially harmful to this family is completely out of the realm of possibility."

Well, that went well. I cranked the minivan, but sat for a few minutes before heading home. Clearly the Lauderbachs would be no help in ridding their farm of a pack of dangerous trophy hunters. In short, I was on my own. Well, maybe not entirely.

I put the van in gear, then had a thought and called Bud. A plan was forming in my mind and it required his assistance. Most importantly it had nothing to do with trying to find Clinton's murderer. I'd said I wouldn't do that any more.

I was just trying to provide a safe environment so my good friend Watson and his team of paleontologists could excavate Cecil. Besides, bad as I hated to admit it, Bud and I still had some issues from way back in our past that needed to be dealt with before we tied the knot again. Tackling this little clean-up job might be just the ticket to set us straight.

SIXTEEN

TULIP AND I BUSIED ourselves arranging a fall display of pumpkins and mums on the front porch until Bud got home. "Nice," he said, admiring it from the yard after he arrived. He took the steps two at a time, then plopped down beside me on the top one and heaved a tired sigh. "I'll sure be glad when we're married again," he said.

"Me too," I said, snuggling under his shoulder. "Any special reason?"

"Well, laundry comes to mind. No one can fold T-shirts like you … Ouch!" he grinned at me and grabbed his wounded pectoral muscle. "That's going to leave a bruise."

"Serves you right," I laughed. "Come inside. I've got something that'll make you feel much better." Bud's grin turned wicked.

A few minutes later, scooping hot crab dip onto a chip, he groused, "Well, not quite what I had in mind, but tasty."

"Thanks," I said, offering Tulip a chip, sans dip. Now it was my turn to heave a heavy sigh.

He gave me a concerned look. "I know you didn't call me over here for chips and dip. What's up?"

I took a deep breath, "Since I started this job on the Lauderbach farm, *everything* reminds me of our past. How we ... well, how we started life together in such a traumatic way ... "

"I wouldn't exactly call it traumatic."

"You don't call my dad getting arrested for murder and you having to hire a lawyer for him, the father of a young girl you barely knew, traumatic? Not to mention—"

"In the first place," Bud interrupted, "I didn't *have* to do anything, and secondly, I knew you plenty well. I knew I loved you from the moment I saw you that day, standing by the drill rig, all tall, and willowy ... "

"Not to mention," I continued, "you having to literally put me back together when Mom died. I couldn't even function, I was so afraid ... "

"You've never been afraid of anything in your life. Anyway, while all that might have been a tad traumatic for you, it wasn't for me." Bud smiled, then added, "Turns out it was all just preparation for living with you."

"See," I said, the pressure of truth causing me to stand and pace. "You keep making light of the way things really were, but face it, Bud. My dad blackmailed me into marrying you and you went along with it because you felt sorry for me—"

"I never did any such thing!" Bud boomed indignantly. Tulip whined.

"Bud!" I snapped back while giving Tulip a reassuring pat on the head. "I need to say this. Please, hear me out. I might have been a pretty young girl with a big education, but I was a nobody from nowhere with a dad facing a murder charge and possibly a death sentence. Not exactly what your folks, Mr. and Mrs. Pre-Revolutionary Blueblood, had in mind. You felt sorry for me and I, well, I would never have considered marrying you if my dad hadn't made me."

The look of hurt on Bud's face was not what I wanted. I wasn't handling this well at all. "Are you saying you never loved me?"

"No. Yes. I mean, no, not at the time." Silence fell between us until I continued. "As I said, we were polar opposites socially, but more than that, I couldn't feel anything but intense fear at that time. Fear like I've never experienced in my life before or since. And, no, I didn't love you then but I did later. But it was later, Bud. Much later. I got pregnant immediately after we married. I was so young, so immature, so unprepared for children. And I didn't want to give up my career. Trying to do both ... "

"You were a great mother, Cleo," Bud said softly.

Suddenly I felt very tired. "Yes," I exhaled deeply. "I was a good mother. But that's just the point, don't you see? I gave them and my work everything and you got what was left. Looking back, you never got all of me in any sense. Our marriage was unfair and unbalanced. What I'm trying to say is, I'm so sorry. You deserved so much more ... "

"Clearly you've forgotten all the times I had to dash off unexpectedly and leave you alone to cope the best you could."

"It was still one-sided ... "

"I never asked for more or expected it," Bud cut in. "Life is what it is and I was glad for any little bit of you I could get. But, let's go back to the blackmail thing. Maybe that's why you're having such a hard time getting your dad to come home for our wedding. I hope you don't let him know you call his insistence that you marry me before he'd agree to let me help him with a good lawyer, blackmail."

"I don't know what he thinks," I said dismally.

"He was just being a good father," Bud said solemnly. "Try to put yourself in his place. With your mom suddenly gone and him quite possibly going to jail for life … or worse … it was only natural for him to take any and all means available to protect you. Any fool could see how crazy in love with you I was. He saw that love as a means to get you to a safe place, being my wife. Of course I happily agreed to his terms. You were the one in the middle, not me. Turns out, in order to get your dad out of a jam, you had to agree to marry someone you didn't love. I think you got the sharp end of that stick."

"No, Bud, you did, " I insisted, as my emotions finally got the better of me. Tears pooled. My chin trembled. I turned away and said. "It's important to me that we start out this time knowing that we're marrying for one reason and one reason only."

Bud stood up behind me and put his arms around my waist. "And the reason?"

"Just plain old love," I said.

"Sounds like a plan," he said, carrying me upstairs to my bedroom. Tulip opted for a snooze on the couch in her favorite afternoon sunbeam.

Much later, pulling rumpled sheets around me, I sat up in bed. "Say, Bud," I said.

"Uh-oh," he smiled. "Two words that strike terror in my heart."

"Two words?"

"'Say, Bud,'" he mocked me in falsetto voice. "But go ahead. What were you about to say?"

"That I need your help."

"Doing what?"

"Well, remember that guy that used to live down the street from us with the wild animal trophies on the wall in his den?"

"Jack Newsom," Bud answered quickly. "Dr. Jack Newsom. Heart specialist. Moved his practice to Cary. Built a big stone house over off Kildare Farm Road. Why?"

"Well, I was wondering if you would mind calling him. Maybe chat for a while about big game. Maybe let him think you've become a big game hunter, too, and you are just dying to kill a local wild boar."

"Oh, I see where this is going…"

"All I want you to do is find out if he's heard anything about clandestine trophy hunts on the Lauderbach farm. If he hasn't, maybe he knows someone who has."

Bud squinted. "I'm afraid to ask, but why do you need me to do this little acting job?"

I described my visit to the Lauderbachs and their reaction to Luther's having anything to do with a hog operation or a trophy hunting scheme. Then I pointed out to him I wasn't trying to solve a murder case, but instead, making a safe environment for extracting Cecil from his 250-million year old rock bed.

"You may remember," I said, pulling my clothes back on, "that Watson's due in on Friday. Five days from now. Works out good for me time wise since I'm not needed on the site while the crew is busy changing to a directional bit. I was thinking maybe I—or we—could catch them in action. Then Chris could bring in the wildlife people and they'd put a stop to it."

"Your reasoning makes sense," Bud said. "And it doesn't sound dangerous to either one of us, so I'll get up with him as soon as I can. But do tell, how do we catch them in action?"

"I haven't thought that far yet."

———

In the days following our confrontation with the past, I had scant time to spend with Bud. Tuesday afternoon I took the opportunity of downtime at the well and headed east to the coastal plain to do a small piece of consulting work. Bud still had to take care of a backlog of office paperwork that had piled up while he was in Greece.

Following a bathroom break, I was heading back into a conference room at one of the leading banks in New Bern. I was about to finish my report on the geologic structures underlying a proposed shopping center out on Highway 70 when I got a call from my son. Hoping it wasn't a wedding-related problem, I took a minute to answer it.

With trepidation, I said, "Hi, Will. What up?"

"Well, for starters, I'm trying to run my business here and Henri has completely dropped her end when it comes to helping the event planner make decisions about the wedding. I don't know what's gotten into her."

Can you say Chris Bryant? "I'm in a meeting, right now," I said. "Specifically what's the problem?"

"She won't even answer her phone, Mom. I think she's screening her calls and ... "

"The problem," I prompted again. "Tell me the problem."

"Seems one of the vendors, the sound and light people, went out of business and now we have to start all over and pick someone else. Before she stopped answering her phone, Henri said she didn't have time to handle it and for me to get you to choose someone else."

Sound and light people? "What in the hell do sound and light people do and why do we need them at a wedding?"

"Uh. Actually, I'm not exactly sure. I thought you'd know. It's kind of a girly thing."

"As it happens, I'm a girly and I don't know so here's my quick answer: ask the event planner to pick one. That's what she's paid for. Then go with who she says. Gotta go now, sweetie." I tapped him off and went back to my meeting. Sound and light people? A horrifying image involving those light beams used at grand openings on used car lots flashed before my eyes. It took a few seconds for the feeling that I might hurl to pass. I pushed all thoughts of the wedding from my mind. Right now, someone was paying me for my expertise in geologic matters. That I could do!

———

Later that same day, while driving home, I'd had plenty of time to come up with a way to catch the hog hunters doing their thing. It was simple. To expose a trophy hunter, act like one.

I didn't know if the man in the Toyota truck knew who I was, but Luther did, so that let me out. When Bud was a young man, he used to be quite the hunter but there was no way in hell I'd let him anywhere near a bunch of hogs and crazy hunters. Chris, on the other hand, well, it was his job to catch the bad guys. I'd already told him how important it was to have a safe place for paleontologists to work. He'd seemed to understand. Besides, what I wanted him to do wouldn't take much time.

I pulled over at a Kangaroo station and tapped Chris's number on my iPhone. "Hey," I said when he picked up. "Got a minute?"

"That's about what I've got," he said, "a minute. I was just finishing up a Coke break. What can I do for you?"

"Remember when I told you about the green Toyota truck?"

186

"Right," he answered.

"Well, I have a question."

"Let's have it." I could hear him shaking ice in a paper cup.

"Okay. Since I guess I'm still considered a murder suspect, and since you and I are in agreement that a hunter is the most likely candidate as the murderer of Clinton Baker—being shot with an arrow and all—I'm wondering why you haven't made a search for the green truck. I remember seeing a scoped rifle in a rear-window rack. If you found the truck and him, you might learn that he has a truckload of ... oh, I don't know ... neon-green arrows."

"Who says I haven't?" he interrupted.

"You have?"

"Yes. And, just to remind you, I've never considered you a suspect. The sheriff does."

"Speaking of him, has he said any more about arresting me? It's been a couple of days since he said he was going to."

"Not a word. I put out a rumor that you thought he'd shot your tire and caused you to wreck your car and you might be looking into having him arrested. Could be that's causing him to cool his jets for a while."

"Could be ... "

"Back to the truck," Chris said. "Soon as you told me about the hog operation and the truck, I put every available man scouting Sanford and the surrounding area. We caught a break at TTA, Sanford-Lee County Regional Airport. They reported a Toyota pickup parked in the long-term lot that matched your description. Manager said the guy who owns it is a hunter. He said he frequently flies his friends down in his plane and hunts somewhere in the area."

"He flies down here from where?" I asked, trying to keep the excitement from my voice.

"Baltimore. And I only tell you because I've already run the tags, found the guy and even interviewed him. Matter of fact, I just got back this morning. This guy is a big real estate developer. Builds exclusive residential communities, most of them with some type of unique concept. You know, based on equestrian activities or lake fishing..."

Or hunting. "So what did he have to say?"

"He has an alibi as to where he was the day Clinton was killed. He was in Snowshoe doing a little early season skiing on the artificial stuff."

"Uh," I said, disappointed. "So did you ask him if he hunts with arrows or a gun?"

"Not that it made any difference, but yes, I did. I found out those things prior to him telling me he had an alibi."

"So, was it boxers or briefs?"

Chris chuckled. "Neither. He said he doesn't hunt. Just takes friends and goes along with them because he likes the outdoorsman lifestyle."

"Well, that's a little weird, because he had a scoped rifle in his rear window. I'm sure of it."

"I'll have someone run out to the airport and check it out, but his alibi was pretty solid. I haven't actually verified it, but at this point I don't feel it's necessary."

"If you don't mind me asking, what was the guy's name?"

"Butcher," Chris said. "Maybe that's why he doesn't hunt. Sounds rather brutal, don't you think? A hunter named Butcher."

"So what now?" I asked. "That doesn't mean there isn't hunting going on out there. They're still your best bet for finding the killer."

"I understand what you're saying, that because of the arrow, a hunter is the most likely person to be the killer, except for one thing. Motive."

"Maybe you just don't know the motive yet. If you'd expose these hunters, you might find someone with a motive."

"Maybe," Chris said around another mouthful of ice. "But, meantime, I *have* found someone with a motive. Unadulterated hatred, in fact."

"Seriously? Who?"

Ignoring my request for a name, he said, "One of our computer researchers has come up with quite a bit of back and forth between Clinton and one of the creationists you mentioned earlier. I've been going over it and believe me, this guy, the creationist, is a serious nut case. The discourse between the two started after Clinton blogged on their site, *The One Truth*. At their invitation, I might add. Following that, there were a multitude of very nasty emails from the site creator to Clinton and vice versa. Anyway, I feel very strongly that I need to look into this. And, remember. We're shorthanded. We've been over this."

"Sure, I remember. If there's anything I can do."

"There is," he said. "And we've been over this too. Nothing. You can do nothing."

"Got it."

SEVENTEEN

WHEN I GOT HOME around six, I went straight to my kitchen computer. It didn't take much research at home to discover that Butcher was in fact one Fredrick James Butcher of Fred J. Butcher Homes; Fred Butcher, Incorporated; Butcher Realty World; and several other companies under the umbrella of Butcher Enterprises, Incorporated.

The Fred J. Butcher Homes site had a photo gallery featuring photos of Mr. Butcher shaking hands with happy customers in front of McMansion-style homes. No doubt about it. That was the man I saw get out of a green Toyota truck in the clearing beside the hog pens. I was staring at the screen when I heard Bud's Porsche as he downshifted into the drive.

"We building a new house?" he asked, kissing the back of my neck and looking at the screen.

"See this guy?" I said, pointing to Butcher. "He's the one I saw at the hog pens. It was either him or Luther that chloroformed me, Bud. Had to be! And my money's on him. Every interaction I've had with Luther since I've been on the farm has been to help me in one way or another."

Bud pulled my rolling chair back a few feet and spun it to where I faced him. "You said you fainted," he said with forced calm. "Now you're saying..."

Oops. "As I recall, our conversation was interrupted by Henri and Chris. Speaking of which, have you heard from Henri lately?"

"Don't try to change the subject!" he snapped as he moved to the refrigerator for a beer. "I remember the conversation, and yes, we were cut off so now's a good time to finish it. Did you or did you not faint?"

"Not," I said. "I did *not* fain..."

"Cleo," Bud said in exasperation. "This is serious..."

"Exactly! And why I need to insist on taking action now to expose these hunters before someone, namely me or one of the paleontologists, gets hurt. Seems to me these guys are fierce about protecting their little hunting club. Even to the point of lying to the police!"

"What do you mean?"

I brought Bud up to speed regarding what Chris had learned about Fred Butcher and how he learned it. "During his interview, Butcher told Chris he was snow skiing in Snowshoe, West Virginia the day Clinton Baker was killed. And that he doesn't hunt. But I know for a fact that I saw a scoped rifle on a rack in his rear window!"

"Okay, okay." Bud said. "Calm down. I know you've got a plan brewing in your head to prove what you say is true..."

"No, I don't," I said glumly. "I was thinking of suggesting to Chris that we find someone to pose as a hunter. Provided you're able to get the contact information on setting up a trophy hunt out there."

"That's where Dr. Newsom came in?"

"Right. Only now, Chris is off on another avenue of investigation, which could be a valid one, only I don't think so. I mean, I just have this gut feeling. There's more to all this than hogs and hunting..." My iPhone buzzed on my desk. I scooted over and, after checking the screen, picked it up. "Hey, Jackie," I said. "Everything okay?"

"No. We've got a serious problem. I've already reported to Overmire, but it looks like we might be down for good on this hole."

I sprang up, knocking my stapler off my desk. "What in the hell happened?"

"S'what I'd like to know. We had a small alignment problem with the threads on the directional bit so the boys and I were back at the machinist truck working on it and the rest of the crew was taking a break at the canteen tent." He paused to suck in a giant gulp of air. The crunching sound of grit let me know he was pacing nervously.

"When we came back," he continued, "ready to mount the bit, well, I guess that's where a guardian angel was looking down on us 'cause someone noticed sneaker prints in the mud on the deck. Don't none of us wear sneakers, so we got suspicious. We ran a camera line down the hole and sure enough there was something down there. We can't tell for sure what it is."

"Can't you just fish it out?" There's an old saying about shit happening. Junk can end up stuck in a well any number of ways. The drill string can get wrung into, cement can break off the sides of the well. Tools, nuts, bolts, and pieces of pipe from the drill deck above can even fall in. The problem is so common that a name has been assigned to this type of junk. It's called a fish. And, special equipment has been designed over the years to fish or lift a variety of odd-sized objects from the hole. "You've got a fishing operator out there. I remember talking to him. Name's ..." I snapped my fingers trying to recall.

"Willie is the guy you're talking about. He does a little bit of everything. In fact, he was the one who operated the camera. Thing is, he says it's more complicated than just fishing it up. Like I told Overmire, we've already tried that several times. Each time, it drops off. Now, it's jammed in sideways."

"Oh great," I breathed. "Well, OSHA says everyone working out there, including me, wear steal-toed boots, so it sure looks like sabotage to me. What do you think?"

"I'm afraid you might be right."

"Any idea how they got in? The gate was locked, wasn't it?"

"Yes. I checked it myself. Of course, that wouldn't stop some-one from walking in. They'd just have to climb a few fences and it'd be a helluva walk. We're a long ways from any public road."

"You don't think the damage could be irreparable, do you?"

"Could be. That's why I'm calling. You're the liaison between Greenlite and the Lauderbachs. They need to know the shale bed we're in now is very friable. Could collapse. If that happens, well, I'm just letting you know we may have to abandon this well. If we do, there'll be weeks with reclamation, then new site prep. All of it may be more than the well owners can take financially. Know what I mean?"

I knew exactly what he meant. Financially, the Lauderbachs were already pushed to the limits. They were counting on this well not so much for extra funds to make repairs and upgrades necessary to keep the dairy operating, but to pay off creditors. I'd gotten the feeling in my talks with them that bankruptcy was looming. It would take subsequent wells to provide income to bring the dairy up to par. My heart broke for them and for all the folks that would be out of work if the well collapsed.

"So what's the plan?"

"We're waiting on Overmire's orders. He's going over the downhole images now."

"Where is the fish located in the well?"

"All the way down. It ain't like it hung up a few hundred feet down and we could just cement off that section and drill a dogleg to the good portion and go on from there."

"Okay," I sighed. "I'll check in with you early tomorrow morning, before I speak with the Lauderbachs. Anything happens before then, call."

"Will do. Oh, and Ms. Cooper, the person who threw junk down the hole?"

"Yeah?"

"They wore New Balance tennis shoes. I found more prints in the soft dirt at the bottom of the stairs. The NB logo was very plain."

Deliberate sabotage of a well is a rare occurrence. And it's a big deal if the perpetrator can be found. Jackie seemed positive that Lauderbach #1 had been sabotaged and so did I. "Do me a favor, Jackie," I said. "Be sure to take good pictures of the sneaker prints."

"Already done it," he said. "Greenlite is going to blame us for this and two things I know for sure: there ain't no way we dropped anything down there and there damn sure ain't no way any of us would be caught dead on the site wearing tennis shoes ... aside from the fact that it's against OSHA regs."

"I believe you," I said, then, thinking aloud, I muttered, "What kind of nerd wears New Balance tennis shoes anyway..."

"The kind that throws junk down a wellhole," Jackie growled before signing off.*Or the kind who wants to end drilling on the Lauderbach farm.*

Bud set a glass of chilled white wine in front of me. "Bad news?"

"The worst," I said and relayed what Jackie had told me.

"Who would do such a thing?"

"Normally, the first inclination is to suspect environmental activism, and that could be the case here. It's just I have a bad feeling that the person who did this knows that the Lauderbachs have one chance at this and one chance only. Question is: who wouldn't want them to succeed in saving their farm and a family business that has helped support the community for generations? It doesn't make sense." I pulled at my bottom lip.

"And I have a creepy feeling that this incident is connected in some way to the murder, I just don't know how. But, more than that, the murder and the hog operation are tied together. I know it!" I banged my hand on my desk. "Ouch!" I yelped. Bud gave me a calm-down look. "I've got to figure this out, Dammit! And when I do, I bet you the answer is very simple..."

"Drink your wine," he said, moving it to the kitchen table and cracking open a beer for himself. "Relax a minute. We'll work through this together."

We sat and sipped in silence, thinking. Tulip, who'd spent the day at home in her back yard kingdom, came in and curled up at my feet.

Bud fiddled with his Bud Light bottle, turning it, defining segments of a circle. "Let's go back to our conversation about the trophy hunters and Dr. Newsom. We were interrupted just as I was about to tell you that I was able to get up with him . . ."

"You were?"

"Of course. You asked me to didn't you?" I gave him a lopsided smile. "Anyway, it was interesting to catch up on old news. He's still quite the hunter, but he didn't know much about hunting feral hogs. He said he'd never had much interest in them. When I told him I'd heard that this hunt is somewhat of a secret—a you've-got-to-know someone-who-knows-someone kind of thing—he got interested and said he'd call around."

"Great," I said.

"There's more. He called back yesterday, all excited. He said he'd found a hunt that's very hush-hush. Very expensive too. My ears really perked up when he said they hunt this aberrant strain of feral hogs. I got the feeling he wanted to call them Hogzillas but the term was just too redneck. Anyway, the story goes that these hogs are only found in this one area."

"Oh my gosh!" I whooped. "I knew it. Why didn't you tell me sooner?"

"He just got back to me a few hours ago."

"Did he give any particulars, like where the hunt is and who runs it?"

"No. Unfortunately he didn't have a name. He was going to find out and call back later." I poured another glass of wine and started pacing. Bud cleared his throat and said, "Last time we talked about this, you said if I could find the contact person for the hunt, you were going to ask Chris to find someone to pretend to be a hunter and find out all the pertinent information to catch them. Now Chris is off on another scent so may I make a suggestion?"

"No," I said. "Because I know you're going to suggest using yourself as a plant."

"And the problem with that?"

"It's too dangerous," I answered, the irony of our reversal of roles not being entirely lost on me.

"What's dangerous about it? Look, say we do find out this Butcher guy is arranging expensive hunting safaris out on the Lauderbach farm for some type of crossbred, souped-up hogs? All we're talking about doing is buzzing up to Baltimore to have a little chat with him about them. Like you said, you need to get these guys off the farm and the Lauderbachs are no help. They're basically in the dark or turning a blind eye because of their feelings for a loyal employee." He got up, retrieved a bag of pretzels from the pantry and set it on the table. I munched on one and contemplated his plan.

"And as I said," he added, "our detective friend is following what he believes to be the stronger lead and, we know the Sheriff's Department is dealing with staff reductions. Looks to me like we'd just be helping old Chris out. You know, creating a safe work environment for a bunch of squints."

"Squints?"

"Academic types who squint at books all day."

"You are absolutely watching too much TV …"

"In the end I'm only after one thing."

"What's that?"

"You out of the sheriff's crosshairs, of course."

What a good man I'm marrying. "Well, when you put it that way," I said, "how can I reject your plan?"

"Then it's settled. If the good doctor, Newsom, says Fred Butcher is the contact man, we'll head on up to Baltimore and have that little chat."

———

Wednesday morning, October 16, a little over three weeks to go before the wedding and what I'd hoped would be the successful end of operations at Lauderbach #1. Unfortunately, what had once been a high-probability well had now been reduced to only a maybe. My first obligation that morning was to get with my employers, Schmid and Medlin, in case they had any special instructions for me other than paying the Lauderbachs a visit to explain what was going on.

Since they had contracted Greenlite Energy not just to drill the well, but to handle production and maintenance during its lifetime, I was sure they'd probably already gotten the bad news from them, it was up to me to explain it.

Jackie and I stood back from the well, watching the activity and having a lengthy discussion regarding plans for the next few days. When we were done, I called Tulip to the minivan for a trip over to the Lauderbachs'. She was reluctant to leave the crew who were basically doing what they could to assist Willie, the "fishing" expert, as he tried to work a miracle. Jackie assured me Tulip was fine remaining with them while I was gone, so I let her stay.

As was the usual procedure upon arriving at the Lauderbach home, I was ushered into the sunroom. The grimfaced couple stayed seated when I entered.

"I can tell from your expressions that Greenlite has informed you of the problem at the well," I said, following polite greetings.

"Yes," Arthur said, reaching for Annette's hand. He looked tired and drawn. "I thought Greenlite was supposed to be the best. How could they be so careless?" Annette wailed. "Don't they realize how much this well is costing us?"

Assigning blame was above my pay grade and now wasn't the time to go into the possibility of sabotage. They were too upset for that. I gave her a few seconds to compose herself, then said, "Greenlite is one of the best energy exploration companies in the business and the company they hired to drill the well, Schmid and Medlin, besides having an impeccable work record, also has a very long history of success in their field."

"It sure doesn't seem so, now, does it?" she screeched. "How could they let something just fall down the well? It's sheer incompetence I tell you!"

I took a deep breath. I needed to be very careful in my wording. They already felt I'd insulted Luther, a trusted employee. If I wasn't careful, I could make it seem that I was on the side of a company that didn't give a fig about wasting their money. "Both companies have spotless records when it comes to safety and accidents … of any kind," I said. "I can understand your frustration, but before we accuse anyone of incompetence, let's see how this situation plays out. Also, you can rest assured that the incident will be investigated. For now, though, let's talk about what happens going forward."

Annette crossed her arms over her chest and looked away. I continued to try to mollify her, saying, "I'm on your side here, and I can assure you that every attempt will be made to save the well. Here's the plan. Using a formula devised years ago, a certain amount of time will be allotted to trying to fish the junk out of the well."

Before I could go any further, I needed to explain what fishing meant in regard to well drilling and how it's done. That accomplished, I said, "If, after that amount of time, it's determined that the junk can't be retrieved without risking collapse, it is possible that portion of the well can be cemented and drilling is restarted at an angle farther back up the borehole."

Annette was still pouting so I addressed my remarks to Arthur, who was paying strict attention. "Since we were getting ready to make the turn anyway, this could work out. I don't want you to get your hopes up, but don't give up either. We're just going to have to take a wait-and-see stance here. But you should know, these things have been happening since 347 AD when the Chinese drilled for oil using bamboo pipes. Trust me, there are still lots of options available to us."

"See, Lovey," Arthur said, giving Annette's hand a squeeze. "There is hope after all."

Annette dabbed tears at the corners of her eyes. "I'm sorry," she said. "Just when we thought we were about to see the light at the end of the tunnel, this happens. Perhaps I need to take the advice of our oldest son, Arthur, Jr. He was here earlier. You just missed him. He came home when we told him what had happened and you know what his advice was?"

"What?" I asked

"Pray," Annette said. "And I think he's right. You know, it's something we often forget to do what with the fast-paced lives we all lead, but when faced with odds such as we've had lately ... well, maybe we should be doing more of it. Junior says God always has a plan and if we trust in Him, everything will work out for the best. That's sound advice, don't you think?"

Also way above my pay grade. "Sure does," I said.

"Indeed," echoed Arthur before turning to me and asking, "Can we offer you anything? Coffee? Tea?"

"Thanks, no," I said. "I'm going back to the well before I leave. I'll be in and out for a while but as you know, I can always be reached at the number I gave you. Remember, stay calm. This is going to take a few days, but everything humanly possible is being done to minimize costs and, at the same time, save the well."

Feeling I'd left the anxious Lauderbachs somewhat less anxious, I hurried back to the site to pick up Tulip and then head home where I was meeting Bud. I checked in with Jackie. They were preparing to make a mold of the object at the bottom of the well, thinking another type of fishing tool might work better. He followed me back to the van as I called for Tulip. I had to call her several times, but she finally trotted up, sat at my feet, and gave me a look I'd seen before. "What have you been up to, girl?" I asked. She just blinked dolefully.

"I saw her earlier out in the pasture eating grass," Jackie said. "That's what my dog does when he don't feel good."

I bent to give her a closer look, but she got up, wagged her tail, and hopped in the van. "She's fine," I said. "Call me if you need me. I'll never be more than a few hours away."

"Will do," Jackie said as I waved goodbye.

I couldn't wait to get up with Bud and find out if he'd heard from Dr. Newsom yet as to whether Fred Butcher was indeed the mastermind behind the hogzilla hunts, as we'd taken to calling them.

EIGHTEEN

Before meeting with Bud, I had one small matter to attend to: the minivan. I'd rented it on a week-to-week basis and it had now been a week since I'd wrecked my magic Jeep. I needed to either renew the rental agreement or buy something else. Picking out a new vehicle would be a daunting task. I simply didn't have the time it would take to look through all the models available and sort through the pros and cons of each. Besides, my heart still wasn't in it.

My text tune chimed just as I pulled onto the rental lot. It was an appointment reminder for the final fitting of my wedding gown. Just then, I saw the nice little rental agent that had taken care of me a week ago. A diminutive little fellow, quiet and unassuming, he dashed out the office door and hurried in my direction. I climbed out to greet him.

His mouth was agape. He held his head with both hands, a look of total astonishment on his face. "Oh my gosh!" he exclaimed. "Are you alright?! What happened? How did you roll the van?"

"Roll it?" I asked curiously. Then, looking back over my shoulder at the vehicle, I realized what he was referring to and added, "Oh, I see what you mean, but really, it's just a little dirty, that's all." Little man's gape got wider. "And, there may be a scra—"

Now his eyes were rounder than the rims on his Ben Franklins. "Madam!" he rudely cut me off. "Are you saying you weren't in an accident?"

"No," I said in exasperation. "I mean, yes, that's what I'm saying. I wasn't in an accident. I've just been using the van during the course of my normal work day."

"Wait," he said, holding up both palms. "You're saying you did all this damage by driving to and from work?"

"Yeah. Sorta…."

"Where do you work? Afghanistan?"

"As I was trying to say, it might have a scratch or two, here and there, but…" I stepped back and gave the van another look. Tried to see it from the eyes of the person responsible for maintaining it. "Okay," I relented. "There's the occasional dent, too, but nothing I'm sure one of those dent-remover tools and a good wash job wouldn't fix."

"Seriously?" fumed little man. "I'd be hard put to find an inch of space on the entire exterior of this van that isn't damaged. And, what about the interior? I shudder to think what that looks like!" He marched to the van's door and slid it open. "Oh, my goodness! What's this?" he asked, startled at being met—practically nose to nose—by Tulip. She gave him a half-hearted wag of her tail and he backed up a few steps.

"Oh, that's only my dog," I said dismissively, stepping to his side. I hadn't meant for him to see her. I'd thought I could just run in the office, renew my rental contract, and be on my merry way. This called for more finesse on my part.

Planning an all-out assault on any weakness he might have for feminine charm, I turned to face him. All at once, and without warning, Tulip barfed up a belly full of slimy green cow dung and grass in the doorway. A few globs oozed down onto the courtesy step with a plop.

The smell hit us first. Little man and I jumped back as though we'd been blasted by the pressure wave of an exploded grenade. Then Tulip, apparently feeling much better, hit us next. Stepping into the muck on her way out of the van, she leapt forward to greet the little rental agent, who by now was ruing the day I drove onto his lot.

"No!" I yelled, grabbing her collar just as she planted both front paws on his crisp, white shirt. "Tulip!" I jerked her back. "What on earth has gotten into you?" Then to little man: "I am *so* sorry, sir. She never jumps on people. She must be feeling much better, having relieved herself of that … guck … " My voice trailed off at the sight of the agent, grimacing in horror at the green smears down his once-pristine shirt.

"Eww," he breathed, narrowing his eyes at me as if his fondest desire at that moment would be the ability to shoot lasers from them. "I can assure you, Ms. Cooper, you'll pay for this … this … disaster. If you think you can just waltz in here and turn this car in, suggesting all it needs is a dent popper and a good wash job, you're sadly mistaken. No one screws G.W. Harris and gets away with it. I'm calling the law!"

Oh, great! Just what I need. Another policeman after me! "Wait, er … G.W. I'm sure I can satisfy you!" I called after him, wincing at my poor choice of words after just being accused of trying to screw him. Hurriedly, I shoved Tulip back in the van, slid the door closed, and followed him into the rental office. He was just lifting his cell to his ear when, checkbook in hand, I asked, "What would you say to a quick sale?"

He looked at me like I was a worm. "What do you have in mind?" he asked and snapped his flip phone shut.

———

Fortunately, Suds Car Wash was only a few blocks down from the rental lot. I couldn't get Tulip and my new minivan there fast enough. After I'd given the attendant the keys and dutifully warned him, I sprayed Tulip's feet with a nearby hose, retired to one of the picnic tables provided for customers, and called Bud. "I'm going to be a little late," I said, and explained what had happened.

"So you had to buy that piece of crap?" he asked.

"'Fraid so," I sighed. "But it's okay. I'll just trade it in when I decide what would work best for me."

Silence for a few seconds. Then Bud said, "How much longer do you think you'll be there?"

"Not much. Have you heard from Newsom?"

"Yep, and it was just as we suspected. Fred Butcher is the man to see to book a hunt for the rare and illusive hogzilla."

"Did he say it like that or have you been watching too much cable TV?"

"Too much cable, but it is nice to know you were right. Not that I ever doubted you. Now all we have to do is book a hunt and have Chris notify North Carolina Fish and Wildlife as to when and where it's going to be held and we'll shut them right down."

"Perfect," I said. "Maybe in the process he'll pick up additional information that'll lead him to Clinton Baker's murderer." Another few seconds of dead air drifted between us. "You still there?" I asked.

"Yes, but I've got an idea. I'll be down there by the time they finish with the van. Then you can follow me to a place where there's a vehicle I think you'll really like. A few modifications to it—which can be done while we're in Baltimore—and it'll be perfect for you."

I was intrigued and truthfully, now that the magic Jeep was gone, I didn't have anything in particular in mind so his suggestion, at the very least, would be a good starting place for me.

A short time later, I followed Bud onto a GM car lot. "Good grief!" I exclaimed as he unfolded himself from his Porsche. "You can't seriously be thinking a Hummer is what I need."

"That's exactly what I'm thinking," he said. "Take a look at your van, fireball, and tell me you don't need something indestructible."

"Well, that was part of the problem, you see. The van was too big." I pointed to three gargantuan vehicles parked side by side. "But look at *those* monsters. They're even bigger. How could I squeeze one of those tanks down a little overgrown logging road?"

"Follow me, babe. I'll show you," he said. We headed for the back lot. "You may not know this, but they don't make Hummers anymore. However, before GM stopped production in 2010, they came out with a smaller version, the Hummer H3 Alpha." We reached the lot and he scanned the rows until he saw what he was looking for.

"I've been giving some serious thought as to what you need and doing some shopping around for you. I found this one. It's a 2008 model." We'd stopped in front of a grey Hummer that was indeed smaller that the mega SUVs out front. "It has a towing package big enough to pull one of your drill rigs out of the mud if you need it."

"Get out! Really?"

"Really," he laughed. "Plus its wheelbase isn't much wider than your Jeep's, but it's plenty bad-ass and just as durable. We can add a heavy-duty grill and a wench to the front and you'll be good to go. I know the general manager here and he can take care of trading in your ... lovely van and have everything ready go by the time we get back from Baltimore. What do you think?"

For some reason the fact that, like the magic Jeep, this car was no longer being manufactured endeared it to me. That Bud had clearly gone to a lot of trouble to find it was also touching. Besides, if it couldn't stand up to my demands, I could always try something else.

I looked up at him. "Okay," I said. "I'm liking this idea. Let's get the trade-in done and then go home. We've got other fish to fry. It's time to see if you can convince Fred Butcher that you're one of North America's great wild boar hunters and you've just got to bag a hogzilla."

———

Bright and early Thursday morning, Bud and I flew to Baltimore in his plane, landing about nine miles from the center of downtown at Martin State Airport. Our plan was simple: Bud would meet with Butcher—he'd arranged the meeting before we left, claiming to be interested in adding an up-and-coming residential development to his family's business—and I would rent a car and drive down to DC for my gown fitting. We'd spend the night and return home the following day.

After checking into our hotel, we drove the rental to one of the downtown plazas and parked in front of an impressive office building that housed Butcher's flagship company, Butcher Enterprises, Incorporated. "I've got his office number right here," Bud said, pulling a post-it note from his pocket. "And we're on time."

"Good," I said, searching my iPhone for the location of the boutique where I'd bought my gown. "You're going to catch a cab back to the hotel after your meeting. I'll meet you there after my fitting and we'll make dinner plans, right?"

"Right," he said as I finished locating my destination and prepared to move to the driver's seat. Then I noticed a Starbucks on the ground floor of the office building. A coffee for the road seemed like a good idea. We exchanged kisses and I hopped out to get my jolt of java.

As I reached for the glass door, someone pushed it open for me. Stepping back, I looked up and realized the gentleman who was holding it was none other than Fred Butcher himself. I froze. Talk about a plan going south in a hurry. Or had it? Butcher smiled benignly and nodded for me to enter.

"Thanks," I said, slipping past him. I went directly to the order counter, which, as luck would have it, was backed with a large mirror. Between the giant coffee urns and stacked cups, I could see Butcher's reflection at the checkout station and realized he must have stepped away from paying his bill to open the door for me. He was now completing his transaction. Keeping my back to him, I watched in fascination as he counted out the correct change for his purchase and left. He never even glanced back at me.

Forgetting my coffee, I rushed back to the car to catch Bud before he left. "I can't believe it," I said and told him what had just transpired. "You know what this means?"

"Offhand, I'd say he's never seen you before."

"Exactly! He wasn't the one who gassed me. That leaves Luther as the culprit and honestly, I just find that hard to believe."

We stewed on the ramifications of this latest development for a few seconds. Then Bud said, "Or, someone else is involved."

"Either that or I'm a very bad judge of character. But, there is a plus side to his not knowing who I am."

"What?"

"I can come to the meeting with you," I smiled. "You know what they say, two heads are better than one. That's why they usually put police detectives in pairs when they question suspects."

"I don't like it," Bud said. "Let's stick with the original plan and keep you out of it. Besides, I don't want anything to interfere with you getting your gown fitted. It makes me very happy that you're taking a real interest in our wedding."

———

Despite worrying about Bud's ability to segue from a phony interest in residential development into he-man talk about hunting feral hogs, and feeling guilty about the fact that buying the gown was the only real sweat equity I'd put into the wedding, I made it to the boutique in record time. That it wasn't rush hour was a big factor.

I'd forgotten how wonderful the gown made me feel as I slipped into it again. Fanny, the French saleswoman who was seeing me through the complicated process, zipped me up and a very talented pair of seamstresses went to work, making sure no other altera-tions were necessary to make it fit like a glove. Later, after a hug good-bye from Fanny, I made my way back to Baltimore.

Bud hadn't returned when I arrived at our hotel so I stretched out on the bed and clicked on the television. I didn't want to call him and interrupt his meeting, but after about thirty minutes of surfing cable channels, I reconsidered and reached for my iPhone. "Hey," I said. "Where are you?"

"Hi, hon," Bud said over background sounds of laughter and clinking dishware. Obviously he was still role playing. He never calls me "hon." "I'm at a waterfront bar with Mr. Butcher. Remem-ber, I was seeing him about perhaps investing in a residential property?"

"Uh, yeah … " I said.

"I'm Mr. Butcher's last appointment for today, so we'll be here for a while, discussing some properties. Talk to you later." Bud clicked off.

Was he trying to tell me something? Like maybe Butcher wouldn't be going back to his office? I turned my attention back to the television just in time to catch a self-lubricating catheter com-mercial. I grimaced and punched the power-off button. After changing into a pair of skinny designer jeans and a cashmere tur-tleneck, I grabbed my little leather bomber jacket, and headed back to the shopping plaza.

Butcher Enterprises was a plush affair. However, the spacious reception area, featuring mural-sized renderings of past residen-tial accomplishments, was deserted. I was observing each mural in turn: Horseman's Ridge—A complete equestrian community— and Taylor's Landing—The good life on the Outer Banks—when a perky young lady with a dangerously short skirt, nose-bleed heels, and enough makeup to go on camera, came up behind me. "Hi!" she said. "Can I help you?"

I jumped, startled by her sudden appearance. "No," I said, wishing I'd had more time alone. "I was expecting to catch up with my ... husband here. He was meeting with Mr. Butcher. I dropped him off earlier and I'm returning to pick him up."

"Oh, there must be some mix-up," Perky said. "They went out to grab a drink and I'm just holding down the fort. I understood Mr. Butcher to say he'd make sure your husband got back to his hotel. Would you like me to double check?"

"No. That won't be necessary, but if you don't mind, I'll wait for a little while just to make sure. Husbands can get grumpy if their plans are upset."

Perky wrinkled her brow. I had the feeling she didn't want me to hang around, but didn't want to refuse a possible client a simple request either. She seemed to deliberate, then said, "Sure. There's coffee in the urn on the credenza. Make yourself at home, but ... uh, I have to be in and out so ... "

"No problem," I said, trying to put her at ease. She twittered about the reception area while I took in the rest of the gallery of residential renderings. After straightening the magazines at least twice, she said, "I have to step out for a minute. Will you be alright?"

I thought you'd never ask. "Sure," I said. "Take your time." I gave her my most trustworthy smile.

She hesitated, then grabbed her purse and booked it for the elevators.

Since she didn't grab the only jacket hanging on the cloak hanger in the corner, I surmised she was going somewhere in the building, just not on this floor. I nosed around in the reception area a little longer, keeping a close eye on the glass sidelight beside the door to see if she was coming right back.

After a few minutes, I made the executive decision to check out the only hallway that broke off from the reception area. Surely that's where the ladies' room would be. Always a good excuse for being discovered wandering about where you shouldn't be.

Impressive brass lettering on a raised panel walnut door let me know I'd found the office of Fred J. Butcher. I turned the knob. Imagine that. It was unlocked. I gave the door a stiff push and listened. The silence in the complex of offices was deafening. I felt sure I'd hear Perky if she returned, so I moseyed on in but didn't touch anything.

It was a large and swanky office with lots of cerebral gadgets and glossy architectural magazines scattered about on glass and brass tables. Very impressive, and very uninformative. I left, quietly pulling the door closed behind me and moved on down the hall.

I found the ladies' room and several other offices, all unlocked, all boring. When I got to a large conference room, however, I hit the jackpot. Scattered haphazardly on an end table were early conceptual designs for another residential community, including several informal sketches done in colored pencil. One was an aerial view. Even though the rendering bore no catchy name, I knew immediately I was looking at the Lauderbach Farm. The notes jotted along the margins made the theme for the development clear.

They were planning an exclusive hunting community.

NINETEEN

FRIDAY MORNING, FIFTEEN THOUSAND feet above the ground, zipping along at three hundred miles an hour in Bud's King Air 350, I sipped my Dr. Pepper and thought about the drawings I'd seen in Fred Butcher's conference room.

Someone had big plans for an exclusive hunting community on the Lauderbach farm and I was pretty sure it wasn't the Lauderbach's. My common sense gene gave me the ability to reason that they wouldn't be risking all they had in gas wells to save the dairy business if they were planning to sell to a developer.

Bud returned from the cockpit where he'd gone to confirm our arrival time, flopped back in his seat facing me, toed his shoes off, and propped his feet in my lap. "Are you excited about your new ride?" he asked.

"Kind of," I said, giving him a foot massage. "The minivan was getting on my last nerve, although I'm sure Tulip will miss it. I'm just worried the Hummer won't be ready and I'll have to rent something else so I can keep my appointment with Watson. We're getting together out at the site around three o'clock."

"You'll make it with time to spare," he said. "I've been thinking about those drawings you told me about last night after my meeting with Butcher and I agree with you. It makes sense that the Lauderbachs aren't the ones contemplating developing the land. It takes big bucks to even break ground on a project like that. From what you've told me, they don't have that kind of cash or credit. But Butcher definitely does."

I tilted my head in agreement. "By the way, I meant to ask you something ... "

"Yeah," Bud said, taking his feet back and leaning over to nibble my ear, "were you going to ask if we could pick up where we left off last night?"

"Uh...I don't remember leaving anything unfinished last night. Actually I recall a grand finale ... "

"I can start there if you want," he said, his voice getting all low and sultry. A jolt of sexual energy shot through me at what that implied. "Stop," I snickered, pushing him back into his seat. "You'll get me all hot and bothered up here and then what would we do?"

"Ever heard of the ... er, three-mile-high club?"

"Umm, I've heard of the mile-high club."

"Well this one is three times better," Bud said, heading for the cockpit door to close it, shielding us from the pilot's view.

"Bud Cooper," I laughed. "Get back here. We need to finish talking about your meeting with Butcher. For one thing, I want to know how you managed to worm the conversation around from investments in residential communities to hunting hogs."

Bud returned to his seat. "You aren't going to turn into one of those boring wives that doesn't want to have adventure sex, are you?"

"Of course not," I played along.

"Prove it," Bud said, calling my bluff.

I glanced over my shoulder to make sure the door was closed, then flashed him with two *almost* perfect Ds—I have had two children, after all. "Later, I promise. Right now, tell me more about Butcher."

"Okay, but I'm like an elephant," he said petulantly. "I never forget. Actually, it was pretty easy to maneuver the conversation. Especially after I regaled him with a few hunting stories from my past and told him about how bow hunting had brought a new excitement and tension to the experience. It didn't take long before he suggested we go to the waterfront bar, where, the more we talked, the more he drank until finally, with a wink and a nod, he told me he knew of an undiscovered place where very large, very aggressive wild boar can be hunted for a fee and how he might be able to arrange something for me."

"But he didn't say when?"

"No. He said he might have some good news about that when he calls me back in a couple of days with the information I requested about investing in one of his communities."

"At the risk of sounding like Nancy Drew," I said. "I think maybe we should keep our little trip and what we found out about Fred Butcher to ourselves, at least until we know more. No sense ruffling anyone's feathers."

"If you're talking about Chris Bryant, I disagree," Bud said. "I think we should meet with him as soon as we can after we get

215

home. This could be a big break in his case, especially if he ran up a blind alley chasing that other idea he had ... "

"The ticked-off creationist?"

"Yeah, that one."

"And what do you propose we say when he asks why we did exactly what he told us not to do?" I asked.

"We did no such thing," Bud said indignantly. "Remember, I helped you with this not because we were trying to solve his case, but rather to get rid of folks who could be a danger to you and your paleontologist friends. I'm trying to get you out of harm's way, not let you follow your usual path and fall right into the middle of it."

"Hey!" I snapped.

"Seriously, you don't think he can imagine what would happen if one of the paleontologists that you and your friend Watson put out there got shot accidentally? Especially if it ends up having some connection to a case he's in charge of solving. Trust me. He understands your predicament and my natural desire to help you out of it."

"I hope you're right," I sighed. "We'll set it up soon as we get home." I checked my watch. "Do we still have time for me to change my mind?"

Bud frowned. "About what?"

"The three-mile-high club."

"Sure thing!" he said, pulling his sweater over his head.

———

"Dang, Jackie," I said upon seeing the rig back in operation. "You're a miracle worker!"

The site foreman beamed and, eyeing my new vehicle, said, "Maybe, but I can see I don't have anything on you. Somehow you've managed to turn a piece-of-crap minivan into a piece-of-art Hummer."

Tossing a skeptical look back at the Hummer, I said. "You like it? The jury is still out for me." Luxury *and* functionality would definitely take some getting used to.

"How about you, girl?" Jackie said, rubbing Tulip's sides vigorously. "You like it?"

"As long as she can slobber out a window, she's happy," I said. "So tell me what's going on."

"Well, nothing much to tell, we just did what Greenlite told us to. Cemented the bottom hundred feet, put the directional bit on, and went back to drilling. Basically, just starting the turn 100 feet earlier, lessening the bend in the curve, you might say."

"Simple. Uncomplicated," I said. "Hey, as long as it gets us to the right spot, I like it."

"Me too. No sense throwing more money at trying to hook that fish."

"And risking collapsing the well," I added.

"Amen to that," Jackie said. He lifted his hard hat and scratched his scalp. "We're making good time now, though. Another day for the turn. Then, when you tell us we're on target, we'll run the horizontal sections and be ready for fracking."

"What about the Lauderbachs? Has anyone notified them yet that they can stop worrying?"

"Overmire did, but if I were them, I'd rather hear it from you. He's usually short on explanations."

"I need to speak to them about Lauderbach #2, so I'll take the opportunity to make sure they understand everything that's happened here. By the way, did you ever find out what was down the hole?"

"Yep. We could tell by the mold we made it was a short piece of pipe. I'm surprised it went all the way to the bottom, but it did. It was about three feet long and bent in such a way that every time we'd get hold of it, it'd flip and dig into the side wall. Whoever threw it down there knew it would give us fits. I still wish I knew how they got through the gate."

"I don't know," I said, "unless, like you suggested, they simply climbed gates and walked in overland."

We were contemplating that thought when, from the direction of the gate in question came the sound of a car horn.

Watson had arrived.

I hopped back in the Hummer and drove up to let him in. He was as excited as a kid on Christmas morning. I got him into the doghouse long enough to show him the location on the aerial. "Also," I said, opening the floor safe, "this is Tulip's contribution to the project." I removed the bone she'd found from the safe and handed it to him. "As far as I know it's the only bone that isn't with the skeleton."

Jamming the Jungle Jim hat he'd been famous for wearing while at UNC on his mostly bald head, he said, "Let's hurry! I can't wait to meet Cecil!"

Then Tulip, Watson, and I set off in the Hummer for the clay pit. Now was as good a time as any for it's maiden voyage into the woods.

———

On the way there, I gave Watson a brief explanation of the hog operation and how, since it was only the two of us, I wasn't too worried about our safety. "We'll be in and out pretty fast," I told him. "Today is really only so you can see Cecil for yourself and verify his existence for our extraction team, whoever they may be."

As we bumped across the pasture, Watson chattered about who he thought might make a good member and my thoughts went to how dramataically things were going to change in a relatively short time.

Economically, the Lauderbachs were only days away from tapping into an asset, which would turn them from debtors into millionaires. Scientifically, the world was about to be introduced to the find of a lifetime—albeit a short one—for Clinton Baker, a heretofore unknown paleontologist.

Not wanting to take Watson past the crime scene, I skirted the first patch of woods, then crossed the second pasture. A short distance into the second patch of woods, I stopped the Hummer.

"Something wrong, my dear?" Watson asked impatiently. "Are we waiting for someone?"

"No," I said. "It's only a quick walk from here to the fork in the trail I was telling you about—the clay pit lies to the right and the hog pens to the left. I think it'd be a good idea to be as quiet as possible."

"Good idea," Watson grabbed his satchel and hopped out. "Lead on!"

I wanted Watson to get the full effect when I unveiled Cecil, so I placed him between the front and hind legs of the beast. As I untied my hitch knots on the twine securing the canvas tarp to the ground, I realized I'd forgotten again to bring more twine to replace the bottom left piece. I looked at Watson. "Ready?" I asked.

"My dear, I've been ready for this day all my life!"

I pulled the tarp back.

A huge inhalation of breath from Watson. Tears sprang to his eyes. I went to stand beside him and patted him on the back. "Not in my wildest imagination did I expect it would be this … perfect," Watson said, dropping to his knees. He reached out and ran a trembling hand over the exposed skeleton. "And what a masterful job someone already has done in getting the excavation started. Why the entire length has been exposed to a depth of 18 inches or more."

"Yes," I said. "And, I want you to know as much as possible about Clinton Baker, the young man who discovered Cecil and did all this work. "

"I'd like that very much," Watson said quietly as he took in Cecil's perfect form. I let him soak in the miracle before him. Shortly he said, "More often than not it's impossible to understand why things happen the way they do. We can only react to what we are given in life, and I for one intend to do everything in my power to see that young man gets the credit he so richly deserves for this monumental find."

As we gazed at Cecil, stretched before us in plain view, a weak autumn sun shone down on us. I closed my eyes momentarily, imagining the world when he'd been the top predator in a tropical paradise. When North Carolina was located just a few degrees above the equator, part of the giant continent, Pangaea. When the Atlantic Ocean was forming, creating the rift valleys known today as the Triassic Basins. Back then they were vast inland lakes and swamps where creatures like Cecil lived and died and became the gas the Lauderbachs now sought.

Watson pulled his calipers and other measuring tools from his satchel and we set about measuring every imaginable detail about Cecil. He took more photographs as well, and all the while we discussed who would get a coveted position on the soon-to-be prestigious excavation team. When we finished, I pulled the camouflage tarp back into place and proceeded to tie down the corners that had twine.

Watson stopped repacking his satchel long enough to look at his watch. "We need to hurry along, dear, if we're going to get me to the airport in time for my flight back home."

"No problem," I said, holding the bottom left corner of the tarp in my fingers. "You don't happen to have some twine and a knife in your satchel do you?"

"Twine, yes. A knife, no. I had to bring my things through airport security, remember?"

"Right. I'll bring one next time I come and you're right. We'd better hurry." We hustled back to the Hummer and booked it for the airport, all the while jabbering about our next meeting—Watson said he'd email the date and time—and who he would be calling in the next few days.

———

Detective Sergeant Chris Bryant was having a drink with Bud, Henri, and Will when I got home. The first thing I noticed when I sat down on a bar stool in the kitchen to join them was that Henri was even more radiant than usual. She sat on a stool opposite Chris, casually swinging a leg clad in skin-tight, designer jeans and sipping a glass of white wine. Glossy red toenails peeked from her black, cutout suede Prada booties.

My practical mind went to the fact that they cost more than Chris made in week, but hell, that wasn't my problem. She was happy and glad to see me and that was all I cared about right now.

Our upcoming wedding dominated the conversation. Surprisingly, Chris seemed eager to join in a discussion of such foolish trivialities as to a change in the lead singer of the band they'd booked and how a different china pattern had to be chosen for the dinner as their first choice had been discontinued. As their laughter and banter bounced around me, I studied Chris. Not for the first time since I'd met him, I wondered what his life had been like in the military. Had he seen combat?

I would have thought talks of china, linen, and puff pastries would seem silly to him. But then, maybe that was why he seemed to be having such a good time. Maybe he had seen the worst of the worst and now, spending time among those he'd spent most of his life protecting in one way or another, was what he wanted.

"What do you think, Mom?" Henri asked, tossing her silky mane of blond hair over her shoulder with a flick of her hand.

Totally clueless of what I was supposed to be thinking about, I took the easy way out. "I think I'm lucky to have a whole family of party animals who can take care of planning all this *and* have fun doing it."

"I think that was a left-handed compliment, kids," Bud said dryly. "But we'll take it, right?"

"But that still doesn't answer the question of whether she wants to order P.F. Chang's and start the weekend here or if we should go out. What say you, Mom?"

"Definitely P.F. Chang's!" I said.

TWENTY

OUR ORDER ARRIVED AND as we dug into the delicious food Henri said, "Chris has been keeping me up-to-date on what's been going on with you, Mom, and I've been relaying everything to Will. All about the fossil and the game poachers…"

"Oh?" I said.

Chris shrugged. "Henri's been worried about you," he said, "and there's no need for that. This is a simple case of workplace chicanery that needs to be addressed before someone gets hurt."

"I've been wondering, Mom," Will said. "Why don't you just tell the landowners about the poachers?"

Workplace chicanery? "I have, but it's more complicated than poachers. One of their long-time, trusted employees is involved and they refuse to believe me."

Lifting a barbecued shrimp from the carton with his chopsticks, Chris said, "I've got several friends who are enforcement officers for the North Carolina Wildlife Resources Commission." He placed the shrimp on his plate and continued. "They tell me almost anything you do to a wild hog on your property is illegal except shooting them. The season is open all year long because they do so much environmental damage, not just to crops, but to indigenous species. If you enclose them, transport them—even on your own property—it's illegal and you can face stiff fines or jail time."

"So all you have to do is catch one of these guys in the act of moving a wild hog to a release location," Bud said, "then arrest them, or have your friends do it, and the Lauderbachs will have to face reality and kick them off the property."

"Easy peasy," Chris said.

"That's way better than your plan, Cleo," Bud said, slathering his egg roll with hot Chinese mustard before taking a giant bite.

"What plan?" Chris asked.

"The same one I still think you'll need to use," I said indignantly, tossing eye daggers at Bud. "How else do you propose to know when they are going to move one of the boars?"

"That's true," Bud said thoughtfully.

"What plan?" Chris asked again, more firmly this time.

"Well," Bud said. "We were thinking that it might be a good idea if we had Butcher, the guy who sets up these hunts, set one up for me. Then I'd be privy to all the particulars you'd need as to when and where on the farm such a move would take place. Speaking from an efficiency standpoint, it would save lots of man hours for your friends at Wildlife Resources."

"Wait," Chris said, clearly trying to keep his temper in check. "We don't know for sure that Mr. Butcher is the point man on this scheme..."

I jumped in. "Remember how you said it was okay for me to accidentally find out things?" I said, but didn't wait for his reply.

"Well, a neighbor of ours—an avid hunter—was passing on one of his hunting stories to Bud, and mentioned that he knew of a real estate developer in Baltimore who arranged trophy hunts for an aberrant strain of wild boar right here in North Carolina. Well, that was just too much of a coincidence, and I had to be in the area anyway—a fitting for my wedding … attire—so we thought we'd kill two birds with one stone and drop by and see if this guy was the one I saw at the hog pens that day."

Chris looked at Bud and me like we'd both sprouted full beards. I could feel the tension mounting in the room like a pressure cooker suddenly turned to high heat.

Fortunately Henri let some steam out of the pot. "Oh, Mom!" she gushed. "You've had your final fitting? Who's the designer?"

I was about to answer her when Chris lifted his shoulders, holding out both palms. "Well?" he asked. "Was Butcher the guy you saw at the hog pens?"

"Sure was," I said, proud I could offer at least one piece of concrete evidence regarding the actual existence of a rather bizarre scheme that up to now, only I had witnessed.

"And more than that," Bud said. "She found conceptual designs in Butcher's office for turning the Lauderbach farm into an exclusive hunting community."

Chris sat back in his seat, his anger replaced by confusion. "A hunting community? Did the Lauderbachs hire him?"

"Not that we know of," I said.

"So, Dad," Will said. "Are you going to pretend to be a trophy hunter?"

"No!" Chris said emphatically, giving Bud and me another stern look. "He's not!"

"Good," Will said, "'cause that sounds like a plan that could turn into a real cluster..."

"Finally," Chris cut in. "A voice of sanity at the table."

"Well, how should I answer the email Butcher sent me right before I got here?" Bud asked. "He offered me a hunting time on Wednesday at dawn and wanted a response. I told him I'd get right back to him."

Chris sighed heavily. "Jeez Louise. Ask him where he wants to meet you. Depends on the place, but if it's somewhere I can work with and if I can get everyone in place in time, well, I might be willing to let you help us."

———

Saturday morning, as soon as I felt a call would be appropriate, I phoned the Lauderbachs and asked if they'd like to have a well update from me. I didn't know what kind of reaction I'd get from them and was relieved when Annette sounded delighted to hear from me and invited me "down to the house" for coffee.

Both Lauderbachs were seated in an eating area off the kitchen. The table, which seated six, was oriented long ways beside a bay of windows. Ruby bustled through a swinging door from the kitchen carrying two large, steaming bowls.

She placed the buttered grits and scrambled eggs on an antique sideboard beside a large platter holding piles of bacon on one side and stacks of pancakes on the other. Sara and Mia were just finishing their meal as I entered the room.

"Hi!" said Sara brightly. "Mia and I were just coming to see if you'd mind if we ask Jackie a few follow-up questions."

"Sure," I said. "Are you helping on the paper, too, Mia?"

"Only in an editorial capacity," Mia said seriously. "Sara isn't known for her grammatical brilliance!"

"Sad but true," Sara said. Then to her parents: "We're going shopping later. Mia needs more shoes."

"That's good, dear," Annette said. "You girls just be sure you don't get in Cleo's way while you're at the well."

"They're fine," I assured Annette. "And Sara, you'll be glad to know I'm here to tell your folks that fracking is just a few days away. You don't want to miss that part of the operation. It's the most controversial and the part I want you to be sure to get right in your paper."

"Sounds good," Sara said as she and Mia pushed through the swinging door, which bounced right back in as a young man I hadn't met yet entered.

"Oh, how nice. Junior's here," Annette said. Then, smiling proudly, she turned to me. "Cleo, I'd like you to meet our oldest son, Arthur Junior. We call him Junior."

"Nice to meet you," Junior said, offering his hand for a shake. I found it damp, limp, and disappointing. Not at all like his father's. I couldn't help noticing his mom jeans, black tie-ups, and white socks. Again, no comparison with his dapper dad. "Junior," Annette addressed her son. "Ms. Cooper is our liaison with Greenlite Energy. She keeps us informed on all matters of importance about our well."

"We hope she's here to confirm some good news," Arthur said from his wheelchair at the table.

"I am," I said. "Everything's back on track. The company decided to take the junk at the bottom of the hole as a good thing and cemented up about a hundred feet and started the turn again, using a wider arc. When they've completed the horizontal run and perforated the different sections of casing, it will be time to do the actual fracking. At that time, the trucks will start coming in."

"So you're fairly certain that our first well, the one all the other wells are riding on, is going to come in and save us?" Annette asked, her eyes sparkling with joy.

"There's never a guarantee until the commodity starts flowing, but I can say I feel very good about it." Everyone at the table but Junior clapped and shouted hoorays.

"What kind of trucks," he asked seriously.

"There will be several kinds," I said. "Some will be dump trucks carrying sand. There will also be chemical trucks and trucks bringing the items we require to actually fracture the well. Then there could be as many as twenty high-powered pumping trucks and they'll operate for three to five days, twenty-four hours a day."

Junior pulled a face. "I imagine we'll get some neighbor complaints," he grumped.

"If the high-frequency noises created every thirty minutes by the crew beating the rust off drill pipes before connecting them hasn't bothered anyone, I doubt the trucks will. They mostly create low-frequency noise. There will also be noise related to building enough water pressure to make fissures in the shale so the gas can be released.

Junior grunted and I continued. "This will be the most unpleasant phase of the operation, but the good news is it's over in a few days. After that, the well will produce for thirty years or more and during that time, besides an occasional maintenance truck, there will be little activity around it and no noise created by it.

"When will production begin?" Junior asked.

"Just as soon as a connector pipe is laid by Greenlite. It's the pipe that connects your wellhead to the line that runs to the compressor station about 40 miles from here. In order to keep natural gas in the lines at the proper level of pressure, it has to go through the compressor station."

Hoping I'd satisfied the family curmudgeon, I looked back to the Lauderbachs, "Any more questions?"

Junior persisted. "You didn't mention the underground explosion that actually fractures the rock."

"I believe you're referring to the perforation gun," I said. "After we complete the horizontal length of the well, we'll case the hole. Once the cement is dry, a perforation device is lowered into the hole all the way to the end of the horizontal run. A number of shaped charges, set at intervals along the pipe, are then fired, using a detonation line.

Those charges blast holes through the casing and shatter the surrounding shale so the gas can escape. Then the sand, water, and a very small percentage of chemicals are pumped into the well and out into the surrounding shale to hold the fractures open. This procedure is repeated until the entire horizontal portion of the well is perforated and fracked."

"So for the next few days," Junior said, "there will be just the drilling crew at the well, then after that there will be lots of activity, then thirty years of peace, quiet, and money?"

"That pretty much sums it up," I smiled. "Until we start Lauderbach #2. The company will probably change out crews for that. Give these guys some home time, or they could just send them right to work on it."

Junior served a plate and pulled up a chair. Annette said, "Won't you have some breakfast, Cleo? Ruby always makes plenty."

"No thanks," I said. "I've got to get back. Call me if you have any questions."

When I left, I noticed a faded red Honda Civic parked beside me. Its sides were banged up and the backseat was littered with fast-food bags, suggesting it was a student's car. Then I noticed something else. On the back seat was a device, which looked like a clamp set at a forty-five degree angle on a wooden stand. It briefly intrigued me because it struck a cord in my memory banks, as though I should know what it was, but I didn't, and with so much on my mind, I quickly forgot about it.

———

Sara and Mia were still at the well when I got back, so I invited them in to watch me analyze one of the samples taken while I was gone. Following that, I let them spend a few minutes looking at samples under the microscope. While they did, I made small talk, asking casually, "How much longer before Junior gets his degree in animal science?"

"Oh he's not studying that stuff," laughed Mia.

"Mia!" Sara said. "That's a secret. You know you're not supposed to tell anyone!"

"Sor-rie!" she said.

Sara looked at me and said, "Junior hasn't been able to bring himself to tell Mom and Dad the truth. He's actually finishing up his bachelor of arts in ... religious studies at the end of this semester ... "

"Yeah!" hooted Mia. "There's oodles of demand in the workplace for graduates with a degree in religious studies!"

"Stop it," Sara snapped. "He has a minor in business." Then to me she said, "You have to understand, my mom and dad have had lots of, well ... issues with Junior. He's dropped out of school several times to, as Mom says, 'find his way.' When he went back this last time, about three years ago, he basically just told them what they wanted to hear. That he'd get a degree in animal science and come home and run the farm."

"He's the black sheep of—"

"Shush, Mia!" Sara huffed. "He's just different that's all."

"What do you think will happen when your folks do find out?" I asked. "I mean, he won't know anything about animal science for one thing. And, if he's planning on using his minor in business, more than likely he'll find he needs an advanced degree."

"Well, that's the good thing. Maybe they won't be too disappointed and angry at him because he already has a job offer working in an office with some company up north," Sara said. "But please don't mention anything. This is a storm they'll have to weather together."

"I agree," I said. "Now, I believe there are some shoe stores awaiting you girls and I need to get back to work."

———

After the girls left, I worked steadily through the afternoon. From time to time, whenever my thoughts would go back to my conversation with Sara about Junior, my heart would feel a little heavy. One day soon the Lauderbachs would find out they'd been lied to by their own son and their dream of having him take over the farm wasn't going to happen.

I felt sorry for them all over again. At least by that time they wouldn't have bankruptcy looming. I was sifting through my last sample, searching for just the right chip to place on the microscope stage when Overmire chimed in on my iPhone.

"You saved me a call," I said. "I need to talk to you about the new location you chose for Lauderbach #2."

"Is there a problem?" growled Overmire. He had one of those gravely voices indicative of a lifelong smoker. "Between the two locations, I like the seismic on this one better. All except for the topography above ground, that is."

"Well, that's what I thought I'd mention," I said, still not wanting to reveal the real reason—Cecil—for keeping the first location. "I've been over the seismic again as well, and I agree, your second choice offers a somewhat higher potential of success, however, the difference is scant. Considering the fact that your clients, the Lauderbachs, are looking at bankruptcy if #1 doesn't come in ... "

"That's not happening is it?" he croaked. "Samples are still looking good aren't they? Gas shows in all the samples now—"

"Yes!" I cut him off before he had a heart attack. "You misunderstand. I'm simply saying that they've got everything riding on this first well to pull them out of debt and finance the other wells. Therefore, it would be best if we choose the second site with the least possible capital expenditures in mind. If we go back to your first choice, in the middle of a totally flat cornfield, we're way ahead on the cost of site prep."

On the other end, Overmire wasn't saying anything, but I could hear the sound of shuffling paper. "Okay," he said, amicably enough. "I don't have a problem with that. So you're saying once we get #1 set up, we could move right over there?"

"I drove by it yesterday and they haven't harvested it yet, but they could anytime. The corn is plenty dry. I'll check with the Mr. Lauderbach right now and get back with you."

"Good deal," Overmire said. "There's enough acreage on that one farm to sink at least seven wells, considering the 160-acre drainage area required for each. Anything that'll help us move along more efficiently is fine by me."

Feeling good about dodging another bullet regarding Cecil, I whistled for Tulip and set out for my second visit that day with the Lauderbachs.

I parked the Hummer and was heading to the front door when, once again, movement through a gap in the foundation shrubbery caught my eye. I stopped and watched Junior step out of the same outbuilding I'd spotted Ruby leaving two weeks ago.

He slung a knapsack over his shoulder and walked briskly toward the pond. I watched until he descended the earthen dam on the opposite side and disappeared from view.

Curious. For a building no longer in use, a home for rats and bats, that old chicken house certainly got its share of activity. What really stood out was Junior's body language. He appeared just as suspicious as Ruby had that day. And where was he going on foot on a 2200-acre farm? Now days, most young people expect some type of wheels to carry them wherever they go.

Double curious.

I continued to the house and rang the doorbell. When no one answered, I was disappointed. Though Luther, as farm manager, probably made decisions regarding when to harvest crops, I'd have preferred to ask Arthur. With limited time, Luther would have to do.

I found him in a yearling lot behind one of the smaller barns. He was standing in the bed of his pickup along with several bales of alfalfa hay. "Hey there, Miz Cooper," he said with a friendly smile. "What can I do for you?"

"I was looking for Mr. Lauderbach, regarding getting one of the cornfields cut—"

"I handle the cutting and picking schedules," he said.

"Then I've come to the right man," I said and gave him the location of Lauderbach #2 and explained why I needed it cut.

"Be glad to!" Luther said, astonishment plain on his face. "Truth be told, I was a little skeptical about the boss being able to pump gas outta the ground and make enough money to put the farm back right and here you are, ready to drill a second one."

"It's happening around here more and more every year," I said, leaning against the rear fender of the truck.

"Oh yeah, I hear about it on the local news and read about it in our little paper, but until it actually happens, it just seems like a fairy tale. I'm glad for the boss. He deserves a break. He and the missus have had a right tough time of it here lately . . ." Luther's voice trailed off as he patted his pockets.

"Lose something?"

"I think I left my knife in the cab," he said. "You mind looking? Try the dash. Or, it might be on the seat."

"Sure," I said, seeing it immediately upon opening the door. It was identical to the knife the kid had in the barn the day I spoke to the Lauderbachs about the hog operation. Same hooked blade, same serrated edge on the top. I handed it to Luther.

"Thanks," he said. "I swear. I buy more of these knives than any piece of equipment on the farm. The kids use them, you see. They put them down, then forget where. I have to keep mine with me or they'll get it too." He chuckled and sliced through the hay twine holding the bale together, then shoved it over the side where it scattered on the ground.

"I'll let you get back to work," I said, resisting the urge to make a remark to the effect that I hadn't fainted lately or seen any imaginary wild boars. Better to let him think I'd forgotten all about the incident.

"Don't you worry none about that corn being in the way. We'll start tomorrow and have it done for you by Monday lunch. That be good?"

"Perfect," I said and returned to the Hummer. I gave Tulip a pull on the ears when I got in. She was in her favorite spot, front seat shotgun. "Ready to slobber on the window?" She gave me a good old dear hound grin and wagged her tail. "Alrighty then, let's go home."

TWENTY-ONE

SUNDAY AND MONDAY FLEW by with little variation either in the weather or in the level of activity at the well. Immense fracking trucks had arrived in preparation for that phase of the operation. Bulldozers, front-end loaders, and other equipment used to level the ground and dig pits for Lauderbach #2 had been moved to the cornfield, which Luther, true to his word, had picked and cleared. The site-prep crew would start work there Tuesday morning.

Since the junk-down-the-hole incident had precipitated a change in the drill plan to accommodate the new kickoff point, I wanted to be sure our projection for running the horizontal part of the well in the horizon where the gas content was highest was correct. The test had gone well. We were right where we wanted to be.

Both days, from early morning until evening, I was on site, running tests on the samples as they came up. An anxious Overmire called often during those days to check test results, including my favorite, the vitrinite reflectance test.

The reason I favor one test over the others is because this one always kicks my imagination into hyper-drive. When I immerse a tiny crushed sample of the Cumnock shale in oil and gently lay the slide under my microscope, the grains of vitrinite, once woody plant material, reflect the light. I use the percentage reflected, not only to measure the amount of hydrocarbon present, but its maturity.

Invariably, the shiny irregular shapes of vitrinite evoke images of a lush land long gone. When the tiny pieces of compressed wood tissue—seen as the shiny streaks in coal—and flattened plant spoors, gleam up at me, I can all but see the vast lakes and swamps that existed in this very spot 250 million years ago.

No matter how many times I do it, it's still mind-boggling that by using this simple test, I can prove definitively what the environment was like in a certain spot millions of years ago. I can know the temperature, what kind of plants and animals existed, even what the atmosphere was like. The truth is important to me. I wished there was a test I could run to find out who killed Clinton Baker that was as simple as this one.

———

By six-thirty Monday evening it was obvious I wasn't going to get home in time to cook the romantic dinner for two I'd been thinking about all day. Still, I was famished, tired, and ready to call it a day, so I gave Bud a ring to let him know I'd be late and for him to go ahead and eat.

"No problem, babe," he said. "Tell you what. I need to get some new jeans. Why don't we meet at that Italian bistro on the upper parking deck at Crabtree Mall? You know the one I mean?"

"The Brio Tuscan Grill?"

"Yes. That's the one. We'll have a late supper, and if there's time we can pick up some jeans for me."

"That's a great idea," I said, checking my watch. "I need to make a few purchases myself. I'll meet you there at seven-thirty."

The baked chicken at the Brio was as delicious as always, and afterward we did some shopping inside the mall. We were strolling along, holding our shopping bags and window shopping when I saw something that caught my attention. I'd seen one just like it on the seat in Junior Lauderbach's car and now I thought I remembered what it was.

Stepping back to see the store name above the window, I realized I was looking at hunting and outdoor camping equipment. I pointed out the piece of equipment to Bud. "Do you know what that is?" I asked.

Bud studied it quizzically, then said, "I give up. What is it?"

"I think I do, but I want to be sure," I said. "Because if it is what I think it is, it casts a new light on things." We entered the store only fifteen minutes before their closing time so few shoppers remained. I grabbed the first salesperson I could find, a young man with acne and enough dandruff flakes sprinkling his shoulders to qualify as a display for skiing equipment. "Hi," I said. "I'm wondering if you could identify a piece of equipment in your window. I'd like to know the proper name for it."

"Yes, ma'am," he said as he followed me.

"That," I said, pointing to the aluminum object. Flakes looked at the object and I could tell immediately that he didn't have a clue what it was either. "Uh," he said. "I'll have to ask someone. I'll be right back." Ten minutes later, when he still hadn't returned, I began to worry the store would close before I had my answer.

"Great!" I fumed. "I had to pick the only person in the whole store that didn't know what in the heck that thing is."

"Relax, babe," Bud said returning from the interior of the store. "I saw one just like it in a case in the back and the guy manning the counter looks to be about ready to wrap things up with his customer. Let's go ask him."

"Okay," I said. "I'll be awake all night wanting to know for sure if I'm right."

Just as Bud predicted, the salesman, who had a large purple nose, the kind you can only get by drinking gallon-sized cocktails, was free. "Pardon me, sir," I asked him, pointing out the odd device in his case. "Could you please tell me what this is?"

Booze Nose leaned over the glass counter to look where I pointed. "That's a Bitzenburger fletching jig," he said. "A left-handed one. Could I take it out for you? It'd make a nice Christmas present. The holidays will be here before you know it."

"No," I said, positive now that I remembered where else I'd seen one like it. "That won't be necessary. This is a tool used by bow hunters who want to customize their arrows, right?"

Booze Nose shrugged. "Or just save money by making their own. Some of the guys even prefer to make their arrows in the more traditional way. Not like the mass-produced ones." Despite my saying it wasn't necessary, he removed the jig and sat it on the counter so he could demonstrate as he talked. "This little piece of equipment is actually a clamp," he continued. "Once your arrow is cut to the exact length for your arm ... "

"Wait," I said. "Arrows have to be ... sized ... to fit your arm length?"

"Absolutely," he said. "Say, for instance, your arm length measured 29 inches. You'd buy arrows 33 inches long and cut them to

239

31 inches. The arrow has to be two inches longer than your arm. Then, say you wanted to get fancy. You'd buy arrows without fletchings..." He paused, looking at my furrowed brow, and pointed in the case to the colorful feathers at the slotted end of an arrow and explained, "The feathers on the nocked end of the arrow."

"I see," I said.

"And that's what this tool is for. It holds the feathers in place on the arrow while the glue dries. Then, you custom-wrap the fletching with sinew or synthetic twine. The twine is what actually holds the fletching in place. Most of the fellas who make their own arrows have a special way of wrapping theirs so they stand out from anyone else's."

Bud and I thanked him and left. "Why were you so interested in that jig?" Bud asked.

"Because I saw one in the back of Arthur Lauderbach's oldest son's car. And, though I couldn't remember for sure what it was, I knew I'd seen one somewhere. After Booz...I mean, that nice salesman told us what it was, I remembered that a well-driller friend of my dad had one. I saw it in his shop not long ago and he told me what it was, but, it's not an everyday object so it slipped my mind."

"That's not good," Bud said, his expression growing serious.

"What? You think I've come into my dotage at an early age?"

"No," Bud laughed. "It's not good that the eldest son of the Lauderbach tribe is into compound bow hunting and an old friend of the family, his sister's best friend in fact, was killed with an arrow."

"Yes, well, there's that to be worried about too." I said. "But, to be accurate, Clinton was killed by a stab wound to the belly that caused him to bleed out. And that's something else that's been nipping at the back of my brain."

"What?"

"I don't know. That's the problem. It's just that every time I think of him being stabbed to death, I feel I'm missing an important … clue or … I'm failing to connect the dots somehow. One thing's for sure. We need to tell Chris about this."

"We'll do it tomorrow. He wants to introduce me to the wildlife officers who will be working with him to catch the hog operators in action."

"When and where are you meeting him?"

"Besides somewhere in Lee County, I'm not sure. I'll call you when he lets me know."

———

Tuesday was a foggy, cool day. The horizontal run had been completed, and the pipe and bit were withdrawn from the wellbore for the last time. Technically, that meant my job at this well was completed. Once the production casing had been set and cemented, Jackie and his crew would take down the rig and move to the next wellsite and the perforation and frack crew would go to work.

It would be another couple of days before the crew would move the doghouse to Lauderbach #2 and I was content, even with the extreme noises created by the fracking trucks as they arrived on site, to stay put and use it as my base. They wouldn't start the actual process for a few days, but the low-frequency noises of their massive diesel engines so close to me could cause a headache. Still, as long as I kept the doors closed and my industrial-grade, noise-canceling headphones on, it was a great place to go over Overmire's orders for new site locations and write up my reports.

Standing in front of the aerial of the farm, studying the location Overmire had picked for Lauderbach #3, I felt my iPhone vibrate in the back pocket of my jeans. It was Bud. "Hey, hold on a minute," I said, removing my headphones. "Okay, What's up?"

"I'm headed your way."

"I take it Chris got up with you," I said.

"Yes, he did. In fact, I'm following him now. We're headed to a café to meet with a couple of wildlife officers. Are you still planning to join us?"

"Definitely," I said. "It's not that I think Chris would put you in danger, it's just that I'd feel better hearing what the plans are. What's the name of the café where you're meeting?"

"The Spring Chicken. Chris says you know where it is."

"I do," I said. "I'll meet you there."

As I was the last to arrive at the restaurant, Wilma had already seated Bud, Chris, and two wildlife enforcement officers and taken their orders. They were laughing about some type of shooting contest in which Chris had apparently won more than his share and been jokingly referred to as a "ringer."

The men stood at my arrival and Bud, who'd ordered for me, pulled out my chair. Chris introduced me to the wildlife officers. Before sitting, I shook hands with each man, noting that their appearance matched my expectations.

They were fit, outdoorsy types wearing crisp brown uniforms and field boots. One looked to be in his mid-twenties and the other a little older, maybe late thirties. Their ball caps, bearing the Wildlife Resources Commission logo, hung politely from the backs of their chairs. Each was outfitted with a hip holster encasing a .357

SIG Sauer pistol, a shoulder-mounted radio, and a collapsible baton.

As I took my seat, I said to Chris, "Did I hear these guys say you're a crack shot?"

Chris flushed a little and grinned as the two exclaimed over his prowess at a local turkey shoot the night before. "I wouldn't have a clue how to cook one so I always give my birds to the Baptist church for a feed they put on at Thanksgiving. But, enough of that, let's get down to business," he said, taking his seat. "I've already explained to Bud that he'll be part of our operation but only in a very limited capacity."

"Right," said the older of the two wildlife officers. "All we need to do is catch someone moving a wild hog from one location to another on the property or confining it in an enclosed pen. Those two things are illegal in the state of North Carolina. Shooting the hog with a gun or a bow is not. Point is, there's no need for him to be involved except to let the hunt organizer put him on station. More than likely, that'll be a tree stand. We'll have the pens staked out. We have a good idea of where they are."

Wilma brought our orders—chicken-fried steak, mashed potatoes swimming in gravy, and green beans cooked with fatback. I gave Bud an incredulous glance. He gave me a "what?" look. Leaning over to him, I whispered, "If my gown doesn't fit, it's your fault." He smiled and gave me a pat on the knee.

We all dug in and the younger of the two officers washed down a mouthful of cornbread with his tea and said, "We certainly appreciate you bringing this activity to our attention, Miz Cooper. You know, some states allow so-called 'sporting swine' to be relocated on a piece of property, but North Carolina does not. In fact, feral swine are considered a non-game species in this state."

His buddy said, "The only thing you can do to a feral swine in this state is kill it by gun or bow or trap it, but you have to have a permit for that. We've made a thorough search and no one with authority on the Lauderbach farm has applied for such a permit."

"I've looked at the laws too," Chris said. "And as far as captive hog facilities being allowed in our state, the Wild Hog Working Group says that the state doesn't offer a permit to run such a facility. But, they do have some nebulous wording under the law to the effect that, if a landowner has some type of facility that wild hogs 'just happen to be in,' then hunting would be legal there. This is why we have to catch these guys in the act of breaking the law where it is clear-cut, by actually moving a feral swine from one place to another on the farm."

"I can help you there," I said and stopped eating long enough to reach in my canvas tote for a set of 8 x 10 photocopies of the farm aerials. I handed the top one, showing the location of Lauderbach #2, to Chris. "We've just moved the site prep crew to this cornfield. I think that means that the hunt organizer would want to steer clear of this area." Each man looked at the photo as it was passed around.

I handed Chris another. "If you look at the clearing in this photo, you'll see it's very accessible to this small farm road, which connects to the state road not far from the service station where Butcher asked Bud to meet him. Of course, I haven't actually been to the clearing to see if there's a pen there. But if there is, it'd be my guess they'll station Bud somewhere nearby and let the hog go from there."

One of the officers looked at Chris and said, "That's one of the clearings we'd already planned to stake out. There were a few others too. But, she's right, about the one near this cornfield probably being a waste of time."

We were just about to finish our dessert when Chris's iPhone vibrated. Fortunately I can read upside down, which is helpful, being the nosy person I am. I just had time to read, "Henri calling" before he picked it up, checked the screen, and discretely put it in his pocket. I counted back to when they'd first met and was surprised to realize they were coming up on the two-week mark. Henri's usually bored by a man by then. Maybe that's what the call was for.

I gazed at Chris across the table. Lucky for him he was drop-dead gorgeous. He'd find someone else soon enough. Too bad, though; I kind of liked him.

While I was glad we were finally going to rid the farm of the dangers involved with an illegal hog-hunting operation, I still felt a little uncertain. I said, "Just to be sure I understand, Bud's to meet Butcher at the service station. Butcher is personally taking Bud to a hunting station—probably a tree stand—where he's highly likely to see a wild boar, a so-called sporting swine."

"Not really my idea of sporting," Bud said under his breath.

"Right," Chris said. "Only once Bud gets on station and Butcher leaves, he calls us, returns to his car, and then *leaves*." Chris said. "Soon as we see someone moving a hog or releasing it from a pen, an officer will move in."

"Let's underscore the word, *leaves*," said one of the officers. "We don't use civilians in takedowns and arrests where things could get dicey. In the long history of our branch of North Carolina law enforcement, there have only been two hunters killed. And before the last incident in 2009, it had been twenty-nine years without a tragedy, so we don't want to take any unnecessary risks."

"And since you know where we'll likely be staked out, Ms. Cooper," Chris added, using my surname for emphasis, "you know where not to be, too, right?"

"Right," I said.

Following lunch, we all made our way to the parking lot. The wildlife officers went off in separate directions—in unmarked cars, I noticed—and Bud and I went to where we'd parked side by side.

"Where'd Chris go?" Bud asked. I looked around, thinking he'd been right behind us. "There," I said, pointing discretely. The detective was standing on the café porch beside a fall display of dried corn stalks, pumpkins, and mums arranged artfully on a bale of straw. He was grinning foolishly, holding his iPhone to his ear, oblivious to the rest of the world.

"We need to pass on the information you uncovered about the Lauderbach's oldest boy being a compound bow hunter," Bud said, moving in Chris's direction.

Touching Bud's arm, I said, "Just wait a sec. I think he's talking to Henri."

"Really?" Bud said and stopped. "How do you know?"

"I have my ways. Thing is, he seems happy, and I'd have thought she would have kicked him to the curb by now."

"Yeah. I'm surprised at that too."

We were both staring at Chris when, seconds later, he looked up to see us. Ending his call abruptly, he came our way. "Anything else?" he asked upon reaching us. We told him about the feather clamp I'd seen in Junior's car and I explained how that was significant. "It means that he is a very serious bow hunter," I said.

I noticed how intently Chris listened when I passed on my new knowledge of arrows and how their length had to correspond with the size of the hunter.

"We thought you should know," Bud added.

Then I had a thought. "When you took statements from the Lauderbachs regarding Clinton, did you ask them if anyone in their family was a bow hunter?"

"Yes, I did, and they said no. There were some small boys in the house at the time and I met the daughter. She said she wasn't a hunter, either. When they told me they had another son, Junior, who was in school at State, I asked if he was a bow hunter and they all said no. In fact they acted like the notion was ridiculous."

"Yeah, I can see that," I said, the mom jeans and dorky shoes coming to mind.

"Why do you say that?"

"He's just not what I would describe as the outdoorsy type, that's all. I guess it just goes to show you shouldn't judge a book by its cover. What about the lead you were chasing, the creationist with a motive? How's that going?"

Totally ignoring my question, Chris turned to Bud. "You got a compound bow and quiver of arrows for tomorrow . . . the proper hunting attire?"

"Yep," Bud said. "All set. I borrowed them from my friend, Dr. Newsom. We're about the same size. I gave him a plausible excuse as to why I couldn't use mine."

"Okay then," Chris said. "Remember. You won't see me until after everything is over tomorrow. Just go back to Raleigh. I'll get up with both of you in the evening. I'll be in Raleigh anyway and let you know how things went." With that he gave us both a friendly wave, angled into his Crown Victoria, and left.

Watching him exit the parking lot, Bud said, "Have you heard from Henri lately?"

"No, not even any wedding questions. What about you?"

247

"No. Not a word. It's just like her though. If she's happy, you never hear from her. It's when her love life is in the toilet that she needs us and calls. I wonder if this means dashing Detective Bryant doesn't bore her to tears?"

I let out a deep sigh. "Give him time. It may take a bit longer than her usual two weeks, but he'll get there. See you at home later tonight?"

"No. I'm staying at my house so I can turn in early. I've got to be back over here at the crack of dawn. What's on for you for the rest of the day?"

"Not much now that my job on #1 is done. We'll be able to make some good estimates on production once fracking is completed. But if it's like other wells in the area, the Lauderbach's will be in fine shape to pay off their debts."

"I'm glad for them. From what you told me, they seem like nice people."

"Yes, they are, and to answer your question, I'm going to catch up on some paperwork, connect with Watson and find out how our associate search is coming, and flag the site for well number three. Then I'll head home."

"Okay, I'll call you tomorrow after my starring role as Bud Cooper, big game hunter, is over."

"Thanks for doing this for me, helping me get rid of the bad guys. I'll feel much safer."

"No problem," Bud grinned at me. "Watching after you is a dirty job, but someone's got to do it. Besides, I'll collect payment later."

———

Back at the doghouse, I started to leave the door open so Tulip could go out. She rolled up on her elbows from the nap she'd been taking on the cot and hopped down. Then on second thought, I closed it. "Too many trucks barreling around out there, girl," I said. "You might get squished. I'll take you with me when I flag Lauderbach #3."

I had plenty of time to take care of this task, but the fog had lifted, the sun was out, and I needed to walk off the fattening lunch I'd just consumed. I felt ready to burst as I strapped on my Beretta. Pinching my sides, I was suddenly convinced the beginnings of a muffin top were trying to creep over my jeans.

I bustled about collecting what I'd need to flag the site, grabbed my canvas tote still packed with the same aerials I'd used to show Chris different sections of the farm, and headed for the great outdoors, Tulip in the lead.

TWENTY-TWO

IF I WERE TO superimpose an equiangular triangle on the map of the Lauderbach Farm, which itself was shaped somewhat like one, there would be a well located in each corner. Subsequent wells would fall out toward the interior of the farm, keeping in mind the 160-acre drainage field needed for each one.

Number one had already been drilled in the northernmost corner. The site for number two in the southwest corner was now being prepped, and I was headed for the southeast corner to flag number three.

We crossed small creeks that fed off the larger Pocket Creek, fields with crops and pastures with milk cows. I'd been told that most of the pastures also contained a young bull and this gave me pause to check each one before crossing. There might be more different kinds of danger in the woods, but I'd learned how to protect myself from most of them. A raging bull, on the other hand. Not so much.

As we reached a large tract of woods, easily encompassing three hundred acres or more, I breathed a sigh of relief and began scouting along the edge, searching for a way in, such as a game trail or an old field terrace. Not finding anything, I unsheathed my machete from where it dangled from a loop on my canvas tote and began chopping my way toward an area that appeared less dense.

At intervals within sight of one another, I'd tie a marker of flagging tape to a tree. Presently, I reached the spot I was aiming for and the woods did indeed seem to open up, letting in more light. Then, using my compass, I chose a southeast coordinate and headed off in that direction, marking my trail with tape as I went. The site for Lauderbach #3 lay almost in the middle of this patch of woods.

When I'd covered about half the distance to the site area, I stopped to check my line. I wanted it to be as straight as possible so the crew and I could easily follow it again when the time came. I'd chosen my entry point at the edge of the woods based on the closest distance on a straight line to the site. The bulldozer operators who would cut a road to this site would appreciate my efforts. Often I'd have to change a path because of terrain, but so far, everything was looking good. No unexpected creeks or boggy areas.

Just when I thought everything was going according to my plan, I suddenly stepped out of the woods and onto a newly pushed road. The portion I could see ran almost dead north/south. "What the hell?" I said to Tulip who was already sniffing the tire tracks. "There's not supposed to be a road here," I said, pulling out my year-old aerial and checking it against today's reality. "Nope, no road on here." Tulip whined and gave me a curious look.

"Well, obviously it was cut fairly recently, at least after this aerial was made." I was torn. While I needed to complete my task of flagging #3, I also wanted to see where the road went. The intrigue of the unmarked road won out and I decided to follow it so I could mark its course on my aerial for future use. I marked the point of exit from my southeast line with a piece of tape and pulled a pencil from my tote. "Come on, Tulip," I said and struck off to the right, the southern part of the road, hoping it would intersect with open land first.

As we trekked along, Tulip kept her nose to the ground, sniffing constantly, more than she ever does in the woods. This was not a good sign. In my mind, it meant she might be picking up an unsettling scent. Like that of something being transported in a trailer?

A hog, perhaps?

I mocked myself for letting my imagination run wild, but 2,200 acres is a large piece of land. When it has been continuously owned by one family for generations, well, any number of things can be hidden on it, especially if the owners have gotten old or unable to stay watchful. Moreover, knowing what I knew about this farm, finding an unexpected road far removed from the working part of the dairy operation made me more than a little curious.

After about thirty minutes of steady walking, the road stopped where the woods met a vast field of corn stubble. I saw no sign of a road across it, although I did see what looked like tire tracks here and there. I turned and headed back the way I'd just come. When I reached the exit marker I'd left where my line intersected with the road, I debated whether to continue on and find where the road came out on the other side of the woods or turn southeast and plant my site marker flag. I decided to plant the flag first, then I wouldn't have to come back. After all, it was after three thirty and this time of the year it got dark early.

I picked up my southeast coordinate and marched to a clearing where I tied three ribbons of flagging tape like stripes around a nice, straight tree, and wrote "Lauderbach #3" in indelible marker on the middle one. Then I headed back to connect with the road and follow it.

In walking the northern component of the road, I got the feeling it was used recently, although not often. The weeds that grew in the center were mature, but they were flattened in places. Moreover, where humps existed, they had been scraped away altogether, exposing the red, gravelly earth. This end of the road wasn't nearly as straight as the one I'd just walked and probably wouldn't be suitable for use by the site crew. Still, I marched on. I just wanted to see where it came out.

As the road took an abrupt left turn, Tulip, a few feet ahead of me, stopped and backed a few steps. Then she turned and trotted toward me, her ears cocked back in a wary manner. Ahead of me, half-hidden in a thick stand of young pines was a small wooden shed. I chirped and pulled Tulip with me into the brush at the side of the road, where I could watch and listen.

No vehicles were present and no sounds emanated from the shed, which looked like the pre-built kind they sell at Lowes. There was no marijuana growing around it and I didn't see any signs of a moonshine operation, so I cautiously approached.

Upon closer inspection, what stood out was the fact that whoever drug it here wasn't very competent. For one thing, red clay from the road still clung to the bottom edge of the back of the building. I pictured it teetering on a too-small trailer. For another, it was sitting directly on the ground. Insects and the humid conditions in this part of the world would make short work of it.

I opened the double doors to have a look-see inside and saw a chilling sight. Red clay footprints on the bare plywood floor bore the same NB imprint I'd seen in photos Jackie had made of footprints found at the well when it was sabotaged.

I blinked, adjusting my eyes to the dimmer light, and laid my canvas tote on one of the wide wooden shelves that occupied both sides of the twelve-foot-long shed. A rustic workbench had been sloppily nailed against the back wall. Two NC State beanbag chairs, both with cigarette holes, were stowed in a corner. I sniffed the air.

There might not be marijuana growing outside, but there had damn sure been plenty smoked in here. I was getting the distinct feeling that this shed was being used by kids as a "grass shack."

I moved to the shelf on the right and poked through the junk scattered there, looking for clues to identify the potheads. All I found was a few porn magazines, empty drink bottles, snack bags, and candy wrappers. There were also two hurricane lamps, matches, and a variety of marijuana pipes. Prizing open an old coffee tin, I found a sandwich bag of grass and a couple of doobies. Apparently these kids had access to money.

Moving to the shelf on the other side, my anxiety meter suddenly pegged the red line. Now, I've spent a lot of time in quarries and learned a thing or two about blasting and explosives. I definitely knew visco fuse, a slow-burning fuse commonly used by pyrotechnic engineers, and det cord, a high-speed explosive fuse, when I saw them. Also—and maybe I've seen too many episodes of *Burn Notice*—but several dissembled cell phones, some hobby shop wire, sawed-off pipes, and empty containers of smokeless gun powder screamed only one thing to me: bomb! These creeps—no longer did I think of them as kids—had made a bomb.

My first thought. Call the law. Gas wells and bombs don't mix. I jerked my iPhone from my pocket, then saw I had no signal. Thinking maybe the shed was blocking the signal, I spun around to step outside but when I got to the doorway, the door slammed shut in my face!

Since there was no window, my world went from light to pitch black. Dumbstruck, I heard a brief fumble with the bolt latch, then a clack as someone rammed it into place. "Hey!" I yelled, pounding on the door. Then I heard Tulip growling—snarling, more precisely—some scuffling noises, a smacking sound, and one startled yelp from her.

I went ballistic, pounding and beating on the door until I heard what sounded like a car door opening, then nothing for a few seconds, then the worst sound I've ever heard. The sound of someone nailing the door closed.

I continued to beat on the latched door and hurl insults at the parentage of whoever was out there, until the hammering stopped and I realized I was hollering to no one. Silence enveloped me. Several minutes went by and all I could think of was Tulip. Fearing the worst, I called out to her.

Within seconds I heard snuffling and whimpering at the bottom edge of the door. Relief washed over me. "Tulip!" I said. "Don't worry, girl, I'll get out of here in a jiffy." I heard her whine again and lean back against the door. She was sitting guard. I turned back to face the interior and tried to feel my way to the right-hand shelf. I needed to remedy the light situation right away.

I felt around until I found the matches and one of the hurricane lamps. After a bit of fumbling, the interior of the shed bloomed into view. I tried my iPhone again. Still no signal. Either the shed was hampering the signal or I was too far from a tower ... or maybe both. I pulled out a beanbag and flopped down to take stock of my plight.

I was miles back in the woods of North Carolina and no one knew where I was ... except Bud. He knew! Sort of. I tried to replay our conversation with Chris and the wildlife officers after our lunch, remembering I'd told him I'd be flagging Lauderbach #3 before I came home. That's when it dawned on me that he wouldn't miss me because he wasn't coming home. He'd said he was staying at his house since he had such an early start tomorrow. *Well, damn!* At least when he did notice I was missing, he'd have some information to work with.

I tried to quell my panic when I though of how long that would take and I already had to pee. Bad! I had to get out of here. If all else failed, I had my Beretta 380, my baby nine. That would be a last resort for obvious reasons, ricocheting bullets hitting me or Tulip outside. Also, I didn't want to use bullets I might need later. After all, the jerk or jerks who locked me in here weren't very nice and might need a baby nine lesson before this evening was all said and done.

I pulled the little gun from its holster and checked the clip. It was full and I had one in the chamber, so thirteen in all. Then I tried to think of other explanations as to why someone would make a bomb except to destroy the well.

Terrorism was the only other reason I could come up with but that wasn't logical. The woods of North Carolina aren't exactly known as a hotbed of fundamentalist radicals. No. It made more sense that the bomb was meant for the well. We'd already been subjected to a sabotage attempt. I was convinced of that. By someone who wore New Balance tennis shoes. Seemed obvious to me that someone, not being able to stop the well from being drilled, was now determined to stop it from producing.

It's impossible to get into the mind of anyone insane enough to build a bomb with the intention of harming people or the economy, so the why wasn't important right now. What was important was that at this critical time, when the well was fitted with only a temporary cap, it was at its most vulnerable. Twenty thousand pounds per square inch of pressure was sitting right out in the open with only a chain-link fence around it. In a few days, the well would have a six-foot-tall piece of equipment called a Christmas tree fitted onto the casing and a sturdy enclosure built around it.

If a bomb were to go off now ... well, what came to mind was old films of the Devil's Cigarette Lighter—the natural gas well fire that burned out of control for six months back in 1961 and could be seen from outer space. We'd definitely be wishing firefighter, Red Adair, was still alive.

Mental images of raging gas wells sprang to mind. I got up and frantically searched the shed again, hoping to find something I could use to get myself out of the creepy little space and go for help. After thirty minutes of sifting through everything, I was as disappointed by what I didn't find as what I did.

I did find a small package of hobby-grade gunpowder—primarily used in making rockets. What I didn't find was any more fuel for the lamps. I checked each of them. At most there was a few hours of fuel left in them.

What I desperately needed was a tool of some type that I could use to prize open the door, but I didn't find any. No claw hammer, no crowbar. Even if I could have pulled up the floor, I'd still have needed a shovel to dig my way out since the damn thing was sitting flush with the ground. There was a small amount of space where roof and rafters met and though one of the sections of pipe was about three feet long, it wasn't stout enough to use as a pry bar. Moreover, strong as I am, I seriously doubted that I could prize the roof away from the rafters.

I did solve the potty problem with an empty plastic drink bottle. Exhausted and suffering a raging headache from breathing unventilated air laden with smoke and fumes from the hurricane lamp, I shut off the lamp.

Once my eyes adjusted to the dark I could see all the cracks in the shed, lit from the outside by the bright light of a full moon. I curled up on the bean bags in the back corner for a short nap but couldn't get comfortable, so I got up, unstrapped my Beretta, and stuffed it in my tote bag.

Before I closed my eyes, I called Tulip through a quarter-inch crack between the floor and the wall until I heard her sniffing back at me. We commiserated until I dozed off.

My nap lasted a few hours and helped clear my thinking. I woke resolute that the only option left to me was to blow the door open. I relit the hurricane lamp and went to work.

It took another hour to come up with a contained explosive, which I hoped would serve to simply blow off the latch as well as the board that had been nailed to the door. I made a handy dandy little bomb by pouring a small amount of the hobby-grade gunpowder into one of the short sections of pipe. A little visco fuse and some tape from my tote and I was ready. I taped the bomb to the crack in the middle of the double doors, right over the latch. Before I lit the fuse, however, I had to be sure that Tulip would be behind the shed. I went to the far corner and called her to our communication crack. "Stay, girl!" I told her in my I'm-not-kid-ding-around voice.

I removed the glass from the lamp, took three quick strides to the door, and lit the fuse. Then I blew out the lamp and jumped back into my corner. To keep Tulip from going back around to the door, I counted out loud to her as I pulled the bean bags over me. "Five. Four. Three. Two. One."

Nothing.

I pulled my fingers from my ears but kept talking to Tulip. "Stay, girl, you know, fuse burn rates can vary greatly." I lay still, but kept talking to keep her with me.

Still nothing. Just when I was about to peek over my quickly improvised blast shield ... Kaboom!

"Whoa!" I yelled to Tulip. "That was way bigger than ... "

"Lawd God!" screamed a familiar voice outside.

What the hell! I threw back the bean bags and a zillion Styro-foam beads flew everywhere. Apparently shrapnel, pieces of the exploded pipe, had ripped into them. Staggering to keep my foot-ing on a sea of white beads and swatting furiously to clear the heavy smoke from the air, I stumbled toward the light coming from the now wide open doors.

In the bright moonlight, I saw Luther Green sprawled on the ground, a two-by-four laying across his chest and Tulip on his head.

"Luther?" I yelled, noticing immediately that Tulip wasn't at-tacking him. She was licking him! She wouldn't do that if he posed a threat. "Where the hell did you come from?"

He gently pushed Tulip aside, groaned, and sat up. "Ugh. I come looking for you. I was worried when I saw your new car still at the well but you wasn't around. Wasn't no one around, so I went back to the house and asked Ruby what she thought I ought to do and we got to talking about all the things what's been going on around here and ... well, I was worried something bad had happened to you. Tried to think of where you might be. Checked down at the pens. Thought you might be snooping around there again. When you wasn't there I went to the old clay works, but you wasn't there, so I come here ... "

"Wait. You know about the ... "

"Them bones that Clint was digging up? Of course, I did. Ain't nothing goes on 'round here I don't know about."

"Really?" I huffed. "Well, if you know everything that goes on around here, maybe you can enlighten me about a few things. First and most important right now, whose shed is this? What are they planning to do with the bomb they made in here?"

"Bomb ..." Luther breathed as he took my proffered hand and allowed me to help get him on his feet.

"Yes, bomb," I said. "Check this out." I stood aside as Luther stepped into the shed. I followed him in, relit the hurricane lamp, and pointed to the bomb makings on the shelf.

"Oh, lawd, what has that child done now?"

"What child? Who are you talking about?"

"Junior," he said, shaking his head. "I'm talking about that sad excuse for a son. A son who is supposed to take over this business. That child ain't never been nothing but a miserable failure at everything he tried. His momma and daddy know it too. And Ruby, she'd know it if she'd jus open her eyes. But she won't. He was the first baby born here and he might as well have been hers. She's doted on that boy every second of his life. He can do no wrong ... "

"What time is it?" I interrupted, checking my watch. "Jeez! It's almost dawn."

I knew Bud, Chris, and the wildlife officers would soon be in place to conduct their bust of the illegal hog hunting operation. But that wasn't important to me now. I had to reach them. I jumped back outside the shed, jerked my iPhone from my jeans, and was relieved to see that I now had a signal.

I tapped Bud's number and waited. Then there was a bleep and the phone cut off. I checked the screen. The battery had died!

Great. Now what? Luther was watching me, rubbing his chin studiously. "Luther!" I snapped. "Tell me honestly. Do you really think Junior is capable of making a bomb?"

"Yes 'um," Luther sighed. "I 'spect he could've. He's smart enough and if he's been doing that crack cocaine..."

TWENTY-THREE

"Cocaine?" I wailed. "He's a crackhead too? Please tell me you don't think he wants to blow up the well!"

"I can't tell you that," Luther said without hesitation. "I don't have no proof and he ain't never said anything to me, but I know from Ruby that he thinks it's evil. He's very religious, you know."

Panic shot through me like I'd stepped into an empty elevator shaft. "Give me your cell phone," I demanded. "Mine's dead and I've got to call the site foreman."

"I ain't got no cell phone. Ruby does. Just to keep up with the kids, you see, but I don't need one. Too new fangled for me ... "

"Come on," I said impatiently. "We've got to get to the well. We can talk on the way. I want the truth about the hog operation. I want to know if Junior is involved in it, too, and if so, how. Where's your truck?"

Luther floored the old Chevy and we careened along the dirt paths I'd never tried to navigate. Tulip and I braced ourselves as best we could on the bench seat—she didn't seem any the worse for wear from her encounter outside the shed—as Luther told me about how Junior's being a sickly child had contributed to everyone spoiling him.

"Uh-huh," I said impatiently. "Let's skip his early childhood and how he got to be the way he is and jump right to what's eating him now. Why do you think he built a bomb?"

"Well, I noticed some big changes in him once he started going to college. He was home most weekends 'cause his daddy insisted he help in the dairy. In the last couple of years, he's been quoting scriptures to me. Avenging kind of scriptures, you know?"

"Not really," I said as we broke out of the woods and made a 90-degree left turn that plastered me against the window before we straightened up and skirted a field planted in winter wheat. "What's that got to do with the well and why he'd want to destroy it?"

"I don't know that he does," Luther insisted. "I'm just saying it's a possibility because of the way he feels about it and because he's been acting crazy lately. Like maybe he ain't on his meds."

Good Lord! Can this nightmare get worse? "Meds?" I asked tentatively.

"Yes 'um. He's been ... er, um, hospitalized several times over the years. The Lauderbachs say he suffers from depression and mood swings but as long as he takes his medication, he's able to, you know, deal with life. But, if he don't, he'll fall into ranting about the devil and how everyone's out to get him. I don't know if there's a name for his problem. I just know he can get real sick at times."

Paranoid schizophrenia comes to mind. I rubbed my temples. My head was still pounding from breathing lamp fumes. "What about the hog operation," I asked as we rounded a corner of the wheat field and cut a sharp right into the woods that sheltered Cecil's fossilized bones. "Was he involved in that?"

263

"Now, Miz Cooper, I done told you..."

"You can skip trying to make me think I just dreamed seeing feral hogs in some of your pens. I know all about Mr. Fred Butcher and how he organizes expensive hunts for 'sporting swine,'" I said, making air quotes he probably didn't see in the dark cab of his truck.

"Don't nobody know about that," Luther snapped, losing his soft southern drawl. "Not even Mr. Lauderbach and it needs to stay that way. I've got two girls at expensive colleges and my boy gonna be attending in another year. I need extra money and what we've been doing ain't hurting no one but them sorry hogs and they *need* killing! They're tearing up crops, even lost a sickly calf to one."

"Be that as it may," I said. "I tried to get you to tell me about it that day when I found the pens and you wanted to play dumb. When I told Mr. Lauderbach about what I suspected..."

"You done told him about it?" Luther asked incredulously. "Now why'd you want to go and do something like that?"

"Because in case you've forgotten, someone has already been killed by a hunter and I'm bringing in a team of paleontologists to finish excavating the fossil Clinton found—with the blessings of the Lauderbachs, I might add—and I can't take a chance of someone else getting killed. Come hell or high water, we're getting that fossil out so that kid, Clinton, will have accomplished something lasting in his life!"

"If that's the case, then seems to me like you'd want me to kill all the hogs. Ain't you seen their tracks down in the clay pits? It's a wonder they ain't rooted that creature up by now. And for your information, Clint wanted 'em dead. He knew they were a danger to his work."

"He talked to you about the fossil?"

"Yes 'um." Luther said, pulling to a stop in front of the very hog pens where I'd been chloroformed.

"Why are we stopping here?"

"I got something to show you," Luther said, climbing out and heading to the feeding shed.

"Come back here!" I shouted, but he was gone. I jumped out, closing Tulip in the cab, and followed him into the dark shed. I grabbed his arm and shook him. "Don't you understand? We've got to get to the well! What if Junior strapped a bomb on the temporary cap? People could be killed! Your boss will be wiped out financially and you'll be out of work!"

"Just one sec, Miz Cooper," he said as he reached in a bag. "You need to see this." He stepped around me and stood silhouetted in the doorway holding something in his closed fist.

"Okay," I snapped. "Then, please, take me to the well!" Pointedly, I looked down and fell for the oldest elementary school trick in the books. Luther tossed some type of funky hog feed in my face.

Blinded and choking, I staggered backward and tripped over my own feet onto my butt just in time to hear the shed door slam! "God dammit!" I yelled, scrambling to my feet. "Not again! Luther! Let me out!" Rubbing my hands against the rough wood, I tried to find the latch in the pitch dark. It didn't take long to ascertain there wasn't one. "What's with you people?" I yelled. "You've never heard of two-way latches?"

The only response from the other side was the snap of a hasp closing, but my intuition told me Luther was still standing on the other side. Maybe he was considering whether he'd made a big mistake. Thinking maybe if I just talked to him, he'd come to his senses, I bit my tongue and sucked in a deep, calming breath.

"Please, Luther," I begged. "For the love of God, help me. Don't let this day dawn on a tragedy so catastrophic it can never be set to right." I gave him a few facts about gas well fires, how hard they are to contain, thus the need for the Red Adair types who are few and far between. The silence between us was deafening, but dammit, I knew he was standing just inches—and a stout wooden door—from me.

There was a shuffling noise—sounded like grit under work boots on the concrete blocks that acted as a step—then nothing. My face protested as I mashed it harder against the rough wood, straining to hear. Was he leaving?

My heart sank as I distinctly heard the creak of the truck door open. But hope sprang up again when I didn't hear it slam shut. Suddenly I heard Tulip sniff at the door. She must have jumped out. Then I heard footsteps back my way!

"Luther, come on, buddy. Please, help me," I pleaded.

There was no mistaking the sound of his boot on the step or his deep sigh. "Miz Cooper," he said sadly. "You got to believe me. I'm leaving you here to keep you safe. That boy can go plumb crazy sometimes. And you're wrong. I *can* fix all that's happened. Make it right again. There's other things going on that you don't know about that I got to take care of…"

"If you're talking about this morning's stupid hog hunt, I know all about it. In fact," I smacked the door with my palm to get his attention, "I'm doing you a favor. Because you aren't there, you won't get arrested with your good buddy, Fred Butcher. Wildlife officers are going to catch his ass in the act of moving and confining a feral hog. As we speak they're staking this place out at my request!"

"Arrest Fred Butcher! Oh, now you've really gone and done it!" Luther cried out. "Junior loves him better than Peter loved the

Lord. Ain't no telling what he'll do. I've got to stop this from happening..."

"Luther," I pleaded. "Fuck the hogs! You aren't hearing me. You can't imagine how bad it'll be if Junior sets off a bomb on the gas well!"

I pressed my face hard against the door again, straining to hear what was going on. For a moment everything was quiet on the other side. Just when I thought Luther might be having a change of heart, I heard a grunting noise from him, then something slammed against the door—and my face—so hard I saw stars.

Tears sprang to my eyes as I struggled to remain standing but failed miserably. I sunk to my knees and curled into a ball. Fighting to stay conscious, I turned my face toward the only light, the crack under the door. Moonlight greeted me. Within seconds, I heard the truck start. Someone gunned the engine and roared away. I didn't move. I just stayed there, trying to gather my senses.

I used to think the saddest sound in the world was that of a far-away train, racking down a track somewhere deep in the night. Now I know that's not true. Trust me, the saddest sound you'll ever hear is someone in dire pain, moaning, "Help me, help me." Only you can't reach them.

I pushed myself to a sitting position and shook my head, hoping to dispel the confusion. Darkness spun around me. It helped to rest my hands against the door, so I did.

Luther moaned again.

Blinking hard to hurry the return of all my faculties, I reached for my Beretta. No time to worry about ricochets. I patted my side. Oh, no. My gun was back in my canvas tote in the bomb-making shed. I'd been so worried about the well being bombed, I'd forgotten it. Now what?

I struggled to my feet, but with nothing except moonlight shining through cracks in the boards for reference, I promptly careened into a corner, knocking over a bunch of tools. Tools! Grappling blindly, I felt each one in turn.

Imagine my joy at finding a pick ax! Supporting myself with the stout wooden handle, I pushed myself up. My head cleared and I swung the ax like a major leaguer at the brightest crack, the one that marked the opening of the door.

It took three swings, but on the last try, wood splintered, the hasp broke, and the door flew open. For the second time in only a few hours, I witnessed Luther sprawled out before me in the moonlight. Only this time he didn't sit up. Tulip whined and licked his face.

He didn't move.

Kneeling over him, I slapped his face softly and called his name. Someone must have come up behind him and knocked him out, but who? I had a sinking feeling I knew. He groaned and said something. I leaned closer. "What?" I asked.

"Look out for Junior," Luther whispered, confirming my fear. "He's gone crazy again...." Then he slipped back into unconsciousness. I tried to rouse him, but when he didn't wake up, I had to face reality.

I was going to have to leave him.

I was the only one who knew what was probably about to happen and I had no phone. "I'll be back with help," I told him and stood up. "Come on, Tulip,"

I ran a few steps but she didn't follow, so I returned to Luther and knelt over him again to feel his brow. It was clammy. He was going into shock. Jeez. What to do?

I scrambled around in the shed and found a stack of empty feed bags.

I carried the whole stack out to Luther and spread out a few of them beside him, then knelt on the other side and pulled him toward me. The idea was to slide the bags under him, then cover him with more bags to keep him warm and prevent him from going deeper into shock.

When I rolled him up, however, my hands came away bloody. Very bloody. "What the hell?" I said aloud. It didn't take a brain surgeon to see that he'd been stabbed in the back. Immediately, the fact that the coroner had said a stab wound to the stomach killed Clinton came to mind. I took one of the feed bags, folded it into a compress and mashed it against the wound. The good news: it had missed his spine by several inches. The bad news: I was pretty sure his lung was punctured.

I ran back into the shed, grabbed the corners of a fifty-pound bag of feed, lugged it to Luther and laid it beside him. With a little he-woman maneuvering, I managed to lay the top half of his body, wound side down, on the bag, the idea being to keep his lung from filling with blood. I covered him with more feed bags, tucking the edges under him. "Come, Tulip!" I commanded. "We've got to get help and we've got no wheels!" This time she seemed to understand and loped off ahead of me.

Her mostly white coloring made her easy to follow in the moonlight. We ran hell-bent through woods and fields until my lungs were screaming. When we finally reached the base of the low hill where the rig had been, I dropped flat and crawled until I could see the doghouse and my Hummer. Rows of Diesel trucks and massive generators loomed in the moonlight, silent now. Since the reclamation crew hadn't come in yet and both drill crews had moved to Lauderbach #2, the place was deserted.

At least I hoped it was.

I wanted to charge up the steps of the trailer and plug in my iPhone so I could call for help, but I knew I couldn't. I had to be sure Junior wasn't lurking somewhere waiting to jump me. After all, I couldn't help anyone if I was dead.

After a few seconds, when I saw no movement anywhere, I took a chance and dashed for a stack of oil drums. From there I could see the rest of the site, including the temporary well cap. It was silhouetted in the early dawn light. I almost gasped out loud when I saw the Cyclone fencing enclosing the wellhead had been cut open and a man-sized hole gaped where the wire had been pulled back. And, there was definitely something strapped to the temporary cap.

My nightmare had come true!

Rage, that anyone, crazy or not, would do such a destructive deed overwhelmed me. Blood pounded in my ears. It was difficult to know what to do next, but one thing was certain: I had to reach my phone charger. If I didn't, Luther was going to bleed out back at the hog pens.

The fact that I'd made it this far gave me hope that Junior wasn't hiding somewhere, watching the well, especially if he was intending to ignite the blast with a rifle shot. But I didn't think that was his plan. When I saw the phone parts and det cord back at his man cave, I got the idea that he was going to use a home-made remote detonator, so I made a dash for the doghouse.

I took the stairs in two steps, jerked open the door and dove in. Tulip jumped right over me and I kicked the door closed and locked it. I didn't turn on any lights. I didn't really need to. It was getting lighter by the minute. Keeping my head below the window level, I crawled to my drafting table, reached up, and felt around for my charger.

As soon as I plugged in the iPhone, I dialed 911, explained the desperate nature of Luther's wounds, gave them instructions on how to reach him and what to look for. Then I called Jackie's cell and laid out the grim facts for him, including who Junior was and what I thought he'd done.

"Sooo, we're dealing with a mental patient who's also on crack?" the unflappable Jackie asked against background shuffling that sounded like he was pulling on his clothes.

"'Fraid so," I said. "What's company protocol with a possible bomb?"

Without a second's hesitation, Jackie said, "We're to keep the well area clear of all crewmembers and civilians and be available to render assistance to a professional bomb squad ... oh, and keep a record of everything that transpires."

"Good to know. I want *you* to call 911. I've already called them about another emergency at the other end of the property, but I didn't mention the bomb to them to avoid confusion. I'll meet you back here at Lauderbach #1 as soon as I take care of it."

"Another emergency?"

"I'm pretty sure Junior stabbed Mr. Lauderbach's farm manager, so be careful. Keep your eyes peeled."

"You too," clipped Jackie.

Still crouching, I gathered what I thought I'd need: my phone, its charger, Schmid and Medlin's first aid kit, a handful of survey flags, and a packet of hand towels from the bathroom. Wishing I hadn't left my canvas tote in Junior's shed, I shoved what I could into my jacket pockets. Then I booked it for the Hummer, praying Junior wasn't taking a bead on Tulip and me through the scope of a rifle.

I skidded to a stop on the side of the road at the location I'd given to the 911 operator, turned on my hazards, and unplugged my phone, hoping it had been plugged in long enough to store a little charge. Then Tulip and I took off at a dead run again, heading for Luther. Every fifty feet or so, I'd stop and jab a survey flag into the ground. I knew I needed to call Chris, but I couldn't talk and run, so I just kept running. It wasn't long before I could hear a cacophony of sirens from the direction of the well.

When I reached him, Luther's condition was unchanged: unconscious, but still breathing. I tried to rouse him several times, but couldn't. Though the feed bag I'd placed under him was soaked with blood, the bleeding had stopped. I placed a thick pad of paper towels over the wound and called Chris.

"What the hell's going on?" he blurted. "I just heard the call go out for the bomb squad out there. Everyone's been called in … "

"There's a bomb strapped to the well!" I said, cutting him off abruptly. "And Luther, the farm manager, has been stabbed. Both acts, I believe, done by the same … maniac, Junior. Remember, the one you were told wasn't a hunter."

"Slow down. Start at the beginning," Chris sputtered.

"Just get to the well," I said, hearing the voices of the EMTs coming through the woods. "I'll meet you there."

"Wait! Where are you now?"

"Down by those hog pens I first told you about … with Luther. Gotta go!" I disconnected and waved frantically for the rescuers.

As soon as I'd told them who I was and how Luther came to be injured, Tulip and I hustled back to where I'd left the Hummer.

TWENTY-FOUR

NOTHING'S WORSE THAN WHEN you need to get somewhere in a hurry, but everything seems to be moving in slow motion. That's how it was for me heading back to Lauderbach #1. I gunned it down straight stretches and slid around curves but the dirt roads still felt like salt water taffy. After what seemed like an eternity, I made it back to the site, but I couldn't even get close to the dog-house for all the emergency vehicles in the way.

———

I parked behind a horde of Lee County law enforcement cars, fire trucks, and other emergency vehicles, and Sheriff Stuckey's Interceptor. After I'd cracked the windows and locked Tulip in, I scanned the crowd of firemen for Jackie. Then I saw him and the rest of the crew. He had called them off Lauderbach #2 in case they were needed. Their familiar Schmid & Medlin hard hats were clustered together in a tight little grouping. I headed toward them but only got a few steps. A fireman rushed up to me, wanting to see my identification.

I showed it to him, explained who I was, and asked if he knew where I might find Detective Sergeant Chris Bryant. "No, ma'am," he said. "But you're free to proceed at your own risk. Turn your cell phone off and keep it that way until the device has been disarmed. Also—" Just then, someone connected with him through his helmet phone. He listened, then said, "Chief says everybody has to move back another hundred feet as quickly as possible. Oh, and better move your vehicle too."

Not a good sign. I jogged back to the Hummer and moved it where Jackie and the crew were relocating the company pickups. I reassured Tulip again, got out, and went to stand with them. "Can you believe this shit?" Jackie asked bleakly.

"No," I replied. "I guess by them moving us farther away, it pretty much confirms that the object I saw taped to the cap is a bomb."

"Looks that way," he said, his eyes glued to the proceedings taking place at the well. "Ever seen a blown well?"

"Thankfully, only on television and company safety videos," I said.

"Same here."

About that time I caught sight of Chris pow-wowing with Sheriff Stuckey. After a brief conversation, the two of them walked to within a few feet of us and Chris motioned for me to join them. I did.

Stuckey had nothing to say to me—apparently Bud's strategy of an arrest for an arrest was still working—so I turned to Chris and asked. "How bad is it?"

"Pretty bad," he said. "It's big enough that we don't have a bomb disposal unit sufficient to take care of it, so we're waiting on one from Raleigh." He checked his watch and continued, "Once they get here, we'll know more. Now, tell us what happened with the man who was stabbed and start from the beginning."

I relayed the events of the long evening, starting with flagging Lauderbach #3, then on to Luther finding me and what he told me about Junior's mental health issues and use of heavy drugs. When I got to the part about Luther tricking me into getting locked up a second time, Chris gave me one of those looks like Ricky used to give Lucy when she'd really botched things. "What?" I said, daring him to say anything.

"Nothing," he sighed. "Go on."

"Well, the rest of the story is simple. After he locked me in, he stood outside the door and told me he was going to set everything right. But here's the weird part. When I told him I knew about Butcher and the hog hunts and that you guys were going to put a stop to them, he freaked. He said that Junior loved Butcher and he didn't know what Junior might do if anything happened to Butcher."

Stuckey looked like he was trying to put on a game face, but I could tell he was behind in the program. He looked at Chris. "You talking about the kid you've been investigating on the Baker death? The religious nut?"

Suddenly it was my turn to be behind. "Wait. What?" I said, "You mean you've been investigating Junior?"

"Yes," he said calmly. "I told you I was following a lead on a ticked-off creationist. Well, he and Clinton had worked up quite a hatred for each other. They were on opposite sides of the pole, you might say, when it came to evolution. But, my investigation of him only started there. It didn't take much digging before I found clues that his past might have been troubled with drugs and mental illness."

"Good grief!" I practically shouted, my hand planted firmly on my hips. If you knew all this about him, why didn't you bring him in before now, before he strapped a bomb to his parents' only hope for saving the family farm? For that matter, why didn't you say anything at lunch yesterday when I told you he was likely a serious bow hunter? Why didn't you tell me then he'd been a mental patient and had a crack cocaine problem? You might've saved everyone a lot of heartache!"

"Calm down," Chris said patiently. "Most of that information was sealed so it took a few days to get the actual facts. I got confirmation on his mental illness and drug use—the actual sealed files—late yesterday before I left to go home. I was going to ask the sheriff to issue an arrest warrant this morning."

Stuckey gave me a smug look, then turned to Chris and asked, "You have sent someone over to pick him up, haven't you?"

"Wow," I said to Stuckey. "Looks like you're going to have to arrest someone for a murder that isn't even related to me." He wisely ignored me.

"Yes sir," Chris said, answering Stuckey's question. "The moment I got Ms. Cooper's call, I sent a team to the Lauderbach home to bring him in for questioning."

"What about Butcher?" I asked. "Did you arrest him this morning? Did Bud leave the property like you told him?"

"Yes and yes," Chris said. "We weren't planning on holding Butcher, but now … if there's a chance of some association with our murder suspect … " He motioned to a uniformed deputy to join us.

"Harris," Chris addressed the deputy. "Go back to the court-house. Have them hold Butcher over for more questioning."

The deputy went to do Chris's bidding and Stuckey looked at me and asked, "Have you got anything else to add about this situation?"

I had a few more choice comments regarding his finally taking some interest in finding Clinton's real killer instead of trying to nail me for it, but I resisted the impulse. Still I couldn't actually bring myself to have a conversation with him so I said, "Not to you, I don't."

Chris said to Stuckey, "When I took statements from the Lauderbachs, the kid's parents, they told me he didn't hunt. I don't think they were lying, but in light of all that's gone on this morning, I'll do a thorough search of the home again, this time with the arrows in mind."

"I think I may have a good suggestion as to where to look," I said to Chris. "There's an old chicken house out back of the main house. I was told it's never used, but I've seen Junior and the housekeeper come out of it."

Chris shook his head in appreciation. "Thanks for that," he said. "We'll check it out too."

In the distance I could hear the prolonged, pulsing wail of the bomb disposal truck as it blasted down the back roads skirting Sanford. It would be here in minutes. "Good," I said. "Because besides being the creep that put the bomb on the well cap and stabbed Luther in the back, I'd bet my life he stabbed Clinton Baker too. In fact ... " I said, giving voice to thoughts that until now I hadn't put together. "I think I know where the murder weapon is and who helped him hide it and ... "

I was interrupted when an enormous vehicle, which looked very much like a box on wheels, followed by another more specialized Lee County emergency vehicle, arrived on site. As we watched them go by, I deduced the first vehicle was used to detonate bombs because the words, "explosive disposal unit" were plastered across the sides, and the second, more specialized truck, was used for detecting, identifying, and disarming explosives in place. Chris turned his attention back to me.

"What were you saying about the murder weapon?" he asked impatiently.

"I think it was one of the knives they use around the farm to open feed bags and cut hay twine. They've got fixed blades, are about six inches long, and have black plastic compound handles. The blades are hooked on the end and serrated on top. Luther told me he buys quite a lot of them because the kids tote them off and forget where they put them ... "

Chris made a rolling motion with his hand.

"Anyway, seems logical that's what Junior used. He probably keeps it in the canvas knapsack I saw him sling over his back when he came out of that chicken house I told you about. Or, he could have been very clever and put it back in the barn. If I were you, I'd round up all of them I could find and test them for blood."

"We'll take your suggestions under advisement," Stuckey said snidely as he turned on his heel and abruptly left our company to join a group of deputies, the fire chief, and one of the bomb disposal experts. Jackie and his men joined Chris and me. We watched the activity at the well for a time.

"You know," Jackie said. "I spent some time with Sara, the sister of the guy y'all think did this, and I remember her saying he was majoring in animal science and would one day run the farm. That doesn't sound like your average run-of-the-mill bomber."

"That turned out not to be so," I said, figuring all Junior's lies and deceit were about to be made public anyway. "He was actually majoring in religious studies with a minor in business."

"Business was likely what he and Butcher had in common then," Chris said.

"Good point," I said. "Butcher is a businessman. He had an elaborate plan for a hunting community on this property. He probably started hunting out here, became friends with Junior, showed an interest in him maybe his dad hadn't."

"Right," Chris said, following the thread. "Therefore the deep attraction for Butcher that Luther told you about. When I interviewed him, he struck me as a very slick guy. Kind of the used car salesman type. Maybe he saw a weakness in Junior … his knack for failure, addiction to drugs … whatever, and exploited it. Probably told him he'd make him a business partner if he'd help him get the land developed."

"I think you're on to something with Butcher dangling a partnership in the land development business as a carrot," I said. "Maybe Junior saw a big flashy residential community as a way to prove himself. And more importantly, Sara said Junior already had a job lined up. *And*, she said it was up north somewhere. Baltimore is north of here. Do you think this infatuation with becoming a big land developer could have led him to kill Baker?"

"Maybe," Chris said. "After all, we're talking about a mental patient with a penchant for cocaine. Still, I caution you, we're only speculating here."

"Understood," I said. "But you'll get to the bottom of all this. I feel confident of that." I wasn't sure, but it could have been that the detective blushed a little before he turned his attention from me to a sheriff's deputy who'd jogged over to our little group and asked for the site manager. Jackie held up his hand. "Head of bomb disposal wants to go over with you what they did to the well cap," he said, then turned and addressed the rest of us. "The area has been secured. It's safe as far as the bomb goes and you can use your phones now, however, the sheriff wants the whole farm locked down until they catch the bomber."

"I'm afraid that won't be possible," Jackie said to him.

Nonplused, the deputy answered "The sheriff won't take no for an answer."

"Then take me to the sheriff," Jackie said, but I could see that wasn't necessary. Stuckey was headed back our way.

"Is there a problem?" he asked.

"There's no problem," Jackie said. "Just a slight conflict. I understand you have our safety in mind what with a lunatic on the loose, but I have our jobs in mind. We're under orders to keep working 24-7 as long as the rig is on site. We were right in the middle of setting it in place when this happened. We've lost enough time already. Now, I'm glad to hire private security to stand guard, but I figure in the time it would take to do that, you'll have your man. It'd be a lot simpler if you could spare someone to watch over us and it sure would be appreciated."

Stuckey stiffened his spine and glared at Jackie. Jackie did the same right back.

"I reckon you already know this, Sheriff," I said. "There's at least three of these crewmen and maybe more that have relatives in this area and they all vote."

Stuckey eyed the crew. They nodded affirmatively.

"Jasper," Stuckey said to his deputy. "Keep a man posted with these gentlemen."

"Okay, fellers," Jackie addressed the crew. "Miz Cooper and I'll make sure everything's squared away here and then I'll be right along. Now get back to work."

Jackie and I listened as the disposal expert explained that the bomb, while deadly and packing more than enough explosive to blow the temporary cap to kingdom come and ignite the highly pressurized gas below, was amateurish and easily disarmed. He was telling us that the well cap itself had suffered no damage when suddenly there was a flurry of excitement among the sheriff and his deputies.

Radios crackled messages unintelligible to me, orders were barked by Stuckey, and like magic, all the cars, including Chris's Crown Vic, took off, leaving behind only a cloud of dust.

Jackie looked at the explosives expert and me. "Reckon that means they found their man?"

"Looks like it to me," the expert said. Jackie and I started to leave and he added, "Before I go, I'll make a few more photos for our records, then cordon this area off as a crime scene. The D.A.'s office will have to clear it before we take it down."

"Sure," Jackie said. "Take your time."

In the doghouse, he and I quickly made things shipshape for the move to the new site. One of the crew would pick it up later. Knowing I wasn't needed there and considering how little sleep I'd had in the last twenty-four hours, I had plans of my own. I was going home to see Bud, hear all about the hog hunt, and maybe grab a few hours of sleep before Chris came over to fill us in on the capture of Junior.

As soon as we'd finished, Jackie headed back to the rig and I went to the Hummer. Tulip was napping. I let her out for a potty break. While I waited, I worried about the Lauderbachs. I had a feeling the police had caught Junior at their home. I felt instantly sad for them. On the other hand, he'd probably be locked away permanently for an offense as serious as intending to use a weapon of mass destruction. Homeland Security would have to be notified and they take of dim view of anything involving bombs. Heartbreaking as it was, the Lauderbachs would learn to live with it and their farm was now safe ... in more ways than one. Tulip finished with her business, jumped back in the Hummer, and we headed home.

———

I used the main farm road and had to pass the Lauderbach home. I slowed up as I did because I was just in time to see Junior, hands cuffed behind his back, being led to a waiting deputy's car. Ruby and Annette stood on the front porch, their hands clasped together, and watched their baby leave their lives, likely forever.

The sight was so disturbing, I had to turn away.

A short ways up the road, the shoulder widened and I pulled over. Seeing the two women had so distressed me that I needed a minute to calm myself. I rested my forehead in my palm. If only I could do or say something. Then I realized they'd had no report as to the well status following their son's attempt to destroy it and that was, after all, my job.

I waited until the caravan of deputies and the sheriff's Interceptor went by, then executed a u-ey and went to the Lauderbach home.

———

Ruby opened the door and silently took me to the sunroom. As I slipped past her to enter, she spoke. "Before I fetch Miz Lauderbach, I want to thank you for what you did for Luther last night. The emergency folks said if it weren't for you, he'd be dead. I'm going to the hospital to be with him soon's I get Miz Lauderbach."

"How is he doing?"

"The doctors said it'll take some time, but he'll make a full recovery. I just wanted you to know how much I appreciate all you did for him and how sorry I am for … believing in Junior when I shouldn't have."

"Sometimes a situation can be so difficult, it's hard to know what to do."

"Still, I ought to have cottoned on to the signs that he was off his meds," she choked back a sob before saying, "I'll go get Miz Lauderbach for you."

When Annette joined me, her face was twisted with stress. Mothers the universe over share a deep connection when it comes to their offspring. Often, no words are necessary. She took one look at me and fresh tears welled in her eyes. I held out my arm. She leaned into me and I led her to the couch.

As I lightly rubbed her boney, frail shoulders, she fought to regain her composure. Once she did, she proceeded to relay to me all that had happened. How a group of sheriff's deputies had banged on the door and demanded to be let in. How they swarmed the house and grounds, some even going to the barns, searching for Junior. The more she talked the more upset she got. My attempts to calm her failed and she vented on.

It was surprising to hear how long the search had taken and that Junior might have escaped entirely if Ruby—having had time to think about how sick he really was—hadn't suggested they go back and look in the chicken house again. The detectives had given it a cursory glance on their first search, but found him the second time. He'd hidden himself behind a burlap screen in the overhead roosts.

I asked Annette if she was aware that Junior had changed his major from animal science to business. "I am now," she sobbed, dabbing her eyes with a worn paper towel. "He told the sheriff and his detective all about how he'd had to change majors to business because his father and I were too stupid to know what was best for us. He thought our plans for tapping into our own resources on this farm and using the money to update a business that served this family for generations was a pipe dream that would all blow up in our faces."

She inhaled a shuddering breath, then said bitterly, "And what did he do when it looked like our plan was going to be a success? He stacked the deck, planted a bomb, and nearly blew himself and lots of innocent people up!" Dropping her head in her hands, she cried softly.

"Could I fix you a cup of tea," I offered. "I know Ruby has gone to see Luther, but I'm sure I could manage for you."

"I'm way ahead of you," Arthur said from his wheelchair in the doorway. "I was just coming to see if I could get anything for you, lovey. " Annette tried yet again to pull herself together, blowing her nose and taking a deep breath. Arthur surveyed his wife sadly, then turned to me. "Cleo," he said, "what a kind gesture you've made in coming to see us."

"I hope I haven't made things worse," I said. "It's my job to see that you are kept in the loop on all affairs pertaining to the well. So, for your peace of mind, please know that neither it nor the temporary cap were damaged in any way. The gas will flow on schedule once the pipeline is connected."

"At least we have that," Arthur said with a sigh. "Life sometimes deals you a hard blow. You just have to face it and move on. To tell you the truth, we've lived in fear for years, haven't we, lovey?"

"Yes, dear," Annette said with a sniff.

"Particularly when we'd see on the news where a mentally unstable person off their meds wreaked havoc somewhere, taking the lives of the innocent. It seems to happen more and more often these days. At least he didn't kill Luther and I understand we have you to thank for that, Cleo."

When I couldn't think of a proper reply, he continued, "And we have one other thing to be grateful for."

"I can't imagine what," Annette said sorrowfully.

"Well, it's a small thing really," Arthur said. "But when a person is as sick as Junior, they need all the understanding hearts and open minds around them they can get." Annette gave him a confused look. "The sheriff, of course," Arthur said. "Remember, he's been in practically the same situation."

Huh?

"Oh," Annette said and turned to me. "He is referring to the sheriff's daughter. She's at Mary Hill Institute, it's a home for ... well, let's say the mentally challenged, and will be for the rest of her life. They say she is very dangerous. She attacked several people before the sheriff and his wife finally got her committed. In their defense, it is quite difficult to get someone committed, even if you are the person's parent."

She got up and fussed with the throw over Arthur's knees as I struggled to take in what she'd just said. "Anyway," she continued, taking her seat beside me again, "recently a rumor started around that she had confessed to a murder. It was quickly quelled. The sheriff's wife is quite influential in social circles around here. Folks just dropped it so I guess there was no truth to it, but still, with the sheriff trying to get reelected, I'm sure it was embarrassing."

Annette could have turned purple and levitated from the couch and I wouldn't have been any more shocked. "I ... I've never heard a word about the sheriff having a daughter, mentally disturbed or not. How old is she?"

"Well, let's see now," Arthur said, clearly relieved to be talking about someone else's problems. "Maybe mid-forties if the Stuckeys were in their mid-twenties when they had her and that's just a guess based on the sheriff being close to sixty-five now. From what we heard, she's been out there on and off since she was a teenager. They say she is completely and dangerously insane."

"I'm just stunned," I said. "I've lived around here all my life and I never heard of her. Of course, way back then I was skipping grades in high school on the fast track to college. Naturally, I had a lot going on in my life at that time."

"Very few people knew, dear," Annette said. "She was so unstable, the Stuckeys kept her hidden away. She didn't even attend public school. Thelma Stuckey home-schooled her. We would never have known about her either if it weren't for seeing the Stuckeys with her out at Mary Hill from time to time when we'd have to take Junior..."

"The point is," Arthur continued, "he's bound to be kinder to Junior knowing that he's unstable and not responsible for his actions. It's not like he's some criminal."

Time for me to leave. I stood and patted Annette on the shoulder, and as I shook hands with Arthur a thought crossed my mind. It probably wasn't the best time to bring it up, but it needed immediate attention. "Arthur," I said. "I hate to bring this up right now when you're dealing with such a difficult situation, but last night, before he was injured, Luther told me he'd noticed pig tracks close to the clay pit..."

"Oh my!" Arthur exclaimed. "Sounds like feral hogs have made it to our land. We can't have them damaging ... what was his name?"

"Cecil," Annette offered.

"Thank you, my dear. Yes, we can't have hogs damaging Cecil. What do you propose?"

"A fence," I said. "Actually I'm on my way home right now and I could stop by Lowes in Sanford and have enough fencing and a gate sent out here to do the job if you have the men to install it."

"I have the men and I will also take care of sending them to purchase the fencing. And, I'll supervise the installation. No need for you to worry about any of this. It will be just the ticket to occupy me."

"Are you sure? I mean with Luther hurt... "

"Nonsense, I have plenty of men on the farm who can drive me where I need to go and I'm getting stronger every day," Arthur said and reached for my hand again. He gave it a gentle pat. "You run along, now, I'll take care of it."

The Hummer purred to life with a comforting rumble—a sound I was learning to enjoy—but I didn't leave immediately. Instead, I sat, thinking, my wrist resting on the steering wheel. The sheriff had a daughter confined to a home for the criminally insane? I wanted to know more about this intriguing bit of information and I knew just who to ask.

TWENTY-FIVE

THOUGH MY DAD HAD never mentioned that the sheriff had a daughter, I had a feeling he'd know something about her. Another call to him was definitely in order. Besides, he still hadn't told me whether he was coming to the wedding and now it was only weeks away. I pulled him up on my iPhone and marveled at the clarity of his ring halfway around the world off the African coast. Already anticipating being dumped into his voicemail, I was pleasantly surprised when he picked up.

"Hi, honey," he said.

"Dad!" I blurted, checking my watch. "Are you off work? What's the time there, about six?"

"Uh … actually I'm kind of in the middle of something right now. Can I call you back?"

"Well, yeah, I guess. When? Dad? Dad?"

Cyberspace buzzed between us, but not before I'd heard the distinctive sound of a flock of crows. Now, last time I checked, there were no crows fifty miles off the coast of Mozambique. Seagulls? Yes. Crows? No.

Where was my dad and what was he up to?

I put the Hummer in gear and pulled back onto the main farm road. Zipping along, roiling a trail of dry dust, I was contemplating the surreal nature of the events of the past twenty-four hours when I happened to pass an unfamiliar path on my right. Or was it?

I slammed on the brakes and backed up to it. Looking out the passenger window, I realized it was one of the shortcuts I'd taken last night with Luther. Suddenly my memory kicked in and I banged my fist on the wheel. Shit!

I'd forgotten all about my Beretta. It was still in my canvas tote back at Junior's bomb-making shack. Rerunning last night's trip through the woods as best I could considering my fatigue, I was pretty sure the shack could be reached using this very path.

If I was right, it intersected with the newer road I'd encountered. The one Junior had used in hiding his shed where he thought no one would find it. In truth a blind man could have found it. Or, in my case, a geologist flagging wellsites.

My stomach rumbled. I hadn't eaten since this time yesterday when I'd lunched with Bud, Chris, and the Wildlife officers. Deciding it was more important to retrieve my Beretta than feed my face, I backed the Hummer and turned down the path. It wouldn't take but a few minutes and I take ownership of a gun very seriously. They are a big responsibility. No matter how upset I'd been late yesterday, securing it should have been a top priority.

The shed came into view just where I'd thought it would. Rolling to a stop in front of it, I was surprised to see both doors still hanging from their hinges relatively undamaged. There was, however, a huge hole where the latch had been. I also noted the 2 x 4 board—formally nailing the doors shut—was still where I'd tossed it after taking it off Luther's chest. I shut off the Hummer but left the door open while I stepped into the dim light in the shed. My first thought: don't be a chump again. I went back out and, using the 2 x 4 board, I jammed the door open.

Back inside, I was struck at how empty the spot was where I'd left my canvas tote. I blinked in confusion. Where the hell was my canvas tote? Definitely not where I'd left it. I wanted to scramble around through the trash and junk on the shelves but it wasn't necessary. I could clearly see that the tote was gone, and besides, this was a crime scene.

Evidence samples would have to be taken from the bomb-making materials in case they were ever needed in court. I gingerly lifted the tattered bean bags, one at a time, and looked under each one but I knew the tote wasn't there. I had a clear memory of where it had been situated when I'd tucked the little gun in it for safekeeping while I napped. There was only one answer as to what had happened to it. Someone had toted it off. But who?

Had the sheriff's deputies already been here? Logic said no, since there was no tape up yet denoting the area as a crime scene. I was trying to think of how to go about reporting a gun missing when outside Tulip started barking ferociously. Then I heard the rumble of a car with a large engine.

Stuckey! I moved to the shack entrance just as his Interceptor pulled up behind my Hummer. Tulip jumped out and ran to my side, her lips curled over her teeth.

"Nice dog. Friendly too," Stuckey said as he sauntered over to me, my canvas tote swinging from his fingers. "Looking for this?"

"As a matter of fact, I am," I said with way more bravado than I felt. "In all the confusion last night, I accidentally left it behind. Since it has my 380 in it, and being the responsible gun owner that I am, I came to retrieve it as soon as I possibly could."

"Guns," Stuckey said, nodding in agreement, "are useful and dangerous all at the same time. And for a civilian like you ... well, you never know when the dangerous part might outweigh the useful part. You know what I mean?"

"No," I said flatly.

"Well," he said, removing the belt and holster from the tote before letting it fall to the ground. "It would be very easy for a person in your line of work to trip over a branch way back in the woods and have the gun fly out of its holster and go off accidentally. A thing like that happen ... no telling where the bullet would go. Why, it could hit you in any number of places that would be fatal." He withdrew the Beretta from the holster, which he let drop on the bag. Then he pointed the gun right at me.

"Stuckey ... " I said with as much don't-do-it inflection in my voice as I could muster.

"Why, you could accidentally be hit in the groin," he said, adjusting his aim to hit mine. "You know, a direct hit to the femoral artery and you'd bleed out in eight minutes. Or," he shifted his aim up to my chest, "a shot through the heart and it's lights out instantly."

I was standing in the doorway to the shed and got that feeling—the one you get when a confrontation with someone is inevitable. You try to avoid it, but suddenly, for whatever reason, you just can't anymore, the time has arrived. Well, this was the time for Stuckey and me. Deciding to force his intentions, I hopped out of the doorway and took a few strides toward him. Sure enough, he swung my little Beretta right up in my face and took a two-handed stance. With my Krav Maga training in mind, I stopped a foot from the muzzle of the gun. "I'll take my chances," I said. "Now give me my property."

"I don't think you fully appreciate the severity of your predicament, here, Miss Margot..."

"Cooper," I corrected him. "My name is Cooper."

"Right, how could I forget that fancy pants smart aleck who paid for another fancy pants smart aleck to get your dad off with only a few years in the pen when he should have gotten the big sleep."

"You know my dad didn't kill Francis Gary Wayne. You know it today same as you knew it back during the trial," I said. "Why'd you do it Stuckey? What was in it for you? Sure, you two had a little high school vendetta going, but that was hardly reason to send a man to die like a dog by lethal injection."

"Why don't you ask him? He and his buddies think they've got all the answers. They just keep nosing around. I tried to send him a message by letting him know how chancy life is, how one minute you have it and the next it can be taken from you. Apparently he didn't get it. Maybe he needs for me to send a clearer one ... "

"You crazy bastard, you shot my tire, didn't you?"

"I'm not the one who's crazy," Stuckey growled. "Pete's the one who's crazy. He should've heeded the message that something might happen to you if he didn't end his ignorant quest to clear his precious name. Like anyone around here would care! My reputation is the one that counts, missy, and whatever it takes to make your dad see that and back off, I'm willing to do!"

"I've got news for you, old man. You most definitely *are* crazy." Then, thinking a quick dose of reality in the form of a sarcastic insult would let him know he wasn't scaring me and cause him to back down, I added, "You're as crazy as your daughter. Now holster my gun, place it on my bag, and go back where you came from."

Stuckey's face turned three shades of purple and instead of doing what I asked, he firmed his stance and stiffened his arms. Not exactly what I had in mind. Time to find out if all those Krav Maga lessons were worth it. I'd already taken step one. I'd assessed my situation.

I was facing an attacker with a gun pointed at my face. I had to count on two things being certain: If I touched the gun, it would go boom! And, Stuckey would back up a few steps.

With those two things in mind, I dropped my head below the level of the gun simultaneously grabbing it with both hands and kicking him in the balls with my right foot. As promised by my instructor, it went off, straight in the air, but I didn't let that slow the forward momentum of my right leg.

I kept pushing Stuckey backward, while rotating the gun and shoving it downward toward his belly. The instant I felt his fingers give, I jerked my Beretta free of his grasp, threw a fresh round in the chamber and opened the distance between us. The entire maneuver took less than five seconds.

Seeing Stuckey crumpled in a ball on the ground didn't make me feel much better … well, maybe a little, but I imagine it would have made my instructor proud as a peacock. With baby nine aimed to kill, I commanded, "Let go of your balls. Take your Glock out of your holster. Hold it straight out using thumb and forefinger."

Stuckey groaned but did as requested.

Using my left hand, I took away the big revolver, tossed it in the underbrush on the other side of the path where it'd take him a while to find it, and said, "What now, maniac? Where should I shoot you to make it look like you were checking out the bomb shack with gun drawn, tripped coming out of the shed, and accidentally shot yourself? Maybe the stomach? Does a nice slow bleed out sound like a good way to spend a beautiful fall afternoon?"

Stuckey didn't respond, just remained wadded in a ball, his face red as a beet. Still taking dead aim with arms outstretched, I sidestepped to my tote, picked it and the holster up, and draped them over my shoulder. Then I moved closer to the door of the Hummer and said, "Or, maybe I should just drive off and leave you to consider the fact that you *are* crazy. You've done crazy things. Maybe ponder what to do about it. What do you think?"

His words were muffled, but it sounded like "drive off" to me.

So I did.

———

I couldn't put down the miles between me and the insanity that had become the Lauderbach Dairy Farm fast enough. That I had just escaped being killed by a lunatic sheriff that had hated me and my father for over half my life was more than I could take in at the moment. All I could think of was Bud and the deep feelings of safety and peace I got whenever I was with him.

Had it really taken being back here in the same area where he and I first met and experiencing yet another living nightmare to make me realize this? Apparently so. And still, there were so many hurdles to jump before we could be together again. Not the least of which was the wedding itself. I shuddered at the thought as I pulled into my drive. It was a little after one in the afternoon and I was exhausted. Thank goodness no one was home.

Foregoing food or drink, I passed through the kitchen, Tulip dragging behind me—she was whipped too—and headed upstairs to my room. Slashes of sunlight beamed through the plantation shutters and played across my bed. I flopped face down on them and closed my eyes gratefully.

I heard Tulip spring into her favorite chair. She scratched her mohair throw to suit her exacting specifications and exhaled a contented sigh. I sighed too. Then my iPhone rang. I opened one eye to see who it was. Bud.

"Hey, hey, hey," he chirped. "You won't believe everything that's going on in Cooperland!"

"Bud," I said, smiling in spite of my fatigue. "Right now, I'd believe anything. I'm so tired and I have so much to tell you about what happened today and I want to hear all about your adventures as a big game hunter. I just need to rest for a few hours."

"Rest?" he asked. "You mean you're home? I thought you'd be busy making arrangements for the paleontologists to come in, and setting everything up so your replacement can take over as wellsite geologist while we're on our honeymoon. You said you'd need days to do all that."

"I will," I yawned. "And I'll get it all done. Just not today. Like I said, right now I need a few hours rest."

"Do you need me to come over and help you ... rest," he offered provocatively.

"No!" I insisted. "You can come over later. Say around suppertime."

"Well, that'll work perfect then. We'll all get together at your house for a Cooper family spaghetti dinner, okay? But first, before I let you go, you'll never guess who's sitting here in my office."

"Uh ... " My one open eyelid drooped.

"Pete!" he chirped, unable to wait for my guess.

"Who?"

"Your dad, babe!"

I knew it! "I had a feeling he wasn't in Africa," I said. "When did he get in?"

"Oh, he's been here for about a week and does he have a tale for you."

"I want to hear it now!" I sat up. The room spun and my head pounded. *Ugh.* "On second thought ... "

"Get your rest, babe. Your dad and I still have a lot to talk about. We'll be over about seven with Will and Henri and Chris. Henri has some news for you too."

I laid back down. "More wedding news, I bet," I said, trying to stifle another big yawn.

"Yes, more wedding news. Rest now. We'll see you later."

I went to sleep, smiling, already knowing what Henri's news would be. She had been agonizing over whether to spend $800—the sale price—for a pair of Jimmy Choo shoes she desperately wanted for the wedding. My guess: she had.

———

I woke six hours later to the aroma of spaghetti sauce. I showered and spruced up before going downstairs. Bud met me on the landing with a big hug and a kiss. "I was just coming to get you. Your dad's in the den."

Though I hadn't seen my dad, Pete Margo, in years, he hadn't changed one bit. He still stood straight as an arrow and was fit as a prize fighter. I ran into his embrace.

"Daddy," I murmured into his chest.

"My little Cleo," he said, rocking me in his arms and kissing the top of my head.

"Let's have a toast," Bud said, holding out three tumblers, each with a healthy dose of Jack Daniels. "Here's to you and your dad being together again."

"Here, here," my dad and I said. We all took a sip.

"Here's to you and Cleo and your upcoming marriage," my dad said, raising his glass.

"Here, here!" Bud and I said, and we all took another sip.

My turn. "Here's to Bud and me getting married for the right reason this time," I said.

"Here, here!" the three of us said in unison, then slugged down the remainder of the booze.

"Arrgh!" my dad grimaced and growled like a bear, "That's good stuff!" He motioned for me to sit with him on the couch. "And your toast brings us to what we need to talk about before the kids get here."

"Okay," I said. "But it isn't necessary. Bud and I have come to grips with why we first got married and why we are now—"

"Yes," Dad said, "but I want to have my say in light of what I've been doing the last several years to clear my name."

"Clear your name … is that why you came back, when Johnny Lee saw you and Buster together?"

"Yes, but let's go back a little ways," he said. "Buster Gilroy and I have stayed in touch since I first went to prison, and after, when I got out and went to work overseas. You may not remember this, Cleo, but Buster's sister was a very close friend of your mom's and a clinical psychologist at the Mary Hill Institute."

"I remember her and mom being friends," I said, "but I never knew what she did and I just found out this morning that Sheriff

Stuckey and his wife had a criminally insane daughter who was hospitalized there. Did you know that?"

"A small number of folks in our community knew about her, but she was never seen. Buster's wife was working at Mary Hill when they finally got her committed. Thing was, she had home visits. They were on a limited basis at first, then more often as she proved herself not to be a problem. Everything went pretty good for a while, until she got a secret boyfriend. She'd sneak out while on home visits and see him. One night she became wildly unstable and killed him..."

"Oh my God. Who was it and when did that happen?" I breathed, already knowing the answers.

"Francis Gary Wayne, and she killed him in February of 1987..."

"Dad," I said sadly, feeling the tears pool in my eyes. "Why didn't anyone know what happened? Why wasn't she charged? Why did you get blamed? I don't understand."

"Sure you do," Dad said, rubbing at the tears that escaped down my cheeks with his rough thumbs. "Think about it. Stuckey was sheriff. He could manipulate facts and plant evidence all he wanted. When his daughter came to him after she'd killed Gary, all covered in blood and needing help, he'd helped her. Seems she'd taken her mother's car and met Gary at the drill site where no one would see them. Things got out of hand, she went nuts and killed him, stabbed him to death with a nail file, so she told Buster's sister."

My dad stood up restlessly and made himself an iced water at the wet bar, then continued. "When Stuckey saw where Gary's body was situated and realized he could implicate me, he jumped at the chance. He put some of Gary's blood on a wrench from the toolbox on my rig and tossed his body in the hog pen, where he knew the hogs would make short work of any evidentiary wounds. Then he got rid of the car and refused to let his daughter come home ever again."

"Then all he had to do was talk to your crew," I said. "Everyone knew about you yelling at the kid the day before."

"And don't forget, he had to *find* the murder weapon in the toolbox on my rig."

"Right," I said. "Mom used to say your temper would be your undoing one day."

"She sure did," Dad said wistfully.

I smiled thinking of her and, though he'd never turned his temper on us, how she'd worried about him. "She called it your famous temper. And turned out, she was right," I said honestly and gave him a crooked grin.

He smiled—years in jail and living in a third world country had mellowed him somewhat. "It definitely made me an easy mark," he said sheepishly.

Thoughts of those dark, desperate times consumed us until I asked, "But why now, Dad. Why did Buster's sister come forward now. Why not back then?"

"She didn't know back then," he answered. "The daughter had enough of her wits about her to believe Stuckey when he told her that if she talked about her boyfriend and what she'd done, her days at a nice place like Mary Hill Institute would be over."

"Apparently her mental condition deteriorated as time passed," Bud jumped in, "and a few years ago she told Buster's wife and a couple of her friends at the institution how she'd killed her lover, Gary Wayne, and how her dad had covered it up for her."

"Long story short," my dad said, "Buster got up with me. Told me what his sister had heard. I went back to the same New York lawyer Bud hired for me all those years ago. He's still going strong. Anyway, lots of legal maneuvers—depositions and such—have taken place, papers have been filed and now we're waiting on a judge to have a warrant served on Stuckey."

"What about Johnny Lee?" I asked. "Has he been helping you? Stuckey thinks he has."

"Not in the beginning," my dad said. "Buster and I just happened to run into him one day at lunch. Later we told him what was going on. He's been real supportive and helpful."

"So how long has Stuckey known about this?" I asked.

"Over a year at least," my dad said. "But it was only recently that we actually took papers out on him."

"But if he knew this freight train was coming down the tracks at him, why did he file to run for sheriff again?" I wondered out loud.

"Maybe he thought aiding and abetting for someone in his position, a parent of a mentally impaired person, might be something he could politically survive," Bud suggested, moving into the kitchen to stir the sauce. "You know how people are. Even manipulating evidence and lying can be overlooked if you get the right jury, especially when the love and protection of a child is involved. We'll just have to see how it goes."

Dad and I followed him so we could help with dinner since the kids would be arriving soon. I thought now was as good a time as any to drop my bomb. "Not after I add my two cents worth," I said.

"What's that mean?" my dad and Bud asked in one voice.

I told them about my latest run-in with Stuckey.

"And that was just a few hours ago?" Bud boomed. "We need to call Chris! Good lord, Cleo, why didn't you say something?"

"I'll kill that son-of-a-bitch!" Dad roared.

I turned to my dad. "Stop!" I said firmly. "I was going to say something. I was just waiting until Chris got here. Besides, Stuckey can't go far with an ice pack between his legs." The two men in my life gave me curious looks. "Krav Maga," I explained.

"Ahhh," they said, nodding in agreement.

"And," I said. "I still need to fill you in on what happened during the time after I had lunch with you and Chris and the wildlife agents until I laid Stuckey low."

TWENTY-SIX

BUD AND MY DAD set the table and I made a salad while I told them how Luther got stabbed and the well had almost been turned into a very large cigarette lighter. We'd just finished when Chris arrived. He didn't even get through the door before Bud bent his ear about Stuckey drawing his gun and threatening to murder me.

"So that's where he went," Chris said. "When we left the Lauderbach home, I was behind him in our caravan and he was following the deputy carrying Junior. Not too long after we passed where you were pulled over down from the Lauderbach's driveway, he pulled over, too, and waved me by. He'd given orders to secure all the relevant locations on the farm that were crime scenes, so naturally I thought he was probably going to do some of his famous supervising. He must have doubled back and followed you to Junior's shack."

"It's possible," I said. "He could have easily waited where I couldn't see him until I left the Lauderbachs' and then followed me."

"All I can say is he wasn't in the office and his second in command, First Deputy Carter, had to fill in. Of course, that's been happening a lot lately. I was seriously ticked, too, 'cause I was ready and waiting with proof that he was the one who shot out your tire."

Better late than never. "Wow!" I said not wanting to take the wind from his sails. "That's great work. How'd you manage that without having me swear out a warrant?"

"I didn't need one. Remember I told you right after your accident that I was going up on the ridge overlooking the spot where you lost control of your Jeep and did a header into Pocket Creek? I believe you cautioned me about a bull."

"Yeah."

"I went up there and found a rifle cartridge. Now, you may not know this but a spent cartridge from a bullet is a very telltale item when ascertaining if a particular gun fired that bullet."

"Really?"

"Yes, because when a gun is discharged, the firing pin hits the cartridge and the resulting ... explosion, if you will, propels the bullet forward and the cartridge backward into the breech of the gun. When that happens, the impact leaves a distinctive stamp on the cartridge. Moreover, the injecting mechanism that flips the cartridge from the gun leaves marks or scratches on the cartridge particular to that gun and that gun alone. In other words, if I have two spent cartridges that have the same unique markings on them, it's undeniable that they were fired by the same gun."

"So," I said. "Wouldn't you need another cartridge fired by his rifle, which means you'd still need a court order to get his rifle and have it fired in a lab?"

"Ordinarily," Chris said. "But recently I participated in the fall turkey shoot put on by our county to raise money for purchasing special equipment for the sheriff's department. The sheriff participates and encourages everyone in the department to do the same. He always uses his favorite hunting rifle, the one he keeps on his wall. It was pretty easy for me to pick up a shell…

"Which you compared to the shell from the ridge and—"

"Perfect match. No ballistics expert on the planet would deny that. Sheriff's rifle is old, the pin is slightly off to one side and it leaves a very unique stamp on the spent cartridge."

"So, when are you going to confront him with this information?"

"I already have. When Sheriff Stuckey finally did show up, he went straight to his office. I marched in right behind him and confronted him with the cartridges and asked him, man to man, why he did it."

"What did he say?"

"He told me to get out. I told him I was going to call for an inquiry and about that time there was a knock at the door. It was a bailiff who promptly served him with papers. No one knows what they are about and Sheriff sure wasn't saying. He just told Carter he had a few matters to clear up and that Carter was in charge until further notice."

"Thank the Lord!" whooped my dad with a smack of his hand on the counter. "For a minute there I thought this young whippersnapper was going to do what I've been trying to get done for as many years as he is old by simply picking up a cartridge and shooting a few turkeys!"

"Oh, my gosh!" Bud exclaimed. "Excuse our manners, Pete, but it has been one helluva day, starting before dawn for me." He turned to Chris and made the proper introductions.

"It's an honor, sir," Chris said, shaking my dad's hand. "Cleo told me all about what happened with you and the sheriff back in

1987. So, you're saying the papers the sheriff got today have something to do with that incident?"

"Yes, they do and I'll bring you up to speed on that before the night is over, but right now, I want you to continue with your explanation of how you're going to put that lying son-of-a-bitch where he belongs—in jail."

"In order to do that," Chris said. "I need to back up to the last time I saw you, Cleo. I went back to the office to fill out the paperwork following the hog operation arrest..." Chris hesitated, looking at my dad.

"No need to fill in there," Bud interjected. "I told Pete all about that earlier this morning," Bud said.

"I don't know what happened!" I complained.

"It was very uneventful," Chris said. "Your husband... to-be was never in any danger. Nothing compared to the experience you were having at that time, only we didn't even know it."

"Yeah," Bud said. "I feel bad. I thought you were home in bed asleep."

"Anyway," Chris went on, "we had agents in several locations. Everyone had their nocks trained on Butcher. Right after he got Bud installed in his tree stand, he made a beeline to a hog pen containing a gigantic feral boar. The guys tell me he'd go 400 pounds or more. Anyway we had the pen staked out. It was about a quarter of a mile through the woods from Bud. Soon as Butcher put his hand on the gate to release the hog, the guys arrested him. Then Bud went home and I headed back to the office. That's when I got the call from you and all hell broke loose."

"So what happened when you finally did get back to the office after arresting Junior?" I asked.

"As I've said, the sheriff wasn't there. Turns out he was getting a nut crunching from you, but I didn't know that, either. That doesn't mean I wasn't busy, however. You see, I'd been working with the BPD, the Baltimore Police Department, and they finally got our search warrant for Butcher's house served. In it they found a compound bow and arrows and a rifle along with a rifle rack presumably removed from his green Toyota truck. They noted that the rack was broken, so maybe that's why he removed it."

"Sounds plausible," I said.

"BPD measured the arrows for us and sent us digital photos. I had just received them the night before the hog hunt. Now here's where I thought I was going to have a problem. As you know, I was working on the premise that Junior was our killer. That he'd shot Clinton with an arrow and then finished him off with a knife to the stomach."

"Yeah ... " I said apprehensively.

"But according to the information you gave me about arrows and how they have to be sized to the person shooting them, they were far too long to have been Junior's. And, when we searched the chicken house, we found where he'd stashed supplies for making arrows and a few he'd completed. They were orange, not green."

"Junior wasn't the killer?" I asked incredulously. "I was so sure."

"First let me tell you this," Chris said and took a long pull from his beer. "Junior's lawyer was waiting for us when we arrived. Mr. Lauderbach had called him before we even left his house with Junior. So, on the way to take Junior to his laywer, who was waiting in an interrogation room, we marched him right by the holding cell where we'd put Butcher. Let me tell you, they both got a case of the round eyes."

"So they really did know each other, just like Luther told me," I said.

"Yep," Chris smiled. We told the lawyer what we had on the kid, regarding both the attempted bombing and the death of Clinton Baker. Meanwhile, Junior was having a jumping up and down fit to explain what really happened to Clinton Baker and ranting that Mr. Butcher should not be held in jail because 'he was too important.'"

"So did his lawyer let him talk?" Bud asked incredulously.

"Actually, he did," Chris said.

"So what did he say?" I said, impatiently. "What did happen to Clinton Baker?"

"First, regarding Bud's question, while I was meeting with his lawyer, Mr. and Mrs. Lauderbach joined the party, too, and they all decided to let Junior give us his version of what happened. The first thing he admitted to was placing the bomb on the well."

"Oh how sad," I said, "his parents had to hear it."

"Yes," Chris said. "It was sad, one of the saddest things I've seen involving kids in my career. They were completely crushed when he told them to their face that he thought they were 'ignorant of the ways of the modern business world.' He jabbered wildly about how they were opting for short-term gains with the natural gas wells, while the development of the land would give them instant returns that could be invested to last for generations, yada yada. I felt so sorry for his folks."

"Jeez," Bud said. "He had it exactly ass backwards! When land is sold to developers, it's gone forever and the money, if poorly invested could be lost too. The gas play will bring solid, large returns for thirty years or more. I know of wells that are still in play after eighty years and in the end, the land is still theirs to run the family business. What a dolt!"

"I think he just got his head turned by Butcher," Chris said. "He is a slick realtor who came along, saw a big fat goose just ripe for roasting, and realized that Junior was his access to it."

"Do you think he had anything to do with the bomb," I asked. "Because I believe there may have been someone involved other than Junior."

Chris looked surprised. "He vehemently denies having anything whatsoever to do with it and I tend to believe him. He's just a slick hustler, not a mad bomber. Do you suspect anyone else?"

"Not really. I just know no one on our site wears sneakers and there were New Balance sneaker prints around the well and the shack where Junior made the bomb."

"Oh," Chris said, relieved. "Junior had on New Balance shoes."

"Huh?" I said. "When I saw him he had on black tie-ups."

"New Balance makes black leather sneakers," Bryant said matter-of-factly.

"Oh, well that answers that," I said.

Chris smiled. "Good detective work, though."

I shrugged and he continued, "We'll turn everything over to the DA and they'll decide what to do from there. As far as the sheriff's department is concerned, though, we have our man and the case is closed." Chris crushed his beer can and walked to the trash can. When he came back to the stove island where we were still seated, waiting with bated breath, he just stared at us. "What?" he asked, knowing full well what we were waiting to hear.

"Who killed Clinton Baker?" Bud and I shouted.

"Oh, sorry," Chris said. "Well, it sure wasn't what I expected, but, according to Junior, no one murdered Clinton Baker. Junior said he was with his friend, Fred Butcher, on the day Baker died. Fred was teaching him how to bow hunt..."

"So apparently Fred lied to you about not being a bow hunter when you went all the way to Baltimore to interview him," I interjected.

"Yes, he did." Chris said. "When I asked him why, he had the same reason most everyone in trouble offers—he was scared to tell the truth. I tend to believe him. Again, he's just a hustler, not a murderer, but as I said, that's up to the DA."

Chris took his seat again and continued. "Butcher accidentally shot Clinton in the back with one of his neon-green arrows, which *are* the correct length for his body size. They mistook the kid for a boar, apparently he was kneeling, tying his boot. All they saw was his mop of dark brown hair. Junior said they didn't even know who it was until they rolled him up on his side. That's also when they saw he had been fatally wounded by a knife."

"So poor Clint was tying his boot, got shot in the back and fell face forward onto his knife?" I asked dubiously. "What? How was he holding a knife and tying his boot at the same time? Doesn't sound possible to me."

"He had the knife in his canvas carry-all bag and fell on it when the arrow took him down. We have it now and, as it happens, it was exactly as you described it—fixed blade serrated on the top, so it probably was one of those used on the farm. Plus, we have the bag and it does have a hole in it and blood on it. Don't worry," Chris assured us, "the DA's office and the forensics folks will verify everything Junior said."

"Where did you find all his stuff?" I asked.

"Once both men saw what had happened, they panicked. Junior pulled the knife out, which meant he had touched it. Butcher, realizing he put his fingerprints on it, told him to take it and the bag and dispose of them. We found everything up in the roost of the chicken house with Junior. He told us, in his haste, he'd pulled the carry-all from around Clint's neck. Again, this matches with the coroner's evidence."

I remembered the angry wheal on Clint's neck, probably where the strap had been jerked across it. "Makes sense that Clint would have the knife in his bag, I guess," I said, explaining how, when I'd found the camo tarp, the twine on one corner was broken and I couldn't fix it because I didn't have a knife. "Sad to think he was very likely on his way to fix it when he was killed," I said. "That's why he had the knife in his carry-all."

"What doesn't make sense," Bud said. "Is if the arrow was so unique, it seems to me like the man who made it, Butcher, would have taken it with him."

"They were trying to, but the shot was poor. A properly executed shot with a compound bow can bring down a cape buffalo. This one hit the kid in the shoulder bone, which is why it didn't blow right through him. This was also consistent with the coroner's report. I spoke with him myself and he told me the head of the arrow was sunk so deep into the scapula bone, no one could've removed it by simply pulling." I grimaced. "They were trying to decide what to do when they heard someone coming and ran. I'm figuring that must have been you," Chris said, looking at me.

"What about all the email arguments regarding evolution versus creationism? Did you ask Junior about that?" I asked.

"Yes, and he admitted there was a huge divide between Clinton and him. He likened it to the divide between Republicans and Democrats. But he rightfully pointed out that while the differences are insurmountable, most of us don't go around murdering each other over them."

"Sounds like a cleverly well-thought defense considering its coming from a mentally disturbed person," Bud said.

"Oh, you can be sure his parents got him on him meds soon as he got back home early this morning and told them what he'd done. By the time we got to him, he was manageable and entirely lucid."

We were silent for moment. Then I said, "That answers most of my questions, except for one."

"Which is?" Chris said.

"Who chloroformed me and why?"

He smiled and pointed knowingly at me. "I thought of that question right before I left the office so I went back down to the holding cells. Junior was having his dinner and I asked him if he'd done it and he freely admitted he had. When I asked him why, he said he was afraid you'd mess up their whole plan of turning the farm into a premier hunting community. He said Butcher was angry at him for doing it but Luther came along to feed the hogs and told them he'd take care of everything."

"Did they, by any chance, say how he moved those wild hogs so fast?"

"I ask him that too. I knew with your inquiring mind you'd want to know. Interestingly, Junior said they didn't move them. There wasn't time. They just let the wild boar and the mixed ones go free. Then he and Butcher left and Luther simply waited until you woke up and told you he'd found you passed out. If you think about it, it was a pretty good plan. No one got hurt and you couldn't prove it wasn't true."

"No, I couldn't," I said. "But it still makes me angry—mostly at myself—that I let the little creep sneak up on me like that ... " Just then, I heard a car door slam. "Henri and Will are here!"

"We're late!" Henri called as she and Will trouped in the kitchen door. "But we have an excuse. We went by the bakery at Whole Foods and picked up some dessert."

"Great," I said, taking a box from her with one hand and giving Will a hug with the other. I watched as she moved into Chris's waiting embrace like a cat curling up in a favorite chair. Right off, I noticed two things: she was wearing an engagement ring, and there was a difference in her demeanor. Besides being happy and radiant, there was a peace about her. Gone was the subtle tension that I'd seen in her since she'd moved out on her own.

"Did we miss anything?" Will asked.

"Not as much as I have, apparently," I said, indicating Henri's engagement ring, sparkling like a headlight on high beam.

"Oh, you mean this?" Henri said, nonchalantly holding out her left hand and inspecting its third finger.

Over dinner I heard what everyone else in my family—including my dad who lives in Mozambique, for heaven's sake—had known all day. Henri and Chris were getting married in a civil ceremony a few days before Bud's and my wedding. They weren't going on a honeymoon because Henri had promised to housesit and take care of Tulip for me while Bud and I were away, and because she wanted to help Chris look for a house in Raleigh. He was leaving the force in Sanford and, according to him, "pursuing other opportunities in Raleigh."

"Like what?" Bud asked. "If you don't mind my asking."

"Not at all," Chris said. "I've had several offers from the law enforcement community here as well as a few private security firms."

312

That prompted more excited questions from everyone but me. Oh, I joined in occasionally, but I was still trying to get over the initial shock. This was not what her dad and I'd had in mind for her since she was a little girl. I didn't want to put a damper on things, but I had so many questions. Plus a plan was starting to form in my mind. Finally I said, "You know, Henri, your dad and I always thought you'd want a big wedding. You have many friends and an extended family that will be crushed when they find they weren't able to share in such a special occasion."

"God no," Henri laughed. "I never want to go through planning an event of that magnitude again. Yours was enough for a lifetime!"

"What about you, Chris," Bud asked. "What are your folks going to say about a civil service?"

Chris took a sip of wine and set his glass down. "Actually, my folks died in a plane crash when I was thirteen. Since they both traveled often in their jobs, I lived at a military academy in Virginia. Neither of them had family, so when they died, I had no family."

He paused as though considering whether to reveal more of himself, then added, "Fortunately, they had life insurance. That, along with a modest settlement from the airlines, was enough to take care of me. I was able to stay at the academy and continue living with the same faculty member who'd always taken care of me during the summers. In fact, he adopted me, took care of my finances and set up trusts for me. But he has passed on now too."

"So, you see," Henri said, patting Chris's shoulder affectionately, "a small wedding works best for us."

"I do have some buds from the military that I'd like to be there," Chris added, "but it's good we don't have a big wedding to plan.

We'll have our hands full finding the right house. We might even build one. I still have some money from a couple of trusts and all my salary I put away during my tours in Afghanistan and Iraq."

The conversation and questions took off again and the plan that had been forming in my mind crystallized. I tapped my glass and without prior conference with Bud—that's the good thing about soul mates, each knows what the other is thinking—I said, "I'd like to offer a proposal to the family."

Conversation stopped and everyone looked at me.

"Henri … and Chris, how would you two like to trade places with Bud and me at our wedding?"

The expressions on the faces of my family at that moment will forever be seared in my memory. *Platinum wedding—five hundred thousand dollars. Giving it all away—priceless!*

"What?" Henri croaked. "Mom! What about you and Dad?"

"We'll take your place at the civil ceremony. That way, your parents will be a married couple at your wedding."

"I love that idea!" my wonderful husband-to-be shouted.

"Makes sense to me," my dad said.

"It's perfect!" Will laughed and turned to his sister. "Don't you see, Henri? Mom gets to be herself—no drama momma. You get the wedding you've always wanted and don't say you haven't, because all the ideas that will make this one so spectacular came from you. And Dad, Granddad, and I get the one thing we've been wanting—the family back together."

"But, this is crazy," Henri sputtered. "The invitations went out months ago with your names on them. People are coming to see you two get married … "

"All the people that are coming to the wedding are coming because they love us, Henri," I said, with an inclusive wave of my hand around the table. "Our *family* is the reason they're coming. They won't care if it's your wedding or ours. And remember, our invitation requested no gifts so there's nothing to return."

"Well," she said, contemplatively. "I guess we could have a cute card made up. Sort of like a save-the-date card only we'll call it a change-of-cast card and send it out to everyone … including Chris's friends. It'll serve as an invitation for them and of course Chris will call them, too, right?" She looked at her fiancée.

"I'm happy to go along with whatever makes you happy," Chris said.

A smile started to break across her lovely face and she said, "I … I think it could work … " Suddenly, her smile was replaced with a look of horror and she wailed, "Oh, no!

I don't have a dress! I'll have to wear off-the-rack!"

"As it happens," I said, "I know just the woman who can fix us right up."

TWENTY-SEVEN

Two weeks and three days later on November 9th, I bent to straighten the chapel-length train of Henri's lace and beaded wedding gown. We were standing before a three-sided, full-length mirror Bud had added in the guest suite at Seahaven, his family's beach home overlooking the ocean at Wightsville Beach. Henri and I admired her reflection in the lace and beaded sheath gown.

We had gone back to the couture boutique in DC, and Fanny, the sales associate who had helped me with my dress, had stepped in to save the day for us. She had seen to it that a beautiful ivory Romona Keveza floor sample from last year's collection was altered to a perfect fit for Henri, cleaned and delivered to us just days before the wedding.

"What do you think?" I asked her reflection in the mirror. "I couldn't be happier," Henri said, turning to hold both my hands. "I just love it . . ."

"Knock, knock, girls!" Anthony, our hairdresser for the last twenty years, called from the door. "Are you ready for me to set the veil?"

"Ready and raring to go!" Henri said.

It was a happy time and I gratefully lifted the chapel-length piece of illusion, studded here and there with crystals, from its hanger and handed it to him. As I gave her a peck on the cheek, Henri caught my arm and said softly, "Thanks, Mom. Thanks for everything." Unable to speak, I just chucked her chin, gave her a wobbly smile, and left to find Bud in our master suite.

Resplendent in his black tailcoat, white shirt, vest, and tie, he looked up from struggling with one of his kid gloves. "Time to get dressed, Mrs. Cooper. Need any help?"

"Nope," I said, taking his wrist in my hands and poking the mother-of-pearl button into its tight hole. "I'm all set. My makeup and hair are done so all I have to do is throw on my dress. Anthony's assistant is here to help if I need him."

"If I haven't told you today," Bud said, "I want you to know how much I love you and how happy I am."

"You have, but if you still feel the need to convince me further, you'll have thirty days in Bora Bora to do it," I said. "Now go be with Henri. She wants to see you one more time while she's still your little girl."

He left and I took a minute to gaze out the window at the festivities below. Guests were filing into a large white 40' x 80' frame tent on the beach. It was floored to accommodate ladies' heels and oriented on its long axis to face the sea. The wedding couple and the officiant would stand on a dais on the east end, flanked by banks of peonies and, yes, even some garden roses. Miles of gauzy white fabric, draping the ceiling and hanging in loose curtains at the tent sides, wafted gently in the mellow evening breeze. A classical quartet began playing some of Henri's favorite pieces.

Once the service was over, guests would move by way of a boardwalk, festooned in flowers and festively lit with Tiki torches, to a round cocktail tent. It was also richly draped in sheer white fabric and featured soft accent lighting, plush silk lounging furniture, and elegantly covered cocktail tables. The couple's favorite songs would be played while hors d'oeuvres and drinks were passed until it was time for dinner and dancing in the main reception tent, another short boardwalk stroll away.

Taking in the massive 60' x 180' clear tent, twinkling with literally thousands of tiny lights across the ceiling, I marveled at Henri's creativity and ability to pull together all the fine details that had made this whole wedding weekend so magical, like a fantasy, really. Then, hearing the classical piece that was my cue to get dressed, I moved to the closet.

I tossed my dressing robe aside, lifted my glorious gown from its hanger and stepped into it. Anthony's assistant came by just in time to help me fasten and zip. Moments later, I gave myself one last inspection in the mirror and got a thumbs-up from the assistant. I left my room to go take my place with the wedding party just as Henri, assisted by her Maid of Honor, was exiting her suite. Upon seeing me, her jaw dropped.

"Mom," she whispered. "Holy cow! I love your gown. It's ... it's so you!"

"You aren't upset I'm not wearing a suit?" I asked, turning so she could get the full effect of shimmering, pale gold, sequin-studded, chiffon creation, which featured a neckpiece of gold cording that reached from my chin to my breastbone, the strands increasing in length until they hung in loose loops to my waist.

The dress itself was fitted, sleeveless, and backless, and flared at the hem, which was slightly longer in the back.

"Heavens no! Not after seeing you in that. Umm, can I borrow it when Chris and I get time to take a short honeymoon?"

"I'm counting on it," I laughed. "Now let's go get you married."

———

Next morning Bud and I were winging our way to San Francisco, the first leg of our trip to Bora Bora. We were seated side by side in his King Air. "By the way," he said, turning to me, "was that dress going to be your wedding gown?"

Reclined and about to fall asleep, I opened my scratchy eyes, a difficult job considering the champagne hangover I had, and looked at him. "Yep," I said.

"Well, it was perfect for you. I couldn't take my eyes off you all night."

"I'm glad you liked it."

"I especially liked the way it slipped so easily over your head about three this morning," he yawned. I gave him a weak smile, but even that made my head pound, so I scrambled through my tote and came up with a BC powder. Mercifully, Bud offered to get me a Coke.

"Here you go," he said when he returned. "I meant to ask you during last week's mad scramble, getting ready for our trip and taking care of last-minute wedding details, how everything went for you at work."

"What do you mean?"

"Were you satisfied with your replacement as wellsite geologist?"

"Oh, absolutely. The Lauderbachs are in good hands and frankly, I'm glad to be out of the country when the ramifications of what Junior did start falling in place. You know, Homeland Security and the good folks at ATF might not be too quick to let him cop a plea in return for being placed in a mental institution; although, in the end, I think that's what will happen. Regardless, his full confession and willingness to talk with a whole slew of government psychologists will ensure that his days as a commingler in the general population will be over forever.

"Butcher probably won't get anything more than probation on an involuntary manslaughter charge, but at least his smarmy tactics will be out in the open," Bud said. Then he quipped, "Some people just give business a bad name."

Feeling a tad better, I dug around in my tote again and pulled out a bag of southern blister peanuts, took a few, and handed the bag to Bud. "Thanks," he said before asking, "What about the paleontological team? Were you happy with the final selection?"

"Absolutely. Just think, in about two weeks, six of the finest paleontologists that academia has to offer as well as their assistants and staff will descend upon the site and start the long, painstaking and meticulous process of removing Cecil from his bonds. It'll take years, but then he'll be free for all the world to see."

"That's great," Bud smiled and cracked open a Coke for himself. He took a sip, then picked up my hand, gave my palm a kiss, and said, "I know how important that fossil is to you."

"Only because it gave some meaning and permanence to the life of a young man who won't get any more chances at claiming fame. Whenever I think of him, I'll forever be reminded that life is short and everyday should be lived to the fullest." I finished my drink, leaned back, and gratefully closed my eyes again.

Beside me I felt Bud's seat drop back even with mine. I heard him blow out a contented sigh. "What about when we get back home?" he asked. "What are your plans as far as your work goes? Got any new prospects on the horizon I might be interested in?"

Too contented to even open an eye, I said, "Maybe."

THE END

ACKNOWLEDGEMENTS

I couldn't have written *Saving Cecil* without lots of help. First let me thank everyone at Llewellyn Worldwide/Midnight Ink, especially my editors, Terri Bischoff and Nicole Nugent. Besides being very patient regarding delays due to my two children getting married in the same year, both are excellent at what they do. Kimberley Cameron, my agent, deserves a big hand for sticking with me.

Russ Patterson, founder and past president of Patterson Exploration Services in Sanford, NC, was an endless font of information and imaginative ideas. No one knows more about the history and lore of Lee County gas exploration than he. On all questions of a geologic nature, my good friend Lee J. Otte Ph.D., C.P.G., Senior Geologist at Otte Enterprises, was quick with answers. My husband deserves a nod for tirelessly answering questions about cars, trucks, and things that go vroom! As always, Mardy Benson, retired captain, Johnston County Sheriff's Department, was generous with his time and advice on criminal matters.

Without Bob Murray's maps to pique our imagination, the Cleo Cooper Mystery Series wouldn't be half as much fun. And, lastly, Tammy McLeod was invaluable as an early reader and should definitely quit her day job to become a line editor.

Thanks again to all of you!

Finally, any mistakes in the book are mine entirely.

Sue Mitchiner of Zoom-In Photography

About the Author

Lee Mims holds bachelor's and master's degrees in Geology from the University of North Carolina–Chapel Hill, and she once worked as a field geologist. Lee is a member of Mystery Writers of America and Sisters in Crime. *Saving Cecil* is her third novel. Currently a popular wildlife artist, Lee lives in Clayton, North Carolina. Visit her online at LeeMims.com.